THE HIT

Other stories by Alex R Price

Secret to Life Series
Novels
Anger to Rage

Short Stories
Forgotten Dreams
Marbles
The Games People Play
T.B.E.D.
Frank's Lesson

Other novels
The Scholarship
The Classroom
The Diploma

One More Thing

Other Short Stories
The Newlyweds
(a six-word short story)
En Pointe

Squaretop Mountain Publishing, LLC

ISBN – 13: 978-1-7332557-9-0

DEDICATION

To the parents whose children are far—

keep being the parent and role model they need.

ACKNOWLEDGMENTS

I would like to thank my editor, Tracy Locken, for stirring this manuscript into the cauldron of grammatical sense. I applaud my editor in the magic she does on my novels. Sometimes I think she is a wicked witch stirring punctuation into a cauldron and ripping unnecessary words out, creating an aftermath that looks like a war zone. But with a season of rain, the story blossoms into a beautiful world I am proud to get lost in over and over. It is at this time that I realize she is not a wicked witch, but a fairy godmother. I'm grateful for everything she does to help make this dream a reality.

I would like to thank my beta readers, Tammy and Angela, for their valuable insight into finding all the plot holes of my story. They've shown me how to analyze sentences and read them from a new reader's perspective.

A shout-out to MiblArt for an amazing cover. I gave them a try and they pulled through with an amazing work of art.

I also want to thank every person who bought my previous books. You are the inspiration for me to keep writing and turning this into a full-time career.

Alex R Price

THE HIT

ALEX R PRICE

This was just another job, another death and another cash payment. Tracer moved the lever ever so gently and watched his foot touch down on the balcony. His fatigues and tactical gear blended into the night, and his pockets were filled with an assortment of ordinary tools for his mission. To anyone else, the map in his breast pocket would appear to be an electrical schematic, but it was coded with characters only he could interpret.

Taking a quick peek through the window, he saw a neatly made bed. He hadn't seen the typical light-flipping of anyone moving from room to room. The only recent activity had been on the lower levels.

The tools he carried were typical of a communications repairman. He didn't need any special tools—not for this job anyway. The utility clothing and tool belt he wore for this assignment were sufficient to complete his objective. Any tool he had within his tool belt could aid him in completing his task. His overall goal was a subtle hint if any at all, never an outright statement. The statements he did leave were reserved for the worst of the worst. He believed children should be allowed to grow unhindered, not forced into any type of adult situation.

The harness loosened as he brought the drone down then landed it on the roof high above. The long cable kept the whirl of spinning blades and their noise at a distance. He wanted to let himself in, not make an announcement of his arrival.

He unsnapped the cable from his harness and gathered it into a coil at the edge of the balcony. A large head suddenly appeared in the window. Tracer cracked the door and put some liver treats down for the fluffy dog, followed by a fist-size ball of peanut butter and rolled oats laced with sedatives. He scratched the large noggin as the dog's attention diverted to the drool worthy snack. If he had to leave in a hurry, it was one latch and a spin of eight powerful motors—he didn't need an extra hindrance from a dog.

Entering the master bedroom, he left the overfed Newfoundland and pulled a taser from a holster. Turning this way and that, he checked every corner carefully to prevent a surprise by the owner of the house. The man's wife and children had gone away for the extended holiday weekend, leaving his target home alone. Tracer had watched them pack the large SUV and leave. By the amount of luggage they rolled out of the house, it looked as though they would be gone for several weeks and not just the weekend.

THE HIT

It didn't matter if they would be back the following day. Tracer just needed this night to finish the job. A pronouncement of death from the authorities would precede a text from his contact's burner phone, and Tracer would have the code to access the final payment he was owed. After that, he would disappear as if he were never there.

He swung the pistol into each room, ready to deliver a painful jolt to any occupant. Skirting the occasional light in the expansive house, he was careful not to silhouette himself against a window. The lights weren't enough to see into every dark corner but were enough that he could step silently through the house without disturbing more than the air.

Checking each room, he found no other inhabitants on the top level. A personal elevator connected all three levels of the home. Peering down the glass tube, Tracer could see the top of the elevator car nestled just below the main floor. Its polished internal workings were meant to be viewed and not hidden as most elevators were.

But he wasn't interested in the extravagant mechanics. He wanted to know where the sole occupant of the home was.

Bright light leaked into the tube from the basement. It wasn't proof that his mark was in the lowest level, but the haunting quiet of the rest of the house suggested that he was. After thorough inspection of the upper levels he confirmed that his target was in the basement.

The faint noise of children laughing and shrieking made Tracer pause. He waited, straining his ears, hearing two distinct children's voices. He had watched two children leave. Could the couple have more than two? Moving silently from room to room, he verified that no one else was on the subsurface level.

The laughter drew him closer to a door with glowing light around its edge. There was activity inside, as he saw a shadow move across the door. This was the last room. He'd checked all the others. But the additional voices of children gave him pause, challenging his decision to complete his job this night.

The flush-mount door was hidden by a sliding bookcase, displaying the skill of a master carpenter. Quality lumber with a pristine fit and finish covered nearly every inch of the house. Tracer didn't have to guess that the bookshelf, once slid back to its home, would look as if it were built into the wall, completely concealing the hidden room.

Moving to the side of the entrance, he peeked through the cracked door. Sheets of polished stainless were glued to the concrete wall, giving the room an industrial feel. Flashes of pink and black from the projected image refracted onto the stainless wall, and a blurry, warped reflection of a figure showed movement in the room.

The laughter and excited play from the children continued. Sounds from a squeaking swing and stomps from little feet pounding against a slide drifted out of the sterile-looking room.

The blurred figure seemed to be turned away from the door, so Tracer inched it open a little further.

The movement stopped.

Tracer stopped also. He couldn't tell what the person was doing. He had to wait.

He wouldn't force his hand if he didn't have to. He had patience. He could stand there for an hour, or two, if need be. Much of his skill required him to wait for the opportune time to make his move. He patiently watched the blurry pink reflection as the figure moved equipment from one place to another.

The video ended, and the resulting silence would expose any sound Tracer might make.

He saw movement again. This time the figure moved toward the door. Tracer didn't know if the person had heard him or not, but they were coming out of the room and he was standing directly in their path. He took a few quick steps and flattened himself against the wall, using the sliding bookshelf as cover.

Bright light flooded out the door. The figure walked out and stood just outside the entrance to the hidden room. Tracer caught himself holding his breath, then cautiously eased it out. Several seconds passed and the man still hadn't moved.

Drawing in a breath ever so slowly, he waited for his target to go one direction or the other.

He watched the man's shadow against the far wall lean to one side and turn as if to listen for the slightest sound. Tracer continued his controlled breathing—listening, watching and waiting to be discovered.

The man disappeared back into the room.

Tracer stepped behind a large plush chair and crouched out of sight. Music began playing. The noise gave him a chance to catch his breath. But when the light escaping the room dimmed again, he could only guess that his target had returned to fill the door. Seconds ticked into minutes as he waited.

Footsteps returned to the inside of the room, followed by a clink of glass and a gurgle of liquid. Tracer thought he could hear grumbling, but he couldn't make out what was being said.

It didn't matter—he had a job to do.

Tracer watched from his hiding spot as the whiskey bottle dwindled from several mixed drinks and concluded with the man drinking straight from the bottle. The man cried, yelled and even begged while watching his family's home movies. In a fit of rage, he leaped from his chair and fired a pistol at the image dancing against the back wall. The image the man shot at was his wife. Tracer didn't care. He had a job to do, and at that moment, his job was to wait.

The man moaned, then with a drunken crash, he fell back into his chair. Slurred cuss words echoed through the shooting range and back out the door. A few minutes later, Tracer heard the sound of heavy snoring.

As soon as the breathing became consistent, Tracer walked through the hidden door. The elongated room housed a collection of guns and a short firing range ideal for shooting handguns. Several safes were anchored against one wall, while a workbench stood adjacent to it.

With his target in a diminished state, it was too easy. His phone was filled with an unsent text message admonishing his soon-to-be ex-wife that her affairs would be brought to light and that his onetime activity was after learning of her multiple escapades.

Without moving the phone, Tracer pulled a stylus out of his pocket and erased the text. In its place, he typed out a message telling the wife and the world goodbye and left it unsent.

Tracer stood in front of his target, watching him snore away the alcohol in his system. With slow and gentle movements, he placed the gun left on the table back in the man's hand, wrapped his finger around the trigger and placed the muzzle to the man's temple. The man was oblivious to anything Tracer did to him.

The smell of gunpowder hung thick in the air. It was done.

He watched as the last muscle flinches subsided from the father of two who would have been a good husband and father had he only picked a spouse who wasn't so greedy.

Retracing his steps, Tracer gave one last treat to the big fluffy dog before attaching the rigging to the harness and picking himself up off the balcony. He sailed through the air, avoiding the cameras that looked for intruders coming across the grounds but not from the sky.

The night air whisked around him as he glided through the darkness to await his next job.

2

Halen Kettleman woke to her mother pounding on the door of her lavish pink room. She moaned as she pulled a fluffy pink pillow over her head. The insistent pounding continued.

Dragging her feet from under the covers, she sunk her toes into the thick pink faux fur rugs that adorned the cream-colored carpet. With a push off the bed and eyes barely open, she stumbled across the expansive room. The extra-thick rugs made walking from the bed to the toilet feel as if she were walking on the softest of clouds.

Photos of Halen with various celebrities decorated one section of her expansive room. On another wall, more pictures of Hollywood celebrities, mostly from various red-carpet events, hung in matching frames organized in order of favoritism and were rearranged on the occasional whim. They surrounded an enlarged poster of her first major film, *The Golden Gate Slasher*, where she was a little girl and the sole survivor in the film.

THE HIT

The film hadn't landed her nationwide recognition. Her third film did, however. *Twilight the Sky*, a film about a young teen stranded on an island and nearly going crazy finding her way back home, had elevated her career. Three more films brought her worldwide recognition, but it was far from the megastar status she sought.

She placed her thumb on the integrated bathroom computer. A small beep of acceptance launched the lavatory into a life of its own. Perfect 103.6-degree water blazed out of the massaging showerhead. Music rose from the silence with the sound of songbirds chirping out a favorite melody. A polished stainless steel lazy Susan spun out of the corner next to the white marble sink, with nearly every conceivable shade of organic makeup ready to paint any mood.

Halen didn't acknowledge her reflection in the mirror, as the smeared makeup and after-party dishevelment that her face now bore would soon disappear down the shower drain, saving her from the truth of what her life actually was. The preprogrammed LED lights remained barely lit, allowing Halen to navigate the bath before being coaxed to meet the day.

"Halen. Are you up?" Halen's mother, Kimberly Rossi, beat on the locked door. Her insistence on being punctual only drove Halen to be more defiant and less caring of what the clock said. "Come on. You have an appointment with the director to go over your next script."

Halen slammed a fist against the wall, spouting unintelligible cuss words at her mother. She had been Halen's manager since she was little. Now she was an annoying nuisance who held her money in trust, only allowing her a couple thousand each week.

Steam fogged the mirror, preventing Halen from seeing her drooping, hungover face. Her makeup was smeared across one side of her mouth, and a bit of vomit had dried on her chin. Sifting through her makeup bag, she pulled out a tiny vial. After twisting the top off, she sprinkled a small bit of white powder on her hand and quickly stuffed it under her nose. Sniffing deep, she closed her eyes and waited for the jitters to go away.

A moment later, she relaxed and stumbled into the marble tub and let the water cascade over her. Her blond hair turned a dark brown as the water soaked it through, washing away the guilt of overindulgence from the night before.

Prancing down the stairs in her parents' mini-mansion, Halen felt a rejuvenation from the shower and the white powder.

She entered the kitchen to find her mother staring at a scandalous news article. Halen met her mother's eyes across the polished white and lavender kitchen.

Kimberly pushed the tablet across the counter. "What the hell are you doing, Halen?"

"I'm having a great time." Halen looked down at the digital newspaper. "Aww. They got my bad side," she said, spinning the tabloid around and around until the picture of her falling out of a limo and planting her face in a puddle of water turned into a circular blur.

"You're embarrassing yourself and everyone around you." Kimberly huffed in disapproval.

"When are you going to grow up? You have an appointment in thirty minutes and you're not even ready."

"Duh, Mom. I *am* ready." Halen popped the gum she had doubled up on to help mask her morning breath. She grabbed an apple and a Mountain Dew out of the refrigerator and stumbled out the door with her mother on her heels.

A car waited in the small circular driveway in front of the house. The short palms and tall block wall surrounding the yard hid much of the building from the street. Taller trees to either side of the property discouraged random fans from taking a quick snapshot of the celebrity home.

"When will you be back?" Kimberly called as Halen sank into the back seat of the rented car.

The door shut without a response from Halen.

Kimberly stared after Halen for a moment following the car's disappearance around the corner. Then, shaking with frustration, she walked back inside. She couldn't discipline her. If she did, Halen would remove her as her financial manager.

She had to come up with a solution, but feared the potential consequences of any action. She reached for her phone and selected a contact, then hesitated. Her hand was hovering over the send button when her thoughts turned to her husband. Kelson Rossi was a brilliant and seasoned lawyer. Maybe he would have an idea.

Kelson, Halen's stepfather, had been a lawyer in his father's Georgia law firm, but a falling-out sent him west to California, where he met Kimberly. She was a young college junior at the university. He had bought her a cup of coffee and began kindling a relationship of convenience. After Halen's birth, Kimberly graduated from the university, and they moved east to Miami, where Kelson began his career at Sterling and Beckman.

He'd helped many clients out of sticky situations, and he'd written all the contracts they used in their personal endeavors. Maybe he could come up with a contract to hold Halen accountable or she would lose her money and lifestyle.

Kimberly still needed somebody to talk to. She couldn't face the day knowing that the world would be laughing at her parenting skills. She pressed the button on her phone. "Hey, Tabs. It's Kim. Could you come over?"

She walked around the counter to retrieve the tablet. Even though the paparazzi made things up, there were still some elements of truth twisted in. For Halen, the truth didn't have to be stretched very far to make a good story, if it was stretched at all.

"Yeah, it's about Halen again." Kimberly spun the tablet so it was square with her. "Could you come help me figure it out?" She swiped back and forth between the cover and the damaging story about her daughter. "Great. See you soon." Tapping her manicured nails on the counter, she ended the call, then stared vacantly at the coffee cup.

When the front door opened again, she sighed, certain she'd have to deal with more of Halen's outlandish behavior. Instead, Kelson walked around the corner and set his briefcase on the floor next to the kitchen counter.

"My office is being renovated," he said. "I'm working from home today."

Kimberly met his suddenly concerned eyes.

"What's wrong?"

3

Halen stepped into the conference room. The magical white powder still tingled in her brain, staving off any skin-crawling jitters. She paused two steps into the room, striking the subtlest red-carpet pose, and scanned the faces to see who she would be working with. She saw a lot of faces she didn't recognize, and a few that only worked B-list films, but there were also a few lesser-known A-listers. Those A-list talents were all business and didn't take their eyes off their scripts. The one A-lister who did, Regina Benton, gave her a polite smile.

"Welcome, Miss Halen." Regina set her folder down, giving her undivided attention to Halen.

"Ugh. What's with the cheery attit—"

"Your script, Halen." Hank Figland, a short, bald man in his fifties extended his arm, folder in hand, interrupting what could become a heated exchange. He all but shoved the pink folder into

THE HIT

Halen's hand—probably to distract her from Regina.

Halen accepted it and stepped around a cast member to get to her contracted pink chair. She opened the folder and settled in to review the script.

Halen's contract included personal time to herself every three hours. In the past, when her break was up, she sometimes didn't return to the set, causing frustration among the cast and crew. Her delays had put the previous film over budget and behind schedule. If it weren't for the ambitious crew working late almost nightly on the set, they wouldn't have finished at all.

One day, while shooting that movie, a crewman had run over her pink chair. Halen sulked in her trailer the entire day. The incident cost the production thousands of dollars. To add to the frustration, a power outage shut down the set, letting the heat evaporate the tolerance out of everyone, including the two bears that had performed perfectly that morning. Halen had refused to come out of her trailer and ruined the critical shot they needed for the movie. Hank was forced to send the cast and crew home until he could get things reset and everyone on the same page.

Since that day, Halen had noticed the hushed tones and whispers when she was near. She also noticed that her every wish was quickly fulfilled. She ordered a fluffy pink rug to put her feet on. Within an hour, one was placed in front of her chair. Now she was always equipped with her pink chair, pink water bottle, pink rug and a pastel pink script with her lines neatly highlighted.

"N-now that we have Halen here, we can go over the f-first scenes that we w-will be shooting." Hank pulled at his neck, where the only remaining hair clung to the back of his head. He had been a child actor forty years prior, but a terrible car accident as a teen had ended his acting career. Some said the accident had brought out his brilliance as a director as well as the stutter that took him years to get under control.

Halen snapped her fingers and pointed to the table. "Where's my orange cranberry and my iced coffee? Oh, by the way, seven out of ten doctors say that rubbing the back of your neck that way will lead to hair loss."

"Good to see that you haven't changed," Hank muttered.

"Didn't the company have enough budget for a full case of Febreze?" Halen peered at some of the B-list celebrities who had been trying to get into the bigger films.

She made the mistake of allowing her gaze to linger on Mrs. Benton.

Regina pulled in a breath, ready to spew her opinion.

The room grew thick with tension. Cast and crew held a collective breath, waiting for what would surely be an explosion.

"Welcome e-everyone," Hank interjected. The hostility in the air eased as Hank continued. "In your folders you will find a copy of your script and the shooting schedule. We have access to the ice arena for the next two weeks, so we will be shooting those scenes starting tomorrow. Halen, Jeff, Celic and Pam, we will need you on day fourteen. If there is a change in the schedule, you'll be notified two days in advance."

"You brought me in here just to say you don't need me for two weeks?" Halen tossed her pink folder onto the table. Its loud slap was an audible expression of her disapproval.

"Yes." Hank turned toward Halen. "I like to think of this as a team sport." He watched her carefully. She felt the challenge in his posture, and she gently settled back in her chair, picking up her folder again.

Hank waited a beat, then continued. "Joanna Steel will be heading up costumes. Be sure to stop by her office before you leave so she can double-check measurements. Try on anything she asks you to so we don't have any malfunctions on set." Hank looked over his cast and crew for any objections. "We have a new camera crew we will be working with."

"A new one. Did the old crew die?" Halen commented in a huff.

"No. They elected not to go to jail for murder," a cast member offered up.

"Just what is that supposed to mean?" Halen glared at the tall, thin actress who then retreated behind her script.

Regina leaned forward and rested her heavy dark-skinned arms on the table. Her fifty-year-old eyes peered over a pair of reading glasses and stared at Halen. "It means they might mistake that huge bobblehead lump atop your shoulders as something to throw knives at, and there are plenty of knives in this script."

Halen inhaled, getting set to throw out her own wave of unjust remarks, when Regina dipped her reading glasses lower.

"Go ahead, girl," she challenged. "I've bent my adult son over my knee and paddled his backside. You ain't nothing special. I expect I'll have to spank your bottom before this film is done."

Only the clatter of a pen falling against the hardwood floor reverberated through the room.

The camera crew supervisor, Jim, cast his eyes back and forth between the two actresses. He had been warned about the blond stick of dynamite, and knew Mrs. Benton wouldn't take BS from anyone, especially a young know-it-all nineteen-year-old.

Outwardly, he was holding his breath just the same as the other eighteen people in the room, but inside he was grinning ear to ear. Jim happened to have been dining a few tables away from Mrs. Benton the previous week. She'd had an argument with her son. Jim couldn't hear what was said, but the tone was unmistakable.

She grabbed her adult son by the hair and ripped him across her lap. Drinks, food, candles and all the floral arrangements clattered across the floor. Her son, too stunned to fight back, endured the pummeling. Regina swung hand after hand, blistering his backside. Jim hadn't counted her swats, but he was sure she had to have hit him over a dozen times. Her other hand had him by his hair in what looked like a death grip. By the way she pulled on his hair, he wondered if the man was about to have his scalp separated from his body.

As a fitting end, she shoved her son onto the patio. She straightened her clothes and picked up her purse. Leaning down close to his ear, she growled a message, then straightened. Without a word, she started for the cash register.

Another man in the restaurant grinned and began to clap. Jim quickly joined in, followed by some of the patrons on the patio. Jim let out a quick whistle as he saw Regina walking away from the café. Her face was stone serious except for a quick curve at the corner of her mouth where she accepted the crowd's approval.

She wore that same expression now as she faced off with Halen. Jim continued watching the two women, wondering who was going to yield first.

"I don't need this." Halen stood, leaving her folder on the table. She turned and walked out, leaving the stunned group to ponder the future of the film.

Hank trailed after the young actress. "Halen, you're needed on this film!"

4

Halen stood on the sidewalk outside the studio, fuming over her limited role in the film. She was to play the girlfriend of a sound tech who was intentionally left out of the credits when he was the genius behind the sound bites. *A Sound Revenge* was a movie where she was to meet her own end while trying to stop his killing spree.

Halen tapped her watch, autodialing her latest friend. "Spearsey? It's Halen. We need to go somewhere . . . No. Nowhere here. Someplace out of town." She fidgeted with her bracelets while looking around. "Everyone's on a broom. Mom doesn't understand what I have to go through to maintain the standards my fans expect."

Tapping an app on her phone, she placed an order for a car.

"Montana? Eww, what's up there? . . . Your uncle owns a resort? . . . Wait, you're leaving tonight? . . . Fats." Halen shot her friend an energetic acceptance.

She walked to the end of the street, filling her time with movement until the Mercedes arrived. "Great. Pick me up at my place in two hours. See you soon, Spearsey."

"Halen, you can't leave for the next two weeks," Hank pleaded to Halen when she told him she was leaving. "Your contract says that you have to be available to shoot some of your scenes if time becomes available."

"Hankie. You know as well as I do that nothing is ever done on time. I'll be back when it's my time to amaze you." Halen looked at her app again for the black sedan to turn the corner.

"Halen, look, we need your talent for this film. No one can do it better than you."

"Aww. Thank you, Hankie." A black Mercedes pulled to the curb. "I'll see you in two weeks. Thank God I only have two scenes with that old bat," Halen said, referring to Regina. "I should have held out for more, but I like you, Hankie. When I get back, we'll get this film done and you will be the first one I invite to the postproduction party. It'll be fun. I'll invite a bunch of old single women, or guys if that's your thing. You can come hang, make and wake."

"Hang, make and wake?" Hank asked.

Halen waited for the driver to open the door for her. "Yeah. Hang out, drink some wine, make out with any of the older hotties that will be there and wake up with a big smile on your face." Halen stepped into the car, and after the driver closed the door, she let down the window. "See you in two weeks, Hankie, and I promise we will make another blockbuster movie."

"Halen, you've never been in a blockbuster!"

The window rolled up and the car drove away, leaving Hank standing on the sidewalk.

On the private flight to Montana, Halen complained of the indignation she had suffered when Regina Benton lashed out at her.

"Really?" Jamie Spears sat stunned by the story Halen was telling. "It's not like she's your mother. Besides, you're an adult now—you make all your own decisions. She doesn't have room to talk. I hear she goes home alone every night. No husband, no kids."

"I heard that she killed her husband to get his life insurance money," Halen said, inventing a new gossip thread. Halen had long been conjuring tales about other people for her own amusement.

"And the police just haven't caught her yet?" Jamie asked. Her gullibility made her easy to manipulate.

"No," Halen said. "They said something about not having enough evidence."

"Dang, that must be some really good rat poison," Gillian Trent said. Gil, as everyone called him, was a native of Whitefish, Montana and a professional surfer. If he had a chance to be on a board, he was on one, whether it was on snow or surf. "And some even better cookies," he added.

Halen took a sip of her fruity mixed drink. She cast a side glare at Gil.

"What?" Gil shrugged. "If she can make rat poison taste good, imagine how good her cookies would taste without it." He flashed a Cheshire grin. "You got to get me her number."

Halen flung a pillow at him. She didn't like his mockery, but she liked the life and energy that followed him around.

"So, what's she doing on the set?" Gil continued. "Is she the caterer, the assistant, Grubhub, Uber driver or . . . ?"

"I don't know. Maybe they need an anchor for the set so it won't blow away," Halen said, showing her disdain for the heavyset actress.

Jamie changed the subject. "How's the conditions at the resort, Gil?"

"Let me look," he said, pulling his phone out of his pocket and scrolling through the apps.

5

"Where to?"

"Miami and Tenth," the passenger answered as he settled in for the short ride across the city.

He looked at the driver's face in the mirror. A white scar almost circled his right eye. He wasn't a large man and was plain and unassuming.

The passenger, a typical-looking business professional, clutched his new tailored briefcase. He fidgeted with the lock, which was just a digit away from opening. His heart raced at the precarious situation he was entering into—one that he hoped would solve a number of problems he and his wife had. He'd gotten the contact information from an old colleague, and he'd prepared for the encounter. A couple of thick, plain envelopes and a lump of cold steel housing six lead-tipped cartridges were close at hand. But now he wasn't sure if he could go through with this deal.

The driver looked a bit gaunt for his profession. The contact name he'd received—and the number he'd found on the website—was Daniel Smith. He didn't think this man was capable of much, but he surmised that even a child could pull a trigger.

He hadn't done anything like this before but knew of it by subtle suggestions given by others in his field. The card he had gotten from a colleague was for a mutual acquaintance of someone who had used Daniel's services in the past. The random set of characters on the card led him to the dark web and a message board where he posted the specialized job.

"I must prepare for a trip," he said, using the code phrase.

"Trips are fun," Daniel answered, adjusting his mirror so the passenger couldn't see him, though he already had.

Awkward silence stretched on with only the tires beating themselves against the divides in the concrete. The sound reverberated into the black Cadillac, where it was barely perceptible. The passenger shifted in the seat after the car took a right a little faster than what he thought was necessary.

"Now, where is the destination of this trip?" Daniel asked in a serious tone.

"Whitefish Mountain Resort, Montana." He watched the driver's head as it shifted back and forth looking for an opening in traffic as they sped along the 874.

"It's cold up there. Lots of snow. I don't like the snow," Daniel said.

"Would you go if you had a really warm coat?" he said, tripping the lock and lifting a bundle of cash out of his briefcase. He slid it onto the seat next to the driver.

He watched as the driver took the fat bundle, twisted it in his hand, then set it back on the seat. His thumb glided across the stack of hundreds. "Where's the rest?"

"When I see some positive headlines on the news, I'll call for another car." He made sure his voice didn't waver in his conviction to remedy his problem.

"How do I know you will call for another car?" The driver slowed and stopped for a red light.

"When news headlines suggest a remedy for tension headaches."

"Let's hope the headache doesn't become contagious," Daniel said in a serious and deadly tone.

The passenger looked at the mirror but could only see the roof of the car. Concern creased his brow. "What if you had top-of-the-line gloves and a hat to go with it? You know, the kind you could retire with. One that *accidentally* makes you look great anywhere in the world."

Daniel accelerated from the green light, easing onto Miami Boulevard. The passenger slid a second, thicker envelope onto the front seat.

The driver opened the flap and thumbed the three-inch stack of hundreds. "I hope you have a good time on your trip," he said as he slowed the car and stopped. "I might take a trip also. Maybe go visit some friends and family in Northern California."

THE HIT

He nodded to the driver, who returned the slightest of nods and tucked the two bundles of money into his pocket.

The passenger stepped out of the car and grabbed a quick glance at his driver. Seeing no discernible feature from that angle, he shut the door and straightened his suit. The tightness in his chest and gut would eventually go away. For now he turned and walked down the street to the local stores. He needed to find a nice gift for his wife to commemorate a turning of a page and their new freedom. He began thinking of a tropical climate far away from the mundane tasks of the world they currently lived in.

6

"Sir, is everything alright?"

Tracer looked up to see a gold-and-blue badge attached to the belt of an imposing and very capable air marshal.

He was momentarily stunned by the sight. Even with all his practiced patience, his heart still skipped a beat. But it quickly returned to normal once he noticed the air marshal wasn't addressing him.

The man who was the focus of the air marshal's attention looked to be a mix of anger, disgust and fear. His antics had drawn the air marshal's attention when two stewardesses struggled to calm the man. The air marshal was poised and ready to handle any confrontation.

They were well into a four-and-a-half-hour flight, but Tracer had noticed the man when he boarded. It was a giveaway when an ordinary-looking passenger talked to the crew a few seconds longer than customary pleasantries, asking about services that weren't commonly available. Now the marshal had been alerted to the significant problem and was standing in the aisle, waiting for a response to his question.

Tracer put down his cup of soda. He had anticipated the confrontation after reading the crowd, and noted the position of the marshal near the back versus the man who leaned far away from the woman and her child. He hadn't known when it would start, just that it would happen before the flight was over. Now the marshal was easing his hand onto his extendable baton. Things were either going to escalate out of control or simmer down to compliance.

The stress of the confrontation radiated through the plane, especially in the seats immediately surrounding the conflict. The man had become agitated by an infant who wouldn't stop crying. Those in first class were oblivious to the commotion, while passengers in the far back were probably curious but would have to wait to deplane before finding out what transpired. Tracer and the passengers who were immediately seated around the mother, the child and the irritated man quietly watched the events unfold.

After a few tense moments, another woman volunteered to change places with the agitated man. Tracer heard his neighbors mutter their disapproval of the situation. The woman who took his place picked the infant up and paced the aisles for several minutes before the baby slipped off to dreamland and was reunited with her mother. The man was escorted to the front seats, right behind the first-class seating and next to the door, where he would be steered off the plane as soon as the door opened.

After the plane docked with the airport terminal, Tracer grabbed his bag out of the overhead storage and stood quietly.

"Can you believe that?"

Dirty blond curls shook in front of Tracer as he waited for the woman's husband to pull their bags out of the overhead storage. "That man gets to leave first when he caused all the disturbance. See, this is what I was talking about. People are rewarded for misbehaving."

"I'm sure that's not the case." Her husband pulled two bags from the overhead that strained at the seams. By all accounts, they should have been checked in as luggage.

"It *is* the case. That's how these airlines work. The more idiotic you are, the more privileges you get."

"Wow, lady. You must get bumped to first class all the time." The voice from behind Tracer reached around him in a taunting tone.

Blond curls flung out, fanning the air as the woman whipped her head around. Her gaze dropped on Tracer. If steam could have rolled out of her ears, he was sure he would have seen it. The woman pulled in a deep breath, ready to exhale a blast of words to assert her self-imposed authority.

"I'm sure that if the air marshal could hear your thoughts," Tracer started, "you would be sharing a bunk with the man they just hauled off. So be careful what you say. You might get an unexpected souvenir with multiple charges." He stared her down as her husband slung the second piece of their luggage set over his shoulder. She flipped her hair at him and marched down the aisle a moment later when the crowd in front began steadily moving off the plane. The husband paused and shot a look at Tracer, sending him a solid thank-you with a nod of his head.

The ambling step-and-wait would have been frustrating, but Tracer wasn't in a hurry. Outside the gate, airport security talked with two young men who had apparently been traveling with the man who the air marshal had escorted off the plane. The offending passenger had been taken behind closed doors until security could be certain he wasn't going to cause any more problems.

Tracer made his way to the vehicle rental counter, where the couple who sat in front of him on the plane argued with the attendant.

"Are you sure you don't want an all-wheel drive or a four-by-four?" the attendant asked.

"I can't believe the prices here. Just give us this one." The woman pointed to a picture on the counter.

"Ma'am, with the winter storms that are due to—"

"It's been warm and my daughter said she's been wearing a T-shirt for the past week," the woman interrupted. "We don't need that gas-guzzling monster."

The rental car attendant opened his mouth to object, but the woman immediately held up a finger to silence him. "Just the car. I'm not gonna let you upsell me. I've read several articles and know how you guys work."

"Just the car." The attendant turned to his computer. "Yes, ma'am."

Tracer waited a fair distance away so as not to insert himself into the woman's line of sight. When the couple had turned the corner with their papers and car keys, he stepped up to the counter.

"Welcome to Billings. Can I help you, sir?" the man behind the counter said as he finished filing the previous customer's papers away.

"I need a car," Tracer said.

"Sure. Do you need a four-wheel drive?"

"Yes, sir."

"Your name?" the attendant asked.

"Mike Smith."

"Welcome, Mr. Smith. Will it be just you this evening?" the hostess asked.

"Yes," Tracer said, pushing his camera behind him.

"This way, please." The hostess led Tracer to the middle of the dining room. "What brings you to Whitefish Resort?"

"I'm doing research for an article."

"Oh? What kind of article?"

"It's an in-depth report on dining establishments. I'm just compiling information at the moment. I analyze the similarities and differences and try to find something unique and exciting," Tracer said, bluffing his way through the impromptu interview. "As for the scope of the project, it just depends on what I find to write about. Editors are always looking for new and different things. So it's my job to find a new angle on a story."

"That sounds exciting. I hope you find many great things to write about during your stay here." The hostess paused, ready to answer any questions he might have.

"Thank you. So far I have a great atmosphere and a wonderful smile to start things off with." He sat down and accepted the wine list.

"Your server will be right with you," the hostess said, her smile becoming a little brighter from his compliment.

He pulled a pair of reading glasses from his pocket and gave them a flip before sliding them on his face. He scanned the selection briefly. A moment later, a waiter dressed in a white shirt and a black vest approached.

"Good evening, sir. Can I get you something to drink?"

"I'll have a glass of Sangiovese," Tracer replied.

The waiter gave an approving nod. "A good choice, sir." He wrote down the selection. "Can I start you off with an appetizer?"

"Can I get a plate of fresh vegetables with a small bowl of vinaigrette?" Tracer asked.

"Of course, sir."

"I'm a vegetarian, and I also have a nut allergy," Tracer explained.

"Yes, sir. I'll make a note and see that the chef prepares your meal as requested."

"Thank you." Tracer toyed with the menu, pretending to take in the options. A small corner of its real estate held only a half dozen vegetarian dishes. In just a few seconds, he had all but memorized the section.

Loud laughter and conversation trumpeted from the entrance. Tracer looked up to find a party spilling through the door, likely from a nearby tavern.

Six young adults stumbled to the waiting area, and the hostess struggled to wrangle the group into a more reasonable mob. Two young women leaned on each other for support while a third clung to a tall, lanky man—apparently not because he was endearing to her, but because he seemed to be the only sober one of the bunch, and cut from a different cloth than the rest of his party. He worked with the hostess to usher his party to a table.

"Your wine, sir," the waiter said, holding out the bottle and reciting the producer and vintage for Tracer's approval.

"Oh." Tracer looked up with a start. "Sorry. I was distracted." He leaned back, giving the waiter room to pour the wine into the glass.

"Is that group bothering you? I can have management remove them if they bother you," the waiter offered.

"No. That won't be necessary. This is all part of writing—reporting on what is and what isn't," Tracer said, explaining his view.

"I heard that you're a writer. May I ask which magazine you're writing for? I'm studying journalism and working my way through college."

"That's admirable of you. I'm a freelance writer, self-taught. For this article, I have several magazines that I'll send my findings to. Sometimes they'll ask that I rewrite my original article with a specific narrative."

"Why would you do that? Isn't it your work? Don't they have to accept it as is?" the waiter asked.

"I could do that, but I would have to trade my hotel room for a broken-down car."

"But you're deceiving your audience," the waiter said, trying to understand the concept.

"Not really. Everyone knows there are multiple sides to a story, and then there is the truth. Most stories have an element of that truth, and everyone tells a version that usually favors themselves. Even if you watch a video of an incident, you may interpret it differently than the person standing next to you," Tracer explained.

"I see. What if two opposing magazines seek opposing views?"

"I rewrite it with two different viewpoints. I use all the same data, but highlight a different take on the subject. It's up to the reader to objectively digest the information."

"Do you sell to only one of them?"

"All of them, if I can. Multiple paychecks for the same research," Tracer said.

"Nice. Very clever, sir," the waiter said. "I'll check on your appetizer. Do you know what you would like to order?"

Tracer ordered, then pulled his camera off the chair next to him, adjusted the wine glass and snapped a photo.

Picking up a pen, he wrote down a note in code to help him remember the details of each of his target's companions.

"Halen. Halen. You gotta see this." Heather, Jamie Spears's longtime friend, leaned over her date's lap, extending her phone to Halen. "This guy is creeping on you."

Halen sucked water through her straw while still dancing to the lingering music in her head. She wasn't ready to slow down, but the rest of her company complained of hunger. She leaned forward and scrutinized the video after feeling a tap on her arm. "Oh my god. I have a stalker."

"Didn't we see him downtown earlier today?"

"That's right. He was following us through the boutique stores," Halen said.

"Yes, and he looked at the same clothes that we looked at," Heather added.

"That's really annoying." Halen sat back, disgusted that she would have to deal with another stalker. "I'm on vacation. That's enough of this. I'm going to take care of this creep."

She stumbled out of her chair and stared across the room at the man sitting by himself. His eyes darted to their table and back to his plate. He toyed with his food as if he was trying to find a way to discreetly hide the vegetables he didn't want to eat. Being caught was the ultimate embarrassment.

Halen did her best to march straight toward the man, but three Blue Hawaiians and a chocolate martini challenged her balance. Weaving through the tables, she approached him. His idle, semi-relaxed movements became more fidgety before he suddenly froze in place.

"What is your problem, old man?"

The patron sat back in his chair, wide-eyed and speechless.

"You never seen a celebrity up close? Stupid nit," Halen spat.

The man was dumbfounded, struggling to utter a sentence.

"You want a peek, don't you?" Halen stared down at the man, whose forehead was starting to glisten with a few drops of sweat.

His chubby jaw dropped. It scissored up and down as if trying to form words, but not a sound made it out. His eyes grew wider when he looked up to see her scathing face staring down at him. The man froze, unable to speak. His time to respond quickly deteriorated until it was too late to do anything.

"Everyone wants to see," Halen blasted. "So here's your own private show." She stared at him for a moment longer, then reached down, grabbed the hem of her shirt, turned her side to him and ripped it up.

The man's eyes grew wider yet at the image presented to him. His features became fixed in shock and wonderment as he stared at the discoloration on her side.

The alcohol in her system and rage at the man's unhealthy obsession had triggered her wild impulse to expose something that she'd always fought desperately to hide.

"Your salad, sir," the waiter announced as he set the plate down.

Tracer pulled his attention away from the young woman and the man she had cornered on the far side of the restaurant.

"Thank you." He moved his camera out of the way. "Could you ask the chef if I can get a few snapshots of some other vegetarian dishes so I can use them for my article?"

"Of course, sir," the waiter said, and returned to the kitchen to relay the request.

Tracer turned his plate one way then the other while hovering a fork above it to see if the salad would look better with the fork sunk into it or if it would be best undisturbed. He decided to take a picture without a fork first. Standing, he angled his camera toward the plate, focusing the lens. The leafy salad jiggled and the wine glass tipped over, casting the ruby liquid across the table and his dinner plate.

Tracer looked up to the bloodshot eyes of the tipsy actress. Her mouth twisted into a smirky smile while she laughed, which was really more of a snort.

"Oops," she said to Tracer as she pushed herself back up off the table. Gasps and muffled snickering came from her group's table.

Tracer shot her a glare, but it didn't have a chance to be received, as the young woman was already strutting back to her friends, light-years away from reality.

7

The following day, Tracer flipped through the images on his camera, studying each on the television in his room. The photos of the restaurant dishes were immediately deleted, but the photos of Halen's group of friends lingered on the TV or several minutes. He studied their faces, the intelligence in their eyes, their watchfulness of their surroundings—or lack thereof. He wanted to be able to easily pick them out of a crowd by recognizing their mannerisms and determine who they looked to as their general leader.

One young man seemed the most intelligent, almost as if he were playing shepherd to the drunken flock. He seemed to know many people at the Montana resort. The only way to know that many people, especially people from all levels of social status, was to be a frequent visitor. Or, he was the local guy who gained notoriety beginning here in Whitefish and later spread his face and talents to other parts of the country. Tracer concluded that it was most likely the latter.

He had heard them mention that they would hit the slopes around midday. His fourth-floor balcony gave him a commanding view of many of the runs. Jamie, the one friend who seemed to be financing the bulk of the trip, didn't take to the slopes. Instead, Tracer found that she frequented the high-end shops and loved to buy a plethora of needless things using her father's bottomless credit card.

The group stayed in a collection of suites just a building away from Tracer's room, even though Jamie's father owned a vacation home just down the mountain. Apparently, their trip required space to frolic outside the immediate supervision of the girl's father.

Jamie's companion was a gopher, as Tracer liked to call him. He was the lovestruck boyfriend who did anything she asked just to be her lapdog and spoon her in bed—probably while remaining fully clothed. He ran for food, alcohol and drugs, keeping a buffer of protection for the elites so they wouldn't have to associate with the common populace or be noticed by the police.

The dry and warmer-than-usual weather had beaten down on the resort for several days, threatening to end the ski season as the snowmaking machines struggled to maintain the slippery slope. Much of the snow around the buildings had melted, leaving paths dry and welcoming for sandal-clad feet. Many on the slopes wore T-shirts, with a few women wearing just a bikini and their skis.

Taking a cup of tea outside, Tracer easily found the local friend's bright yellow shirt. He had already taken a dozen photos of the group as they made their first run down the slope. The pro surfer had already made two runs before the rest of the group joined him. Tracer watched the hand gestures pointing toward a restaurant, and the group turned their skis toward the establishment and finished the run down the slope.

Tracer walked back inside, grabbed a light vest and headed out the door.

Chatter abounded inside the restaurant as Tracer stepped through the entrance. A snowboard with a please-wait-to-be-seated sign stood just inside the entrance at a second set of sliding barn doors. The warm smile of the approaching hostess contradicted the *Welcome to Hell* words on the front of her podium.

"Just one today?" Her dark curly hair bounced with each step as she strode up to the welcome podium.

"Yes please." Tracer scanned the inside of the restaurant for the bright yellow shirt.

"Is the bar okay? We're a little busy today, and a number of groups are on a waiting list."

"That's fine." Following behind the hostess, he saw people from all walks of life congregating on the mountain for one reason. Dozens of skis and snowboards leaned against the wooden racks outside the old chalet.

"Have you been into town to see the winter carnival?" the hostess asked.

"No, I haven't."

"You should check it out. There are contests and a lot of fun events. I'm taking my kids down later." She waved a hand at a barstool.

"Thank you. I'll look into it. I've been meaning to head into town to explore what Whitefish has to offer." Tracer sat down and turned on the barstool to find a young woman ready with a drink list and a menu.

Suddenly a yellow sleeve reached in next to Tracer. He glanced out of the corner of his eye and noticed the tall local who had accompanied the group up from Florida. Tracer turned to him and leaned away to give him some room to collect his drinks.

"Hey, Gil. Are you competing in the skijoring this year?" a young man seated next to Tracer asked.

"Oh, hey Walt. Yeah. I planned on it. Does Dimsy still have that stallion we won with two years ago?"

"Yeah, but he's being lent out as a stud down on his buddy's ranch in Wyoming."

"That's a bummer." Gil pulled the sipping straw to his mouth.

"But there's a foal born from that stallion that lives just a few short miles from here."

"That doesn't tell me anything, Walt."

"I think he's about three now. Dimsy's been training him up for something."

"Does he have a rider?" Gil asked.

"I don't know. You'll have to call him."

"I'll do that. First thing in the morning. Thanks, Walt."

THE HIT

"No problem, man. See you at the track."

"See you." Gil turned back to the bar and finished collecting the drinks for his friends, then disappeared through the crowd.

Tracer turned his attention back to the bartender and ordered a club soda and lime, then perused the menu, deep in thought.

To murder someone was one thing. To get away with it was entirely different and near impossible, especially with modern technology. To make it look like an accident was easier in some ways, yet harder in others. If done right, he would simply have to place the proverbial stick in the right place for the victim to trip on of their own accord.

Dealing with reckless teens would be easy, as they typically didn't listen to the whispers of caution. Those in their early to mid-twenties had a growing sense of caution, though their intuition to fully calculate life's consequences wasn't fully developed. It also mattered how sheltered the individual was. A young woman he had known in college still believed in the tooth fairy, Santa Claus and the Easter Bunny. The girl's roommate made short work of that and educated her on multiple other things her parents had neglected to prepare her for. This type of person would have been the easiest target, as opposed to a child surviving on the streets of Moscow or in the Middle East, where growing up suspicious of everything was second nature.

Detectives had now become infinitely smarter than they were twenty or thirty years ago. Technology had advanced by leaps and bounds. Anyone who wanted to commit a murder should be dissuaded from doing so because of all that had been developed and all that would be developed in the future—not to mention any laws that might change to make it easier for the authorities to probe into one's personal life. Now it depended mostly on time. Time the authorities could spend on each case.

If someone wanted to kill a junkie on the street, the detective might just dismiss the death as an accidental overdose and not look further than the needle in their arm. A higher profile case like a celebrity death would have police and private detectives swarming the town, overturning every rock they could find, because of public influence and the money involved. This was the challenge, and this was why he had to hide in plain sight just behind the front line of the crowd. He had to be just another innocent spectator, curious to know what had happened.

A low-level magazine writer was typical of touristy areas. The kind of publicity a good writer could draw to the area helped everyone in the community. If just one article brought one family into town for a weekend, they could potentially spend a thousand dollars or more, helping the community prosper. But Tracer wouldn't be influencing any type of community growth.

All these thoughts tumbled through his head as he sought the right spot to place the stick. He turned back to the menu before him as the bartender returned to take his order.

"Have you decided, sir?" the bartender returned ready to take his order.

8

Tracer's curiosity about skijoring had grown from mild to genuine enthusiasm, causing him to visit the event regardless if Halen Kettleman would attend or not. His alias and subtle prosthetics altering his appearance gave him the confidence to explore the many different events in the community. If he didn't already have a one-way profession, he probably would have taken a keyboard along with the camera to produce quality travel articles.

He took photos as he approached the collection of various vehicles. A dozen horse trailers were parked at one end of a large gravel lot. The spectator parking was at the other end. Inside the temporary barricade, heavy equipment stood off to one side, distanced from the public. Tracer took pictures of most everything, asking simple questions of the locals and really filling the shoes of a journalist.

The persistent warm weather made driving and outdoor activities easy but hampered the planning and logistics of the winter festival. It was unheard of in the northern states to have a winter carnival without freezing temperatures and snow. This year, Montana had seen its warmest February in a decade or more. The parks and recreation department hauled in a dozen truckloads of snow just to create the course that Tracer had become mildly enamored with.

He approached the crowd, surveying each person and noting whether they were a sheep or a wolf. He thought of himself as a coyote, surveying his target and watching for anything or anyone he could persuade to do his dirty work.

Anything could be manipulated to cause harm. A jittery horse, an inattentive driver or a person's own clumsiness could be used against them. A skittish horse could be bumped in the ribs, but who was to say if the resulting kick would be placed well enough to kill? Even more luck would be needed for a distracted driver. Tracer didn't have what it took to receive a favor from God, so he'd have to look for something more dependable—like the stupidity of youth.

If they drove fast, challenge them to drive faster. If they did drugs, encourage them to do another line. And if they're stupid enough, invite them to walk across your newly built invisible bridge.

There were thousands of ways to die. The trick was to present an environment that was conducive for the reaper to come knocking.

Tracer skirted the horse trailers, taking random shots of the riders as they prepared to make their runs. The skiers checked their equipment and talked strategy with their teammates. He wove through the crowd, returning a nod here, a wave there and exchanging an occasional smile with a toddler. He didn't advertise what he was doing; he just blended in as some reporter taking photos and writing notes.

He had bought a set of quality outdoor hearing aids for this job. Through the engineering marvel, he eavesdropped on random conversations. From a distance, he mentally cataloged any important information or events his target might attend.

Contestants milled around the starting line along with their support roadies and cheer squads. Tracer found Halen mixed in with a few locals and the rest of her group. Like her, they wore the latest fashions. The shy one of the group had even neglected to remove all the tags from her designer pullover. Gil quietly approached her and motioned at the tag. The young woman discreetly pulled the tag off and dropped it in the trash.

The act of kindness didn't go unnoticed, but Tracer was too busy to give it more than a blip of acknowledgment. His job was much like a safety officer's, but instead of trying to prevent an accident, he was looking to cause one. He noticed a light pole that seemed a bit loose. With some subtle persuasion, it could fall and injure or kill someone. It wasn't a good idea, and he didn't want to be around for any sort of investigation. There were too many eyes that might see what he would do. He screwed down the loose nut so it wouldn't accidentally come apart and topple. People being on guard for potential accidents was the last thing he wanted.

Peering through the fence, he saw that Gil was up next. He had captured a half dozen other contestants on his camera—photos he would erase later that day. He squatted on his heels in the slushy mud and prepared his camera as Gil readied his grip on the rope.

Capturing some preliminary shots, Tracer took pictures of the vapor coming from the horse's nostrils, the clumps of mud and snow lifting in the air from the dancing hooves and a glance from the rider as she checked her teammate for a nod.

The nod came and the horse launched. Steel-cleated shoes hammered into the semi-frozen ground. Slack disappeared from the thirty-foot rope dallied to the saddle horn as the rider spurred her horse into a gallop.

The barrel-racing horse made short work of getting up to speed. Gil guided his skis through the blocks, effectively starting the clock and beginning the run. Cutting to the right, he made it around the first pole and began the short slalom before hitting the first of three jumps. Pulling himself closer to the four-legged stick of dynamite, he launched up and over the first jump.

People held their breath as they watched the former champion sail off the edge, his hands frantically feeding slack back to the horse and rider to allow himself half a beat to land and recover before accelerating to the next set of poles and the second jump.

Three horses had slipped on the corner as they attempted to turn their forward momentum around the horseshoe-shaped course. Tracer zoomed the camera in to catch an exciting moment or mishap, should one occur. Clicking the button, he shot a four-round burst in an attempt to capture the perfect stunning moment in time as Gil cornered around a gate pole.

Through the second set of slalom gates, Gil choked up on the rope, letting the tail follow behind. Like the tail of an enthusiastic dog, the cotton rope whipped back and forth frantically. Gil landed the second jump with a wobble but quickly recovered and reoriented his skis toward the next gate.

Passing the next set of poles, he lined up his skis to capture the bonus ring hanging an arm's reach away just past the final jump. The only way to snag it was in midflight from the third jump. But it could be detrimental, as it left precious little time to grab the rope again and secure a solid landing to race through the final two gates and the finish line, stopping the clock. If a racer captured the ring, a half second would be deducted from their overall time. With the race measured to the hundredth of a second, a half second could boost the team several placements in a close race.

Gil swerved for the ring, taking a longer path. He reached the top of the ramp and jumped. Tracer followed his movements, snapping a shot right as the rope sizzled through his left hand as he reached for the ring.

9

Though people migrated up and down the sidewalks, the majority were drawn to the vibrant music coming from Casey's rooftop bar. The tall rock-and-wood structure was bathed in colorful lights, drawing in patrons. The seared meat, deep-fried onion rings and fruity flavors from the kitchen and the bar added to the elixir that separated customers from their money. So many people had said it was the best place to be for after-hours entertainment. Tracer knew that the young adults wouldn't miss spending time at Whitefish's hot spot.

Blue light glowed like ice against the translucent frosted glass. High-quality liquor stacked on the tiered terrace created its own light show through the various colors of alcohol. The bartender's pressed shirt and vest flowed with him as he made drink upon drink for the thirsty crowd.

Blue flame towers and their reflecting shields speckled the roof along with a dozen or more tables.

Light illuminated the dance floor, pulsing with the beat of the music and the steps of the dancing couples, sending ripples of light out like pebbles tossed in a pond. The unseasonably warm weather allowed the owner to open the rooftop during the festival and attract more clientele *and* more income.

Tracer watched for his target from a block away. He had arrived at sundown and found access to a nearby rooftop, where he leaned against a fan inlet and surveyed the party from a distance. With a view of the entrance, he watched Halen arrive with her entourage and enter the building. Minutes later, they emerged on the roof and settled into the hastily made VIP section.

Tracer waited by the air duct several minutes after Halen's group had settled into their corner of the roof. The party was in full swing as a DJ mixed the music from his corner. Thumping dance music vibrated the bones of the festival participants as they capped off a day of fun.

A small VIP sign hung on the velvet ropes, isolating the area from the rest of the patrons. To each side, tall potted evergreens created a living wall and held their spiny needles on point, ready to cause discomfort to any who decided to crash through them.

Tracer watched the party on the roof for a while and noted the magnetism of the local celebrity. The local snowboarder, Gil, seemed to be the proper host, bringing selected locals up to meet Halen and her friends and not overwhelming her with a barrage of unwanted attention. Tracer watched for a few moments longer, then backtracked off the clothing store roof and made his way to the rooftop of Casey's.

He found a recently vacated table just beyond the VIP section and close to the bar. He arranged the empty glasses on the dirtiest side of the table and brushed a crumb off the side closest to him. In short order, one of the waitstaff came to collect the glasses and wipe down the table.

"What can I get for you, sweetie?" the young woman asked.

"Honestly," Tracer began, "I'd like twenty years shaved off my driver's license and your phone number."

The young woman smiled at the compliment.

"But since we both know that's impossible," Tracer continued, "How about a watered-down scotch and twenty years shaved off my driver's license?"

She smiled again and disappeared to get his drink. When she returned, Tracer placed a twenty-dollar bill on the edge of the table to pay for the drink.

After a bit of small talk with the waitress, Tracer was able to con his way into getting a few photos of the bartender mixing drinks. Returning to his table, he flipped open his notebook and sketched the layout of the Sky Bar. He didn't know if he would need it to plan an accident, but it was better to have it than not.

"Excuse me, sir."

Tracer jumped. His mind had temporarily been fixed on the details of his map.

"Didn't I see you taking pictures of the skijoring today?"

Tracer looked up to find Gil holding three empty glasses. "What? Oh, sorry. I was taking some notes. What did you say?"

"I was wondering if you were out at the skijoring today?" Gil asked.

"Yes. I was. It's an interesting sport. I have heard the name around town but didn't know much about it. So, I thought I'd see what it was about."

"Did you get some good pictures?" Gil asked.

"I hope that I did. I take pictures mostly of food and drink. They stand still long enough for me to focus and get the lighting right."

"I'd like to see what you got. If you don't mind, that is," Gil said.

"Ahemmm." A woman's voice reached through the shrubbery to blast Gil with an admonishment and a cue to retrieve the next round of drinks.

"I'll get them, cool your jets," Gil barked back through the shrubbery.

"Sorry, sir. My friends seem to be more insistent than usual," Gil said.

"Good friends are hard to come by," Tracer offered.

"Gil," the woman's voice said insistently.

"I'd better get these refilled before the sands of Hades bury me," Gil said in a hushed tone.

"Stop by when you get a minute. I can flip through them for you."

"Let me get these refilled and I'll be back in a few minutes."

"Sounds great. See you in a bit." Tracer watched the second-place holder of the skijoring event wander off through the crowd with empty glasses.

The drinks flowed like water, and soon Tracer's target dragged the tall Montana boy out on the dance floor along with two of her girlfriends. The beat thumped on through the night and Tracer watched as the youngsters danced. He made small talk with others who passed by to make it appear that he wasn't a threat, though he was likely the deadliest man in attendance. The bouncers stationed around the rooftop weren't deadly; they were babysitters. They were there to put the disobedient children in a timeout off the establishment's property. Of course they didn't want to kill anyone.

Tracer watched for his opportunity to kill, or rather nudge an accident to happen. It would be a miracle if he found it on the rooftop, so he wasn't too intent on looking. It was a hopeful thought, but the walls around the edge were just too tall to trip and tumble over the side to the ground. What he was after was information that would give him the opportunity to set a trap. Something that would allow him to be ahead of the game. Something that would allow him to place that stick in the right spot.

She was too high of a profile. Lawyers would dig for years to find the truth. Which was why making it look like an accident was so necessary. The more natural and obvious it looked, the more likely it was to be ruled an accident.

As the party wound to a fevered high, Tracer saw Halen exhibit the behavior that his employer wanted to dispose of. The woman dropped her pants and urinated in the middle of the dance floor. The fluid spread across the floor, where dancing feet began to spread it. Some saw it and immediately left. Others thought someone had just spilled a drink and continued to dance through it.

After Tracer killed her, society would only mourn the nineteen-year-old until the next commercial break.

He felt no emotion for the young actress and was eager to collect the rest of his paycheck and move on to his next assignment. He had watched her films in his hotel room and saw a bit of raw talent, but she failed to learn from her craft. It was as if she were substituting her fame for talent. Fame did not impress him. Not much of anything impressed him. Certainly nothing that humankind had done.

Screams erupted from the dance floor. Jolted out of his philosophical thoughts, Tracer looked up to see two women locked together like two stags with their antlers entangled. They each had a fistful of the other's hair while their other fists flew wildly, seeking to hit anything while their nails clawed deep to draw blood. Halen pulled the woman in for another punch. The other woman grabbed her shirt and pulled it over Halen's head. Halen was now topless and still swinging with wild abandon. She continued to fight with her own shirt around her head and the other woman still clenching a fistful of hair.

The two bodyguards jumped to assist Gil and Halen's other friends. They pulled at the women's hands and arms to separate them and stop what could potentially be a very public and costly lawsuit. Gil wrapped Halen in a bear hug, holding her arms up around her head and backing her into their VIP section. With her shirt around her head, nearly everyone was afforded a look at the birthmark on her side.

A dark splotch covered part of her breast. Tracer wouldn't have thought much of it except for its unique shape. It appeared as though it were a fist raising its middle finger. The intriguing shape stuck in Tracer's mind and added an element to his assignment that he hadn't expected and was ill-equipped to deal with.

The shouts and insults continued from inside the VIP area, with Halen using every curse word Tracer had ever heard, plus a few he thought were made up.

"Halen, calm down. It's not worth it," Gil soothed.

"That bi . . . I'm going to kill her," Halen spouted, pulling her shirt back in place.

"Halen, we got your back." Jamie tried to reassure her friend. Once the punches started, she had fled back to their section, out of harm's way.

"Let me go beat her ass!" Halen screamed.

"No. No. You don't need that," Jamie said. "You'll get put in jail and miss our flight home."

"Plus, you'll miss out on Grit's new racing sled," Gil said.

"He'll let me ride it?"

"He promised—one time. I can probably talk him into a couple more." Gil's soothing promised turned Halen's attention away from the other woman.

"When?" Halen asked.

"Tomorrow afternoon. On the lake."

10

"What do you need, Grit?" Gil asked.

"Hand me that laptop." Grit pointed to a work bench in his trailer.

Gil stepped into the trailer, grabbed the laptop and handed it over, then tipped his aluminum beer bottle up for another pull.

Grit plugged the computer into his sled and pulled up the diagnostics and tuning system. A two-stroke zing turned Grit's and Gil's attention away from the technical issues. The engine of an approaching machine cut off just outside the trailer.

Squeals of delight and breathlessness replaced the loud engine. Halen and Jamie stepped off the machine, laughing and stumbling through the light snow that announced the beginning of a major storm.

Grit finished tuning the engine and disconnected the laptop. "Try that," he said to his driver. The scrawny man grinned, exposing his jack-o-lantern teeth. He stepped aboard the sled and rapped the throttle. The track whirled, sending bits of snow backward into the darkening sky.

Gil set the jack down so the machine sat fully on the frozen lake. The driver inched his machine forward to their temporary starting line. Halen did the same. The stock sled that Halen rode couldn't hold a candle to the custom snow machine that Grit had been continually tinkering with, but competing against another racer helped imitate the conditions on the track. It also gave the girls some fun in the pretend competition.

Halen's heart hammered as she lined up on the starting line. Her nerves weren't buzzing nearly as much as the first couple times she had thumbed the throttle. Next to the highly modified snow machine, she didn't expect to win any races, but that didn't stop her from pretending that she was an elite racer. She copied her opponent's every move and stored them in her brain in the off chance she might get a part where she played something similar.

Halen stole a sideways glance at her opponent. Demon of Speed vinyl stickers decorated the sides of the machine's hood, announcing to the world the bravado and intent behind the label.

She hugged the seat with her legs. Jitters traveled through her body, culminating in her left leg, where her calf pumped them out as nervous energy.

"Worm, you ready?" Gil yelled through the noise of the revving two-cycle engines.

The city's local daredevil nodded.

"Halen, are you ready?"

Halen nodded.

"This one's the last one of the night!" Gil shouted, then flipped the switch for the starter lights.

The lights counted down. Halen's muscles tensed in anticipation for the start. The yellow lights flashed, and she and Worm slammed their throttles to the max.

Worm lurched to a sled-and-a-half lead. Halen started gaining and surpassed the Demon of Speed. She kept the throttle pegged, accelerating toward the finish line.

Heavy flakes of snow flew up over her helmet and matted against her visor, severely limiting her vision. As the machine found its own top-end limit, she stole a glance to the side. Demon of Speed and the crazy man they called Worm weren't there.

Halen slowed and stopped just across the finish line. The snowman they had made earlier that day stood with his smiling face. Two checkered flags protruded from its body, and the pointed ears on the top of his head made him look like a NASCAR Batman.

She turned on her seat to look back. Heavy flakes blocked all but the faintest of glows coming from the trailer and mobile workshop. Worm had already circled back around to diagnose the problem with his machine. Turning again, Halen stared at the checkered flags, deciding whether or not to pluck them from Frosty as he sat there with a silent cheer. It was as if he was mocking her with a joyous grin.

She took off her helmet and set it above the handlebars, leaning it against the windscreen.

"You win."

Halen turned toward the voice. A white mass rose up out of the snow next to her snow machine. A jolt to her head stunned her, and the world went dark.

11

Ice-cold water jolted Halen awake. She instinctively gasped for breath, only to suck plastic tightly over her mouth. Water soaked into every fiber of her clothing, pressing death's embrace tighter around her body. She could hear the gurgle and pop of bubbles. The crack of ice added to her fear of confinement.

Knowing that ice wouldn't allow her to resurface struck a chord in her brain and demanded that she lash out. The shock of the cold had numbed her limbs to inaction as panic continued to scream inside her head. Instant uncontrolled shivering took hold of her body. Icy shards of water stabbed at her, shredding her conscious effort to move her limbs.

No light leaked into her vision, though she strained to peek through her eyelids. It was blacker than a moonless night with heavy clouds. She couldn't see. There wasn't an inkling of light to be found anywhere. Panic flooded her mind even more—being blind had been one of her childhood fears. Now it seemed to have come to life. She clawed at the heavy plastic again, trying to rip it open to get a glimpse of light, but she could barely control her hands and arms as they shook violently from the cold.

The water pressed in further around her, and she clutched at her face, trying to tear the plastic away. This time she was able to grip the plastic, but not enough to cause any damage. She tried finding the seam around her neck and tore at it but found layers of duct tape. The plastic bag was there to stay, and she would soon suffocate. Maybe this was how her life would end. Suffocated in a plastic bag at the bottom of the lake.

There was a tug on her body and she felt herself being dragged through the water. A more pronounced fear suddenly overcame her.

No one would find her for years.

Slipping in and out of consciousness, Halen strained to identify the sound of a droning engine in the distance. As she began to wake, she felt repeated lurches and a side-to-side sway. The limited movements she could make didn't reveal much about her current surroundings or what was happening outside her cramped enclosure, only that she wasn't in the water anymore, though she was still wet. Boxes and cold steel pressed in on her as the weight shifted inside her prison. Sometimes there was a jolt, but she mostly felt a soft sway back and forth like rolling across a pile of pillows.

THE HIT

The muffled rumble of the engine sounded familiar, like a distant snow machine, but in another way it sounded very close, like it was just on the other side of a thick wall. The machine kept its steady hum, sometimes almost lulling her back to sleep. It seemed she had been listening to it for hours as she climbed out of her unconscious state, but she soon realized that was the least of her worries.

With consciousness came the bone-chilling cold. It seemed to have frozen her limbs down to the bone. Shivering hurt with every violent jerk and compounded the fear inside her. Something pushed in on all sides around her. She began to breathe hard as she remembered the plastic bag covering her mouth. As she sucked air in, she tasted the cold frosted air with a hint of pine.

The plastic bag didn't suck to her face as she breathed, but she could still feel it around her as it agitated the lump on the side of her head. Metal cans and plastic boxes pressed in from all angles, preventing her from moving more than a couple inches. Her mind began to race, trying to make sense of her surroundings.

The bag around her head prevented her from seeing anything, but somehow she could still breathe. The plastic wasn't up against her mouth anymore. With a few anxious breaths, she drew in more cold air. She could breathe, but she couldn't see and she couldn't move.

Time passed and Halen shivered, sometimes uncontrollably. She tried moving her hands but they were tied together. She tried moving her feet. They too were tied together. She tried to straighten her body from her hunched posture. Her feet pulled on her hands. She'd been hog-tied. Pressing her shoulders up and out, she found that the items around her also limited her movement. Whatever was around her wasn't allowing her to stretch. She was stuck in one position, shivering, wet and cold.

More moments passed. If it was hours or minutes, she couldn't tell. Time blurred as Halen tried to piece together how and why her world had been flipped on end. The numbing cold slowed her thoughts to something akin to hardening concrete. She had been abducted, and whoever had kidnapped her had someplace to get to as if the devil himself were on his trail.

She had just come to confront the why of her situation when a desperate urge to pee outweighed the necessity to stay quiet. She screamed and beat her head against the roof of the compartment she was crammed into.

The machine slowed, then stopped. A few seconds later, the engine turned off and the world was suddenly dead silent. The elimination of both sound and movement amplified the cold and the screaming demand of her bladder, not to mention the pain in her bottom from hitting every bump on the trail.

Halen held her breath when she heard the sound of latches unbuckling on either side of her followed by a grunt. Part of her enclosure lifted and fell into the snow with a soft poof. She felt the platform shift and thought her kidnapper had climbed inside with her. Her heart thumped in her chest, then her throat. She would soon come face-to-face with the person who dared kidnap a celebrity.

Someone worked at a knot that held a large canvas bag up around her body. The knot jerked loose and the bag dropped around her shoulders. Her body shuddered as much from the cold as from what would soon be her first glimpse of whoever was responsible for her dire situation and the fate they had in store for her.

Her breath quickened as fingers tugged at the tape that had sealed air around her head while she was underwater. The tape came loose and the plastic bag came off, taking several strands of hair with it. Halen looked up to see a hooded figure silhouetted against a dark gray sky.

A flurry of large snowflakes whipped through the air as the massive storm raged all around. Trees bent under the storm's wrath and the wind screamed through the branches.

She couldn't tell what part of the day it was, but the large flakes seemed to accumulate an inch with every beat of her heart. It was Mother Nature trying her best to bury her alive. Halen could feel the urge to keep moving or be lost to the thick blanket of snow until spring.

"I have to pee," Halen pleaded.

The figure reached down and grabbed the lid he had just flipped to the ground. Though she couldn't see, she assumed her abductor was a man. He made strong purposeful movements without an ounce of tenderness or concern.

"Please. No!" Halen screamed.

He looked down at her for a moment. His bug-eyed goggles and respirator gave him an otherworldly appearance. He reached and grabbed the front of her snowsuit and lifted.

With her hands bound to her feet and the intense shivering, she couldn't step out of the compartment. He dragged her out and dropped her in the snow, leaving the semi-warm confines of the clamshell sled behind.

"I need my hands free so I can get out of this suit," Halen said.

The man kicked her in the side, turning her face-down in the freshly fallen snow. Cold bit at her cheek as her face pressed into the frozen flakes. The man straddled her, pinning her face to the snow with her bottom to the sky.

Halen puffed air out to keep the snow from collapsing in around her face and suffocating her. The man tugged at her one-piece snowsuit. She wondered how he thought she would be able to relieve herself without cutting the ropes that bound her hands. There was no possible way. He had to at least cut her hands free to wiggle out of the ski suit.

He was tugging on her suit when suddenly she felt something colder than the snow. Steel slid between her skin and the fabric that was meant to keep her warm. A shiver crept up her spine, adding to the tremors of cold she had endured for hours. The knife slid across her back, just grazing the skin, and Halen held her breath for fear that the blade might cut her.

Cold air flooded over her bottom as her backside was exposed to the elements. A fist grabbed her hood and flipped her back over.

Halen stared up at the dark figure. Her insides tightened as she waited for cold steel to slice through more than her clothes. He wasn't gentle. His actions seemed intentional and savage.

"Where's the toilet? she said through chattering teeth.

"Go there or don't go at all," the man growled.

"I can't go here."

When he simply stared at her without comment, Halen continued. "It's not civilized."

"Humph," the man grunted. He turned away from her and took a step toward the trees, then relieved himself. "Is pissin' on the dance floor what you call civilized?" he called back over his shoulder.

Turning back around, he squatted on his heels and took off his goggles and respirator. It was lighter now with the approaching dawn, and Halen could make out a slim face and a two-day-old beard. She noticed the white scar that circled his right eye. She didn't recognize it, but his face seemed familiar.

"Is that something they teach in acting school? Pissing on the dance floors?"

The man picked her up off the ground and hurled her back into the snow machine's trailer, causing her to exhale a grunt.

Wiggling around to sit upright, she looked up at the man. Realization set in that she was far from her element and helpless. "Please sir, I'm cold." Halen cowered in the small trailer, shivering.

He picked up the other half of the clamshell cargo sled and prepared to slam it down.

"Please!" Halen screamed. "I don't want to die." She looked into her captor's eyes, searching for an ounce of empathy. "I really don't want to die."

The lid slammed down, trapping Halen inside.

12

Time had warped reality as the darkness and the steady drone of the machine kept Halen on the edge of consciousness, disorienting her in a twisted nightmare. She had fallen asleep and been jolted awake over and over by her captor's relentless determination to get somewhere.

After their first stop and the humiliation of having her bottom exposed, she'd begged and screamed to stop and get warm, but her pleas were drowned out by the drone of the engine and the raging storm. Sobs and tremors of fear gripped her between fits of restless sleep and shivering. She actively worked her limbs in the confined space to keep some sort of circulation going in her hands and feet. No matter how much she cried and screamed, the machine rumbled on and on through the storm.

When the man stopped again, she figured it to be about half a day later. He opened the clamshell and reached in, pulling at the ropes with gloved hands. She held still so he could work at the ropes. In her state, she wasn't going to argue.

After the ropes were off, he made her strip out of her wet clothes. He tossed her clothes on the floor of the sled and motioned for her to get back in. A quick glance around revealed thick forest layered under a heavy blanket of snow. Seeing no better option, Halen crawled back into the cramped space.

The man pulled a wool blanket from his gear and threw it at her, then fished several hot packs from a container and activated two of them. "Bend the tab of a new one when these get cold." He tumbled several more in alongside her, then slammed the lid down, hitting her on the head.

The latches snapped closed like a jail cell door slamming shut. It was a sobering and terrifying sound for anyone who'd never heard it before. A moment later, the engine started and tugged on the sled, signaling a continuation of a long, cramped ride in what could end up being her coffin.

Halen tugged the thick wool blanket around herself and massaged her hands and feet to work some kind of warmth back into them as well as to soothe the rope burns on her wrists.

Her abductor drove the snow machine on through the forest, stopping only to refuel. He gave her a bottle of water and an energy bar at each short break and allowed her to relieve herself if she needed.

During those short breaks, she saw the change in weather. The snow fell straight down, then later it whipped sideways as the wind tried to uproot the entire forest. Trees bent against the wind, sometimes dumping the vast piles from their boughs with a dull whop. Hard, sharp snaps echoed through the trees as the heavy boughs cracked under the immense weight of the snow.

While trapped in the ice fishing sled, boxes slammed against her as the machine sped up, slowed down and pitched from side to side as the man picked a path around obstacles. She didn't understand his urgency, but it seemed that the devil himself was on his trail and was relentless in his pursuit.

At least two punishing days passed, as she had seen the black of night twice and the dim gray light twice. Her stomach ached from hunger. The bottles of water and the few granola bars did little to curb that problem. Though she only had the blanket, she managed to stay reasonably warm from the pile of other things she rearranged around her body. The hot packs kept her fingers and toes from frostbite. At least she was warmer than in the wet clothes she had been wearing.

When the snow machine stopped and turned off, she waited for the usual opening of the clamshell and the extraction of another gas can, but she was disappointed. Minutes dragged on as Halen waited, still doubled over inside the clamshell. Her anxiety and imagination constructed horrific scenes in her head where the outcome of her demise ended with a blood-soaked field of snow. Everything around her had fallen as silent as death, save for the wind whistling through the trees. They complained with a chorus of creaks and groans, swaying back and forth against their invisible enemy. She strained to hear the outside world, but found nothing but the wind.

Halen's teeth were chattering again. Though the blanket was better than the wet clothes, it was far from adequate for the relentless storm outside. She pulled the blanket tighter but realized she wasn't shivering from the cold. Not like she was before. She trembled from the full terror of knowing that something was about to change. Something horrific lay outside the clamshell this time—something that would make her tiny prison feel like a protective cage. And she could do nothing but wait and listen.

Cold air crept in through the edge of the two sled halves. Halen adjusted her blanket to thicken the insulation on the side of her leg closest to the seam. Tremors of terror racked her body as her mind raced, trying to imagine what she'd have to face once the lunatic of a man opened the cage for the last time.

Minutes stretched on, draining her energy and exhausting her imagination before she slipped off to sleep again.

Bright light startled Halen awake. She threw her arms up to block the light and anything that might come down on her. It was still snowing, but it seemed to have slowed. But that wasn't remotely close to what she feared.

As her eyes adjusted to the light, she squinted up at a figure in a heavy white parka, white gloves, white mirrored goggles and a white mask with icicles hanging off the exhale port. It was a monster more terrifying than any she had faced on the movie sets.

He wrapped his fingers into the knot of hair at the back of her head, repeating what he had done on several occasions when he stopped to refuel and let her out for a short break. In her efforts to stretch, she lost her grip on the blanket. She made a hasty attempt to retrieve it but the grip on her hair forced her onward, flailing through the deep snow. He kept his grip on her and forced her out ahead of himself.

The capsule that held her bent over for the entire trip left her achingly stooped over. She tried working her limbs and stretching from side to side to get herself upright.

In front of her was a set of tracks. They zigzagged up a steep hill through a maze of trees and two feet of fresh powdered snow that rubbed against her thighs and bit into her toes. She stumbled and fell, only to be jerked back to her feet. She grabbed at branches for stability while tears streamed down her face. The rough bark and needles cut into her tender flesh, leaving tiny red welts where her blood pushed to the surface.

Step after step, she was forced ahead like a lamb headed for slaughter. Each turn was met with a steeper climb and limbs that begged her to stop. Her own scream began and ended as a large branch broke, falling with its heavy burden onto her head, shoulders and back, shocking the voice out of her.

The fist holding her hair forced her onward, leaving her tiny dark sanctuary behind. It was obvious the direction the man wanted her to go, and she followed the footsteps from his previous trip up the hill. Turning a corner, she followed the trail into a tangle of trees toppled one way then another by the heavy snow. He shoved her onto the ground to crawl under some of them and then lifted her onto her toes to climb over others. Her shuddering fear was replaced by tremors. The cold caused her to stumble and fall more often. Each time, she was reminded to stand back up by a harsh tug of her hair.

As they pushed forward, the forest became darker with less snow on the ground. In small pockets, the dark ground was littered with pine cones and pine needles. The trees laced their branches together, blocking out the sky and casting the forest floor in a black labyrinth of death.

She gasped and stopped short of a black form lying in the snow. A beat later, she saw that it was some kind of creature with thick black hair. She tried to walk around it but was shoved ahead. The black matted figure looked like it was still breathing. As she stepped next to it, it flinched, drawing in a gurgling sound.

Halen screamed and tried to stop or turn around, but the man's grip tightened and he lifted her onto her toes. He shoved her past the beast, then down to the ground on her hands and knees.

"In," the man barked, shoving her head into a hole. He let go of her hair and kicked her with his boot.

Halen clambered through the hole and into what seemed to be a cave. She felt for the wall and tried to stand up. Solid rock met the back of her skull, and she crouched back down and inched further inside. Cowering against the warm rock wall, she waited, unwilling to explore further.

Movement came from the entrance, accompanied by a few grunts, and she felt the presence of the man next to her. Keeping her eyes closed, she waited for his hand to grab her hair again, but he didn't.

Whimpering and still shaking from the cold, she waited for whatever might befall her.

13

Light cut through the cave like a knife. The headlamp the man wore flashed one direction, then another, and Halen huddled near the wall in a weak attempt to avoid his attention. Dirt, sticks and underbrush were interlaced with mounds of feces from the multitudes of critters that had called the cave home. Its former resident had apparently wanted it for the winter to slumber away peacefully until spring.

"Move," the man said, pointing to the back of the cave.

Halen stepped gingerly over and around the heaps of debris littering the floor. Zigzagging again, she made her way further back into the cave, where she was able to stand a little straighter. Turning the corner, she found a trickle of water flowing across the floor. Her foot slipped on the green algae and landed in a small pool. Quickly she pulled it back out before she burned herself.

"The water's not cold?" Halen blurted out in astonishment, suddenly unaware of her situation.

"No," the man said. "Move."

Halen followed the stream and stopped in front of several stacks of green steel boxes. They were piled to the low ceiling in columns. Yellow lettering identified them as military ammunition cans.

"There." The man pointed to a bare rock next to the small stream. It looked like a small island refuge among the dirt and sharp sticks.

Halen obeyed by stepping onto it. The warmth of it soaked into her toes and the bottoms of her feet. She crouched down on her heels, shaking violently from the cold and the terror of the unknown. She squatted down on the rock and tested the water again, with her hand this time. It was hot to the touch and bit into her skin like a thousand needles. She pulled it back out, afraid of being burned.

The man fumbled with a lock on a steel box. With a quick jerk, the lock came free and he pulled the heavy chain through the steel loops.

"C'mere," he mumbled.

Halen reluctantly stepped off the stone, still shivering, but the warm air inside the cave fought for her and helped warm her blood.

He bent down and locked the chain around her ankle. From the steel trunk, he pulled out several items and set them on the ground at her feet. "Set these up," he said and started away.

"I'm cold and hungry." Halen tried to find her voice to protest.

He looked at her, then down at the items at her feet. "Set them up," he growled, then walked back toward the entrance. The light from his headlamp faded, leaving her in a smelly, damp and dark cave.

Halen stood shaking, waiting in the dark. Seconds ticked into minutes, then minutes ticked into a blur of immeasurable time. Her curiosity grew as the cold shivers left her body. The air in the cave was warm, and before long, it brought sweat to her brow. She looked down, trying to see the floor in the lightless void, wondering what the things were at her feet. He had told her to set them up, but failed to tell her how. How did he expect her to assemble whatever was in front of her, and without a light?

She moved her hands up her naked body, gently feeling her scalp and the tender state it was in. After days of little to eat or drink, it was all she could do to stay on her feet as he'd forced her to climb the mountain through the thick blanket of fresh snow. Even though she felt weak, she didn't want to sit down for fear of sitting on or in something. Her thoughts turned to the man, or rather the beast, who had hauled her into the middle of a frozen forest, spoke very little and held a crude sense of sociability. The harsh treatment during the trip coupled with being forced to walk up the mountain left her still shaking in fear.

Halen turned her mind to the comfort of her home in Florida. Her life was easy, and her notoriety could get her anything she wanted. With a snap of her fingers, she could have it at any moment. Because of the lights and cameras, many young girls wanted to be her, young men wanted to date her, but there wasn't anyone here who could help. She was alone, chained to a steel box inside a cave and at the mercy of a madman. No one could see her now. She would die in a cave in the middle of a frozen wasteland.

Just one step in the dark and she could end her own life. She could smack her head on a rock or fall on a sharp stick. She couldn't see to move anywhere without taking the chance of tripping and breaking her neck. She was also petrified that something would explode out of the darkness and rip open her insides to feast upon them.

She squatted down, wrapping her arms around her knees. She didn't want to lie down for fear of the unknown dangers, bugs and feces that lay on the ground.

Tremors overtook her. She wasn't cold anymore. It was fear, uncertainty and a sense of complete abandonment by her friends. Silent tears streamed down her face at the realization that she was completely alone in the world. She couldn't run to the sanctuary of her mother's house. She couldn't borrow strength from her friends. She didn't even know where she was. How would anyone else know her location? She lost herself to sobbing and wavered on her perch, losing her balance.

Falling forward, she threw her hands out into the darkness. One hand hit and fumbled through the pile she had been told to assemble. A light flashed. She froze, wondering if she had inadvertently made a spark. A fire would provide light, but she had seen all the sticks that had been brought in by unknown animals and reasoned that she was standing on a tinderbox. A fire now would cook her worse than a scorched Fourth of July hot dog.

She pushed off the floor, bumping the object again. This time she saw the source of light. It was a lightbulb. It had given the slightest flicker, then died out. She watched the coil inside the bulb dim and become swallowed by the same darkness that had swallowed her.

Fumbling for the light, she tried to imagine a flashlight and the shape it should feel like. The bulb flickered again and she seized it. Exploring the item with her fingers, she found what felt like a handle and a switch. She pressed the switch. Nothing happened. She pressed it again. Still nothing happened.

Pressing it over and over without any desirable result caused panic and frustration, while rationalization was just out of reach. Pressure built in her mind like a balloon the instant before it reaches its limit and pops. Halen tried to see the puzzle right there in front of her but was only met with a black emptiness. It taunted her over and over until she snapped.

She screamed into the void and hammered the air with the contraption, pressing the button again and again. Her screams only echoed back at her, and her frantic movements created nothing of consequence.

The trickle of warm water gurgled on and on. Its indifference calmed her. It calmed her enough to allow her to realize that screaming and waving the object in the air was not going to work. She forced herself to stop. Slamming it down on the floor, she heard gears whine and saw another blip of light.

THE HIT

The mechanism had just spoken to her and given her a hint. She explored it again with her fingers, this time gently and with purpose. She found a crevice big enough to slide the tip of a fingernail into. Pulling at the notch, she found a small handle. Using one hand to hold the light, she turned the crank like a fishing pole with the other. The gears delivered a high-pitched whine that echoed off the smooth rock walls.

Still there was no light.

Halen growled and cranked the gears harder. Still nothing. She bounced the contraption off the other items that lay before her, then picked it up to examine it again. She swapped ends, holding it a different way. A way that seemed a bit unnatural. She clicked the button again. Bright light blasted from the device.

Halen tipped backward, trying to get away from the sudden light. Sticks poked at her back, and the chain rattled from the sudden movement, but she could see now.

The red walls of the cave lit up, revealing years of claw marks on the walls. She turned the flashlight around, pointing it at what she knew was there—the ammunition cans—and explored what she hadn't seen yet.

14

Halen woke with a start. The air was quiet except for the trickle of water that originated somewhere deep within the cave. It divided the space down the middle and flowed out through a crack in the rock, away from the cave entrance.

She had set up the equipment as she had been told. It wasn't much—just an old army cot and a couple of blankets. Having the light made a world of difference in her progress, and she was able to assemble the items with minor difficulty.

She was going to rebel and fight the man, but he had all the advantages at the moment. There wasn't much she could do in her current vulnerable state, and she thought better of attacking him. She would have to endure this man and his twisted mind until he either killed her or she found a weakness and was somehow able to turn the tables.

Listening into the darkness, she clung to the blanket, creating a barrier between herself and the rest of the world, even though it made her sweat.

THE HIT

The warmth from the hot spring inside the mountain was enough to maintain the temperature just short of that of a sauna, and the air was just as humid. She clutched the blanket, instinctively protecting herself from the unknown. A tiny red dot hovered above her.

She knew something had to be there.

She waited. It didn't move. Her hand gripped the flashlight, ready to blind whatever it was with the press of a button. She had charged the battery with the crank and turned it off, waiting for her captor to return. She hesitated a moment longer, listening for any identifying sound, then mashed the button.

Her abductor loomed over her, his white snowsuit contrasting heavily against the red rock. He ripped his goggles off with one hand. With his other, he backhanded the flashlight across the cave. He was now a shadow against the red wall behind him. She looked up to see dark sunken eyes and hollow cheeks. His stare told her that she was down to her last few breaths, and no one would hear her last scream before he ended her life.

He pulled the thick mitten off his hand and reached through a fold in his coat.

Halen wondered what fresh hell awaited her. She imagined warm, slick blood oozing down her frame and draining into the small trickle of water, diluting and disappearing into the frozen forest. Her bones would lie inside the cave and become the chew toys of animals, only to be discovered years later.

Her heart thumped wildly in her chest as his hand slowly inched back out of his coat. She held her breath. His fist was gripped around something. Halen clenched her jaw, preparing herself for whatever came next.

In a flash, the man bent down, grabbed the frame of the cot and toppled Halen backward, slamming her into the rock wall. He swung the cot around and flung it to the far side of the cave. Returning to her, he grabbed the blanket she clung to and jerked it away from her before returning to the other side of the cave.

He set up the cot and spread the blanket out while Halen cowered against the opposite wall. Turning, he swept up the flashlight, turned the crank a dozen times in rapid succession, charging the capacitor more, then hung the light from a crack in the center of the cave. Walking to the ammunition cans, he popped the lid off one, pulled two packages out and tossed one to Halen before refastening the lid.

Crouched against the wall, she leaned forward and dragged the package to her. MRE—Meal Ready to Eat—told her what it was, but she didn't have a clue what to do with it. She sat with her knees drawn up to her chest and watched as the man sat on the cot and opened his own package of food.

She mimicked him, tearing open the bag and pulling out the bland-looking contents. The package was labeled Chili with Beans. She watched him scoop up some stream water into a plastic bag and slide his meal into it. Soon steam started to rise out of the pouch as the contents heated.

Halen read the packaging and copied what he had done. She crawled over to the stream, filled the bag to the indicated level and inserted her pouch.

THE HIT

When the meal finished heating, she ate it while watching the man.

After he finished, he stretched out on the cot. Halen listened to him snore for what seemed like forever before she curled up against the rock wall and the crate of supplies and slept.

Her muscles complained and she shivered through most of the night. The warmth and humidity from the hot spring made for favorable conditions compared to the blizzard of the century outside. Yet she huddled against the lukewarm stone and drowsily scraped twigs and debris up around part of her body through the night to retain some sort of warmth, or rather security from the monster sleeping in the cot across from her.

She didn't want to sleep. She didn't want to give this man an easy target, but she was still so exhausted. She convinced herself that if she only closed one eye at a time, she could still watch him.

That compromise was her undoing.

She woke to find her clothes in a pile at her feet, along with another MRE. The man shifted on his cot and soon started snoring again. Remembering the rough treatment she received from him, Halen elected to be quiet as a mouse, eat her food and sleep.

The last several days had become a blur. She had been in and out of consciousness, and the lines between reality and her nightmares had blended into one horrific event.

She sat quietly watching for any reaction from the man. Fear of him lurching up off the cot, grabbing her by the hair and dragging her out through the snow blared in her mind. He'd probably abducted her to molest her, to use her for his own personal gratification, or maybe he wanted to dominate her to satisfy his twisted mind. She watched him as he slept, contemplating all the different reasons he might have for dragging her out into the wilderness. His steady breathing and soft snoring continued, and she chanced a look at the clothes that had been placed at her feet.

Slowly she pulled them up to her one by one. They were still frozen. He must have just brought them in while she was asleep. Without a dryer or a fire, there was no way she would be able to get her clothes dry. She did the only thing she thought she could do—build a wall. She placed the clothes between her and her abductor in a pathetic attempt to trip him. It wasn't much of an obstacle, but it served as a small boundary until she could think of something else.

Halen stared at the rock walls, thinking of ways she could escape. She had to figure out where this maniac had taken her and where she could find help. For that, she would need energy. She dragged the bag of food closer and quietly opened it.

15

Halen blew on the flicker of flame. She had found a box of matches in one of the trunks and scraped together some twigs lying around the floor of the cave, placing them in a pile. Several matches later, she was coaxing a finger of a flame to something larger she could work with. She added more sticks, sending the orange tongue higher into the air.

She had done it—she had made a campfire. She could now dry her clothes. A smile spread across her lips at the monumental feat. She had learned about how it was done a dozen years before, but because she lived in a city, she never actually got to try it. Now she had. She had made a fire just like her scout group had promised they would all those years ago but never did. It was one of the many promises that adults all around her would make and break. Sure, they had promised her things before, but this was the first time it really mattered.

Halen had read *Julie and the Wolves* by Jean Craighead George when she was in grade school.

At the time, she had fantasized about surviving in the wild, about how wonderful it would be to live in harmony with nature. It was a short-lived wonderment, like many other childhood fascinations that sat in her heart alongside all the empty promises made to her over the years.

Her career had begun early, leaving little time for friends and other activities. She starred in her first commercial, then another and another. Then came a couple different sitcom pilots, which led her to the stage, where a bloodcurdling scream launched her onto the silver screen. It became apparent that the only promises she had to worry about were the ones she made to herself.

The flame triggered her excitement and became the first self-fulfilling promise she realized from her childhood. The flame grew as she added larger branches. Grabbing two sticks, she began propping up her clothes so they could finish thawing and eventually dry out enough to wear.

A grunt startled her. She looked up to see her captor charging her.

"Goddammit!" The man rushed forward, backhanded her out of the way and stomped out the fire. He grabbed the empty MRE bag, filled it with water and doused the hot coals.

"You'll choke us out. Damn, woman."

"I'm cold," Halen said weakly.

"Get a hotel room and order your damn hot towels." He stomped back to his cot and lay down.

The realization hit Halen that he had been stalking her since Whitefish, at least. A chill ran through her body, making her feel the cold even more.

She stared at the man and he stared back. "How the fuck am I supposed to—"

He lurched up off the cot, took two strides across the cave and backhanded Halen across the mouth. He planted his hands on his knees and leaned down to her level. "Don't you ever say that word again."

Halen retreated against the rock wall, keeping her eyes on the man and cupping her swelling cheek with her hand. The sting of pain followed by his growl paralyzed her.

He stared at her for a long time, taking a slow breath before he turned to an unopened trunk next to her. After turning the tumblers of the lock, he gave it a quick pull, then lifted the lid. He reached in and pulled out a contraption and then a small electric heater. He plugged the heater into the side of the first item and turned it toward her, slamming it into the sticks and mud.

After stomping back to his cot, he lay down, turning his back to her.

Her creep-o-meter had shot through the roof but now remained stagnant as a question lurked in her mind. Why had he kidnapped her? If he wanted sexual favors, he would be leering at her now as she sat crouched against the cave wall. Instead, he settled into heavy, even breathing, which she surmised would turn into a steady snore.

A few minutes later, she heard those exact sounds. The man looked like death warmed over. She wondered if he had slept at all since he'd grabbed her and dragged her through the frozen lake.

His stomping out the fire was like another broken promise from an adult. Her huge achievement of creating a fire was crushed by a boot. It was like crossing the finish line first only to be handed a ribbon for sixth place out of only five contestants.

He had to have been awake for the two or three days she was locked in the sled. Sympathizing for him hung just outside her reach as she watched his back rise and fall with each breath. Though, it was hard to guess how long they had been traveling. She knew it had to have been more than two days, probably three or more, since they had started their journey. She couldn't imagine being awake for three days, working constantly to put distance between himself and where they had come from.

Turning her attention to the contraption at her feet, she saw the bicycle pedals. It was obvious what she was meant to do. A subtle shiver demanded her attention. She put her feet on the platforms and began pedaling. The heater coils glowed red, and the fan began to whirl. She brought the heater close to her and continued pedaling even faster to produce more of what she really wanted: dry heat.

Time ticked by as the heater warmed her, then dried her clothes. When they became dry enough to wear, she dressed and curled up next to the trunk to sleep.

Over the next three days, Halen cleaned all the feces and sticks out of the cave under the glare and instruction of her captor. She pushed the refuse out of the cave opening and shoved it over the edge, where it tumbled down the steep hill.

She had improvised a needle from the wire clip that had held her ski pass and pulled thread from the frayed edges of her suit to sew the bottom of her snowsuit closed. The rough-cut flap had left her feeling exposed along with the feeling that his eyes were on her every time she wasn't facing him.

"What are you going to do with me?" Halen posed the question on the second day of the cave cleanup. Her captor just grunted and continued to point his finger to the next spot that needed cleaning.

Elegant was not a word she would use to describe the cave, but with the debris gone, Halen found the interior more tolerable. It was crude, with uneven pockets and tiny tunnels disappearing into the mountain. If she hadn't been so busy with every issue that her captor ordered, she might have taken some pride in sanitizing their environment.

After moving the bulk of debris out of the cave, she used buckets of water to wash the stone walls and floor. As she worked, she watched the man's subtle movements. In particular, the times he dialed the combination on the lock chaining her to the heavy steel trunk. He had to allow her to conduct her chores outside the door to push the muck over the ledge.

Halen waited and watched for her opportunity to escape. She had memorized the four-digit code on the lock and tested it one night to make sure it worked. After locking it back around her ankle, she started planning her escape.

She still tried to act normal, as in scared out of her mind with a smattering of defiance. Movies streamed through her head as she tried to marry what she saw of the prisoner-of-war movies with her acting talent. She drew from her acting skills and put on the performance of her life, because it was her life that was at stake. There were no cameras, no second takes. It was her against him, locked in a battle of wit and survival. She portrayed a prisoner who could be subject to torture at any moment. She argued with him, called him names, inadvertently barking out the f-bomb only one other time. With that, she'd found herself on the ground, clutching her head and trying to suppress the ringing in her ears. It was a mistake she would never make again.

Her opportunity came during one of his regular long naps. He had turned his back and begun another session of heavy snoring. She quickly dialed the combination, grabbed some bags of food and filled a gallon jug with the fresh, hot spring water.

Slipping out the woven tree-branch door, she started down the hill through six inches of new snow on top of the several feet that had dropped during the massive storm several days earlier. The depressed trail where they had climbed up was easy to follow, as her abductor had been up and down it several times.

She knew she could get away. She just needed a big enough head start, and she could find her way back to civilization. People lived everywhere on the planet. It wouldn't be hard to find someone, even in the remote mountains.

THE HIT

The sun was up, and the air felt decently warm. She could do this. She could escape and tell the world about the maniac who dragged her for days through what the news back in Whitefish had called the storm of the decade. The news clip played in her mind. The storm would be the worst Montana had seen in the past decade. She had survived it, though she had had help.

Stumbling down the mountain, she found the snow machine the man had used to carry her off. She found the key in the zippered bag attached to the handlebars. The engine turned over several times before she remembered that older engines had a choke that needed to be pulled before they would start. She pulled the black knob and turned the key again. The machine roared to life.

With three MREs stuffed inside her suit and the gallon of water tied to the handlebars, she slammed the throttle, and the machine leaped out of the small cluster of trees. She was free of him. She could escape, find help and have him arrested. She vowed to never set foot in Montana or any other mountainous state again. The engine screamed as she raced away across the thick blanket of snow, bobbing up and down over the hidden drifts.

16

The wind screamed like a thousand corpses shrieking a warning to any who would cross the veil of the dead. Halen felt like she might have already stepped over that line, but she couldn't stop. She had to keep going. The blowing snow was like a river of ghosts ready to whisk her spirit away from her body. Each passing gust sank another hook into her soul, preparing to jerk it into the unknown.

The snow machine she had stolen ran out of gasoline just a mile into her escape. She searched the container on the back of the sled and found that it was void of fuel also. Abandoning the machine, she continued on, fighting her way through the deep snow.

Ten thousand icy needles stabbed at her hands and feet as she forced herself to continue. An hour later, she found an earthen wall from the roots of a toppled tree. It created a break from the wind and a temporary reprieve from her plight. She sat in its shelter and ate one of the MREs, then used the flameless heaters from the other two to warm her hands and feet.

After the rejuvenating break, she slogged on through the deep snow, her feet quickly progressing from pins and needles to numb stumps. Each step, she reasoned, would get her one step further away from a madman and one step closer to safety.

When the wind kicked up a ground blizzard, she lost the sun and her direction of travel. Although the soothing effects of using the heaters had been nice, she now knew she had wasted them on warming her feet and hands. It seemed she had been shivering for hours, and she knew she was dangerously cold. She needed to find someplace warm or she'd become just another ornament of the frozen landscape.

"Hey. You there!" a voice called out to Halen.

She looked up to see bright glowing windows, smoke billowing from a chimney and a man draped in an oversized flannel nightshirt.

"You look cold. Come in and warm up," the man called from the front porch. He was gathering a load of firewood and waved at her to come up the steps and into the cabin.

A woman poked her head out the door. "Oh, you poor dear, come in and get something warm in your belly. We have soup on the stove and I'll make you a cup of hot chocolate."

The woman had brown frizzy hair and was wearing an oversized quilted nightshirt that matched the man's. Her grandmotherly glasses framed her bright eyes, and her smile warmed Halen's heart. Halen reached out for the cup she was offering. It suddenly seemed further away. She reached again and again, but each time it was just out of her grasp. She stumbled forward, finally grasping the cup, and lifted it to her face. The steam rose up into her eyes and she drank, but the liquid was cold, and she fell.

The crackle of a fire rang like a song stuck in her head. She heard people stirring in the distance. It was like she was a little girl again, suddenly warmed by the surrounding ocean and sun, but something wasn't right. She looked down to the sandy beach to find that she was peeing through her bathing suit. She thought she would stop, but her urine kept flowing, surrounding her, climbing up over her knees, then up her chest to her neck. She was in a pool of her own urine. The odor reached her nose, causing her to panic, and she began to thrash.

Halen woke. The embarrassing dream turned into a nightmare. She grasped for anything to pull herself up out of the water, but the mossy slime covering the rock kept her flailing and sliding under. Water splashed out of the pool only to drain back in, submerging her over and over. Rolling onto her hands and knees, she pushed herself above the surface and coughed water out of her lungs.

A blackness surrounded her. Blinking did nothing to improve her eyesight. The blackness remained.

Steadying herself, she forced her coughing fit to stop. Phantom light poked at the edge of her vision. She turned her head one way then another, searching for a light source, but saw none. She thought she might have suddenly become blind until she caught a hint of light coming from a passage through the rock.

Scrambling out of the water, she started for the dim light at the entrance to the pool. The light grew brighter as she entered the corridor and brighter still at the other end of the short tunnel. On the ground before her was a neatly folded wool blanket. She looked at the walls and the familiar red rock, and her blood went as cold as the frozen world outside.

She was back in the cave.

"Why?" Halen sat on the metal crate, clutching the blanket around her shoulders. Her snowsuit was neatly folded on the trunk beside her. Touching it, she found it cold and still somewhat frozen. She hadn't been in the cave for very long.

She leveled her eyes at the man sitting across from her. He didn't react or give a hint that he'd even heard her. His hand worked back and forth, scrubbing his teeth. He leaned over the trickle of water that ran through the cave and spit the toothpaste froth out, then sipped from a canteen, swished it and spit it out.

"Why what?"

"Why are you keeping me here?"

He looked back at her. She reflexively clutched the blanket tighter around her body. Minutes passed as he stared at her. He averted his eyes to study the bristles on his toothbrush.

"I don't know," he said and quickly got up and walked to the other side of the cave, putting his toothbrush and canteen away.

"Then let me go," Halen hissed through gritted teeth. When he didn't react, she screamed, "Let me go, you bastard!"

He stomped over to her and slapped her across the face. Halen instinctively turned her head with the slap as she had practiced so many times doing simple stunt work. It didn't prevent the sting, but it did reduce the lasting pain that would have been there. Weeks of coaching had ingrained the movement into a second nature.

The man spun on his heels and retreated to his bunk. He pulled his blanket over his shoulder and stared at the wall.

"Is this what you want, you freakin' pervert?" Halen stood and dropped the blanket around her feet. "Just come and get it over with."

Halen shook with fear and anticipation. She stared at the man, her courage building to confront him further. But he didn't budge from his cot. It seemed that he had no interest in her. His back continued to rise and fall with each breath.

"You're a pathetic loser," Halen goaded, trying for a reaction. She all but screamed at him. "You dickhead freak. You're not a man at all. You're a pathetic little coward."

There was still no reaction to her taunting. His back continued to rise and fall as if he were asleep, but she knew he wasn't. She knew he was listening. She just hadn't found his sore spot.

"Your boyfriend cut your dick off to make you his bitch." Halen began to shake, preparing herself for a fight. She was tired, hungry and had become crazed from fear and uncertainty.

The man remained motionless. Halen wondered if there was anything that would provoke him. She had to find something to fight back with. Something that would clue her in to what would happen next. If she was going to die, she was going to die on her own terms, and she was going to take this man with her.

His lack of response angered her even more. She clenched her fists at her sides and scrambled to think of something that would get to him. "Your whoring mama must have been too stoned to—"

She didn't have time to finish. In a flash, she found herself on the cave floor, her blood dripping into the stream.

She had found his trigger. She found the soft spot that made the man angry enough to kill. She wanted him as crazy as she felt. Maybe then she would get answers, or she would kill him or he would kill her. Either way, the tension between them would finally have an end.

Her eyes caught a glint of steel lying next to his cot, and she lashed out, grabbed the knife and spun in one fluid motion, lunging for the man. She sought any part of him to plunge the knife into. He threw up an arm, but it was too late. The blade dug deep into his flesh, cutting through the thick clothes and into his forearm.

She swung again, but this time he sidestepped and dodged the attack. Halen regrouped and steadied herself on her feet. She was looking for an opening to thrust the hunting knife into him when suddenly it was no longer in her hand. The back of her hand stung, and the knife clattered across the cave floor.

The man grabbed her wrist and spun her around. His other hand gripped a fistful of her hair and slammed her against the wall.

Through gritted teeth, he growled, "You better give me a damn good reason to spare your life a third time. I won't do it again." He flung her onto the crumpled blanket as if she were just a piece of dirty laundry. He walked over to retrieve his knife and examined the edge for nicks. After sliding it home in its scabbard, he tossed it in the steel trunk and shut the lid.

Grabbing a first aid kit out of a different trunk, he stripped off his coat and shirt and sat on the edge of his cot. Blood dripped in a steady stream down his elbow and onto the floor, then slowly made its way to the trickle of water at his feet. He bandaged his arm, then turned his gaze to Halen.

She had pulled the blanket back around her naked body and was sitting on the trunk. She fixed her eyes on him, trying to understand if what he'd said had actually come from a man who intended to kill her.

"Why?" Halen demanded. She worked up her courage to face off with him again. "Why do you say you spared my life when it's obvious that you intend to torture me before you kill me?"

The man huffed. "Torture." He shook his head. "This ain't torture."

"You're scaring the crap out of me," Halen cried, her legs trembling from dread and trepidation. She steadied herself, gritted her teeth and continued with her resolve to trigger him into giving up more information. "You drag me naked into the goddamn wilderness, then up a hill into a bear's den full of shit and who knows what else." Her hands trembled from fear that she desperately tried to turn into anger.

"You should be scared," the man said calmly. "But not of anything here."

"What does that mean?"

"Your fake friends will do worse by you than anything I could do. After everyone ditches you and your endorsements and royalties run dry, you'll be a washed-up has-been with nothing to show for it."

"I've got five hit films—"

"Two," the man snapped. "That were barely worth a shit. One of the two was half decent, but it wasn't because of your acting."

The man got up, put his shirt back on and knelt in front of Halen. He pinched her chin between his knuckle and thumb, lifting her head and turning it one way, then the other. She was about to protest his touch, but decided against it. She already had an album full of bumps and abrasions.

She softened her tone before she spoke. "You kill people, don't you?"

The man looked her in the eye, then flatly said, "Usually."

He got up and dug through the first aid kit, retrieved a green can of ointment and smeared some on her lip. He motioned for her to stand. When she did, he ripped the blanket out of her hand, letting it drop to the floor. He scooped out a generous amount of ointment and spun her around. She flinched at his touch but didn't move further as he smeared it on multiple abrasions on her backside. There was nothing sexual about it. It was more rough than anything, like he was treating her as if she were livestock.

Leaving the can, he went back and lay down on his cot, facing away from her. She picked up the can and began to gently tend to her wounds.

"What's your name?" Halen watched him with a careful eye as she rubbed the ointment on her skin.

The man didn't answer but sat up again and grabbed the unfinished meal at the foot of his cot, rummaging through it to pull out a package of crackers.

Halen turned her back and continued smearing the medicine on the multiple sores. A lump of clothes hit the wall and fell to her feet. Picking up one of the items, she inspected it. It was a thermal base layer. She carefully glanced over her shoulder. When he didn't move, she collected the other piece and put them on.

She sat on the trunk and wrapped the blanket around her again, eyeing what he might do next. He tossed her a meal.

"People who know me call me Tracer."

17

Halen waited for Tracer to continue. When he didn't, she asked, "Is that a first name or a last name?

"It's an only name."

"You have to have a last name. You have to come from somewhere."

"Everyone comes from somewhere," Tracer said flatly.

"You said that you usually kill people." Halen tore open her package of food and gingerly sifted through its contents.

Tracer unwrapped a small butterscotch candy and popped it in his mouth. "I help people have accidents."

Halen looked into his predator eyes, processing the information for a beat. "You were sent to kill me." Alarm rose in her voice, but it was quickly extinguished with a glare from Tracer. "Weren't you?" Halen's finished in a much softer tone.

He nodded and dug through the empty MRE bag, looking for anything to occupy his attention in order to avoid answering her questions.

"Who told you to?" she asked.

He remained silent, studying the empty food wrappers.

"Who told you to?" she demanded a little louder. Halen stiffened her back, ready to take action at a moment's notice.

Tracer looked up at her. "Who wouldn't? You're not a nice person."

"I *am* nice. I have friends all over."

"No." Tracer shook his head. "I'm the nicest guy you'll ever meet."

"You're deranged. You are *not* nice." Halen emphasized. "Nice people don't wrap a garbage sack over your head and plunge you into a frozen lake. They don't lock you in a tiny box and haul you through a damn frozen wasteland. A nice person wouldn't rip you from the safety of a warm cabin with food. Did you kill those people too?"

"What people?" Tracer asked.

"When I escaped this demented prison." Halen shot daggers at her captor.

"I followed you to make sure you didn't do something stupid. Seems you've had a lifetime of doing stupid. As far as this being a demented prison, you should feel at home here. As I'm the only sane one, we'll go with my decisions." Tracer leveled a glare at her.

"You're the insane one."

"This coming from the woman who squats and pees in the middle of a dance floor, then laughs about it?"

Halen sought to steer the conversation away from her obvious shortcomings. "You killed those people who would have saved me."

"Which people?"

"The ones in the cabin."

"There was no cabin."

"Yes there was. They invited me in where it was warm. I felt the warmth of the fire."

"You had hypothermia. You were probably hallucinating."

"I felt the warmth of the fire though!" Halen cried.

"I found you wedged between a boulder and a rotten log. I brought you back and threw you in the hot pool."

Halen considered his statement. If she was hallucinating, then there wouldn't have been a cabin. There wouldn't have been a fire, and she would have frozen to death. "How do I know you're telling the truth?"

"You're welcome to follow my tracks back to where I found you. They've probably blown in by now. I wouldn't try it."

"Why not?"

"It'll be subzero for the next week. It's thirty below right now. You wouldn't last a mile."

"I might surprise you."

"The only thing that would surprise me is if you heeded good advice. But if you're determined, the door's right there. I'm not going to save you a third time."

"What do you mean a third time?" Halen asked.

"You're alive because of me." Tracer leaned back against the wall as if to challenge her to come up with a better reason.

"I would be alive if you had left me alone," she argued.

"And what kind of life would that be?" Tracer glared at her. "Pissing on everyone's Cheerios. Buying the next set of friends. Pissing them off and alienating them. Is it always what fits what you want? How long before you run out of friends and businesses you can coerce into tolerating you?"

"My friends love me for who I am."

"So they like it when you piss on their floor."

"I don't pee on their floor."

"Why not?"

"Because that would be rude."

"Why'd you pee on the dance floor?"

Halen straightened and heaved her chest out in defiance. "Because it was funny."

Tracer lunged off his cot, grabbed her by the hair and dragged her out the entrance, kicking the door open and sending the woven branches tumbling over the edge. He pulled her out into the subzero air, grabbed a handful of her base layer bottoms and heaved her out into the night.

A fleeting thought of her fluffy pink rugs in her bedroom flickered through Halen's mind. That life was now a world away. If it was on another planet, it wouldn't have made a difference. Even if it was one valley over, it wouldn't have made a difference. All her celebrity photos framed on her wall, the red-carpet gowns in her closet, the glitzy parties, the carefree lifestyle where money could buy her anything didn't matter here. She couldn't buy her way out of this. She couldn't talk her way out. She was at a loss. She didn't know what this man wanted, and she couldn't get away from him.

Halen tumbled down the snow-covered hillside. The thin layer of clothing helped guard against the icy abrasions, but the cold air quickly soaked through the garment to bite at her skin. She stretched out her arms and legs to stop her plunge through the frozen night. She dug a foot into the snow and stomped a couple times to confirm solid footing, then began her climb back up to the cave.

Every icy-cold pinprick biting into her flesh reminded her of how vulnerable she was in her scant clothing and of the short time it would take for her body to become part of the frozen landscape. Her feet would likely freeze first, then her hands and her ears. She'd freeze quickly unless she climbed back into the cave.

The cave offered food and shelter. That was all that mattered. Those two things would ensure her immediate survival. She had made a serious blunder—one that might cost her her life. She had been cast out for a reason she didn't understand. She had been cast out of the worthiness of survival, the worthiness of having some sort of value. She had been cast out as if she were a piece of trash. To him, she was of no value.

He didn't care that she brought entertainment to millions of people. He didn't care about the rich and famous life she lived. He didn't care about the advancement in technology of the film industry, of the artistry in creating an alternate personality, of creating a believable character that would evoke genuine feelings inside the people watching.

There were no silver screens, no fans, no malls, nor any hospitals if she should need one. In her delusion, she thought the film industry would need her, but it didn't. She would be replaced by one of a thousand people eager to step into her shoes. She had been on the edge of being booted for a while and was too naive and stupid to see it. He was right. She was walking down a path, burning every bridge in sight and laughing at the flames. The thought broke the foundation of her life. He had stripped her out of her fantasy world.

She had heard the negative criticism, and in the back of her mind, she knew her acting was subpar. She wanted to be known for her acting, but the attractive lifestyle was easy and alluring. It was exciting and distracted her from her career.

The tabloids didn't matter. They got paid to smear celebrities whether the story was real or not. Most people discounted it as gossip. In the end, it didn't matter in the functionality of the average person's life. They would still go to work, earn a paycheck, go home at night, make their family dinner or fix the broken swing in the backyard.

Halen saw now that she was just a disposable piece of entertainment. She was little more than a prostitute in some ways and far less valuable in others.

Tracer had stripped her mind bare just like he had stripped her of her clothes. She needed those layers of clothes. She needed to survive even if she had to act her way out of her predicament. The man in the warmth of the cave above held all the cards. He held all the aces, all the plays for power. He was trying to best her in the cat and mouse game he had dragged her into. Now she had to pull a Golden Globe out of her backside to match wits with a killer.

18

Halen looked up at the glow coming from the cave opening. Her mind raced to try to figure out what the crazed lunatic wanted from her. She'd offered him what most men wanted, but he hadn't cast a glance at her when she stood naked before him. It was a ruse to get a reaction out of him. She didn't want to be with him, but if offering herself would get her back to civilization, she would reluctantly agree.

But he clearly wasn't interested in sex. This confused her. If he didn't want sex, she might be held for ransom. It seemed a plausible motive, but that didn't explain his disregard for her life or his admission that he kills people. He barely kept her alive. If he had saved her from hypothermia, why would he show her the door and allow her to escape again or to freeze to death on her own? If he helped people have accidents, she was far from anywhere where an accident might be thought of as believable.

THE HIT

Whatever it was that he wanted, she had to give the performance of a lifetime in order to draw it out of him. She knew she had to appeal to him, but she didn't know how. He was a cold blank slate. She had to convince him of something. Something that would prevent him from pulling a big hunting knife across her throat.

With no way of knowing how to deal with this man's erratic behavior, she had to do something or die. She dug her fingers and toes into the snow and climbed back up the slope.

Her feet felt like blocks of ice on the ends of wooden planks that she stabbed into the snow over and over. Her fingers barely obeyed her commands to close around the next handhold that would bring her closer to the warmth if not the safety of the cave. She might get smacked around in the cave, but at least she wouldn't freeze to death.

By the time she reached the ledge, he was gone. The opening to the cave was just a few feet away, but her shivering delayed her from reaching the warmth she needed. Climbing over the edge and to the opening, she looked around for him, subconsciously waiting, anticipating being beaten and flung back out over the edge.

He was nowhere in sight. Violent shivers racked her body, causing her to fumble and lose her balance. She rolled over onto her side and struggled to get back onto her hands and knees. Pushing against the mountain, she forced her knees under her and her palms onto the packed snow around the entrance. The crawl into the cave was slow but wrought with determination.

She expected a boot to her face as she entered the cave, but there was nothing. Her scalp tingled, waiting, preparing for the yank up off the floor, but that didn't happen either. The muscles in her ribs tensed, waiting for a boot to the side, but none came.

She crawled through the cave past the man's cot and the meal rations. She crawled around the stacked trunks and into the corridor that led to the natural hot spring that lay deep inside the mountain. The hot spring was her lifeline, and she had to get to it or chance losing a toe, a finger or a foot. When she had crawled through the snow, she'd felt the sting of sharp, icy razors cutting into her flesh. As soon as the cuts thawed out, they would start bleeding, and as dirty as the ledge was, infection was a serious concern.

She crawled through the narrow passage to the hot pool just inside the next room. The warm, humid air soaked into her skin, bringing back the pins and needles of the returning blood flow. When she reached the edge of the pool, she slid her hands into the water. The heat sent spikes of pain up through her arms, and they screamed for her to draw them back out, but she forced them deeper into the water.

Halen turned and slid her feet into the water next, gritting her teeth in agony from the circulation returning to her limbs. The pain from the hot water subsided, then began to soothe her aches away, and she found herself drifting off and relaxing.

Even as she drifted off, she reminded herself to stay vigilant. After a time, soft pillows and fluffy pink blankets wrapped around her mind and her body. The smell of bourbon filled her nose and warmed her belly from the inside as well. Her friends surrounded her in the hot tub, holding drinks out, waiting for her to make a toast. She raised her glass to the handsome young man from Montana. He saluted her with his glass before twisting his other hand into her hair, drawing her close to his rugged face.

He continued to wrench his fingers into her hair. Teasing her, exciting her, causing her to crave his touch. He clenched his hand tighter, this time causing her pain. His handsome face distorted into one seething with disgust. The pain brought her out of the blissful dream. The face of her fantasized lover morphed into Tracer's angry scowl.

Tracer hauled her out of the water and dragged her through the corridor and the outer part of the cave. Halen kicked and twisted, trying to get her feet under her. Changing directions, he kept her scrambling and unable to get up. Ducking through the entrance, he flung her over the edge again.

The subzero temperatures instantly coated Halen in a layer of ice. As she hit the snow again, she immediately stretched out her limbs to stop from rolling over. She clawed at the snow, trying to find a grip on something to keep from sliding down the mountain. She grabbed at a branch and missed it, but with a second attempt, she found a foothold from her previous trail.

"Close the door next time!" Tracer called down to her.

Adrenaline shot through her body. She knew she wouldn't be able to sustain being tossed down the hill multiple times. She had to comply or kill the man. If by some miracle she could find a way to kill him, then she would be free of him and she could wait out the winter. There seemed to be plenty of food, and the cave was comfortable enough. She just had to outwit the monster that resided inside.

The door to the cave lay off to her left, where it had tumbled down and become wedged against a tree. She would have to climb down, then across to the woven tree-branch door. Violent shivers returned, but this time her blood was raging and fought off the cold. She didn't care about the cold anymore. She was furious about how she was being treated. The games he was playing were getting old. If he was going to kill her, she would rather he do it quickly instead of toying with her for his own amusement.

She reminded herself that he was the one who'd placed a bag over her head and dragged her into a frozen lake. He'd kept her tied up and cramped in a tiny box, then bounced her for days across a frozen wilderness before finally hauling her naked up a frozen hillside into a cave where he could do anything to her and no one would hear her scream.

It was time to force his hand. It was time to make him take her back to civilization or kill her. Either way, she would be comforted by knowing what would happen instead of guessing why he'd abducted her.

Digging her hands and feet into the snow, she grabbed a piece of the door and hauled it up to the small ledge. She was trembling now. Not from the cold, but from what she was about to do. Crawling through the opening, she pulled the door in behind her and wedged it into place. She turned and saw Tracer waiting for her in the roomiest part of the cave. The lantern cast foreboding shadows against the wall.

She stiffened her back and marched up to face him. His expression was blank and unfeeling, as if he didn't have a care in the world. He saw right through her as if she were a ghost, like she was nothing. If he cared so little for her, why would he bother with her?

Sharp pain stung her palm as it connected with the side of his face. The slap seemed to hardly faze him. He still looked through her to the far wall of the cave. She slapped him again. Normally when she did this, gasps from her friends or the people around her helped cow her target into not doing anything. There was nothing like that here. It was just her and this man.

"If you hit a person, you better damn well be fighting for your life. You don't just go up to someone and slap them," Tracer said. "All that does is make you look like a cowardly little bitch."

Halen doubled her fist and swung. She whipped her hand around as fast as she could, gritting her teeth and aiming for Tracer's nose. He lowered his head at the last instant, connecting his forehead with her fist.

A crack in her hand shot pain up her arm, crippling her attack. Tracer lifted his head and watched her reel back in shock and pain. She bit her lip to stifle any cuss words lest her brain should fail to keep that floodgate closed. She looked at her captor. He stood before her as if he hadn't even been hit. A small red welt on his forehead was the only sign that she had done anything at all.

"You're lucky you didn't break your thumb with it tucked inside your hand like that. Hit me again," Tracer challenged.

"I can't."

"Hit me again," he growled, taking half a step toward her.

"I can't," Halen said, matching his insistency. "My hand is broken."

"HIT ME!"

"I CAN'T!" Halen screamed back.

Tracer shoved her. "HIT ME!"

"YOU'LL THROW ME OUTSIDE!"

Tracer shoved her again. "HIT ME!"

Halen looked up into a determined face. He wasn't going to back down until she complied with his demands. She didn't see any other way out of the corner she was now backed into. He'd had full control from the moment he sprang up off the frozen lake and wrapped a trash bag around her head. She had no choice. He was forcing her to swing. He wanted her to, and she knew it was going to be a trap. He was going to hurt her again whether she swung at him or not.

Maybe she could slip one in and at least get a piece of him before she got pummeled. If she could take away his sight, she might be able to outmaneuver him. She struck out as fast as she could with her left hand, aiming for his eyes. Her fist darted toward his face like a scorpion striking for a kill. Her fingers extended into claws, ready to rake across his retinas.

THE HIT

For an instant, her success was right before her. For an instant, she had the upper hand, and that upper hand was going to gain her her freedom. She had control. She was going to show this self-indulging man that she wasn't going to be his victim anymore. She would drag him through the snow, dirt and feces. She would make him stumble through the dark and do chores for her benefit instead.

Her hand suddenly stopped. It had seemingly hit a mound of solid clay and stuck. She tried jerking her hand back, but it barely budged. He had her. She had never really had the upper hand. He just wanted to toy with her and give her a false sense of hope. It had to be part of his psychological manipulation.

"When you punch"—his voice shook with anger as he gripped her wrist—"keep your thumb on the outside, like this." He physically manipulated her hand, tucking her fingers in and wrapping her thumb around the outside of her fingers.

"When you punch, you only hit with your first two knuckles." Tracer pulled her hand into his chest. "When you hit, hit with your whole body. Line up all your energy and send it in a straight line through your arm and into these two knuckles. You won't break your hand like you did on your roundhouse bitch slap."

Tracer pushed her back, putting some distance between them. He stood facing her, challenging her to take him on. "Hit me."

Halen looked at the man, baffled by the lesson she had just received. She wasn't sure what her continued participation would result in. She was sure that he would force her cooperation one way or another. If he was giving her another opportunity, she would take it, but she feared the result of such an attempt. Her right hand throbbed. Any movement she made sent pain racing up her arm, reminding her how vulnerable and inexperienced she was in a real fight.

Pain made her bite her cheek and helped balance her focus. The broken bone opened the door to another dimension of reality. It was her first broken bone. Compared to the choreographed stage fights in front of the camera, this was on a different level. Sometimes the stunts she had to do on-screen faltered, and a solid punch was landed. After the director called cut, most would laugh it off and massage the area of impact. She, however, would complain to the offender about their lack of professionalism and dish out a verbal reprimand while painting herself in a better-than-thou light.

It was different now. There was realism here, with vindictive intent. This was serious—deadly serious. Tracer was a hired killer. He had said as much when he told her he helped people have accidents. From his lack of emotion, she figured he had been doing this a long time. She couldn't fathom that this man wouldn't already be on the FBI's most wanted list.

She swung, almost without realizing she was doing it. Tracer immediately caught her hand and smacked her on top of her head.

"You didn't listen." Tracer pulled her fist to him and re-formed her fingers. "You do that again, I'll let you break your hand."

Halen looked him in the eye, trying to judge his intentions. "Why should I trust you not to break my hand?"

"I didn't break your hand," Tracer said impatiently.

"Yes you did."

"If you had hit me with your first two knuckles, you wouldn't have broken your metacarpal," he reprimanded.

"What?"

He grabbed her hand up, gripped it between his first two fingers and his thumb and pinched her broken bone. "This bone right here," he growled.

Halen screamed and slapped his hand away. She stepped back and then forward, lunging at him. She threw her whole body into her punch, aiming for his heart. She visualized her fist breaking through the rib cage and grasping the man's heart. She wanted to squeeze it until he was dead. She wanted to see the shock in his eyes followed by the horror that he knew his life was about to end.

Her fist slammed into his chest. It felt like she was punching a rock, but she knew that this time she had gotten a piece of him. She made him hurt. The grunt and gasp for air was evidence of that. He would likely beat her into a bloody pile of bones, but she could at least revel in the fact that she'd hurt him.

Hands clamped down on her arm. She prepared herself to be flung against the wall, but nothing happened.

His eyes held a glint of joy, but it was soon replaced by a determined and angry face. "Good. Go eat. We'll fix your hand after."

Tracer walked off as if he hadn't been touched. He rummaged through a supply box and pulled out a can marked with a red cross, then grabbed a meal and sat on his cot to eat.

Halen fumbled her way through the MRE, her broken hand hindering her every step of the way.

Tracer pulled the lid off the medical-supply can and selected a few items wrapped in plastic. "Drag that box over here," he ordered.

"Why?" Halen asked, cradling her arm.

Tracer cast her a look, and she immediately regretted opening her mouth. Grabbing the handle on the trunk, she grated it over the stone floor, bridging the small stream of water that had just started its journey to the ocean. She sat cautiously and waited for the next command.

"Give me your hand," Tracer said as he unwrapped packages of gauze.

"You said eat first." Halen hesitantly reached her hand out.

"Eat first then. I don't care. You want your hand fixed, we'll fix it now or you can fix it yourself later." Tracer grabbed an aluminum splint from the kit and set it on the cot next to him. He walked to the door of the cave, snapped off a short branch and returned to the cot. He smacked Halen across the face. The sudden act surprised her. She opened her mouth to protest, but before she could utter a word, he shoved the dirty stick in her mouth.

"Bite," Tracer barked, immediately grabbing her hand and pinching down on the broken bone.

Halen bit down on the stick, growling through the pain. She swatted at him, only to have a hand grasp her face, and the look from Tracer made her understand that if she interfered again, she would be tossed down the side of the mountain once more.

His strong grip held her hand firmly in place while he set the bone. After securing her hand with the aluminum brace, gauze and several layers of padding, he finished up with layers of flexible tape to hold everything in place.

"Line those three trunks up in that corner," Tracer said, pointing to the opposite side of the cave. "There's some extra blankets in the one you're sitting on. You can make a bed with those."

19

"Again," Tracer barked.

Halen kicked at the pole that had been wrapped in a blanket and tied with cord. Her leg was sore and felt as if it were on the verge of breaking. Her arms were bruised from the previous day's assault. This day, she didn't use her arms except for balance while kicking away an attack, then switching to offense and forcing her foe to back up a few steps.

Weeks had passed since her attempted escape. She'd realized that the cage keeping her there wasn't the chain around her ankle or the man who had dragged her up to the cave. It was the hundreds of square miles of frozen wilderness. The odds of venturing out and flagging down a plane were slim. She understood now that the cave with its hot spring was her only chance at survival until the earth moved around the sun and the snow melted.

The snow machine was useless, as Tracer had used the last hidden can of gas to find and retrieve her. It had taken her a few days to sort through the hallucinations and come to terms with the fact that she hadn't been safe in another cabin. She was alive only because of this demented man forcing her to throw kick after kick into the padded pole. The mystery had deepened as he taught her how to defend herself and how to subdue and kill people, thus teaching her to best him. She imagined a hundred different reasons why he was forcing this training on her but couldn't fit logic to any one of them.

Day in and day out, she kicked at the pole, following Tracer's instructions. He forced her to practice for hours, even when she didn't think she could stand any longer. She had protested at first, but his determination forced her to comply. The harsh lessons outweighed being flung out of the cave again. His usual one-word instructions guided her in correcting her stance, hits, kicks and blocks. The rest of the time was forced calisthenics, eating or sleeping. Halen fell into a routine of waking to a single beep from his LCD alarm.

One particular morning, after making a cup of black instant coffee with the hot spring water and a boost of heat from the MRE heater, she choked down the lasagna from a meal pack and washed it down with the coffee. After making a second cup, she wandered outside to watch the first rays of light as they crested over the speckled landscape.

Tracer had already left the cave, and she found him sitting on a stump of a tree that had long ago toppled. He had hollowed out the center to make a comfortable seat to watch over the valley from. Most mornings she would find him staring off over the empty winter blanket. She took a seat a few yards away on a pile of boughs she had cut to keep herself off the frozen earth, then settled in to watch the morning sun.

"Lynx." Tracer lifted a hand, pointing down the mountain.

Halen had learned to be quick with her eyes to catch the subtle movements of the various critters residing outside the cave. She watched the black-tipped ears bob up, over and around the tangle of trees. A squirrel raced up the trunk of a tree, ready to leap through the branches to survive another day in its frozen world. Halen followed the cat's movements until it disappeared. Searching the surrounding area, she waited for it to resurface, but it didn't.

"Don't move." Tracer's words were as serious as death.

Halen heard a shift in the snow behind her. Her heart raced, threatening to pop the arteries in her neck. She wondered if the creature behind her could hear the pounding drum inside her chest. Out of the corner of her eye, she looked to Tracer for a hint of what to do. He held his hand flat and pressed down.

"Don't look him in the eye. Look at his feet if you have to," Tracer said in a low tone just loud enough for Halen to hear.

She kept her head down but searched wildly around the perimeter of her vision. The snow crunched under the creature's feet as it moved to investigate. A large furry paw spread out across the snow at the edge of her vision. She raised her head ever so slowly to glimpse more of the creature.

THE HIT

The lynx paused every few steps to look at Halen and Tracer. It waited for several minutes, observing the intruders. Its gray-brown speckled coat easily blended into the trees, making it hard to see at a distance. The black tufts of hair stood tall and proud at the points of his ears. The black-on-white muttonchops framed his face, giving the cat a regal look.

It studied Halen, checking for a potential threat, and then walked cautiously over to Tracer. He remained as still as if he were part of the rotten stump he sat on. The furry resident walked around him, stopping to study him at odd intervals. The animal's prey drive had switched to curiosity, as the subjects he studied seemed uninterested in his presence. It circled halfway around Tracer, then turned back to Halen.

Halen's wide eyes were riveted to the animal as it inspected Tracer. When it turned its attention back to her, she lowered her eyes and let the majestic animal advance. His steps were nearly silent as the big paws spread out over the snow. She looked at the place where his foot had been and didn't see a hint of a track. The wildcat paused, then sat just to Halen's left and looked out over the valley as if he were a third member of the forest sentinels. She watched the fluffy animal, drinking in the smallest of details. From the color pattern on its paws to the swish of its short tail, Halen relished every bit of it.

The lynx sat, content to take a break and watch over the valley with Halen and Tracer. Wisps of Halen's hair caught in the air and floated up, tantalizing the predator's instincts.

"Bow your head," Tracer whispered. "Lean down a bit."

Halen leaned forward slowly and ducked her head as if bowing to a king. She could just see the creature's feet from her left eye. It sat there long enough for Halen to stop holding her breath. Her sudden focus on her breathing made her want to breathe heavy and catch up from when the lynx had first appeared. Instead, she eased her breath in and out, slow and steady.

Its breathing was raspy and blended with the hammering of her heart. A long, slow breath left her lungs, and her nerves eased a bit.

Then it lunged.

The cat slammed into her shoulder, almost causing her to topple sideways. The thick, raspy breathing became more pronounced and distinguishable. The cat was purring. It rubbed the full length of its body against Halen, doubled around and came back for another pass. It rolled onto its back, exposing its belly to her and patting her face with its front paws. It lay there looking at her for a moment longer. It was obviously in a playful mood as it writhed halfway onto her lap before plopping onto the bed of evergreen boughs.

For several minutes it lay there, rumbling and content. Halen, too, was content to just sit there as long as the lynx wanted to. It stretched and yawned, showing Halen its razor-sharp teeth almost as if to say *Look what I have and you don't*. A scurry of movement in the trees made the lynx flip and study its surroundings. After a careful inspection, it reached its paw out, placing it on her leg and flexing his claws through her clothes and into her skin.

She shot a look to Tracer, who continued to hold his hand in a suppressing gesture. Halen endured the pain of the five sharp claws stabbing into her leg and forced herself to stay as relaxed as she could. The claws withdrew and Halen eased out a sigh of relief. The beast lay there for a moment longer, then sat up to watch the valley.

As fast as it came upon them, it left. In a few short bounds, it blended into the forest and became all but invisible. Halen watched the speckled coat disappear as the forest swallowed up the lynx, its short tail flicking back and forth as it darted this way, then that.

"Well. At least you know you have one friend," Tracer said with a chuckle.

Halen looked at him with confusion. She was about to protest when he continued.

"His friendship is genuine." Tracer stood to move back into the cave. "He doesn't care about your money, fame or social status. He just likes you for you."

He walked back into the dark cave. Morning light was quickly burning away the shadows, and the warmer weather was ebbing toward the fast-approaching spring.

Halen followed him in. "Are you ever going to tell me why you dragged me into the wilderness? It can't be because you like my company. You don't like anyone's company."

Tracer stood a moment, thinking. "I brought you up here to make a friend."

"You said I made a friend with the lynx. Does that mean I can leave?"

"Sure. It don't mean that you'll survive before you reach civilization though."

"Great. So I'm stuck here with you."

Halen's sarcasm didn't faze Tracer. "Since you're stuck here, might as well learn a thing or two." He started off to the stack of storage containers against the wall. Pulling one after another off the tallest stack, he dug his way to the bottom and hefted the bottom trunk onto the others. He dialed the combination on the lock and opened the trunk.

Plastic hugged the curves of several metallic objects. Halen watched from a distance. The single light cast a heavy shadow on the trunk and its contents, making her guess what she was looking at.

He pulled a knife out and sliced the end of the plastic, allowing air inside, Halen guessed, for the first time in years.

"Here. Clean it." Tracer returned to his near single-word commands.

He set a towel out on a double-stacked trunk and pulled the metal object from the plastic.

"No. Guns are murder machines," Halen protested. "I'm not going to touch that."

Tracer laid the rifle on the towel and looked up at her. "Guess you'll starve then."

"Why? What do you mean?"

"There were only enough MREs for me to survive the winter. Unless you're going to eat pine needles the rest of the winter, you better make a decision about your survival right now."

"I don't believe in killing," Halen admonished.

"Do you believe in eating?"

Halen looked for a way out of or around the decision before her. She couldn't kill anything. Killing was for barbarians. She had elevated herself above the brutal slaying. "Yes." She had a feeling that something more was coming.

"Where do you think the meat comes from in that lasagna you ate?" Tracer asked.

"It comes from the store," Halen blurted.

"Where does the store get it? Do you think that they magically pull it out of their ass?" Tracer said.

Halen stood staring, searching her mind for something she could use to make her argument. "The store gets it from the factory."

"Also known as a slaughterhouse. It's amazing how little history and skill gets passed down to the current generation."

"See, the slaughterhouse makes it," Halen said.

Halen saw his face tighten. It was a subtle change that she knew would have a dire consequence.

He rushed her. His hand clamped around her throat and he shoved her against the wall. The barrel of a pistol was suddenly at her temple.

"The whole world is about survival. The whole world is about imposing one influence against another. That cat knows it better than you or I. The farmer grows what he eats. The guy on Wall Street trades stocks and skims some off the side so the rest can make him more. Politicians make rules and laws that favor themselves and their buddies. They get kickbacks called insider trading by telling their family members to buy into an investment before a new law gives that company an advantage. You shake your ass and tits on-screen and call it art. What are you gonna do when you've scratched your ass off wondering why you don't have another acting gig? Who's gonna pay the doctor bill after you've tripped over your sagging tits and break your hip? Do you have a plan to pay for your lifestyle after the theater is closed?"

Halen stared back. The gun at her temple had little effect on her. He had commented over and over about killing her and ending her *insignificant life*.

"Until you open your mind to how the world actually works, you will have no use for the things I tell you. By some miracle, if you do open your mind, understanding how the world works will scare the shit out of you *and* help you survive. In the end, you can only count on yourself, and if you tell yourself lies, you have just doomed yourself to death." Tracer slammed her against the rock as a final emphasis.

He turned and went back to the trunk. After pulling another rifle out, he cut open the plastic and retrieved the well-oiled firearm. He wiped the excess oil off with a rag, pulled a single bullet from a box, then started for Halen. A quick motion of his hand sent her out the door ahead of him.

"Don't come back unless you have meat." Tracer shoved the rifle into her hand and placed a single .22-caliber bullet in her other hand.

20

Halen had tried to duck back into the cave that morning, but a bullet in the ground next to her foot was a clear indicator that Tracer's decision to send her hunting was not up for debate. She had little to no influence on the things he decided.

Trudging through the snow all day gave her plenty of time to reflect on her life and the few words Tracer had said. His views on survival made her reflect on her own Hollywood celebrity status and see that it was a fleeting blink of time. That she was only as good as her last film. It wasn't enough to frighten her, but it did give her reason to consider what had happened to those who weren't in the limelight anymore. Were the actors and actresses she no longer heard from happy and comfortable with their lives after the cameras stopped rolling?

Though she didn't like the man, Tracer had taught her a few things that wouldn't benefit her here in the middle of the wilderness. She had thought she could use the lessons against him, but it still didn't make sense. It would only benefit her if she were to kill him. But why, then, would he even teach her? He taught her how to fight and defend herself. There wasn't any reason for her to use those skills up here. It dawned on her that he very well might send her back. But why? She could tell authorities all about him, what he had done to her, what he looked like. It made no sense for him—someone who didn't want attention and hid in plain sight, probably for years—to release her. She could easily put the police on his trail. She could give them enough evidence to put him away for the rest of his life. It just made no sense why he was doing what he was.

It had taken her a few minutes to figure out the rifle and how to load the bullet into it. She'd handled movie prop weapons before and they were very realistic, but there were no cameras here. In the wilderness, the lessons didn't get a second take. They didn't have a script or a rehearsal.

Just like the wildlife in the surrounding frozen land, she had one opportunity. One bullet to earn her survival. One chance to live another day. Another day of what? She would only learn that tomorrow.

The outline of the hare was bright against the dark tree trunk. At only twenty feet away, it would be an easy shot. The rabbit stood perfectly still, hoping not to be noticed. Halen steadied the rifle, aimed and fired.

The rabbit hadn't given its life. She was the one that took it. She took it in order to be allowed back in the cave. She took it so she could eat. Now she had to grab the dead animal and find her way back.

Halen admonished herself for sobbing as long as she had. The light was fading fast. If she had shot the animal and grabbed it right away, she might have found her way back to the cave before the sun had set. Since she had cried over killing the rabbit, she was now forced to differentiate the shadows of her own tracks that crisscrossed themselves from the tracks of countless other critters who called the forest home.

She opened her eyes to see the last bit of light casting deep shadows over her surroundings. The temperature had dropped; she felt the chill seeping through her clothes. She would need to start back soon. Her clothes wouldn't hold against a night outside the cave. With the new moon upon them, it would be difficult to find her way back. She could follow her trail through the snow, but she had wandered back over it multiple times. She'd made the mistake earlier that day when she retraced her steps in a circle.

Tracer paced the small landing outside the cave. Looking as far into the growing shadows as he could, he tried to distinguish one shadow from another. He told himself that he didn't care and the world would have to endure the small loss, but he found himself pacing and searching the evening for any movement indicating Halen's return.

The impulse to kidnap Halen hadn't bothered him. He was confident that his plan to stage a drowning in Whitefish Lake would keep the authorities busy with her disappearance until spring when all the ice was off the lake and they could use sonar to search for a body. Even if they suspected otherwise, they would be hard-pressed to uncover snow machine tracks under the many feet of snow.

The modified snow machine with the added muffler had helped to keep the noise low as he'd navigated out of town. With such deep accumulations of snow, the machines were commonly seen on the roads as they towed portable ice fishing shelters back to their homes. Most would view him as one of the local fishermen heading home after a day of fishing on the ice.

He knew this area of Canada, as he had grown up here before leaving home for college decades earlier. He had discovered the cave while hiking with his father. It was a place he wanted to keep to himself—his parents had fought constantly, and he thought it would be of use if he could leave his parents behind. His parent's divorce had caused a lot of anxiety and hatred toward his parents during his teenage years.

After leaving college, he came back to the cave to sort out his thoughts and his plan for the future. It was to be a future of revenge that turned into a way of life and a lucrative career.

The chance of a local sheriff stumbling onto his trail was always a possibility. If that happened, he had blackmail tapes that would persuade a passel of politicians to lend one of their top lawyers. He had become so skilled at his craft that the government hinted at putting him on retainer. If a politician was rocking their boat, he would be summoned to address the issue.

He knew that he could cut and run if the authorities started to close in on him. He had connections and safe houses scattered throughout North America, South America and Siberia. He had no real obligations, yet he was pacing outside the cave, watching for Halen to come back. The last rays of light were gone, and the incoming clouds were going to send the valley into a dark, starless night.

Against the brilliant white of the snow, he saw movement. Tracer quickly ducked back into the cave for his rifle.

Halen kept to the trails zigzagging through the trees and guessed which one led back to the cave. She ripped off pieces of her clothing to use as a cord and tied the snowshoe hare to her waist and the rifle to her back. With her hands free, she was better able to balance and used her hands to climb over downed timber or shake the snow off the pine boughs before crawling under them.

The day had been exhausting climbing through the snow, balancing on logs and looking for anything that moved. She'd passed up numerous squirrels, thinking they were too small a target for her to ever hit. Her confidence with the rifle was nonexistent.

She had spooked a rabbit while stepping over a log, then followed it, trying to get close enough so her one bullet would count. Through half the day, she played cat and mouse with that rabbit, but it had stayed out of her range. As it ran off one more time, she looked around and saw another rabbit outlined against the trunk of a tree just a few feet away. She lifted the rifle, aimed and squeezed the trigger. Nothing happened.

She fought through her frustration, trying to figure out why the gun didn't fire. Night was coming soon and she couldn't return without some sort of meat. She didn't care what it was, she just wanted to bring something back. She wanted to sit in that hot pool and let the water warm her frozen toes.

She had forgotten about the safety button. She clicked it off, squeezed the trigger and began to cry.

With the moment long past and the sun having gone down, Halen wandered through the forest, making her way toward where she assumed the cave was. The darkness made her second-guess everything she did. Every decision she had ever made. Even the ones she'd made as a girl. If she had made a different choice all those years ago, would she be in a different place now? Would she even be a movie star? Would another little girl have taken her role and gone on to be a positive role model for today's youth?

The crunch of snow—not from her own foot— stopped her in her tracks and brought her back to the harsh real world. Despite her exhaustion, adrenaline snapped her back to full alertness. Every nerve buzzed in anticipation of which boogeyman or beast might be out in the night. She knew of one, but he seemed indifferent to whether she lived or died. He showed no emotion other than anger. She couldn't read him at all. He treated her like an inconvenience. She supposed that she was, yet he still kept her around, teaching her ways to defend herself in many different situations.

"Tracer?" Halen called out through the night. "Are you out there?"

She would have given anything for a flashlight at that moment. To cast a light on her surroundings and reassure herself that there was nothing out there. That it was just a clump of snow that had loosened from a tree branch and fallen to the forest floor.

She heard another crunch of snow.

"Tracer. You better not be playing with me," she called out a little louder.

Halen listened for a long moment. There was nothing but an imagined ringing in her ears. Giving up on the fictitious monster in the night, she turned and started off, hoping she was going in the right direction. It was uphill, and she felt she had crossed back over her tracks a couple of times trying to find her way back to the cave.

She stopped and leaned against a tree. She heard distinct footsteps this time. Something was following her. She turned to see a black mass just a few yards from her.

"Get back!" Halen screamed.

The black mass let out a scream of its own. The shrill made her blood turn to ice, and she froze in her tracks.

The beast leaped into the air.

21

Halen screamed again. She brought up the small rifle as if it were a stick to stab at the beast, distancing herself from the outstretched claws.

"Tracer!" she screamed, hoping he was close enough to hear her.

The cat lunged at her over and over, testing and looking for an opening where it could move in for a kill. Halen stabbed at the predator with the muzzle of the rifle. She didn't have a knife to wield but rather preferred the empty rifle anyway, as it helped to keep the beast just out of reach.

She had wasted her only bullet on a rabbit. After feeling for the strap that tied the rabbit to her side, she fumbled with the knot. If she could get it loose and throw it at the cat, it might be distracted enough to leave her alone so she could make an escape.

Deep growls sounded through the night, warning any around that the lion meant deadly business. Halen shrieked at it over and over while continuing to stab at the beast, keeping it at a distance. The dark mass dodged to the side, trying to find an opening.

Halen turned. The cat lunged and Halen fell backward. The mountain lion inked out what little she could see of the sky. Snow crunched underneath her, some trickling inside her collar, but her focus was on defending herself from the claws gripping her arms and the teeth inches from her face. The animal collapsed on her, pushing her deeper into the blanket of snow.

Halen flailed at the beast. Warm liquid ran down her face and neck. Panic struck her as the heavy cat pressed its fangs down on her forehead. She was sure that a tooth would sink into her eye socket and pry the top of her skull off. The warm, wet liquid running down her face concerned her more.

She fought like the lion did, trying to match its ferocity. She had lost the rifle when she fell and only had her hands to use to prevent the cat's teeth from piercing her flesh. She tried to push the thing off her but failed. She pushed again at its head to find that it wobbled back and forth. Bone crunched in its neck, ceasing any voluntary movements, but the remnants of a pulse caused its blood to spew out and down onto Halen.

The warm liquid dripped on her face, some getting into her mouth. She screamed, fighting to get out from under it. Pushing herself to the side in the deep snow, she wiggled out from under the limp body. Huffing with half screams, she scrambled across the snow to a fallen tree. The cat didn't move from where it lay. She kept her eyes on the beast, waiting for it to jump up and attack her again.

"Nice catch."

The words hit Halen like a tree smacking the ground. She jumped up and spun around to face another dark figure standing just a few yards away on the other side of the fallen timber. She stood for a beat, wondering if she had actually heard the words. The figure didn't move. In a way, it looked like just another mangled tree stump.

"You alright?" Tracer's flat, indifferent tone cut through the night air.

Halen breathed a sigh of relief, then shot a look back at the beast lying in the snow.

"Is it dead?" she asked.

"Should be. I know I hit it at least once," Tracer said, taking several more steps and stopping on the other side of the log. The AR15 was still gripped and at the ready.

"You shot it?" Halen asked.

He ignored the question. "Are you alright?" he repeated.

"I . . . don't know. I can't see."

"Lift your chin," Tracer said.

Halen did as he commanded. She couldn't see and didn't know how Tracer would be able to see any better in the now overcast night. He used his hand to move her chin from one side to the other, occasionally wiping away the mountain lion's blood.

"You feel anything else on your arms, legs . . . ?"

"No. I don't think so."

"Can you move your legs?"

She shook her legs, then lifted them one at a time. "My toes are numb from the cold, but I think I'm good."

"Here." Tracer handed something to her. "They're goggles. Put them on."

She fumbled with them, looking for the right way to place them over her eyes. A small screen came into view. It showed her the snow-covered ground with occasional fallen trees crisscrossing her path.

"What are these?"

"Night-vision goggles," Tracer said.

Halen felt for the strap and pulled it up over her head. After a moment of fumbling, she pulled the straps tight and looked up at Tracer.

The green screen showed her the world as if she were watching an ancient television with a snowy green tint. She could make out the whites of Tracer's eyes as they darted about, scanning the scene.

"Your movement along with the blood from that rabbit made him think you were wounded and an easy meal," Tracer explained.

Halen looked down to her side. The rabbit was no longer hanging there. She looked around at the scene. The cat lay in the depression she had made when she fell backward, and the rabbit was impaled with the cat's claws. She realized that those claws would have sunk deep into her leg if she hadn't killed the rabbit. Realizations hit her, one after another. If she hadn't killed the rabbit, the mountain lion might not have smelled the blood. She also would have been stuck outside through the night, where the cold likely would have claimed her.

"The essence of survival right there," Tracer said, stepping around the edge of the log and walking up to the kill.

Halen followed him but kept back a step in case the monster came back from the dead.

"What is it?" She asked.

"Mountain lion." Tracer shook out a cord and wrapped it around the cat's head and pulled it out of the crater.

Halen looked in the hole where she had been smashed into the snow and saw her rabbit.

"Get your rabbit," Tracer said, turning back to his trail and starting off, dragging the cat behind him.

22

"If you hate me so much, why did you come after me? Didn't you say you wouldn't save me a third time?" Halen looked across the small fire they had built near the entrance to the cave.

Tracer stared back for a moment. He tested the doneness of the meat he had carved from the mountain lion. Halen rotated the tree branch with the skewered rabbit over the fire. She was hesitant at first, but Tracer had told her that if she wanted to eat, she would have to prepare the rabbit on her own.

Several spells of dry heaves later, she managed to get the rabbit on a stick. With a dash of seasoning, her appetite had returned enough to tempt her to try the wild game. When she engaged with what he was trying to teach her, he was much less aggressive and seemed to volunteer more information—and he seemed to enjoy watching her learn.

Tracer set the strip of lion meat back over the fire. "I know you can get rabbits now."

"You were on your way to find me long before you knew I had a rabbit." Halen tried to corner him into the real reason he had come to look for her.

"I saw the lion. It'll feed us a few days longer than a rabbit."

Halen watched him test the meat, then rip off a chunk and eat it.

"What does it taste like?" Her curiosity had gotten the better of her.

Tracer ripped off another piece and extended the stick over for Halen to pull the last bit off. She took a bite and considered the flavor mixing with the salt and spices. It had a stringy texture and tasted like dog. When she was a child, her friend's father had tricked her into trying canine meat. In her friend's homeland in Southeast Asia, it was commonplace, but here it was extremely frowned upon. After learning the truth, she stopped being that little girl's friend. She saw now that some cultures adhered a little closer to the line of survival than the self-righteous with a river of abundance.

The growl of her stomach convinced her to be a little more open to varied cuisines. The aroma of cooked meat was more appealing than she remembered from her childhood. Maybe she had just been appalled by the idea at the time. Tracer watched her. She nodded her approval at his implied question.

"How's your hare?" Tracer asked.

"Ugh. My hair is a mess. I haven't had a brush to brush it in forever." Halen began rambling. "I wish I had shampoo and conditioner, some bath beads . . ."

Halen looked up. Tracer's face bore an expression of utter disbelief.

"You asked me how my hair was doing."

"No. I asked you how your hare tasted."

Halen stared at the slim skeletal rabbit, then reached out and pinched the thick, meatier leg. "How do you know when it's done?"

"Well, if it's black, then you have overdone it. If in doubt, cook it until it is almost burnt. Then you can scale back to what tastes good on the next one."

"Next one?" Halen's alarm went off. "I was barely able to shoot the first one, let alone skin it out. I'm not going to be able to shoot another."

"First one's always the hardest," Tracer said, stabbing another strip of meat onto his skewer.

Halen gingerly pulled a strip of meat off the rabbit and tasted it. "It's kinda stringy like chicken. The flavor is good though." She picked at another strip. "Will you teach me to make a fire in the snow?"

"Why?"

"I want to escape this place. Isn't that obvious?"

"You're not ready yet." Tracer took another bite of meat.

"When will I be ready?" she pried, trying not to overstep the number of questions he would actually answer.

Tracer cooked the next chunk of meat, ignoring her question.

"Know how to make pemmican?" Tracer asked after he had finished his cup of coffee.

"Make what?" Halen watched him as she dug through a pouch of mixed fruit.

"Pemmican. Dried meat, lard and pine nuts," he explained. "It's a delicacy that the natives made and survived many cold winters with."

Tracer's decorative words seemed to turn Halen's crude introduction to surviving in the wild into a gourmet cooking class.

Together they dried meat, gathered pine nuts and ground everything into a powder. Tracer had saved the fat from the bear he had killed upon their arrival and was now rendering it in a pot over the fire.

"Pour this over the pemmican. It acts like a preservative. It has about four thousand calories per pound. Natives lived for centuries on this stuff," he said, stepping away from the pot of lard.

Halen reached in with gloved hands and lifted the pot off the firepit stones. "How did you learn about this?" she asked as she drizzled the melted fat over the dried meat and nuts.

"My grandmother was a Siksika. Tough as nails. Did everything by hand. Made me help her. If I did something wrong, she beat me with a big wooden spoon that she also used as a crutch. She used that spoon for everything—making soap, making pemmican—she even used it to splint my leg when I tripped over a rock while carrying her laundry. She whipped my ass for getting her laundry dirty before she decided to splint my leg. I think I was about five. My ass hurt worse than my leg did that day."

Tracer took the pot of lard back, poured some in another pot and added some special water he had strained through a bed of wood ash. He placed both pots on the coals and continued to stir.

Halen continued to mix the dried meat with the lard in a tarp suspended from a pole. She twisted her face in disgust at the texture.

"Pretend your grandma whipped your ass and is fixing to whip it again before she decides to splint your leg," Tracer growled.

Halen recognized the tone for what it was and plunged her fingers clear to the bottom, pulling up the dried mix and combining it with the saturated meat on the top. She continued to mix, elbows deep, until her back couldn't take the strain of leaning over any longer.

"How did your grandmother do this day after day and year after year?" Halen asked.

Tracer stopped stirring the two pots for a moment. "Her mother beat her ass and told her not to complain."

"Seems like a family tradition. I feel sorry for any children you have," Halen said.

Tracer fell silent, staring into the pots on the fire.

Stars filled the sky where the trees didn't. The two of them worked through the night in the cover of the trees so as not to send up any smoke signals during the day. Halen's mind continued working, learning and scheming to find a way to escape the forced wilderness survival education. If she had to, she would learn it all in order to escape from him.

Her confidence was growing and she was becoming more comfortable with the rugged and ruthless lifestyle she was living. Ancestors everywhere had lived this way doing the things she was doing now. However far back one could trace their lineage, there was someone who had stood over a fire and prepared the things that would allow them and their families to survive.

When Tracer finished boiling what he wanted, he set the pots aside to cool. He grabbed some of the bones from the lion and went to sit on his stump.

Halen was exhausted. She finished packaging the pemmican and dragged herself to her bed and fell asleep before her head hit the bunched-up blanket.

23

Halen pulled herself out of a crazy dream about Tracer's grandmother standing to the side of a film set, waving a large wooden spoon at her, making sure she had said her lines correctly. The augmented dream swirled and mixed with the surreal life of the cave, making it harder to differentiate between the two.

The lead in her limbs stifled her morning arousal. Every muscle in her body screamed for her to go back to sleep and wake when all the pain was gone. But she knew it was there to stay, and the only way to quiet its relentless scream was to make it scream louder until her muscles loosened up.

Gravity continued to smash her face against the wool blanket and the steel trunks underneath. She had acclimated to the temperature and the humidity. Her tan had faded while her muscles became more defined. There was little time to notice these changes during day-to-day activities, but now she noticed, and it was glaringly apparent.

With or without a blanket over her, she slept without a chill. Most nights she was borderline sweating.

This morning was the same, except for the massive weight that clung to her limbs. She feared the soreness that would wreak havoc on her as soon as she twitched a muscle.

Instead of moving, she shifted an eye to the cot opposite her. Tracer was on his side, facing the wall. His back rose and fell steadily. A relieved sigh escaped her. She was safe from his domineering authority for the moment.

She continued to scan her surroundings. Something caught her eye before the generator light faded from low charge. The rock they used in the generator had reached the floor, halting the flow of electricity and extinguishing the LED light. If it had just gone out, Tracer had to have been up two hours ago doing something.

The object or objects she thought she had seen when the light faded seemed out of place. She hadn't noticed anything that close to her head when she'd lain down. Slowly she moved her hand up to investigate.

Tracer snorted as he readjusted his position, and she froze. A minute later, he started snoring. She continued her exploration of the item next to her head.

She found a soft cloth. Her hand continued across the folded fabric to explore the item and found a thick waxy slab in the shape of a crude triangle. Under it was another item that felt like a skeletal bone. She jerked her hand away. The sudden movement shot pain through her muscles, reminding her of the heavy labor from the day before.

Halen curled herself into a ball to stretch her muscles, then gingerly pushed up off the bed. Steadying herself, she eased up and onto her feet. The generator was just in front of her, and she reached out for the rope and followed it up to the light. Wrapping the rope around the spool, she let the rock hang and start its two-hour descent to the floor.

Light filled the cave and she turned her attention back to the items that had been laid next to her head. The cloth was a folded towel. On it was a waxy-looking triangle and a comb. The thick tines were coarse and marred with cuts from a knife's edge. She picked up the comb and brought it closer to the light.

She could see where the crude gouges in the bone had been polished, creating a simple design. A dozen teeth were cut into the bone, creating the comb. She turned it over to inspect the other side. Halen couldn't imagine what part of the lion the bone had come from. She decided she would rather not know and left it at that. The design on the back had her name etched into the bone with tiny scrolls carved on either side. The bone didn't feel slimy; it felt dry. Though she could see the gouges from his knife, she also saw that the tines were polished, free of any notches that might snag hair.

She turned her attention to the items still next to her bed. Picking up the triangular slab, she pressed a fingernail to it, then sniffed the wedge. She thought she could smell a hint of what bacon smelled like when frying. That and a bit of ash from the fire. She picked at the edge of it again and glanced down at the towel. She looked at the wedge, then back at the towel. It was soap. Tracer had made her a comb and a bar of soap.

Halen spun around and looked at Tracer. His chest still moved up and down in a steady rhythm, and his snoring had quieted.

He must have made the comb while she slept. It was, in a sense, an olive branch of peace. He had taught her many things about surviving in the wild. She still didn't know what his endgame was. He might never tell her. At the moment, it didn't matter. For the first time since she had been dragged into the cave, he'd made her feel like a girl. Though she was still a prisoner and she was still piecing some things together, like why he would do such a thing, at this moment, he recognized her as a girl.

The simple gift seemed monumental, where otherwise it would just be a trivial annoyance. Months earlier, she would have scoffed at the gift. Now, she saw the effort that had gone into the simple items. It warmed her heart to realize that he saw her as more than just an object. She now had an identity. She was a girl.

Halen fidgeted with the rationed MREs. *Waste not, want not* echoed through her head from the multiple reprimands Tracer had given her about the scarce resources. She knew that nothing should be wasted. She had to eat all of it. Sometimes she waited longer or until the next day to eat to give her body a chance to utilize all the calories from the meal packs. It was a mindful balance of eating just the right amount.

She watched Tracer finish his own meal. Though he seldom looked at her, she felt that he always knew exactly where she was. When he did look at her, he held a most inquisitive look, almost as if his soul were crushed.

"How much do you make when you kill me?" Halen asked, breaking the silence.

"Half a million." The lack of hesitation surprised her.

She was also surprised by his bluntness. "Do you collect on it before or after?"

"Half before, half after."

Halen pondered the information. In a way, $500,000 was a lot of money, but she was also a celebrity, and a high-profile case would be sternly scrutinized. For this kind of risk, the reward was likely to be substantial. After a minute of thought, she asked a follow-up question. "Are all your contracts for half a million?"

Tracer got up. The question clearly made him uncomfortable. He picked up his coat and headed for the cave opening.

"Thank you for the comb and the soap," Halen called after him. If he heard her, he didn't give any indication.

Halen pulled her hair over her shoulder and stroked it. The crude comb had pulled most of the knots out that had accumulated over the past several weeks. The soap and comb were small luxuries that had allowed her to feel like a woman again instead of just a captive.

She picked up her comb and wedge of soap, then placed them neatly in a small crevice in the rock. She looked around at the disheveled and scattered cargo boxes. The littering of food packages encroached on the cave's livable space. Usually Halen would abstain from any sort of cleaning, as it violated her personal views. Paying to have someone clean for her was much more convenient and allowed her to focus on her acting and her socializing. She grudgingly had to admit that socializing had taken up a large majority of her waking hours.

Those long hours of socializing had been abruptly cut off, leaving her with time to explore something else. At first, and after she realized that this man who had dragged her to a frozen wasteland would not harm her immediately, she found her mind at times screaming for some sort of entertainment. Anything to fill the mind-numbing quiet. A song from her youth floated into her head from years of dusty neglect as well as the memory of a childhood friend. They had sung that song to the point of driving their parents crazy.

She also remembered being mean to her friend in order to become friends with a more popular group. For almost a year, she had caught sad glances from her former friend as Halen flaunted her new popularity. She remembered that her former friend's mother had made the most amazing cinnamon rolls. Halen's mouth watered at the memory. She wished she could have one right at that moment.

THE HIT

"Deenya." Halen startled herself as the name echoed off the wall of the cave, bringing her mind back to the present.

The cave had been neglected and was in a bit of disarray, mostly due to the long hours of making the pemmican from the lion's meat and the bear's rendered fat. She figured Tracer would make her clean up the mess. If she started now, she could hopefully prevent any harsh punishment if he happened to be in a foul mood. After collecting the food bags into one larger bag, she set it aside and started washing all the mud, blood and other debris down the small stream. Hours passed and Halen looked back over the work she had done to clean and organize the cave.

All the trash had been compacted into a couple larger bags. The walls and floor were scrubbed with a green pine bough. The place was humid and now smelled of fresh pine. She straightened Tracer's cot and the blankets on it, then re-leveled her own bed with varied sticks, propping up the corners of the hard boxes to bring them into alignment.

Tracer ducked back inside the pine-branch door. He looked at the floor of the cave and fixed a hard stare at Halen.

Halen cringed, wondering what his next move would be. She did everything he asked and then some. His expression swung from rage to annoyance to a creepy calm, keeping her guessing whether he would hit her again or simply grunt, lay on his cot and roll over to face the wall.

Looking down at his feet, Tracer followed her gaze and saw that his boots had found some mud somewhere. She had noticed that the days had been warmer for a while, but the massive snow accumulations might cause the high country to forfeit the spring and summer, as it wouldn't have enough time to melt all the snow. Tracer took a long sidestep over to the small stream and stepped down into the shallow water.

Relief washed over Halen, as the small respectful act validated her efforts. She wanted to smile. She wanted to be joyous about anything but was afraid to show any type of emotion. She checked her expression. She was smiling. Fearful of any reaction, she dissolved the smile before he could catch her.

Tracer left his muddy clothes and boots by the entrance and walked to the stack of trunks in his long underwear. He pulled a case down and set it close to Halen's bed. He pulled another and opened it, then fished out a long, flat box whose contents rattled. Fear that it was some torturous device came to the front of Halen's mind. It was something that she couldn't help, and no one could begrudge her of the thought. She tensed as he placed one case atop the other and then put the old, worn flat box on the case. He turned and brought his cot over to use as a chair.

"Ever play a five-thousand-year-old game?" Tracer shook the cardboard top off the game.

24

Halen rolled the dice. "Ha. I win. That's three games in a row."

Tracer glowered at her and grumbled to himself.

"Come on, now. You have to pay up. You made me pay up. Now it's your turn." Winning three games in a row was a monumental accomplishment for Halen. The luck and strategy of her opponent had dominated over her for months, from her first game in the middle of winter. He'd taught her the basics and they played game after game for days on end. When she won her first game, she asked why he liked this game. His response came halfway through the following game when he muttered, *I'll tell you after you win three in a row*. She had learned not to push him for anything. That he would, in time, give her an answer.

"Damn it," Tracer grumbled.

This was the third time he had lost three games in a row, striking a blow to his concealed ego. His agitation doubled each time he lost a game. His three-game winning streaks resulted in a break from the game while Halen mastered one self-defense move after another. He taught her how to get out of choke holds, how to react to a gun being shoved in her face, how to get out of being pinned to the wall or pinned to the ground. He instructed her how to survive a carjacking and flee from a bomb threat.

The more he taught her, the more she realized he truly wanted to help her. He had plucked her from a lifestyle where few could live and truly shine in a positive light. She began to see kindness masked by his crude and inhospitable temperament. A simple grunt had become the equivalent of *good job*, and he spent less time staring at her as if he were still deciding whether to kill her or not. He was a mystery. Halen couldn't figure out what he wanted. He seemed to continually study her like a scientist putting a rat through various experiments and tests.

She looked across the trunk at him, waiting patiently for the agreed-upon wager to be paid. Tracer heaved a sigh of defeat. Halen riveted her attention on him, still uncertain if he would tip the table on edge, spilling the game across the floor, or reluctantly bow to his agreement.

He glanced at her from behind hooded eyes. "My father was a good man. He did his best to raise me right. And he did. He taught me all I needed to be a good and decent man. I admired him for that. Still do. He taught me to put a hundred-ten percent into my work. Never let a job fail in any way. If I made a mistake, he taught me to learn from it, improve from it and to look for other ways I might have similarly failed and to take steps to avoid that potential outcome."

"He sounds like a great father. Where is he now?" Halen asked.

"Dead."

"What happened?"

Tracer lurched to his feet, bumping the chest and scattering some of the game pieces across the floor. Striding to the door, he pulled on his coat and grabbed the rifle that was ever ready for action and threw open the door.

Halen watched him duck out. She had found a sensitive issue and apparently stomped on that nerve. He was gone. She had hit a nerve the first time she'd won too, and she asked why he spared her. He'd said he wanted to see who she was first. When prodded for details, he tossed the game across the room and disappeared for the night.

Halen picked up the game and carefully put it away, then pulled on her own coat and ducked out the small entrance. Scanning the slope, down first and then backward up the hill, she didn't see him. Movement caught her eye and she spun. Far down the hill, she saw his camouflaged body lumbering around trees and over boulders. Worry crept into her mind. Not for herself but for him.

A short time ago, she wondered if she would be able to kill him so she could escape. Now she worried for him for a reason she really couldn't put her finger on.

"He'll be back in the morning," Halen said to herself, and retrieved the .22-caliber rifle he had assigned her to hunt with. She sat on the rock and watched for any rabbits or squirrels that might venture into her limited shooting range.

She had gone with him numerous times on hunting expeditions, practicing each shot as he instructed. She learned to break the simple single-shot rifle down, clean, oil and reassemble it. He taught her when the best time to shoot was and when not to force a bad shot. He was a stickler for one shot, one kill. He told her it was an insult to the animal if she had to take more than one shot, but she suspected there was more behind his reasoning.

He would listen all day to the forest noises and sometimes abruptly go back inside for days on end. He would watch the clouds and predict upcoming storms. She noticed that he would only hunt far away when a storm would soon cover his tracks. She knew he didn't want to be found. It was her objective to fight him and get away, yet she stayed. Mostly because it was winter and she lacked any confidence in finding her way back to civilization, and partly because she was curious about him. He had kidnapped her and revealed that he was to kill her, yet he hadn't.

Something was holding him back from collecting his reward. Of course, she wasn't going to push him into finishing the job, but it didn't stop her from wondering about that all-important answer.

Shadows grew long and disappeared as the sun set. She sat on Tracer's stump and watched the valley below, as it had the best vantage point. Darkness enveloped the mountains she was stranded in as she watched for Tracer's return. Her eyelids began to droop, and she caught herself nodding off and almost fell from the stump. She was becoming accustomed to the night and the lack of lights. Tracer had taught her how to see in the dark. How to understand shadows and not become spooked by what was likely a clump of brush. She found that she preferred the dark over a beam of light. The light would let her see better but blind her to anything outside the reach of the bulb.

Cold air forced Halen back inside, where she replaced the door and wound the string to the light generator, then let it dangle. The LED charged and spread its meager light across the cave. After putting the backgammon game back in the steel case and the cases back on their stack, she straightened her bed and dug an applesauce pouch out of an MRE bag and a handful of pemmican from the collection of empty MRE bags. The meat, pine nut and lard mixture wasn't as tasty a treat as she would have preferred, but as Tracer had told her on multiple occasions, *It'll push a turd*. With a final glance at Tracer's bed, she lay down and closed her eyes.

Morning brought the promise of a new day and most likely several games of backgammon. She'd begun to enjoy the game and studied Tracer's strategy, mirroring it at first, then eventually countering it. It took her days to talk him into it, but she eventually nagged him into betting on the outcome of the three-game streak. If he won three in a row, which was often, she would eagerly learn any lesson he wanted to teach her. But if she won three games in a row, he had to reveal something about himself, which usually meant answering just one question. It was a bit lopsided, but she took what she could get.

His cot was still where she had placed it after his hasty exit. The blankets hadn't been ruffled any more than they were the previous night. He was usually back by this time, but it wasn't completely out of character for him to be gone through part of the next day. Halen made a cup of coffee and went out to sit on her boulder.

Shadows shrank as the sun lifted into the sky. Halen scanned her surroundings, working her way out to the furthest points she could see. Satisfied that there wasn't any immediate danger, she turned her attention to the sky. High cirrostratus clouds showed their wispy lines of crystallized water. The agitated state of the lines ripping from the northwest indicated that a spring storm was moving into the area.

Halen waited through much of the morning, watching for Tracer's return. She saw his tracks leading off down the hill. Worry ebbed into her mind and her subconscious made her duck inside the cave and emerge with the rifle and a pack they had used for the last couple hunting trips. It had an emergency shelter, food and a basic first aid kit as well as a knife, multi-tool, matches and a candle. A flashlight rounded out the pack.

Halen squinted against the bright glare from the snow. Moving slowly and methodically, she followed Tracer's tracks through the trees.

She lost them from time to time, then circled, spiraling out until she picked them up again. With the wet ground, it was much easier to follow, as his feet had sunk into the mud and snow, leaving distinguishable prints.

She thought he would be proud of her for tracking him this far. She figured she was a couple miles from the cave and far lower in elevation. The hill became steeper, and she found balancing on the slope increasingly difficult. Three times she slipped, and three times she went to a knee. The mud soaked through her clothes to her skin. The lesson about hypothermia was all too real for her. She vaguely remembered the hallucinations of entering a warm cabin and curling up by the fire. Every time she felt a chill, she was reminded about her near collision with death.

She didn't rush. Tracer's lesson about being patient was made clear when he'd told her to stay on her bed until he said she could move. She'd had nothing to count the days with. She hadn't known if it was day or night. She tried counting the meals she ate, but the inconsistency of their meal time quickly deterred her from using it as a clock. She got to eat when he did, and sometimes he wouldn't eat for a day or more. Her job was to watch a spot on the wall and be as motionless as possible.

Days passed. The spot didn't move. She didn't know how it would. It was fixed to the stone. She wanted to question his motives but was compelled to stay the course. He was teaching her something but she couldn't fathom what it was. He said that the lesson would be learned or she would face a night outside in freezing temperatures. She slept when tired and ate when he handed her a meal. The rest of the time she watched that spot on the wall. At times it appeared to move, but upon blinking it looked as though it were the same speck it had always been.

Her muscles involuntarily tensed, pushing out a yawn. When she looked back at the spot, it was gone. She got up and crossed to the wall where it had been. Peering into a small crack, she saw a white silky sack. Looking further around the wall, she found the black spot she had been watching. The spider scurried toward the cave entrance and the bounty of food that lay within the forest floor.

Patience had allowed her to see a hidden gem in nature, but it was a lesson that wasn't helping her now. The threat of a storm and the sinking sun had become a direct opposition to her patience. She slipped on the slope again, this time going all the way to her hands and knees. Before her in the mud was Tracer's boot track. There was another track on top of it. One that made her blood run as cold as the approaching storm.

25

The track was more than double Halen's foot size, and the claw marks in the mud were longer than her fingers, from the pad to their tips. She had heard about the monsters and the gory mess they could leave a body in—unrecognizable and scattered across miles of wilderness. Sometimes they didn't leave enough remains to fill a shoebox.

Bolting up off the ground, she looked all around her. Every hair stood on end. Every scent was analyzed for a potential threat. Every thump of a pine cone falling to the ground made her jump. She looked around several times, then back down at the track to make sure she had seen it correctly. Pulling the .22 rifle to the ready, she waited and listened as dread built inside her. The rifle was a simple single-shot that she would have to reload after every pull of the trigger. The extra bullets in her pocket would do her no good, as the bear would devour her before she had a chance to reach for them. Tracer had mentioned that the small-caliber rifle was only good at killing small things. Hitting anything bigger than a medium-size dog with the small bullet would likely just make them mad.

She took a hesitant step forward, watching the tracks as well as watching all around her. She knew she was supposed to make noise but couldn't bring herself to clear her throat, much less whistle a tune. Her whole body trembled as if she had a violent earthquake stirring within her. She couldn't keep her body under control. Her teeth didn't chatter, but her chest vibrated and shook.

One cautious step at a time, she followed the tracks. It had become obvious now that the bear was stalking Tracer.

The dread within her screamed at her to turn around but the anger growing in her chest kept her moving forward. Through the maze of trees, she followed the tracks late into the afternoon. The first flakes of fresh snow drifted down from the sky. The air had turned humid and brought with it a biting chill.

She went to step around a stick when she noticed that it wasn't a stick—it was Tracer's rifle. Checking the tracks again, she saw several desperate footprints in the mud as they turned this way and that. A spot of blood stared up to the heavens as more flakes tumbled down, covering up the trail that would lead her to Tracer.

She looked at the rifle and found blood on the muzzle of the silencer. Picking it up, she pulled the bolt back, ejecting the spent cartridge, then slammed a new cartridge into the chamber from the magazine clip. She slung her own rifle over her shoulder and looked out through the trees.

THE HIT

"Tracer!" Halen called out into the surrounding forest.

Her call went unanswered.

Her heart pounded in her chest, making it difficult to hear anything around her. She looked at the tracks again. Both sets seemed to crash through the underbrush. Broken branches and smeared mud gave indications of the path they'd taken. Long brown hair hung on the broken tip of a tree. Several splotches of blood were smeared across trunks and fallen logs. In a small opening, she found grass that had been matted. Boot heels had pressed into the earth as if Tracer was on his back and trying to scramble away.

Another cold shiver ran down her back. On a fallen log she saw a bloody handprint. As horror filled her mind, heavy snowflakes began to cover the trail.

"Tracer!" Halen screamed louder as panic flooded her. Snow fell in increasing waves, and the wind began its dance, twisting and turning through the trees. The colder air kept the flakes from melting as they began to layer the ground, hiding the trail Halen was following. This new snow sent her mind racing along with her feet as she stumbled through the trees with her rifle slung across her back and Tracer's hunting rifle held tightly in her hands.

She floundered through the brush and over logs, twisting around one tree, then the next, following the trail before it disappeared under the new snow. The snow was relentless, and that made time her enemy. Panic gripped every fiber of her body as she raced, stumbling through the trees. Then it stopped her cold.

She had lost the trail.

There were no more bloodstains or broken branches. The light had faded doubly fast with the heavy clouds overhead, and the snow had covered any sign of Tracer's presence. There was no longer a trail to give her a clue of the direction she was to follow. There was only a blanket of innocent white. The sun had set, leaving her in a wilderness alone and unsure.

Halen spun around and around, frantically searching for a clue. In every direction, she saw the same: hundreds of trees quickly being swallowed up by a blanket of white. She looked for anything out of place or anything that looked familiar. Thick, heavy flakes continued adding to the blanket of white. She knew it could easily pile up a foot or more in the high country even though it was now late spring.

Her heart pounded in her chest, causing her head to throb and her thoughts to jumble. She raced several yards in one direction, looking, searching, listening, then raced back looking for anything in the fading light.

"Tracer! Where are you?" she screamed. Heavy flakes prevented an echo from coming back to her. The falling snow suffocated her voice, limiting its reach. "Goddammit!" She kicked at the ground. Looking back the way she had come, she paused. An idea came to mind. Retracing her steps back up the hill to where she knew his tracks were, she looked for any discernible pattern.

THE HIT

"Dammit, nothing," Halen blurted. She began to circle, pulling the flashlight out of her pack and searching the ground for any hint of the bear or Tracer. Around and around she walked, staying within a few feet of her previous loop. She spiraled out, looking for clues of either one's passing. The new snow quickly filled her tracks, making it harder and harder to see them and keep an even spacing.

Up the hill and then down, she walked in ever-increasing circles, bending closer and closer to the ground as the flashlight's batteries gave out. With a final flicker, the batteries died.

Halen stood in the thick, black night. No light from the heavens could penetrate the clouds and allow her to continue. She was alone. Heavy flakes matted her hair. Some of those flakes melted, then trickled down inside her shirt. She knew it was a deadly combination. She was wet from sweat and melting snow, exhausted from the frantic search, and the air was growing colder, but she didn't care. The shock of cold didn't matter. The shock of losing Tracer did.

She lifted her head to the sky, heavy flakes mixing with the tears that rolled down her cheeks and neck. Her body shook as she stood alone in the dark, miles from anyone except Tracer. She felt he was close, yet she wasn't certain. She hoped he was miles away rather than a few feet. He wasn't her friend; he had kidnapped her. He wasn't her enemy, because he kept her alive and taught her things. She couldn't define what kind of relationship they had. At times she felt as if he were keeping her as one would an unwanted pet. Just going through the motions until a better solution could be found.

Tremors took control of her body. The movements shook her violently. Her knees buckled and she collapsed on the spot. Tracer's rifle folded into her arms as she cradled it like an infant. Bowing her head and hunching her back to the storm, she sobbed into the inky blackness.

She had failed. But she didn't owe him anything. He was the one who had become upset over a simple question. He was the one who stomped off into the night. He was the one who failed to face his own demons. There was no logical reason she should be out here looking for the man who had kidnapped and brutalized her.

The thought of being alone scared her more than being his unwanted pet. At home she always had someone around. Whether it was her mother, her friends or the cast and crew of a movie, there was always someone to praise or ridicule, someone to work with or shun. She had felt some sort of connection with Tracer. She had felt his cold and icy personality through much of the winter, but there were a few moments where he seemed almost human. It was those moments that made her wonder about him.

Here, there was the purest of elements, as Tracer had told her on multiple occasions. It was survive or die. That was the only law that mattered. She wouldn't die if a strand of hair was out of place or her red-carpet gown had a hanging thread. It didn't matter if she responded to a tweet at a moment's notice or if the color of her dress was azure or Bleu de France. From her current blurred world of white, the difference between the two colors was of no relevance.

THE HIT

The only thing that mattered was that she was alone in a world where she desperately didn't want to be. The safety of society was hopelessly out of reach. Now that the storm was dumping inch upon inch of new snow, and with a flashlight that didn't work, she was hopelessly out of reach of the cave's security. The colossal monster that lurked nearby would be welcomed, if only to focus her attention on something other than being alone.

"Use my bones to pick your teeth," Halen mumbled.

She sobbed into her lap as the snow piled a layer of the frozen blanket onto her and everything around her. The heavy wet snow would soon burden the branches, causing them to break under the weight just like her loneliness had broken her. She didn't care if she lived or died. At least if she was dead, she wouldn't be lonely. Whether it be heaven or hell, she wouldn't be lonely.

Resigning herself to the inevitable, she relaxed and invited the world to come and take her. Scavengers could pick her bones clean, then scatter them across the mountainside. She would in turn provide a full belly for some creature so that they might live. She consoled herself with the knowledge that if nothing else, she would be valuable to someone or something.

The wind shifted. It didn't matter to Halen. She would be part of the frozen landscape soon. If only it didn't smell like a dumpster. She wished she could die in peace with the fresh pine scent, but Mother Nature thwarted her peaceful death. It was one last boot to her middle. Her nose curled at the stench.

Bears smell like rotten meat.

The words ricocheted inside her head as if Tracer were standing right next to her repeating it. An icy chill ran up her already shivering body.

26

Halen sprang to her feet, listening for any sound the bear might make. The heavy snow muffled any noise—she might not hear it at all. She knew it had to be close, because the scent was almost overpowering.

Breathing became a conscious decision. She had to force herself to exhale. When she did, she thought it sounded like a jet engine winding up for takeoff. Her heart hammered in her ears. She didn't know how to quiet her breathing. With her senses alert, everything was amplified. A snowflake felt like a collision from a car, while the snap of a stick sounded like a clap of thunder.

She jerked her attention to even the subtlest movement only to find falling snow. The putrid smell stung her nose as if someone had dumped her headfirst into a garbage can. She faced the swirling wind and searched the black nothingness, though she knew there were trees and underbrush. There was also a bear lurking in the dark. Eyes open or closed, it all looked the same. She could only feel the weight of the snow and smell the bear that waited just beyond her other senses.

How dare this bear interrupt whatever relationship she had growing with Tracer. How dare Tracer abduct her and abuse her the way he had. How dare anyone put a bounty on her head and hire a hit man to kill her. How dare Tracer cram lessons down her throat. Anger filtered in and replaced the hopelessness that kept her immobile.

"I don't need your damn lessons. I don't need any of your stupid teachings. I don't need the cold or the starvation or that damn crate for a bed," Halen barked out into the night. "I don't need the pemmican or the backgammon lessons. I don't need you in my life!" Halen screamed.

A grunt reached her ears. The smell became stronger.

"AND FUCK YOU TOO, BEAR!"

Halen screamed, charging blindly toward the origin of the smell. Her numb hands gripped the rifle and her finger was ready to pull the trigger. She felt the power of a hundred screaming women charging toward their freedom. She was going to kill it or die trying.

Into the wind she raced, eager to shove the muzzle of the gun into anything and destroy it. Slamming one foot after another into the heavy snow, she charged. She was sick of the wilderness game. She wanted out, one way or another. She was going to take back control of her life or die.

Branches ripped at her face and clothes. They grabbed at her feet, trying to trip her and bring her down. She wasn't going to let any tangle of branches trip her up. She was going to find that bear and kill it. Then, as soon as it was light, she would walk out of the secluded forest and back to civilization.

Halen's feet beat the earth mercilessly as she plunged through the unknown. Her body ricocheted off trees, causing her to flounder and struggle to maintain balance. Branches continued to rip at her body and face. She closed her eyes to protect them from being gouged out, as they weren't of any use in the black of night anyway. She clutched Tracer's rifle as if holding on to life itself. Her smaller rifle bounced on her back as she recklessly and blindly charged toward what she knew was certain death.

Her feet carried her into the wind and closer to the rotten stench from the beast that had killed the man who was responsible for her situation. She continued her suicidal charge through the night. Her foot slammed against something hard—something that wasn't mud or snow. Plunging headfirst, her body continued forward as her feet stayed behind. She toppled over the large mound of snow. Casting her arms out to break her fall, she flung the muzzle of the rifle ahead of her. Its barrel dug deep into the snow and mud. She squeezed the trigger inadvertently and the rifle exploded.

Shrapnel pelted her head. The loud noise disoriented her, causing her to lurch to the side. Ringing in her ears and the black night prevented her from regaining her balance. Halen flopped from one side to the other, trying to get even one foot under her. The soft earth below the snow left her struggling to stay upright. She turned to see what had upended her. With no light, there was nothing to see. She couldn't even make out the dark trunks of the trees against the white snow. Something had tripped her, and it wasn't a tree.

The odd sensation unnerved her as she fought to regain a sense of logic. Why was that mound of snow so big and solid? It should have been soft. The air wasn't cold enough to freeze everything solid like that. Not yet anyway. She would have been able to crunch through any old clump or wade through any of the fresh snow that was still falling and it wouldn't have piled up in one spot.

She inched her way back toward the lumpy outline. Reaching a hand out, she tested the snow. That was all it was. She scraped at the snow and felt the light, fluffy ice crystals. She scraped again. More fluffy snow. And again.

"Dammit, Halen. Get it together." Relieved that it wasn't something more serious, she breathed a sigh. A thought came to her. "Alright. Here's your photo op, ya flipping vultures." She laughed into the dark night. "Come and get it," Halen cried out, laughing at the absurdity and half crying from the crushing weight of the lonely nothingness around her.

Hatred welled up inside as the emotional pinball game continued. Striking out at the soft snow, she contacted a thick mat of hair. The sudden stench of rotten meat came flooding out from its source. She had tripped over the bear and hit it, thinking it was just a mound of snow.

She beat her fist against the large hump—a hump that was the warning sign to all that it was king. The mound was massive, dwarfing her as she railed against it. Even in the blackest of nights, she assumed that something that large should have been as noticeable as a skyscraper or as apparent as paparazzi at a movie premiere. She could pick one of those camera-toting villains out of a crowd, but she couldn't see a monster even after tripping over it.

Fear of waking the bear spiked her adrenaline and launched her backward, leaving Tracer's rifle in the snow. She scrambled, kicking at the snow and earth until it only pushed out in front of her feet. Her breathing became labored, and her panic tilted off the scale as the bear inched after her. She scrambled away but didn't get any further from the creature. Though she couldn't see it, she felt it, and it was keeping pace with her. She wasn't getting any further away. She didn't want to take the time to turn. Turning would only delay her escape, and she would lose sight of the bear.

The bear groaned. The sound wasn't coming from her, and Tracer was surely dead. She would be too if she didn't get away. She tossed her head back, slamming it into the tree trunk behind her. She hadn't gone more than three feet and she wasn't escaping certain death. The bear wasn't coming after her. Stopping and holding her breath, she tried to listen to see if the bear was making any sound, but she could only hear the hammering of her heart in her ears.

The dimmest of light illuminated the falling snow on the far side of the grizzly, showing an outline of its massive body. Snow removed from toppling over the beast revealed its form. She carefully watched its chest for any movement. A full minute passed. There wasn't any. Was the bear dead? Was it sleeping? These thoughts raced through her mind as she continued to stare at it for any signs of life.

There it was. The chest heaved; snow toppled down. Halen reached behind her, grabbed her rifle off her shoulder and fired the tiny projectile into the hump of the bear. The shot sounded like the smack of a flyswatter, and a flyswatter to this bear would be the best idea for an extremely short life. She watched the animal. Again it moved, and this time there was a groan. Halen's hands ejected the tiny shell out of the rifle and fumbled through her pocket for another shell.

Finding one, she silently cussed at her hands as they shook, making reloading almost impossible. She dropped the shell in the snow. Fishing around in her pocket again, she grabbed two more and tried to funnel them into the chamber, hoping at least one would line up. Another bullet slipped and tumbled to the ground. She tried to slow her heart and her trembling hands. The third bullet tumbled into the chamber. After a nudge and an involuntary shake of the rifle, it settled into the slot. The light was too dim to see if the bullet was aligned, but the bolt slamming home told her that it was.

Pointing it at the bear again, she pulled the trigger. The gunpowder ignited and sent the bullet into it. This time the bear spoke.

"S-s-stop." The warbled and shivering voice reached out from under the beast.

Halen dropped the rifle in the snow and covered her mouth with her frozen hands. She didn't know how long she stood there. She was too petrified to move. Animals didn't talk. She looked over the edge of the bear. Tracer's headlamp lay on the ground, quickly being devoured by the falling snow.

Halen raced around to the other side of the bear and grabbed the light. The scene lit up. Snow piling on the beast made the already massive bear seem gigantic compared to her meager 120 pounds. She didn't see Tracer. A blanket of white encapsulated everything. At her feet, she found a crimson lake spreading from under the beast. Looking at the bear again, she saw no sign of life, and it looked to be lying at an awkward and unnatural angle. It was certainly dead.

An uprooted tree created a divot in the ground where the bear had collapsed and would never rise again. The snow continued to pile up on the beast and all the surroundings, each new flake stacked like building blocks, one atop the other. Halen looked at her feet and the slushy red pool. There still wasn't any sign of Tracer.

"Tracer!" Halen screamed into the night.

She listened. There was no reply, no sound and no signs of life.

"Tracer!" she cried again.

Nothing else around her gave any clue to the man's location. She didn't want to leave without an idea of what to do. She stepped clear of the blood-tainted snow. Moving the snow around her, she searched the ground, inching her way toward the bear. She remembered the voice. She wondered if she had imagined it—if it was a hallucination, or if Tracer was trying to speak to her from beyond the grave.

She had a friend who claimed to hear people speak to her from beyond their graves. Now she was thinking that her friend might not be crazy after all. Moving her foot around, she began clearing the snow away from her and inched toward the mound. Halen pushed at the thick fur with her foot. There was no motion. She pushed harder. Still no reaction. She stomped on the bear. Nothing. It was still dead.

Curiosity piqued her interest and she began removing the snow from the animal. She wanted to see it up close. The smell made her scrunch her nose. It was barely tolerable. She continued to push aside more snow, finding a hind leg. She looked at the place where she had tripped and tumbled over the animal. She had hit it square in the middle of its body. Working around the leg, she started clearing snow off the beast. She found the second hind leg, then a pant leg and a boot.

"Tracer!" Halen screamed. Her enthusiasm ripped through the night. Her fear of being alone evaporated except for a wisp of a thought that he might be dead. She had found her abductor, though she couldn't say what he was to her anymore. From the position of the leg, she assumed that the rest of him would be on the opposite side. Rushing around, she ignored the pool of blood and dug at the edge of the bear, looking for any other part of Tracer. From under its belly, she found a hand. Scooping the blood-soaked snow out of the way, she dug at the earth and pushed the body of the bear back to expose more of the man's arm. Then his face emerged. She quickly put Tracer's headlamp on, allowing the freedom of both hands to dig.

Cradling Tracer's face in her hands, she looked for any sign of life. Blood, mud and ice caked his beard. She lifted the skin of the bear, searching for the rest of him. A slight movement of his chest as he breathed almost made her drop the thick, heavy fur back down on him. He was alive.

"Tracer. Tracer. Come on, you can't . . ." Halen tapped the side of his cheek, trying to elicit a reaction. The shallow breathing continued, but there was no response. Her frustration grew as she couldn't see anything she could use to try to pull the bear off him.

She grabbed the rear leg of the bear and tried to roll the beast off Tracer. The wet and soggy leg seemed to weigh as much as she did. She could barely lift it more than a couple feet off the ground. It slipped out of her grasp and dropped to the ground. She had to find a way to get Tracer out from under the bear. It was spring, and the bear didn't have its hibernating fat anymore, but it was still a massive bear and one she couldn't handle on her own.

Looking around, she found Tracer's rifle. Using it as a lever, she tried to wedge it under the animal and lift. The barrel dug into the soft mud, and the loose skin wadded up against the barrel and the stock. Releasing the gun, she let the beast's skin fall back to the ground.

Staring at the useless gun, she saw that the sling was made of woven cord. It reminded her of a series pilot she costarred in where she had to improvise a hoist to lift a large body. After pulling her knife out of its sheath, she cut the end off the sling and unraveled all the braided cords. Tying the cords end to end and one end to the leg of the bear and the other around a tree, she leaned against the cord, using the leverage to flip the bear over.

After several attempts and shortening the rope a few times, she pulled the massive front paw up and over the stump. Halen grabbed the hind leg and lifted. Slowly, the bear rolled off Tracer. Red blotted the white snow, turning it various shades of pink. Normally she liked pink. Now she wondered if she would be able to tolerate the color ever again without losing her lunch.

"Tracer." Halen scrambled around the bear. "Trace." Lifting his head out of the muck, she patted his cheek again, calling for him to respond. "Tracer."

There wasn't a hint of life other than his shallow breathing. His skin felt like ice against her hand. He had told her about hypothermia, and she knew she had to get him warmed up. She wouldn't be able to pull him back to the cave in time to keep him from freezing to death though.

A large fir tree with drooping boughs stood several yards away at the edge of a small clearing. Its branches sheltered the base of the trunk from the bulk of the snow, creating a small pocket of dry ground. Pine needles, bark and sticks had piled around the base for decades. Halen cleared out what she could to make room for her and Tracer. She knew she had to get him warmed up soon or he would slip away forever.

Using the cord from the rifle sling, she wrapped it around his chest and under his shoulders, then dragged him through the pool of blood, over to the tree. After scraping away wet debris, she found a scattering of dry pine boughs and made a bed to keep the two of them off the ground. She dragged Tracer up next to it and stripped off all his wet clothing. She lay the emergency blanket over her outer coat atop the dry pine boughs and rolled him into it. Then she stripped nearly naked herself and curled up to his icy body, pressing her skin next to his. After arranging both their clothes on top of the shiny plastic, she ducked under the thin blanket. She had done all she could and quickly fell asleep.

"Halen."

The word drifted to Halen's ear. She heard it but thought it was just part of her dream.

"Halen." Tracer said her name again, giving her a nudge with his elbow.

She stirred. A small moan escaped her lips.

He nudged her again. "Girl. We gotta get back to the cave."

Halen opened her eyes to daylight. Matted and bloody hair confronted her. The rotten smell of the bear filled her nostrils. Tracer nudged her again.

She gasped. "You're alive?" she said cheerfully.

"Sorry to disappoint ya," he said over his shoulder.

Halen squeezed her arm around his middle. Tracer jerked.

"What's wrong?" she asked.

"The bear got me. Got me good. I think I'm bleeding again." He lifted his head. Halen pulled her arm out, as he was using it as a pillow.

She looked around; the storm was gone. Birds squawked in the distance, and a squirrel chattered overhead. She lifted her head up higher. The bear was covered in several inches of snow, and it was still dead. A ripple of the plastic emergency blanket let the frozen air inside, and she shivered at the cold.

"Come on," Tracer urged. "We gotta get back to the cave."

"Can you walk?"

"I don't know, but we can't stay here. We gotta move."

"Okay," Halen said.

"You first. I'm trapped in here."

THE HIT

Halen pulled the sheet down tight in a momentary protest. With a reluctant sigh, she scrambled out of the emergency bedding and gathered her clothes, shaking off the skiff of snow that had accumulated on them. Her jaw chattering, she shoved her limbs into her clothes and stabbed her feet into what seemed like buckets made of ice. Her shoes were stiff from being frozen, but she had no choice.

"Can you move?" she asked.

Tracer lay motionless for a moment, seeming to do a mental evaluation, then tested his extremities. Pulling the blanket open again, Halen helped support him as he struggled to his feet. He turned his back to her. Blood had blackened and crusted over his wounds in a large ugly patch on his side, but the simple act of standing up reopened the wound. Fresh blood streamed down his side, spattering on the ground.

As Tracer used a tree for support, she helped get his frozen and blood-soaked pants back on. She handed him the rest of his clothes one piece at a time and finally his coat.

"Where's my rifle?" Tracer asked. "Did you see it somewhere?"

"Yes." Halen looked around. The snow had covered the area where she had rolled the bear off him. The pristine white had turned the previous day's ugly events to a clean, unwritten sheet waiting for life to write its next chapter. All the savagery of what had happened before had been erased. Mother Nature had reset. It was as if she were awarding them another day.

Halen ventured out from underneath the tree to kick through the snow for the rifle. She found it stuck in the frozen mud and pried the barrel out, then collected the cord she had used to move the bear and again to drag Tracer to the shelter. She handed Tracer the rifle to use as a makeshift cane, and they walked back to the cave in silence.

28

"What happened?" Halen asked when they reached the cave. "I saw tracks like the bear was stalking you."

Tracer crawled through the cave opening then trudged straight to the hot water pool—rolling into the water clothes and all. He lay in the basin for almost an hour. Halen checked on him several times, asking if she could look at his wounds. He only grunted and accepted a package of hot chili and a cup of coffee. Halen arranged the first aid kit, preparing anything she felt she might need to put him back together.

Tracer emerged from the back room, stripped to the waist and dripping across the stone floor. He shuffled to the edge of his cot. The stiffness of his muscles hindered his usual fluid movement.

Halen could see the wounds now. The deepest one still oozed blood. Four jagged lines were opened to the world. She thought she could see tissue trying to squeeze out of the openings. Angry swollen flesh told her that infection might have already set in. Black bruises on the front and back of his shoulder looked as if the bear had almost managed to bite into it. Smaller wounds on his face oozed blood too. The bear's teeth had broken the skin there. His cheek looked to have been torn a bit, causing him to favor one side of his mouth over the other, as it had swollen to the size of a golf ball.

Halen addressed the four slashes on his side first as blood continued to ooze out. She handed him a cup of coffee and a stick.

"Have you done this before?" Tracer slurred through his injuries.

"Once," she said, squirting the wound with saline.

"Did they live?"

"No." Halen injected the area around the wound with a local anesthetic, then prepared the needle and thread to stitch the wound closed.

Tracer turned to look at her. She looked back at him.

"It was a dummy," she began. "I stitched him up, then they shot him. A little more bloody than this one."

"That's comforting."

"It seems that this is a replay of that movie. I help save my friend only to find out that he was the bad guy . . ." Halen paused, concentrating as she tied off the first stitch. She snipped the line and started the next stitch. "I played a nurse in the movie. They brought in a real doctor to teach me how to do stitches. They wanted everything to look as authentic as possible."

"Did it work?" Tracer winced from the poke of the needle.

"What? The guy getting better?"

"No. The review of it, did it look authentic?" He gritted his teeth against the next poke.

"The scene never made it all the way through postproduction. They scrubbed it." She tugged the second stitch tight and snipped the thread.

"How do you know that the guy wasn't a quack?" Tracer steadied his arm across the front of him and out of the way so Halen could see to stitch the gash closed.

"Because he was very calm when he explained the stitches to me," she said. "He told me that wounds like this one have to heal from the inside out or they might trap infection inside and cause a whole mess of problems."

"Sounds like a smart man."

"Eight years of medical school and a surgical residency," Halen explained as she dabbed at the wound with gauze. "He had his fill of car wrecks, gunshots and mangled bodies. He said that he was overdue for a career change. He moved to a small rural town where the highlight of the week would be Bobby, who sliced his leg open in a skateboarding accident." She quietly stitched a couple more spots closed. She stopped any openly bleeding wounds first, then moved to the deeper gashes.

"Sounds like a guy for a nice girl to settle down with," Tracer said flatly.

The comment wasn't lost on her. She knew what he was insinuating. "He has a fiancée."

Tracer grumbled to himself. "I know a guy that can fix that."

"No! You will not," she said sternly. She tugged on one of his stitches, causing him to wince. "You will do no such thing."

Halen finished the last stitch and dabbed it with some gauze. She smeared the wound with antibiotic ointment, layered it with gauze and wrapped his middle. She then turned her attention to the puncture wounds and filled them with the antibiotic after flushing them with saline.

Tracer caught her arm and pulled her down. He grabbed her hair and pulled it close, examining her forehead. "What happened here?"

She put a hand up, examining her head. Her hand came away with a bit of dried blood. She touched the area again and found a bump under the skin. When she pushed on it, it stung. "What the . . ." Halen felt the bump again. "How did that happen?"

"Tweezers," Tracer said.

"I have to wash out that last wound."

"Tweezers," Tracer growled.

"Let me finish with your last wound first."

Tracer lurched up off the cot, grabbed her by the throat and threw her on her bed. He rummaged through the kit, spilling the contents on the floor. He came back and straddled her, wincing with the effort of it, and turned her head to the side. Grabbing his headlamp, he adjusted the beam to focus on Halen's forehead. She stared back up at him from the corner of her eye. Tracer wobbled a little, then took a firm hold of her head and pinned it to the crate. Using the tweezers, he dug into her scalp, next to her hairline.

"Ahh. Dammit!" Halen cried out. "What the hell are you doing?"

Tracer leaned on her, gritting his teeth and growling. He stabbed into her wound and fished around underneath her skin with the tweezers. Halen struggled against his prodding, but he pushed his hand harder against her throat. Cussing and kicking, she tried to upend him and toss him onto the floor, but he continued to dig into her skin. He scooted his body forward, almost sitting on her head, and she saw a wave of dizziness try to claim him. She fought against him, but he kept her still as he dug for the foreign object. Exhausted, she relaxed from the struggle, and Tracer took advantage of the opportunity. He plucked something from her scalp and held it up—a piece of shrapnel—and then immediately passed out, toppling off her onto the floor.

Halen held her palm to her forehead as fresh blood poured out of it. She stared down at the unconscious man. The wound on his side had reopened and was soaking through the gauze. Anger flared up in her. He had no right to treat her that way. Especially over a small bit of shrapnel.

Halen growled down at him and paced the floor, then turned back to him. "FLIP YOU! Goddamn asshole!" She looked down at the heap of a man on the floor. Launching into a rant, she stormed around the cave, kicking his cot over, tossing his things against the wall. She stomped through the stream of water, then back over to Tracer. Her head was throbbing from his crude extraction of the metal. His splayed arms and shallow breathing told her he was out cold. She stepped forward and with all her might kicked him in the fleshy part of his rump.

"Do you have something to tell me?"

Tracer opened his eyes to a scowl. He was on his cot and freshly bandaged. He looked from Halen to his surroundings. Her bed was neatly made. His clothes were washed and hung near the entrance, his rifle next to them. The bolt on the chamber was mangled and protruding from the side. He looked at Halen. Her clothes were clean too. She was dressed to head outside. The .22 rifle leaned against the wall, with her pack sitting next to it.

"G . . ." His dry throat ached, and his first attempt at speaking failed. He tried to clear his throat and finally managed to say, "Water."

His raspy request spurred Halen into motion. She reached for his water bottle and held his head while he took a drink. He swallowed and nodded that he had had enough, and she unceremoniously dropped his head back onto the pillow and stared down at him.

"Why does my ass hurt?" he croaked out slowly.

"I tried to shove a stick up it but there was one already there." Halen glowered down at him.

Tracer looked up, baffled by the attitude. The scowl hadn't left her face. His expression twisted as he tried to figure out what she was talking about.

"I kicked it." Halen took a cautionary step back.

He tensed and moved his body a little, testing its limits.

"How long?"

"How long what?"

"How long was I out?" he asked.

"Almost three days," Halen snapped.

He looked around again. The trunks with all the food and supplies were stacked as neatly as possible. The floor was cleaned of all the mud and blood they had traipsed in. "Going somewhere?" he asked.

"Do you have something to tell me?" Halen repeated her question.

"Tell you what?"

"I cleaned up your wound. I saw it." Halen stood on shaking legs, waiting for an answer.

"Saw what?" Tracer asked as he looked around for his pants. He saw them hanging in the far corner. They were clean, though parts looked stained and the holes had been patched.

"I saw your side. There is something you should tell me," Halen said, her voice beginning to quaver. "You need to tell me."

"Hand me my pants," he said in a flat tone.

"No. Not until you tell me," Halen demanded. She stood trembling at the foot of his cot.

"Tell you what?" Tracer circled back around, avoiding her question.

"Goddammit. Why won't you fucking tell me? Jesus Christ. What the fuck is so hard about answering a simple question?"

"Watch your mouth with that word."

"Fuck. You don't want me to say the word *fuck*. Well, fuck, Tracer, what the fuck ya gonna do about it?"

Tracer fidgeted on the edge of his cot. His anger welled up inside him, but the total body aches kept him grounded to his cot.

"Huh? What the fuck are you going to do?"

He tried to get up off the cot. Pain, stiff muscles and extreme fatigue prevented him from getting any further than an elbow propping him up. He collapsed back onto the cot. Pain ran through his body as if he had been run over by a train.

"Well fuck. Isn't that a bitch. Can't even get your own ass off the cot. Guess you're gonna have to say fuck it and tell me."

Tracer gritted his teeth as a muscle cramped in his side.

"Every time you feel that pain in your ass, you can think of me. You can say 'My captive put it there because I'm a fucktard.' "

"Don't say that word," he growled.

"What the fuck ya gonna do, fucktard? You gonna hold me down and pluck out my fucking teeth with the fucking tweezers? Maybe then I'll say thuck. Is thuck better than fuck? You are un-fucking-believable. Ladies and gentlemen, the Grammy for fucktardidness goes to Tracer Fuckhead."

"Don't say that word," Tracer growled, pushing up off the cot. He lost his balance and tipped the cot over, spilling himself onto the floor.

"ARE YOU GOING TO FUCKING TELL ME?" Halen screamed.

"Sounds like you already have the answer in your head. Doesn't matter what I say."

"Why did you kidnap me?" Halen cried. Tears flowed down her cheeks like the spring runoff filling the banks of the streams and rivers.

He ignored her and looked under his blankets at the bandage wrapped around his middle. It was fresh and clean like it had been changed just hours before.

Halen pleaded. "Are you going to tell me?"

"No." He lay still, defeated.

She stared at him. A long minute passed, with each one waiting for the other to say something.

"Fuck off, Tracer. You're a fucking waste." Halen turned, picked up the small rifle and her pack and ducked out the door.

29

Twin streams flowed down Halen's face for much of the day. The secret she'd found had uprooted her mind and churned it into mush. Tracer's encounter with the bear, and the cougar a month earlier, kept her alert and watchful, but the betrayal she felt turned her thoughts inward and away from the dangers around her.

Much of the snow had melted since their encounter with the bear. Halen had nursed Tracer back from a fever, monitoring his temperature and keeping it from becoming dangerously high. She'd propped him up numerous times to feed him broth. In his semiconscious state, he wasn't able to answer questions. It had taken most of her willpower not to drag him out into the cold and leave him for dead. She could think of only one thing. She only wanted him to answer one question. But he couldn't. She had had to wait for his fever to break first. She had to nurse him back to health before she could kill him properly.

THE HIT

The doctor's brief lesson on leaving the wound open had paid off, as the stitches she had put in two days prior were healing nicely. After cleaning the wound, she'd stitched together the outer skin. Though she didn't have a medical degree, she had paid attention to the step-by-step instructions the doctor gave her. When she stitched the final bit of skin together, she sat back on her heels and examined her work. She made sure the edges of the port-wine stain were lined up. She gave it another gentle wipe-down before realizing the significance of its size, shape and location.

It was at that moment she understood. She understood everything. She understood the kidnapping, the rough treatment, the lessons and the game.

All she wanted was to hear it from him. She wanted him to admit what he had done. It had crushed her when he didn't.

Halen stumbled down the trail next to the small stream. Water inched up over the banks, moving slowly, while the center of the stream boiled and churned as it began its journey toward the ocean.

She made camp in a rock outcropping, with her back to the small cliff and a boulder in front of her. The small fire became her best friend and companion, giving her warmth and something to tend. And something to talk to.

"Why can't men say what they feel?" Halen spoke to the crackle of flames, happy to have a friend listen to her. She pulled out one of several meal packs and opened it. The warm flames soothed her emotions like a hug from an understanding friend. As the wood burned, so did her anger and hatred toward the man she had abandoned in the cave.

Guilt had visited her several times that day. Her emotions crashed around inside her like the water bouncing off the rocks in the stream, twisting one way, then another. Many times, she thought about turning back. She had even retraced her steps a dozen paces before turning downstream again toward civilization. Tracer had done horrible things to many people. He was a contract killer. He didn't deserve to live. If he was ever caught, he would certainly get the death penalty, and she could be the one to put him in prison.

She wondered if there was a reward for the man. She also wondered if the authorities even knew about him. If what he said was true, there wouldn't be a shred of evidence that would link him to anything. He of course would clam up like he did when she confronted him; their investigation would be even harder. A bloodhound wouldn't even have an odor to sniff. Detectives might figure out some of what he had done, but they would never figure out all of it.

Two squirrels complained to each other as they raced around in the dimming light. It distracted Halen from her thoughts and allowed her a moment of joy. Beyond the squirrels, there was a slap on the water. She must have disturbed something swimming out in the stream. Dipping the spoon into a pouch of food, she let her mind relax from the day's troubled thoughts.

For the moment, she just wanted to be. She just wanted to share this moment in the wilderness with its residents. Not another moment in the entire universe mattered, just this one and just for right now. No other moment was allowed to interrupt this one.

The light faded and stars came out, sprinkling the sky with diamonds. Halen set her blanket aside and walked out into the night, away from the comfort of the campfire. She turned the corner and stared at the wonderment of the sky above and the surrounding mountains. Night brought an unprecedented beauty to a place that was already amazing. It was a hard life out here, and to be able to survive and thrive was harder yet. And these animals did it every day. She wished she could lie on the ground and stare up at its majesty night after night. It was a sliver of bliss she would cherish, causing her to vow to take at least one camping trip every year. She had never felt so big yet so small at the same time, and she was a part of this moment that nobody could take from her.

Halen felt bad for leaving Tracer before he had recovered enough to take care of himself, but she was still mad at him. How could he not tell her? How could he keep that kind of secret? She shook the idea from her mind. She had friends and family back home. She had a life and a career. She had to get back. She had to tell her friends she was alive.

Sunrise found Halen sipping a cup of coffee made over the revived embers of her fire. She had tended it between fits of sleep, adding stick after stick from her dwindling pile of wood. Rocks held her emergency blanket in place above her bed while reflecting the heat down on her. A collection of pine boughs kept her off the heat-sucking earth. The rocks to either side also reflected the heat from the fire onto her as she curled into a wool blanket.

After finishing her cup of coffee, she stowed her camp gear and drowned the fire by diverting a tiny stream into the firepit. It sizzled and complained about the intrusion but was quickly turned into a black ashy soup.

Following one trail or another, she crossed multiple small streams that fed into larger ones which fed into larger ones yet again. A few ducks spirited away when she happened upon them suddenly. Squirrels were in abundance, and a porcupine lumbered down the trail ahead of her. She waited for him to amble off, but he chose to climb a tree instead. Halen kept her distance and watched from a nearby rock. The mobile pincushion reached for branch after branch, scaling the tree in search of some delectable bark.

Halen thought she'd be in a rush to get back to civilization, but instead she had become continuously distracted by the forest dwellers who lived along her path. She slowed her steps almost as if she were in a gallery filled with fine art. Every step offered an infinite number of shapes, angles and colors to study that coalesced into stunning works of art, from the hard-angled rock to the softest flower petal growing right next to it.

She studied the dazzling colors of a butterfly and the camouflage of a small spider. She soaked in the pine-scented air as she strolled through the trees, and later rotting vegetation filled her nose as she skirted a marsh.

Deer dashed through the trees, and a moose, belly deep in a marsh, stripped fresh leaves off the willow bushes. Some animals she knew, but others were a mystery to her. The landscape around her seemed to infuse her with some of its beauty, making her feel appreciative of taking her next breath. This was that silver lining encompassing a very dark cloud. She would never have been this appreciative of nature if it hadn't been for Tracer.

The thought had broken through the wall that separated her wondrous surroundings from the unpleasant way she had come to such a place. The unsettling feeling she had been shoving back reared its ugly head. She didn't want to acknowledge the truth and revisit that heartache. She didn't want her final words with Tracer to be in anger. He did deserve to be cussed out, and maybe imprisoned, but he also deserved a word of thanks. He had taught her a lot, though maybe in a crude way. She couldn't let things be left as they were.

If she doubled back now, she might be able to camp in her former spot. Though, her bed might now be flooded by the small stream she had diverted. If it was, she would find another place. There were many to choose from. The thought of another night under the stars excited her, and she did want to see Tracer again.

Walking on the edge of a cliff, she peered over at the boiling and churning waters of the river below. The cauldron was at the bottom of a waterfall, and the sight was spectacular. Mist sprayed up, creating a cascade of color as the sunlight filtered through it. Below was the white, milky froth of the falls, where thousands of pounds of water crashed against the unseen rocks at the bottom of the riverbed. She stood in awe, wishing she had a camera.

The moment finally passed and she turned up the trail toward the cave.

Halen froze.

A throaty growl rumbled from the animal crouched in front of her. Its thick, long tail twitched with anticipation.

She had faced one before. Tracer had shot it and shown her how to make pemmican. Now she was alone, but she wasn't as defenseless as before. Pulling her rifle up, she pointed it at the mountain lion and pulled the trigger.

The bullet flew past the cat, shattering a rock behind it. A scream split the air over the roar of the falls. The screech was unlike anything she had ever heard. The silver screen could never duplicate the bone-chilling fear she felt now. She felt as if a hammer had slammed her in the gut, causing her knees to buckle, and her bladder suddenly became weak.

She couldn't let the cat best her. She couldn't die when she had learned and gained so much. She had to fight, because no one was around to fight for her. She was on her own with only an empty rifle to fend off the cat.

The lion lunged.

Halen stabbed at it with the muzzle of the gun, keeping the big cat at a distance. The cat's scream shocked her, and the claws at the ends of its enormous paws were like huge hooked daggers.

THE HIT

The cat swatted at her rifle. Halen jabbed. The cat lunged, trying to hook her foot and upend her. She parried the swat with the barrel of the gun and looked for a way to escape. She didn't want to become its next meal, or worse, its next sporting kill. It lunged again. She stepped back. A rock crumbled and fell to the churning water below. Halen kept her eye on the fangs and claws in front of her and quickly brought her foot back onto solid rock.

The lion spat snarls and hisses at Halen as it looked for an opportunity to get a claw into any part of her. She sidestepped, only to have the animal parallel her. She let out a scream. It was as loud a battle cry as she could muster to try to intimidate the cat into leaving her alone. The beast didn't flinch; it wasn't the least bit dissuaded. It lunged at her again. Halen stabbed the cat in the mouth and sidestepped, turning each of them broadside to the cliff. The cat swatted at the rifle, knocking it free. It clattered across the rock two steps to her side. The deadly claws and teeth could easily grab her if she elected to retrieve it.

Halen retreated a step, giving the lion his opportunity for the kill. His haunches flexed like a spring uncoiling with tremendous force. She stepped forward to meet the challenge like Tracer had taught her to do with an opponent. He'd told her that most times they will back off and leave you alone if you stand your ground and sometimes act crazier than them.

She closed her eyes at the last moment. Fear of the teeth biting into her face kept them shut tight. She waited for the assault. Instead, she heard a thud like two slabs of meat colliding. She opened her eyes to see a blur of motion flash before her. She saw Tracer's dark coat disappear over the edge of the cliff. Claws sank into the coat and teeth bit down into Tracer's shoulder. The cat's tail flipped violently as they descended into the churning water below.

"Tracer!" Halen screamed. Her knees hit the rocky cliff as her hands clutched at the edge.

White froth from the churning river swallowed both man and beast.

"Tracer!" she cried again.

She stared for a long moment at the boiling river, searching for him to reappear where he went in. He wasn't there. He was gone.

"Tracer," she cried to herself.

Movement further downstream caught her eye. Her heart jumped at the possibility. She wanted to see him again. Give him a hug and tell him that he was still an ass but also thank him for all he had done for her. She wiped tears from her eyes and focused on the movement.

The lion emerged, shaking its coat free of water, then looked back as if expecting his attacker to follow and resume their fight. After a moment he disappeared into the trees.

Halen looked further down the river, hoping to see Tracer emerge from the water and collapse on the bank. He wasn't anywhere to be seen. It was as if the river had spit out the mountain lion but devoured Tracer.

She frantically scanned the banks looking for him—his coat, a wet trail, anything. There was nothing. She sobbed to herself.

THE HIT

"DAD!"
He was gone.

The lower elevations of the mountains gave way to warmer temperatures and a lush, green landscape full of life. Though green and vibrant, Halen could only see gray and black. Nothing seemed alive through her eyes.

She hadn't spoken a word since the day she watched Tracer tumble over the cliff. The roar of the water had drowned out her echo as she screamed for him over and over until her voice was no more. She'd walked down the river's edge as far as she could, searching for Tracer, his body or any sign of his existence. The anger she felt over his betrayal a few days before melted into a never-ending pit of sadness. She had discovered her father and now he was suddenly gone.

She had gone back to the place she'd last seen him, hoping against hope that he would walk back up the trail just as cold and grouchy as he had ever been. But with that kind of torrent and no life jacket, his chances of surviving the churning monster were near zero. She had hoped she would find something when she continued her search downstream, but nothing indicated he had emerged anywhere along the banks.

There was nothing to do now except follow the river down. The majesty of the area she had relished no longer existed. She couldn't begin to be excited over the forest and the animals—not without him. Tracer had said it would be more than a few days' walk to reach a road. He was right. It was now day three since Tracer had plunged into the river, and she still hadn't seen an improved trail or a road of any kind. Her tears had run dry, unlike the river. She made a quiet camp next to a stream, close to the water, hoping he would somehow find her as he had before.

She built her fire up to be a companion. It was the only thing she could think of so she wouldn't feel as lonely. It kept her busy through most of the night, before she became too exhausted to tend it. She laid her head on a pile of leaves she'd plucked for a pillow and fell asleep.

Morning didn't bring sunshine and chirping birds. Instead a depressive rain patted her hood hour after hour in a steady drizzle. The rain matched her mood as she slugged through the wet underbrush. If she died from exposure, she didn't care. It would be fitting. She wasn't a nice person. She was a horrible friend. She had used people and tossed them aside as if they were empty candy wrappers. Now somehow she felt as if she were the empty candy wrapper. She deserved it. She deserved the rain, the sorrow, the guilt. She should have done more, done something, anything. If there was something more she could have done, she would be hard-pressed to see it through the choking net of guilt and sorrow.

Stumbling over cut logs, she plodded along in the direction of anything that wasn't this dark, depressing forest. Her feet found the easy path of a heavily compacted trail. Her mind in a daze, she hadn't realized it was a logging trail. Large green-and-yellow machinery sat silently in a row as if bowing their heads in silence for her loss. She plodded on, following the logging road.

"Miss. Miss."

Halen turned her head toward the voice. It wasn't Tracer. She stared at the grizzled face of the man standing in a doorway, searching for any sort of familiarity, but she found none.

"Are you alright?" the man asked.

Halen looked at her wet and muddy clothes. She was dragging the butt of the rifle in the mud. Her pack strap had slipped off one shoulder. Wet and stringy hair draped across her eyes like a set of shredded curtains. She'd pieced together enough from her vision to keep from walking into a tree or off a cliff. There was no color, only a dismal gray like the clouds that sent rain from above.

"Come inside. Have a cup of coffee. Get dried off and warmed up. I think I can talk Jeff into cooking something for ya," the burly man said.

"Jeff?" Halen looked at the man blankly. "No. Where's Tracer?"

"Come inside. You're too cold to think straight."

Halen turned toward the inviting door and the smell of hot bacon.

Halen stared at her wall. Pink was everywhere in her room, from pink picture frames to the thick pink faux fur rug at her feet. The sight nauseated her, but the energy to do anything about it was nonexistent. After arriving home and ignoring the hundreds of paparazzi and the blur of questions, Halen had sulked around her parents' house, eating and sleeping for three days. Officers asked her questions about where she went and what she did during the months she was missing. She had turned numb to the world. She answered their questions with vague one- or two-word answers.

They'd brought in a psychiatrist who grew frustrated when Halen wouldn't even acknowledge her presence. Halen overheard her mention to an officer that she was exhibiting a form of grief. She said that time to process grief would allow her to be more responsive to their questions.

She curled up with a soft blanket, idly flipping through the channels on the TV. Her mother had welcomed her with open arms at the airport when she stepped off the private plane. Kimberly wept into Halen's hair as they rode from the airport to her house. Once inside, her mother brought all the usual things Halen had liked—even a visit from her old drug dealer. Kimberly held her for a time, but the gesture seemed forced. A buzz vibrated the air.

"You'll be back to your old self in no time." Her mother excused herself to answer a phone call.

The words she had said rolled around in Halen's head. Her old self was an impossible fairytale. It wasn't sustainable. How could she pick up and continue after being forced from her home and lifestyle, held captive for months and made to face the harsh elements of life, far away from civilization? How could she suddenly call up her "old friends" when she felt like someone who was ready for a nursing home? The term *old self* even bothered her. She didn't see herself as old. The whole statement seemed an oxymoron. If anything, she viewed herself as young and naive then. Now she felt old. She felt she had aged ten years in the past several months, so how could she return to her *old* self if she was older now?

"I don't care if he's a kid, much less your kid." Kimberly argued over the phone, pulling Halen out of her internal conflict. "He ran the lawnmower over my flowers." Kimberly continued to berate the landscaper.

Halen half listened to the argument and flipped the channel away from a movie she had starred in.

Kimberly's voice became more agitated. "I don't care if it was an accident. I'm not going to pay for it."

Halen turned over on the couch and listened to the heated venom in her mother's voice.

"I don't care if he's only ten. He has to atone for his mistakes. Okay, fine. I'll see you this afternoon." Kimberly ended the call. "I don't care if it was an accident, a mistake on purpose or anything else. He has to learn," she said to the room. She looked at Halen. "Never let the hired help take advantage of you. I don't care how old they are."

Kimberly vanished to another room. There were dozens of things that needed attention to keep the house flawless. Halen looked around the expansive room. Lush white couches, polished tables, integrated digital media—all were meticulously cleaned every week. Halen remembered finding somewhere else to be when they were cleaned, usually on Tuesdays, because her weekend hangovers typically lasted through Monday afternoons. While the service cleaned, she would usually have an afternoon coffee and go shopping with her friends.

When her friends had heard she was back in town, they blew up the new phone her mother had gotten her. She didn't answer any of them. She didn't know who she was. It was as if she had traded places with a celebrity. She had stepped into this woman's shoes and was expected to live like her.

The probability of Tracer's and her birthmarks looking eerily similar was a million to one. She tried to remember the details of his face, like the shape of his eyes, the color and texture of his hair, the shape of his nose. She went to the mirror and looked at herself. This time there was no makeup, no styling gel nor any glitter to hide the real her. She looked for other similarities, but her memory kept bringing back the image of Tracer plunging into the water with the mountain lion digging his claws into him.

Losing him made her feel like she had the first day she'd arrived at the cave. After being dragged through the snow by the hair, her skin scraped raw by the frozen earth, she had felt like she was stripped of all self-worth. She was scared and didn't know what was going to happen next. She was feeling that again, but this time it was in her soul and for a whole different reason. She had been scraped raw on the inside. These wounds didn't require ointment, bandages or stitches. These wounds required something else to heal, if they would heal at all.

It seemed a black hole had opened up in the pit of her stomach, intent on devouring her from the inside. She couldn't think of any other time she had ever felt this way. She had always had a distraction from the real world, and friends who gave their opinion on how to live her life. If she disagreed with their ideas, she would belittle them until they went away or suggested something to bring her out of her glum mood. Regardless, it was always someone else's fault. She knew now that she was responsible for her own life. It wasn't up to anyone else to entertain her or make her happy, sad or indifferent. She had cast aside so many people, taking what she wanted from them, then barring them from any of her social outings. She had lost so many friends. Some of them were just leeches doing anything to be in her social circle. Some used her celebrity status to launch their own careers. But some would have been genuine friends who would have given her the time of day even if they were sick in bed.

She couldn't be that person any longer. She had to change. She had to fix things. She had to atone for her mistakes, just like her mother had said. She had to fix what she had wronged, but there was so much to fix. There were so many things in so many different areas, it was hard to find a place to start. She had to fix her soul but didn't know where to start with that either. She had to start somewhere.

Halen stared at herself in the mirror. "Start at the beginning."

31

"Yeah, that's fine. I can take Mikey and Sandra too." Deenya shouldered the phone to her ear. Her fingers clutched at the grocery bags and wiggled to readjust the loops to prevent them from cutting into her skin. The double load of groceries strained against the straps. "Make sure Chesh has her homework with her. Did she get any work done on it?"

Deenya turned the corner onto her block. Plywood and cardboard filled several windows on the street. Albert was in his usual spot in his front yard, watching children run up and down the street. The paper-wrapped bottle didn't fool anyone. As long as he didn't leave his yard, there wasn't much anyone could do about the eyes that followed little girls up and down the street.

Mrs. Netsbiln watched from her front stoop as well. Her eyes, like those of a momma pit bull's, looked for any creep who would come within a mile of any of the children. She had confronted Albert numerous times, threatening voodoo magic against him if he tried anything. Forever the neighborhood busybody, she was constantly knocking on doors to tell parents about the four-letter word their child said, or who took whose after-school snack. The parents didn't care for the nosiness but tolerated it because she had kept the neighborhood children safe on many different occasions. Deenya mowed her lawn occasionally when the woman's nephew couldn't. Bringing Mrs. Netsbiln her weekly groceries was Deenya's usual chore.

"No," Deenya argued. "I can't drop them off. My car is broken." She turned the last corner onto her street. "I don't know when it'll get fixed. Your brother gonna dish out the money to fix it. It was his fault anyway."

She set the groceries on the porch. "Here you go, Mrs. Netsbiln." Deenya waved and turned, grabbing the phone from her shoulder and transferring it to her other ear. Her right hand still clutched her own sack of groceries. "I don't care if he don't got a job. There are plenty of help wanted signs." She turned down the sidewalk again. "Marco, he don't pay rent at your house. He'd be able to make more than enough to buy what he wants *and* fix my car." She scolded Marco as children raced past her. "Well until he pays for it or hell freezes over, you're going to have to shuttle the kids."

Halen checked her watch and curled her toes over the edge of the step. Her pink tracksuit hung loosely on her. She didn't realize she had lost that much weight. She would have felt more energized than any other time she could think of, but the apprehension she felt waiting for her former friend kept it bottled. She wanted to feel alive like she had the last time she played backgammon against Tracer. It was a moment in their relationship that had brought her pure joy. For that moment, they weren't captor and captive. They were two people enjoying a game. She craved more of those types of moments—genuine happiness with genuine people.

She didn't know what she had to do to make things right. A look back on her life flooded her with examples of all the wrong ways to live it. The drinking and the drugs were an obvious mistake. Her choice of friends was another. There were many other things to fix to correct her life and lifestyle, and she felt she had to start at the beginning. She had to start at the fork in the road that led her on the wild rollercoaster ride that landed her in the clutches of a madman, the eye-opening experience that both literally and figuratively shook every bone in her body. In a sea of wrongs, she had to make at least one thing right. Of all the things to correct, she chose the one where she knew everything had started going wrong. She sat on the tiny porch, stared at her feet and waited.

Though the day was near blistering in the afternoon sun, she kept her hood pulled up tight so the average busybody wouldn't recognize her. She waited with her phone on silent. The nonstop dings were driving her crazy. She didn't want to answer any questions, she only wanted to ask one. One that would determine if she would get to put her life back on solid ground.

"Back from the dead?"

The voice was gruff and short. Halen looked up. She didn't see the bright smiling face she remembered from her childhood. Instead she was met with a scowl. After years of being shunned, coupled with the rough neighborhood, Halen guessed that her former friend had little to be happy about.

"What do you want?" Deenya's flat, emotionless tone pummeled Halen's hopes.

"I wanted to—"

Deenya cut her off. "Whatever you're going to say, save it. I don't have time to deal with this. My car broke down weeks ago. I don't have money to fix it. I do not need this. I have kids coming over in five minutes. I have to make dinner. I don't have time for you, Halen."

Deenya walked past her and into her house, slamming the door behind her.

Halen stared at the door. It was a shock she wasn't prepared for. She needed to talk with someone. She needed a real and legitimate friend. She thought Deenya would be that friend, but maybe she was mistaken.

"Mom. Mikey stole my homework!" Deenya's daughter screamed. The ear-splitting sound rang through the thin walls, alerting the entire house as well as the neighbors.

Deenya rushed into the living room, still holding the spoon she'd used to stir the macaroni noodles. "What happened?"

Cheshlan pointed to the three-year-old boy. "Mikey wiped his nose with my homework."

"Mikey. Come here now," Deenya growled.

Mikey bolted for a back room with Deenya racing after him. She passed Sandra, who stood in her playpen, biting the edge of the cushioned rail and observing the commotion with mild amusement. Deenya cornered the boy under the bed. It was his go-to safe haven where neither his mom nor Deenya could reach him without difficulty. The boy giggled at the game, then screeched as her hand came within inches of grabbing him. A knock sounded at the front door, but she didn't hear it.

"I'll get it," Cheshlan said and raced to see who it was.

Deenya gripped the toddler's hand and pried the paper from it. "Mikey," she hissed. "Give me that paper."

A bloodcurdling scream erupted from the living room. Deenya jerked the paper from Mikey, tearing the math coloring paper in half. Racing into the living room, she found her daughter, Cheshlan, standing frozen just a few feet inside the door. Her daughter trembled in her socks, unable to move as she stared out the door. Deenya saw the corner of a pizza box just beyond the edge of the door. She shouldn't have gotten that excited over pizza. They had ordered some two nights before, and Cheshlan knew she wouldn't allow pizza more than once a week.

She followed her daughter's gaze, and it wasn't on pizzas. "Marco. This isn't a good time. The kids already had junk food this week." Deenya stepped forward to confront her boyfriend. "I don't . . ." Looking out the door, she didn't see the large man she expected.

"I just want a few minutes to apologize." Halen stood just outside the door, her shoulders hunched apologetically. "I was mean and I didn't realize what I was losing."

Deenya looked at her former friend. The effort to maintain her resolve and send Halen away was monumental.

"Mom. Mom. Mom. Mom. Mom," Cheshlan stammered.

"I know," Deenya said as if she had bitten into a rotten apple. "It's Halen Kettleman."

A squeal as loud as a freight train exploded from the back room. A dark-skinned naked body bolted past Deenya, shrieking through the house. "Mikey. Dammit."

Mikey slipped past Deenya and back to the bedroom. She raced after him, slamming the door behind her, trapping the disobedient toddler inside.

"So what color goes there?" Halen asked the first grader as they both leaned over her second page of math homework.

"This one." Cheshlan picked out a pink crayon.

"But the assignment tells us that the ball is supposed to be colored blue if this answer equals five," Halen explained.

"But I like pink."

"Not everything can be pink. Some things have to be other colors."

"No. They have to be pink." Cheshlan continued coloring the ball pink.

"What color is the grass?" Halen asked.

"Pink," Cheshlan said.

"What color is the sky?" Halen asked again.

"Pink," Cheshlan replied with vibrant enthusiasm.

"Why is everything pink?"

"Because that's your favorite color," Cheshlan explained while pointing at Halen's pink tracksuit as if it should be self-evident.

Halen looked up at Deenya, who was picking at a slice of pizza. She gave Halen a *Welcome to my world* look and followed it with a *What ya gonna do now?* raised eyebrow.

"Well that's not true. I like lots of different colors. I like yellow flowers. I like green grass. I like beach balls when they are blue. I like your eyes because they are a beautiful brown. If everything was pink we would all look the same and you might mistake a fat, hairy guy for your mom. Does that make sense?"

"I guess so, but your favorite color is pink," Cheshlan said, sounding a little disconnected.

"Well, I think maybe I should change it. What do you think?"

Cheshlan shook her head emphatically.

"I think I need a new favorite color. Do you want to know why?" Halen asked.

Cheshlan shook her head and listened.

Halen glanced to Deenya, then back to Cheshlan. "Because I went somewhere, and even though I didn't like it at first, it turned out to be the best thing that ever happened to me. I was forced to see all the mean things I did and see how sad it made some people."

Cheshlan stared blankly back at her idol. Halen could see that she wasn't understanding; the depth of the concept was too much for her mind. She could barely do her homework because of her continued starstruck paralysis.

"Does your mom read you books?"

"Yeah. She reads me *The Land of Stories*," Cheshlan said.

"*The Land of Stories*?" Halen looked to Deenya for an explanation.

"It's a series written by Chris Colfer. It takes all the fairytale characters and mashes them into a new series featuring twins, Alex and Conner."

"Oh. That sounds exciting. You'll have to read to me sometime."

"Okay." Cheshlan agreed eagerly, knowing that meant another visit with her favorite actress.

"Well anyway, do you know when Alex and Conner are in a really bad place and they don't know what to do?" Halen recited the all-too-common premise of most children's stories.

Cheshlan nodded.

"They find the thing that's missing so they can fix all their problems."

Cheshlan nodded again.

"That's where I'm at. I found the thing that was missing and now I'm here to make things better." Halen looked to Deenya with her own pleading eyes.

"You're better now?" Cheshlan asked.

"Almost. I have to talk to your mommy first, then I'll be all better."

"Okay. I'll let you talk to mommy so you can be better."

Deenya rolled her eyes at the authority her daughter thought she had.

Halen stood and watched her little student pull a blue crayon out of its box and start coloring the beach ball blue.

"I wanted a chance to say that I'm sorry. I did some mean things to you that I shouldn't have." Halen stood before her former friend. Deenya continued to pluck at the slice of pizza.

"Grab a slice and come sit." Deenya motioned to Halen then turned to a small sitting area behind the couch. A cartoon filled the TV screen for the two toddlers. As they sat, one in the playpen and the other in a toy car, gnawing on their own slices of pizza, they watched the bright, colorful characters sing their song.

"You were in a bad place?" Deenya asked. "The news said they found you in Canada."

"They did."

"They also said that you were abducted." Deenya paused, holding a slice of pepperoni just before her lips.

"I was."

"Do you know who it was?"

Halen hesitated. "No. I don't know his real name."

"What did he do with you?"

"He kidnapped me."

"That was obvious. Everyone thought you fell through the ice and drowned."

"I did. But, I didn't drown," Halen explained.

"You did, but you didn't drown?" Deenya looked at Halen through skeptical eyes.

"He knocked me out. When I woke up, I was inside one of those ice fishing sled, igloo things."

"How did you not drown?" Deenya picked another tiny bit off her slice and nibbled on it.

"He taped a plastic bag over my head." Halen mimicked her childhood friend and picked the toppings off her own slice of pizza.

"If that's all it took, I would have wrapped a bag around your head years ago," Deenya said.

Halen looked up to find a mischievous smirk on her friend's face. She had broken the ice, and a huge apprehensive weight had just been lifted from her shoulders. She returned a smile.

"Somehow you made it to Canada," Deenya continued.

"I'm not sure on that one. I was locked in a dark box. I was only let out to pee and eat a granola bar."

"So you had to have ended up somewhere."

"Yeah. He had a camp," Halen said, leaving out more specific details. She took a bite of her pizza and waited for the next question.

"What did he do there?" Deenya asked.

"He dragged me around like I was a bag of trash. I think to assert that he was in charge."

"And after that?"

"Well, he just stared at me."

"Stared at you? Like a creeper?" Deenya asked, scooting to the edge of her seat, devouring the story.

"No. Not like that. Like he had gotten . . . I don't know. Like a package in the mail or a puzzle that didn't have instructions. Probably more like a puzzle. He just stared at me like he wondered if putting the puzzle together was worth his time."

Deenya stopped chewing and stared blank-faced at Halen as she continued.

"He changed how I thought about life. I used to think that big city lights were magical and mesmerizing. Now I know where the real magical lights can be found. And they're not found anywhere near a big city. They're the stars on a moonless night.

"I don't know what happened to me. I just know I'm not who I used to be."

"You're not. I don't know who you are, but it's a better you. Unless you have hidden cameras here and I'm about to get punked."

"No. No cameras. No makeup. Just me," Halen confessed.

"No?"

Halen continued. "It was a really dark place at first. But Tra—" Halen caught herself. She didn't want to reveal his name. He might have been a bad person, but he wasn't quite as bad as she would have thought. In a way, he was a saint. Rough around the edges, but still a saint. He had opened her eyes to the downward spiral she was on, and the crash at the bottom would be alongside so many other celebrities who'd burned out long before their time.

"I learned a lot about myself." Halen glanced up at Deenya, then back at her pizza. "And I want to make right as many things as I can. I wanted to start with you, since my first and biggest mistake was losing you as a friend. Can you forgive me?"

"I did that when I saw you helping Cheshlan with her homework," Deenya said.

"Oh." Halen squealed. "You let me say all that."

"I've pretty much known what your whole life was about, except for the last few months. Now, I feel privileged to be the first to know. Unless you spilled your guts to the scouts."

"No. I just told them I wanted to go home. How do you know I didn't tell a shrink?" Halen suggested.

"You'd never see a shrink."

"You're right. But I can trust you, right? Please don't say anything to anyone."

"I never even told anyone what you did to me back in third grade."

"What did I do?" Halen asked, searching her memory.

"It's what you didn't do."

"What didn't I do?" Halen plucked the last pepperoni off her slice of pizza.

"You claimed my project as your own," Deenya began. "I worked really hard on that. I was so proud of it. You asked if you could carry it for me. I agreed, hoping to rekindle our friendship. You took it to your classroom and said it was yours. You didn't do your own project, and you stole mine. That's what you didn't do. You didn't do your own project."

"The project about England and the castles?"

"Yeah," Deenya said.

"You got an A for the exhibit. I'm afraid I didn't do well on the report."

"What did you do for the report?"

"I couldn't remember which castle was which and called your castle by the wrong name throughout the presentation," Halen said.

Deenya huffed a chuckle. "I stopped trying after that." She finished her pizza and set the remaining crust on a side table. "If you were going to steal all my homework assignments, then I was going to purposely do bad on them. That's when everyone started calling me dummy. I quit trying once I saw that you no longer wanted or needed me. Everyone started ridiculing me, telling me that I could never be good enough to be your friend, especially after you got started in acting. After a while, I believed them."

"I'm sorry, Deenya." Halen put a hand on her friend's knee. "I really am."

Deenya talked at her pizza. "I just wish I had a chance to see what I was good at."

"You're a good mom."

"I want to be more than a good mom. I want to be a good provider. I want to be amazing. I want my daughter to look up to me like she looks up to you."

"She will."

"How? You're in our lives now. How can I compete with that?"

"I don't know." Halen tried to understand her friend's position, but she had been handed life on a silver platter. She had to work, but she never had to manage her own life.

"My life hasn't been glamorous like yours. I haven't had things handed to me like you have," Deenya complained.

"Yes, it seems like things are handed to me, and sometimes they are, but there's a lot of hard work too," Halen explained.

"Like what?"

"Well, there's—"

A loud pounding erupted on the door.

32

Halen jumped to her feet at the sound. The small confined house unnerved her. She had become accustomed to large houses with open floor plans, and the wide-open spaces of the Canadian wilderness expanded her spatial comfort zone. Now she was in a house that she could probably fit inside her bedroom. It unnerved her that someone was suddenly this close without her knowing about it. Most people called before arriving at her home. Even if they knocked, she was usually out back in the pool house. To have someone beating on the door so close to her and in a stranger's house set her on edge. The months living in the wild had sharpened her senses, and from the emotional pounding on the door, Halen knew it wasn't going to be a friendly visit for Deenya.

Deenya sighed as she went to the door and peeked through the peephole.

THE HIT

She turned the knobs on two deadbolts and unfastened the chain before opening the door. "Yes, Marco?"

Marco stepped through the door, looking down on Deenya. He was a little taller than Halen but three times as round. His weight wasn't attributed to work-hardened muscle unless his work was as an official drive-through tester. He clearly used his size to intimidate those around him. Deenya backed off, hesitating and watching his moves, keeping just outside his reach. She was watching his hands more than his face.

Halen took note of the detail. As an actor, when she wasn't making a fool of herself, she watched people: what they did, how they talked and how they moved. She studied their hand gestures, how they tilted their head and whether they were relaxed or walked stiffly. She watched to see if they favored one side or another and if they were right- or left-handed.

A thick gold chain hung around Marco's neck, and his shirt tried but failed to hide the stretch from his last meal. His arms imitated his barrel chest, with extra padding over the muscle. He looked like a brute and surely was one, at least to some people.

"Where my little 'uns at?" Marco scanned the room, overlooking his children, who were staring at the television. His eyes fell on Halen. "Sup." He gave her a nod with a sly smile.

Halen didn't respond as she slipped into the kitchen, where Cheshlan was paused over her homework. She watched Deenya duck her head and start gathering the bags and car seats for Mikey and Sandra.

"Thought you said you car was broke," Marco said.

"It *is* broke, Marco. It's been broke for weeks. You know that. It still has the freaking grass clippings on it from last week. It hasn't been moved," Deenya said, trying to defend her position.

"What you doing with a brand new car out there for?" Marco peeked around the corner, watching Halen, then turned his attention back to Deenya.

"That's Halen's car. It ain't mine."

"You borrow dat or sumfin?" Marco nodded at Halen.

Halen ignored his question and focused on Cheshlan and her homework. After handing her the proper colored crayon, she leaned to the curtain and peeked out.

"Dis a mess. What choo do all day?" Marco blasted Deenya in an obvious show of dominance.

"Same as I do every day, Marco." Deenya sighed.

"Why you live like a pig? Me and my kids deserve better."

"I don't have time, Marco. I work and take care of these three and you," Deenya said.

"You call dis takin' care of me? You serious? Come on."

"Yes, Marco."

"You gonna give me the cold shoulder tonight too, I bet."

Marco gauged her reaction, then continued when she didn't respond.

"Dat's alright. I gots somethin' somethin' special for ya tonight."

Marco leaned toward the kitchen. Halen caught him sizing her up. Unconsciously, she adjusted her top to cover more of her bottom.

"Hurry up. I got ta take 'em over der moms'," Marco said while throwing glances and a subtle wink over to Halen.

By this time, Halen could smell the alcohol that was becoming all too apparent in the room. She watched her friend put Sandra into her car seat, hoping she would take her back out immediately. Halen took a step into the living room, taking more of an interest in what Deenya was doing.

"Deenya, what's happening?" Halen asked.

"I'm dropping deez kids off at der mommas' houses," Marco volunteered. "Then comin' back here to get our freak on. You welcome to join. I promise that I will not disappoint. You know you slammin' in that pink suit, right?"

"Deenya. Put that baby back in her pen," Halen said, keeping her tone level and serious.

Deenya looked at her, as did Marco.

"Who you, telling her what to do? Dat's my job." Marco stood up straighter, puffing his chest a little.

"Deenya, put that baby back. You have the numbers to their mommas, right?"

Deenya nodded, then glanced at Marco as if asking permission to communicate with her.

"What's choo say? Deez my kids. I'm gunn take dem, 'cause dis bitch don't know how keep her car on the road." Marco inhaled and casually flexed his muscles.

The faux intimidation didn't faze Halen.

"Who are you to comes in here and tell me how to run my house? Huh? Fuckin' scrawny little sack." Marco took a step toward her.

Halen stepped further into the living room and met him partway. "For the next twenty-four hours," Halen began, "I am the owner of this house. I am the boss, the grand pimp, lord and devil of this house. What I say goes. After that, you can reclaim your home and all this lovely and stylish furniture. You can have the torn and yellow wallpaper, the broken lights, the broken window and the brand new and probably stolen game system." Halen looked him in the eye and saw that he didn't flinch when she mentioned that the system was stolen. "For the next twenty-four hours, you will not step foot within a block of this house."

"You talking to me, bitch? You disrespecting me in my own house?"

"Yeah. I'm talking to you. And this ain't your house. Your momma left it to you."

"Don't you talk about my momma," Marco growled.

"Your actions disrespect yo momma. You disrespect your momma's house, letting it run into the ground. You got broken windows over there. The carpet should have been replaced five years ago, and damn, the condition of the furniture. I didn't know you liked floral print so much. What up with all the stains? Your momma be proud of how you take care of her furniture? How many house parties you have here after she slaved her whole life to pay for this house and give it to the likes of you?"

"Shut your mouth, bitch. You don't know me."

"I do know you. I used to be like you. I used to use people and toss them aside just like you do. As soon as a friend became boring, I blocked their number. I tossed them out of my life, just like you're doing to your kids."

"I take care of my kids."

"No. No you don't. She"—Halen snapped a finger and pointed at Deenya—"is the one taking care of your babies. They ain't her babies. They ain't her responsibility. They yours. And, you went drinking with the boys. You shoved your responsibility off onto my friend, and you ain't gonna do that anymore."

"Bitch. I'm gonna fuckin' smack you." Marco's words quavered in his throat.

"You ain't shit. I've faced down monsters ten times your size. I fought off one who held five daggers in each hand. I've looked a killer in the eyes and walked away. What the fuck are you gonna do, smother me with that dough-boy gut? Come on, donut hole, what you gonna do?" She stepped up and bumped against his belly. "What you gonna do, bitch?"

Halen bumped him again. He gave a step. She bumped him again. He gave another step.

"You can fuck up yo momma's house tomorrow. Right now, get fucking lost."

Halen bumped him one more time and he stumbled backward out the door. She shut it but didn't lock it.

Deenya found herself holding her breath when Halen called to her.

"Deenya, get over here."

She looked at Halen, then the door, then back to Halen.

"Get over here. Now, now." Halen snapped her fingers, pointing to the floor where she was standing. She set Sandra back in the playpen and hurried over.

"This is my gift to you. You have to commit to it full force. No holding back."

"What am I doing?"

"You have to commit one hundred percent. Don't you dare hold back."

"What?" she stood in the spot where Halen told her to, shaking with anticipation.

"Just do it. This is my gift to you. Promise not to hold back."

"I don't know. I can't promise what I don't know."

"Yes you can. Now face the door. Not too close. You don't want to get hit when it opens."

Deenya backed up a few inches.

"Now, get mean."

"I can't. I'm freaking terrified."

"Yes you can. You have to or it won't work. You have to get mean."

The door handle turned, first one way, then the other. It wiggled back and forth before the latch released and opened. Deenya panicked, not knowing what to do.

In her ear, Halen whispered, "He raped your daughter."

That was it. That was the trigger she needed. It didn't matter that it wasn't true. He had, however, forced himself on her several times. Insulted and belittled her and suppressed her in every way that he could. She had allowed it because she didn't have any other place to go, but what Halen had said triggered something inside her. And this was likely the only chance she would have to change her situation. Halen was right—this was her gift, a gift of retribution.

Before anyone realized what she was doing, Deenya was already in motion. She took a small step with her left foot and swung her right with all her might. It connected with a glorious thump. It was a connection an NFL punter would be proud of.

The explosion of pain triggered an involuntary jump, giving the illusion that she had kicked Marco hard enough to lift him off the ground. Either way, the message was clearly and unmistakably delivered.

The man's knees buckled and he collapsed. Deenya stared at him writhing in pain on the floor. She had no remorse for what she had done, as he had had even less for her as she'd wept through many nights when he came home drunk. Halen had just given her the courage to take back her life. Halen had given her, as she said, a gift.

33

Halen sat on the couch, scrolling through her phone while idly turning the pages in Deenya's photo album. Cheshlan had curled up and fallen asleep with her head on Halen's lap.

"Think he'll be back?" Deenya asked, peeking out the window. The toddlers had been picked up by their mothers hours before. The house had been tranquil since then. Her constant pacing was brought on by the worry that Marco would surely return. It was just a matter of time.

"No. Maybe. I don't know. Whatever happens, you can't stay here," Halen said.

"I can't just leave. Cheshlan has school to finish up. I have to work."

"What do you do?" Halen asked.

"I'm a produce stocker at Kim's Grocery. When I'm done there, I go to Cheshlan's school and clean. Then I come home and clean. Sometimes I just don't want to clean. Ya know?"

Halen nodded, then turned a page in the album and paused. "Who did your daughter's Halloween costumes?"

"I did." Deenya kept looking out the window, one way, then another, watching for Marco to return.

"Where'd you learn to do that?" Halen asked, the gears turning in her head.

"Online makeup and monster prosthetic tutorials." Deenya glanced back at Halen. "Why?"

Halen held up a finger and dialed a number on her phone. "Hey Beatrice, it's Halen."

She listened for a few seconds, then pulled the phone away from her ear. The scream was audible from across the room. When it faded, Halen continued. "Yes, Beatrice, I am still alive, and yes, I will come by to autograph your daughter's late birthday gift." After a moment of listening, she interjected. "Hey, what's Slappy working on?"

Deenya inched away from the window, her attention now on Halen.

"I don't care if it's chaos there. Put the phone to Slappy's ear. He'll thank me later. Just put it up to his ear." Halen huffed into the phone.

"Slappy." Halen started with an enthusiastic voice. "This is Halen . . . Yes, I've been dead for a few months . . . What are you working on?"

Halen sat up on the couch. "Really. Will you be nice to me if I bail you out?"

A screech of tires outside made Deenya peek out the curtain. "Halen, Marco's back. What're we gonna do?"

"Be there in five minutes. Love you." Halen ended the call and looked up at Deenya.

"Halen? What are we doing?" Deenya stood in the middle of the living room. Her eyes pleaded with Halen to jump to action. The handle turned and the door shook. The deadbolt was barely hanging on by the last few slivers of wood in the doorframe.

"Halen!" Deenya cried.

"We're leaving." Halen shook Cheshlan. "Sweetie, we gotta go. Grab a blanket and something to cuddle with."

A pounding erupted on the front door. "Bitch!" Marco's voice blared from the other side of the flimsy door. "You let me in my house."

"It your momma's house, slut!" Halen yelled back.

"What's going on?" Cheshlan said, rubbing sleep from her eyes.

"We're leaving," Halen said. "Deenya, get your makeup kit and the bags I told you to pack."

Deenya raced to the bedroom. Halen walked to the door, waiting for anyone who would dare walk through. Cheshlan stood by the couch, pulling her blanket tighter around her shoulders. The door blew open with a heavy foot following it into the living room. It wasn't Marco. This man was bigger and didn't have the table muscle that Marco had. The dark skin and dreadlocks along with thick tree trunks for arms and size fifteen special-order shoes made Halen hesitate.

She noticed a small hitch in his knee. He was coming toward her. She shrank back a step. The man was huge, but he didn't look nearly as fierce as the mountain lion she had faced. He seemed indifferent to anything going on around him. He was just there for the muscle and intimidation.

Halen stepped back, feigning cowardice, drawing him in where she had more room to move. She stepped back one more time, then forward, swinging her leg with all her might. Her shin connected with his knee, causing a loud pop followed by the man screaming in pain as he thumped to the floor like a large redwood falling to the ground. Dishes rattled in the cabinets as the whole house shook when he hit.

Marco and his other crony hesitated when they saw Halen bound over their point man. He had seemed invincible. Now he lay in a pile on the floor, gritting his teeth against the pain. Halen stood in front of Marco, who had backed out the door and onto the front lawn. She stepped outside, facing the two men.

"I thought I told you that you weren't allowed back here until tomorrow. Because of your stupidity, you got your friends hurt," Halen growled at him.

Marco's wiry friend focused his attention on Marco. "You said she told you to never come back."

Halen used the opportunity and stepped forward. She feigned a kick to the wiry man's groin. The man bent forward to keep his jewels out of harm's way but met an elbow across his nose. Blood erupted and spilled down his shirt. A stream of tears blinded him. Halen launched a foot to his groin as if she were attempting a fifty-yard field goal. The man crumpled to the ground, one hand holding his nose and the other trying to comfort his groin. She turned her sights on Marco.

Marco swung at Halen. She ducked and threw a quick fist, catching his throat. Her fist did little to deter his advance. Ducking his head to protect his throat, he moved in on her and swung again. This time he caught her in the chest, just under her left breast. Halen grunted from the impact. She continued her battery on Marco. She hit him in every sensitive nerve she could think of: the tender spot under the arm, the nose twice and the base of the throat after he clipped her on the jaw. She attacked his legs and knees next, kicking each in turn as he tried to hit her. Suddenly he screamed and fell onto the patchy dead grass. Halen was surprised. She didn't think she had hit him hard enough to make him scream like that. She looked up to find Cheshlan standing behind him with a baseball bat.

"He always complained of a bad hip. I was just seeing if it was true." Cheshlan let the bat drop to the ground and looked up at Halen standing under the yellow street light. She was panting from the effort of the battle, staring down at the little girl. Marco writhed on the grass, as did his accomplice. The brute with the bad knee tried to get up from the floor, but Deenya kicked him in the groin and he collapsed again.

Deenya walked out the door with several bags over her shoulders and under each arm. She paused to look at her front lawn. "What happened?" she asked, bewildered at the two men lying on the ground, groaning in pain.

"They're starstruck," Cheshlan said, grabbing Halen's hand as she reached out to her.

Halen lifted Cheshlan into the back seat, tucked the blanket in around her and saw that she was buckled securely. Deenya climbed in the passenger seat and struggled into her seatbelt as Halen backed out of the small driveway.

"Sorry," Deenya said, clicking her seatbelt home before quickly checking on her daughter.

"Sorry?" Halen asked, putting the car in drive and pulling away from the house. Marco's friend had managed to pull himself to his feet. He fished for something in his pants. Halen didn't know if it was to cup his injured manhood or if he was reaching for a pistol. Not wanting to find out, she smashed her foot on the gas pedal and sped away from the dilapidated neighborhood.

"Sorry for spilling some fingernail polish in the back," Deenya said.

Halen turned left against a yellow light and sped away from Deenya's past. "Why should I care? It's your car." Halen threw a side smirk at her bewildered friend.

"Oh swell, we have a child—keep her out of the way." The gaunt man leered at Deenya and her daughter.

Anger flared at the challenge of her motherhood while the production set left her feeling intimidated and unsure. The man wore pressed yellow pants and a shirt accented with a black-and-yellow checkered vest. Checkered loafers completed his distinctive style. His reading glasses were absent the arm pieces that would have hooked over his ears, but they were firmly pinched onto the bridge of his nose. He looked down his nose at the details of each costume with an occasional glance around the room to check on other projects.

"Janine, get this ragamuffin a station and some supplies and keep that thing out of my . . . whatever. Just go somewhere where I can't see you." Slappy walked off, smacking his hands to get everyone's attention. "People, our models will be here in three hours. These masks need to be fitted and ready for the afternoon. If they're not finished, find another job."

Slappy walked around the room, looking at and criticizing one aspect or another of each project. Janine took Deenya by the arm and marched her to an empty station. She picked up a head mold and set it in the middle of the station.

"This is Clayton. He's your model. He'll be here in three hours to be fitted for your design," Janine said.

"Who am I turning Clayton into?" Deenya asked.

Janine looked at her quizzically and walked off.

Deenya scanned the room and saw a dozen other artists busy painting or working on various aspects of their costumes. She glanced back to where she had come from and found Halen adjusting Cheshlan's blanket around her shoulders before pulling her into a comforting embrace on a couch. Deenya looked around at the different workspaces. It appeared that the other artists were turning people into fish. She looked over her work space, the bust of the model and the reference pictures of a tiger shark. She understood now that she had to turn Clayton into a shark.

"Hello."

Deenya looked up to see chiseled abs. She looked up further to see the rest of a sculpture that would put a Greek god to shame. His warm smile was the only thing that made him human and made Deenya a little less intimidated.

"Hi. Clayton?"

"Yes." The male model reached a hand out to greet her.

"I'm Deenya. It's nice to meet you." She tried to offer a hand but retracted it, since it was covered in glue and multiple paint colors. The muscles of Clayton's shirtless and hairless body scrambled Deenya's brain and tossed her professionalism out the window. She finally turned her attention to the head and bust and spun it around so he could see her creation.

"I've been playing with your face." Instantly regretting her statement, heat flushed up her neck. "I mean, I've been painting your face." Deenya scrambled to make herself seem more professional by pushing away some of the clutter and tossing a handful of odds and ends into a bucket, out of sight.

"I thought this would be further along." Clayton looked at the rough form that barely resembled a shark.

"Sorry. My friend Halen threw me into the hot seat just a few hours ago."

"Halen?"

"Halen Kettleman," Deenya said, pointing to Halen, who was asleep on a couch with her daughter snuggled up next to her.

"I thought she was dead," Clayton said, taking a few steps to get a better look at her face.

"I thought so too, until I found her waiting for me on my doorstep."

"Is she still the snotty little bi—" Clayton caught his tongue. "Sorry, the rumor mills never really painted her favorably."

"They may have been justified before. Now I think you might have to give her a chance. I think something happened that has made her change," Deenya explained.

"Okay. I guess we'll see." Clayton turned to the creation. "What do you have for me?"

34

Halen stared out the high-rise apartment building window. Three days had passed since rescuing Deenya from her dead-end life. Though she hadn't fully completed turning Clayton into a tiger shark, Slappy was impressed enough with her speed. She had turned out an almost-finished project in just a few hours, whereas the others had two days to get their models ready. When he left without saying a word, Deenya was disappointed. She didn't know how to react to the non-reaction, and she wondered if she'd failed the assignment.

Janine had walked up to Deenya and given a disapproving glance at her ragged wardrobe. "Be here tomorrow at ten. You have one more trial by fire before Slappy will pay you for a third. Try to look a little more presentable."

Halen was proud of her friend. She had helped her by opening a door, one that she would never have had a chance at. Deenya had taken advantage of the opportunity thus making Halen envious of the fortunate turn around. Now Deenya was busy working on another creation. This time it was a paying gig, as she had passed the second audition. Cheshlan was off to a new school, bragging about her movie star best friend and her mom's cool new job creating monsters.

Their involvement in the outside world left ample time for Halen to think about her life, or the lack thereof. With Tracer dead, she had lost her light at the end of the tunnel. She was hoping that somehow at the end of winter, Tracer would have said something to encourage her to continue on. Something that would have given her a direction. Instead, she had only the image of him disappearing into the churning waters of the river.

She thought of all the lessons he had taught her about self-defense. *The best defense against the mean, ignorant and stupid people in life is to surround yourself with good, honest people and treat them right.* Halen thought about his short but meaningful bits of advice. She was in her hometown but now felt as though she were a visitor. She recognized the buildings, the traffic and the mobs of people rushing to live their lives, but she felt suspended in limbo.

She didn't feel she was in command of anything, and she didn't know what she would do next. She lacked direction. It was midmorning, and all her old friends were still sleeping. Her role in the film had been recast after she disappeared and was presumed dead. The film was now in postproduction. Life had continued on without her.

Halen had been told that the news covered her story constantly for the first week after her disappearance, then tapered off gradually as other stories took their turns in the headlines. After the first month and the search teams hadn't found anything, they suspended the search until spring. The ice would thaw, and a more thorough search of the lake would have been conducted.

Halen was lost in a sea of concrete and people. There were no classes or instruction manuals to teach her how to come back from the dead. News and talk shows begged for an interview. She had her media manager politely turn down all requests, leaving the outlets to speculate about her mysterious reappearance.

Finding herself first would make her feel more comfortable giving any interviews if she decided to do so. She grabbed her purse and headed for the door.

Rezzer's was one of the most popular nightclubs for the elites. It was one of her favorite party spots. Even though she was underage, she always made it in. She frequently made reservations, but only kept some of them. On her eighteenth birthday, she had rented out the entire nightclub and invited friends and the crew from her most recent film, thus beginning her downward spiral into nonstop partying.

With no vehicles in the parking lot to indicate where the party was, she double-checked the address. The building didn't resemble anything she remembered. Neatly trimmed hedges accented the tinted glass walls, and the absence of the thumping bass gave the club the atmosphere of a funeral home. That in itself made it more intimidating than three-hundred-pound bouncers standing at the entrance.

Stepping out of the hired car, she walked to the oak doors decorated with heavy brass hinges and handles. Large sago palm bushes stood as sentinels on either side of the double doors. The lights on the outside of the building were barely noticeable compared to the bright Florida sun beating down on the busy Miami streets.

Halen thought she might have spent enough money at the establishment to possibly buy the place. Barry had become an instant friend the day she turned eighteen. The exorbitant price of renting the club for her birthday solidified her place in the owner's heart and wallet. Though she was underage, he would bring her the highest quality drinks and lavish her with free bottles of champagne. She was sure extra drinks were added to the tickets she had placed a drunken signature on. With all the alcohol she had bought in the past, she wondered if Barry would spot her a free drink. She could use one. It had been months since she'd had any alcohol at all.

The atmosphere inside the club was alien to her. The usual loud chatter was replaced by eerie quiet and was void of the usual energy. The only hint of life came from the back, where music played softly alongside the clink of bottles. A young woman crouched behind the bar, vigorously cleaning the nooks, corners and cupboards. She pulled the condiments off their rack and began cleaning under their usual spots.

"Hey. How's it going?" Halen asked, peering over the bar. She pulled a barstool out and sat down.

Without looking up, the bartender continued to wash the back of the bar. The young woman worked diligently at her task until she was satisfied with the results. She looked up and spotted Halen.

"Oh, Jesus." The bartender stumbled backward, knocking a glass into the sink. "You scared the shit outta me." She pulled her earbuds out of her ears.

"Oh. Sorry," Halen said. "I was . . ."

Color drained from the woman's face and she bolted to the back room, where bottles continued to rattle. Halen followed her with her eyes and stared at the doorway she'd disappeared through. The music stopped.

Halen looked around the empty venue. The eerie quiet became unnerving, prompting her to get up to leave. Pushing the barstool back in, she turned for the door.

"Hello." The male voice echoed through the room.

Halen turned.

"Who's here?" the voice called.

"Halen Kettleman." She waited for the man to come closer. He stopped a few feet away.

"You're supposed to be dead," the man said. He walked into the light. Fine lines creased his forehead and around his eyes, but the bulky muscles in his shirt did not allude to his age.

"By all rights, I should be. I wasn't a good person," Halen said. "I'm sure there are more than a few people who wish I was dead."

"Well with that statement, I would say that you're already a better person. What can I get you?" Barry asked.

"Coffee?"

"Yeah, sure. No problem. Anything you need here, you got it."

"Thanks, Barry."

"Oh, I'm sorry. This is Tina, one of my bartenders." Barry stepped aside to allow Tina to step forward and be introduced. Halen reached out and shook the apprehensive woman's hand.

"Sorry," she said. "I thought you were a ghost."

"Horror does run in my blood. I do try to leave it on the big screen though," Halen said, trying to lighten the mood.

Minutes later, Halen found herself in a corner booth, a cup of black coffee sitting close to her fingers while she leaned on an elbow. Thoughts of her recent past churned through her mind. An image of Tracer's lifeless body floating down the Bull River teased the edge of her imagination. She couldn't accept that he was dead. He was smart and resilient. He couldn't just vanish like that. She couldn't accept that he was dead, but she couldn't think of how he could have survived either. He had fought a bear and fought a fever for three days. In his weakened state, how could he track her down and tackle a mountain lion off a cliff and into a churning river?

Shoving one memory behind another became a frequent activity for the evening. People started trickling in and ordering drinks. Music played. People danced. Conversations grew louder to talk over the music. The crowds pushed in closer, while Halen tried to distance herself.

"Oh my god. Halen. Is that you?"

Halen instinctively retreated further into her booth. The siren of a voice sounded her name like a fire alarm. Greta Portnov had been one of Halen's friends that she'd ghosted when she didn't quite mesh with her current crowd. She couldn't remember her original reason for ghosting her, but she guessed it had something to do with her loud, obnoxious voice.

"Hey Greta," Halen replied with considerably less enthusiasm.

"What are you doing here? Oh my god. You gotta tell me. Who kidnapped you? Did they molest you? Gag you and tie you up? You gotta spill."

"What's everyone been saying?" Halen asked, knowing that Greta would be on the front line of any gossip.

"That you drowned. Then I heard that some creep smuggled you into Canada and made you act out all his favorite scenes from the movies you've been in," Greta said, leaning forward as if she were telling a secret.

The whispering reminded Halen why she ghosted her. The girl couldn't keep her mouth shut. If Halen wanted to keep something a secret, she would have better luck giving an in-depth interview with the *National Enquirer*. The woman reeked of gossip whether it was true or not. She had a fan-following ten miles long on social media. Halen had to admit that when launching a movie, she would seek Greta out and get her fan base buzzing with word of the new film.

Halen knew she couldn't escape the socialite, so to pacify her, she decided to allow the lies to continue until she chose to let the truth be known to the general public. Greta wouldn't lose any viewers on her channel. She always had plenty of connections to satisfy the million followers seeking her bits of entertainment. She would somehow twist the truth around, once it was revealed, to show she was in the know and that what she had said was true.

"Well, you're right. I didn't drown," Halen said.

"What happened to you?"

"Well, I was abducted by Sasquatch and made to do his laundry and teach his children to speak." Halen sat up, determined to keep the truth away from this woman.

"Oh, Haley Hay-Hay. You can tell me. I promise I won't tell anyone," Greta pleaded.

"Greta, you and I both know that you can't keep a secret," Halen admonished.

"I can. I promise." Greta cast a hopeful look at her.

Halen sat back, evaluating her former friend's faux offer. She knew the information would be out before morning. She had to come up with a credible lie. Something that sounded plausible. Something that was juicy enough to satisfy Greta's hunger for gossip. And something that was far from the truth. The beginning and end were public knowledge, but the middle was still a mystery. One she didn't want to reveal.

Halen finally surrendered. "Buy me a drink and I'll spill."

She was craving a good drink. Maybe that would take her mind off the spinning thoughts in her head.

Pounding in Halen's head woke her from a heavy sleep. Pulling a hand up to her face, she tried to find where the throbbing was coming from. After several seconds, it lessened when a sudden thud of pain shot across her temples in time with another volley coming from the door.

Go away, she screamed in her mind, expecting the sound to make it out of her mouth, but her lips were dry and stuck together, preventing her from saying anything.

As the hammering in her head subsided, she slipped back into a deep sleep, but the pounding on the door woke her once again. She had to get up to answer the door, but her legs felt like lead, her arms like blocks of solid concrete, and her head felt like the point of an anvil was driving straight between her eyes. Whoever it was would have to wait.

"I'm coming. I'm coming." An irritated voice rattled the empty walls as a door opened and shut.

Footsteps thumped across the carpet like a bass drum beating against Halen's head. She heard someone pass by and cringed internally, searching for the peaceful bliss of unconsciousness. When the pounding finally stopped, she let herself fall into oblivion.

Deenya opened the door.

"Hello. I'm Detective Milton. We're looking for Halen Kettleman." A robust man stood just outside the apartment door; light glinted off his shaved head. A woman stood just off his left shoulder, and a badge hung from her belt, as did her partner's.

"Hay?" Deenya said, looking back over her shoulder.

Halen lay motionless on the couch.

"Halen," Deenya called, walking back into the living room and pulling the blanket off her.

Halen's face had dissolved into the pillow that soaked up the drool coming from the corner of her mouth. Her breathing was slow and even. The pulse in her neck was a steady, rhythmic beat showing the only signs of life. Her hair was mussed, and what little eyeliner she wore was smeared across her face and the cushion. Her shirt had been ripped on the side, showing several angry chafe marks.

"Halen," Deenya called. "Halen?" She shook her shoulder.

Deenya stood up and looked at the detectives standing in the door. She waved them in. The female detective took the lead and inched around to have a look at Halen. She lifted the sleeve of Halen's shirt, then turned her arm over.

"Look," the woman said. "She was shooting up. Call an ambulance."

35

"Do you know this man?" Detective Milton held up a photo.

Halen pushed the button on the electric bed, sitting herself up. Her IV had been taken out an hour before, and the doctors were preparing to discharge her.

She took the photo and looked at the young man in it. "I . . . don't . . . Maybe?" She stared at it. "Is this someone I was with last night?" Halen looked at the detectives over the top of the picture.

"Do you think this man slipped something in your drink?" the female officer asked.

"I don't know."

"Can you tell us what you remember?" she asked in a soothing voice.

Halen thought a bit about Barry, who had set her up with coffee and later soda for the majority of the afternoon. The alcohol began with Greta.

"I know Greta bought me my first Manhattan. I think I remember having two. We danced and talked, or rather screamed in each other's ears. I remember a guy who came over. We noticed him earlier, then suddenly he was there with us."

"Can you describe him?" the officer asked.

"He was quite a bit taller than me. I think he had dark hair and maybe a red shirt?" Halen pulled at the hospital gown where it was ruffled and pinching her. "It's weird. I just don't remember much after that second blue Manhattan."

"Miss Kettleman, Manhattans aren't blue," the female detective said.

"What's your name?" Halen asked.

"My name is Detective Perez. Do you know what happened to you? In a general sense, that is?"

Halen searched her memory but was coming up empty.

A woman came into the room. Her white coat gave her the ranking power of anyone there. The clipboard she held had the information needed to discuss Halen's immediate and prolonged health concerns. "Am I interrupting?"

"No," Halen said with a sarcastic sigh. "I imagine the detectives want to hear everything you have to say, whether it's pertinent to their case or not."

"Do you want me to talk to you alone and then you can decide to tell them?" the doctor asked.

"No, my brain is a little foggy. I won't know how to explain it to them." Halen looked at the detectives, then back to the doctor. "Just tell them what you think happened."

The doctor looked from Halen to the detectives. "Okay. I'll need you to sign a release form."

THE HIT

A nurse stepped forward and presented the paper to Halen, explaining what each paragraph said. Halen scanned the page, then signed the paper. After handing it back to the nurse, she looked around the room. The nurse left, and Detective Milton stepped back and shut the door.

"We found benzodiazepine in your system. It appears that someone slipped you some Rohypnol." The doctor paused to let the information sink in.

"Row-hip-what?" Halen asked.

"Ruh-hip-nahl," Detective Milton said, pronouncing each syllable. "It's a roofie."

Understanding dawned on her. "Was I raped?" Halen asked flatly.

"No. There was nothing that would indicate that," the doctor said.

Halen nodded; her muscles relaxed at the fortunate news.

"There's more," she continued. Both Halen and the two detectives were now riveted to the news of additional findings. "We found diacetylmorphine, more commonly known as heroin, in your system as well."

Halen's eyes grew large. "I know that I have never done heroin."

"The level was dangerously high. High enough to have killed you. Someone must have given you naloxone, also known as Narcan, to counteract the effects of the heroin. We found that in your urine test also."

The doctor looked from Halen to the detectives and back to Halen. "Do you have any questions, Halen?"

She shook her head. "No. Not right now."

The doctor excused herself and walked out.

Halen turned to the detectives. "You guys know more than I do now."

"Is there anything else you can think of that might help us identify this man?" Detective Perez asked.

She shook her head slowly. "Sorry. Last night is a complete blur."

"Halen, you were at Rezzer's almost two days ago."

"Wow. Fu . . ." Halen paused, thinking about the backhand Tracer had dealt her when she had dropped the f-bomb, and changed her mind. "Fun."

"We have a few photos of the man from that night," Detective Milton said.

He passed the sheet to Halen. The sheet of paper had three photos from grainy CCTV images. The first image showed the same man carrying what looked like Halen into the apartment building. In the second photo, he was setting her down in front of Deenya's door. The third showed the man entering the elevator. In each photo, the man held his head so his face was blocked from each camera by his hat.

"Does this man look familiar?" Detective Milton asked.

Alarming thoughts began to form in Halen's mind. Though this man wore the same clothes as the man in the other pictures, he also wore a broad brimmed hat and seemed different somehow.

"He exited the apartment building and left in the same car that he came in."

"Do you know where he's at?" Halen asked.

"Yes," Detective Perez said. "He's dead."

"What was that about?" Deenya asked as she skirted the edge of the hospital bed.

Halen struggled to comprehend all she had been told by both the doctor and the detectives. "I don't know. I can't flippin' put two things together."

"Well, how about you tell me one thing at a time and I'll write everything down?" Deenya offered. She pulled out her phone and opened a notepad. "Tell me any one thing. We'll start by making a list, then organize it later." She pulled a chair up to Halen's bedside.

"Okay. I don't remember drinking more than two drinks." Halen sat herself up higher in the power bed.

Deenya typed into her phone.

"I was talking with a former friend."

"Former friend?"

"Yeah, classic me. I use them and lose them. Well, I was desperate for a confidant. Told her something that ended up on the buzz net's greatest hits." Halen looked at Deenya. "Where's Cheshlan?"

"She's with Clayton."

"Who?"

"Clayton. Remember, you dragged me to the studio to create a shark. The model who I made the costume for?"

"Yeah." Halen looked at her friend's blushing face. "What's going on?"

"I . . . uh . . . We talked for a time after the shoot and before his event the next day. I didn't have him as a model again, but he was in the booth next to mine."

Halen waited. When nothing more came, she impatiently asked, "And?"

"We made arrangements to go out tonight."

"Why are you here?" Halen asked.

"Because of you. I wanted to check on you, and he wanted to know that you were okay also."

"Thank you. Tell Clayton I said thank you for stopping by. You guys are going out?" Halen sipped some ice water, set the cup back on the food tray and pushed it aside. "Where are you going?"

"Well, he asked if I wanted to see a movie. I said sure. I asked if he had a movie in mind. He said whatever Cheshlan wanted would be what he wanted to see."

"A first date and he wanted to take both of you out? Wow. That's something."

"I know. That's a first for me."

"Guard your heart. You know those Hollywood types—they'll love ya and leave ya," Halen joked, giving Deenya a wink.

"I'll take it slow. It was really nice that he wanted to take Cheshlan along too." Deenya focused her attention back to the list. "Anyway, what was this former friend's name?"

"Greta."

"Last name?"

Halen searched her thoughts. "I don't remember."

"What else do you know for sure?" Deenya asked.

"Oh geez." Halen stared into space, thinking. "I remember dancing. There was this guy who I think was handsome. I remember a car. I think it was red. Then I was here. At times I think I was awake, yet I remember wild, crazy dreams. Sometimes they felt real, but when I think of them, they seem totally absurd."

Deenya typed furiously, trying to get everything down.

"The doctors said I had enough heroin in my system to kill me, and the roofie was over-the-top also."

"It sure seems like someone tried to kill you. What else did they say?"

Halen had withdrawn into herself. She stared down at her lap, one hand cupping the other. "Am I that horrible of a person?" She looked at Deenya, distraught. Tears streamed down her face as she sought to grasp anything that would give her a sense of meaning and purpose.

Deenya moved to sit on the edge of the bed. "You are my friend. She picked up both of Halen's fidgeting hands. "Yes, you hurt my feelings way back when, but you made up for it by pulling me up out of a hole I would have died in. For that, I am truly grateful, and you're definitely not a bad person in my book. And for now, that's the only one that counts." She drew Halen into a hug.

"Ow, ow-ow," Halen said.

"Ohmigod. What?"

"My IV."

"Oh. I'm sorry. I'm even trying to kill you here."

Halen gave her a cautionary look.

"At least I'm trying to be nice about it," Deenya said.

"That's not helping," Halen warned.

"Even if I wanted to or did or whatever, Cheshlan would hate me all the way to the grave. I can't have her feel that way about me. She's your number one fan."

"I know. She keeps asking me to have lunch with her at school." Halen leaned back.

"You're gonna have to." Deenya moved back to her chair.

"I know," Halen said. "It'll break her heart if I don't."

"Who would want you dead?" Deenya said, drawing them both back to the current issue.

"Probably everyone that knows me. No one wanted to work with me on the last film I was cast in. I can't blame them. I was a bitch."

"What's done is done. What are you going to do next?"

"Be a better person, if people will let me." Halen mentally shrank from the new path she was forced down. She knew it was better, but it was still very unfamiliar.

"What do you suppose all this means? I mean with being drugged and all," Deenya asked.

"I don't know," Halen said. "Maybe I should move. Ya know, move somewhere where no one knows me."

"Do you really think that someone new might be trying to kill you?" Deenya scanned her notes, looking for a connection.

"I guess . . . it's possible." Halen alluded to the possibility, even though she knew all too well what Tracer had told her.

"Is it possible that the drugs found their way into your system by accident or an accidental overdose?"

"If I took them voluntarily, I really don't remember." Halen took another sip of water. Her head continued to throb.

"How many drinks did you have before you became oblivious to your surroundings?" Deenya scrolled through her notes.

"Two?"

"Two typical drinks?" Deenya asked.

Halen nodded. "Yeah. Depending on how strong they are, two is usually just a buzz for me. How about you?"

"Mmmm. Yeah. Uncontrolled laughter, that's drinks seven through nine," Deenya confessed.

"What happens at ten?" Halen asked.

"That's when I start over."

The sarcasm wasn't lost on Halen. "Only ten. Wow. Such a lightweight," she chided.

"I believe it's the other way around for you, Miss One-Two-Floor." Deenya brought the conversation back around to their investigation. "What else is there?"

"Well, I was roofied and injected with enough heroin to kill me."

"You weren't assaulted?" Deenya asked, then added, "Sexually, that is?"

Halen shook her head. "You would think that I would have been. Isn't that the whole point of knocking someone out? So they can do whatever they want with them without opposition." Halen adjusted the IV in her hand after bumping it.

"You're not wrong. That's the most common illegal use for the drug. What else is there?"

"They said that the Narcan was the only thing that saved my life."

"Okay, I got it." Deenya tapped at her phone. "What else?"

"The detectives told me that the man I danced with brought me to your door and left me," Halen said.

"I remember a loud banging on the door. I got up and went to open it. You fell through the door. I thought you were just passed out drunk. I was so tired, I didn't think to check for more than if you were breathing. So I dragged you to the couch and rolled you onto it, threw a blanket over you and set a trash can next to you, then went back to bed."

Halen sat silent, listening to the parts of her life that she couldn't remember. She realized change was needed now more than ever. She had to do something. She had to change or she would die like she almost had that night.

"Oh. My poor sweetie." The voice was like nails across a chalkboard.

36

Halen's shoulders slumped as Kimberly burst through the door and began moving equipment and monitors to accommodate her distorted opinion of how the room should be organized. She threw her purse up over her shoulder, poked her head out the door and flagged down a nurse who was already hurrying to another patient. "Miss. Miss. Can you get another pillow for my daughter? She isn't comfortable."

"Mom. I'm fine. They're going to discharge me soon."

"Oh, hush," Kimberly said and turned back to the nurse, who was another three steps away.

"Check with the nurse's station," the woman said as she turned and sped away.

Kimberly huffed at the nurse before stalking off to the desk, where a mix of activity was in play.

"Is she always like this?" Deenya asked when Kimberly was out of earshot.

Halen nodded. "Always has her best interests at heart at the expense of my sanity. She's a good mom. Overbearing toward others at times, but good."

"I guess I might act out too. Just to see what I could get away with," Deenya said, saving the list and tucking her phone away.

Kimberly charged back into the room with a wide-eyed young woman in tow. The woman's plain blue scrubs looked as if they had just been pulled off the store rack, while her shoes were scarred and worn.

"Can you move those monitors away from my daughter's head? The electromagnets will damage her brain. And could you organize these tubes and wires? They are all a mess and not color-coordinated." Kimberly turned her attention to Halen. "Oh, you look dreadful. Let me just get into my purse and get some concealer."

"Mom. I'm fine. I don't need any makeup."

Kimberly waved off Halen's comment. "Oh, you're just saying that. Here." Kimberly flipped through the cabinets until she found the one with extra bedding.

"Mom. I'm fine. I don't need a pillow. I don't need the hospital rearranged, and the staff doesn't need to be educated on how you think they need to do their job." Halen scoffed at her mother. The nurse's aide that had followed Kimberly into the room stood wide-eyed and unsure of what needed to be done.

"Oh, you don't know what you're saying. The medicine they have you on is keeping you from thinking straight," Kimberly said as she fished out a container of base from her purse.

"Mom. They have the discharge papers right there." Halen pointed toward the nurse standing in the doorway. The nurse's aide excused herself, likely to tell the tale of the entitled and overbearing mother who had been shut down by her daughter.

"All the more reason to look presentable," Kimberly insisted. "You know that there will be cameras out front."

"I don't care about the cameras, Mom."

"Oh hush. You're still delirious from your night out."

"Mom. Enough," Halen barked.

Seeing that she wasn't going to win the argument, Kimberly came forward for a hug. "I'm just happy that you're alive. Sorry I couldn't get here sooner. I just found out and traffic was bothersome."

"I'm fine, Mom," Halen said flatly, realizing that she could do little to dissuade her intentions. The irksome interruption aggravated her, as it seemed she was on the verge of putting together a few pieces of the puzzle that Deenya had written down. Had it been coincidental, or was someone trying to kill her again? Tracer had said he was paid to kill her, but he hadn't. And he didn't say who had paid him. Instead of ending her life, he decided to kidnap her and teach her how to defend herself. But he was dead now—drowned in a Canadian river. She was on her own to figure out who had ordered her death and whether that person was still trying to kill her, or if one of the many people she had angered in her life was picking up where Tracer had faltered.

Halen broke from the hug. "Mom, do you remember Deenya?" Halen motioned to her friend, who was sitting in a chair in the corner.

"Who?" Kimberly asked.

"Deenya. My friend from third grade," Halen explained.

Kimberly turned and peered down at Deenya. "Oh. Well, it's good to see you again."

"Hey, Mrs. Rossi."

Kimberly looked her up and down. "You're one of those who did this to my daughter?" The kind, endearing voice suddenly dripped with venom. "You pumped my daughter full of drugs, then have the gall to sit there while my daughter is in pain. Get out. Get out now."

Deenya scooted the chair back, trying to inch away. She was defenseless, and Kimberly's almighty scowl could burn any potential threat to ash.

"Mom," Halen argued. "She helped save me."

Kimberly turned to her. "She what?"

"She helped saved me. She let the police in and they recognized that I needed help."

"She did?" Kimberly looked back at Deenya. "Oh. I'm sorry, my dear." Her face lost its scowl and brightened considerably. "Halen seems to run with many undesirable people. I thought you were one of those."

"Oh. No. I'm here trying to . . ." Deenya saw Halen hold a finger to her lips. ". . . help see that she gets back on her feet again."

"Oh. Well, thank you. But I think she needs her mother. I'll see that she gets home as soon as the doctors release her. You can go now." Kimberly shooed her away with a wave of her hand.

"I'd better go check on Cheshlan. Call me when you're better, Hay-Hay." Deenya gathered her bag and straightened her clothes. Kimberly blocked her from giving Halen a hug, so she gripped Halen's hand across the hoses and wires.

Halen turned back to her mother and sighed, preparing for the preening that was about to commence.

"I don't know if you should be hanging out with someone like that," Kimberly said as she rifled through her bag, extracting a flat iron, a curling iron and a brush. "Doesn't matter. You'll be really busy in the next few months. I've gotten Drake Benguardie to consider you for his upcoming film. You need to meet with him tomorrow. Do you want to know the best part? I'll tell you. They're filming in Tuscany. Oh, I can't wait to try the food there. I imagine it will be amazing, and the vineyards . . ."

Halen tuned her mother out and thought about the young man she'd danced with. He had taken her back to Deenya's door, and now he was dead. The shock of information made her dizzy, and her mother pulling on her hair didn't help.

An inspection of her broken fingernails caused her to sigh. Her mother would soon see them, and she'd get another lecture of how important nail care was while she cleaned, filed, glued and painted new ones on her before she could set foot outside her hospital room.

There was a knock at Deenya's door. A squeal followed by thudding feet raced from a back room to the apartment's front door.

"I'll get it!" Cheshlan screamed as she skidded in her sock feet around the corner of the kitchen.

"Tell Clayton to come in." Deenya called from the bathroom. "Offer him one of the cookies we made today."

"Okay, Mommy."

The door opened. "Hey Clayton, I put up all the posters in . . ." Cheshlan's voice fizzled to a whisper, then silence.

"Oh." Cheshlan caught herself. "Hello."

"Hi. Is Halen here? I'm Greta, Halen's best friend."

"Um . . . Mom," Cheshlan called out.

Deenya rounded the corner, fastening an earring into an ear. "Is Clayton here, baby?" She slowed when she saw the trio of girls outside the door.

Straightening her posture and her shirt, she gently guided Cheshlan behind her. "Hello. Can I help you?"

"Hi, I'm Greta. I wanted to stop by and see if Halen was feeling better and to see if she wanted to go with us to Benny's."

The woman smiled pleasantly, though Deenya didn't feel comforted by it. Greta played with a strand of her dark wavy hair. The feathered ends perfectly framed her face and readily inspired a renewed trend. Aside from the modern makeup with a touch of glitter, the young woman looked like a model from a page of a seventies fashion magazine.

Her slight smile broadened to show a row of perfectly straight teeth. "I tried calling her, but it went straight to voice mail. She left early from the club the other night."

"She's not here right now," Deenya said.

"She's in the hospital," Cheshlan volunteered, not comprehending the subtle positioning of the friend-foe relationship.

Greta gasped, triggering her two friends to follow suit. Deenya recognized their phony surprise. The bad acting fit with their style. The clones behind Greta turned to each other, whispering.

Greta leaned forward with mock sincerity. "Is she alright?"

Deenya didn't think they could be any more fake. "I think so. Time will tell though." Deenya shifted uneasily from one foot to the other, eager to find a way to shut the door on the three women.

"Oh. Is she still there?" Greta asked.

"Who are you, again? I didn't quite catch your name." Deenya asked, suspecting she knew who the first of the trio was.

"I'm Greta. Greta Portnov. I was Halen's second last winter, before she disappeared. How do you know her?" The question seemed forced, like a bad interrogator attempting to squeeze answers from a suspect.

Deenya recognized the prying question. Her comfort level dropped even more as if she had fallen on a bed of nails. "Second?" Deenya wanted whatever information she could get and fought the urge to shut the door on the trio.

"Yeah. I'm her best friend and her understudy for a recent film." Greta continued her sweet smile. Deenya still didn't feel any warmth from it. "And you?"

"I met her in class."

"Class?" Greta inquired.

Clayton moved up behind the women. Deenya was momentarily distracted by his tight T-shirt gripping the familiar sculpted muscles hidden underneath.

"Acting class?"

"Yeah." Deenya's voice trailed off as her knight in rippling muscles approached the door.

His deep voice greeted the women. "Ladies."

Startled, the trio turned to see the tall male model. He towered over the three. Greta's friends were sheepish, but Greta looked as though her favorite dish had just been served to her.

"Hey, Clayton." Deenya's heart gave an extra thump of excitement at seeing the kind man who adored her daughter. Cheshlan squeezed past her mom and grabbed Clayton's hand, dragging him inside.

"Excuse me, ladies. I have an appointment with an interior decorator."

Cheshlan and Clayton disappeared inside, leaving Deenya alone with the socialites. "Last I knew, she was still in the hospital."

"We checked. They said she was released earlier. So we thought she was here."

"Why would you think she would be here? I only started leasing this place a week ago." Deenya folded her arms.

Greta's giggle sent a shiver up Deenya's spine. "Oh. Miss D, everyone knows Halen is back, and everyone knows where she's been hanging out."

"Obviously you don't, or you wouldn't be here." Deenya inclined her head, emphasizing the hole in her story. "Is there anything else I can help you with?" Her tone was anything but inviting.

Greta straightened. "Maybe we could go out sometime, have a girls' night out."

"Maybe."

Greta turned to leave.

Deenya looked up suddenly and called out to her. "What was that guy's name that Halen was dancing with?"

"Dill Wesley. Why?" Greta asked.

"Oh. I just wanted to know whose family to send condolences to."

Greta stiffened. She looked Deenya in the eye for a beat, then continued down the hall toward the elevators.

"Mom. You can't hold me hostage," Halen argued.

"Halen, you're not well. You need to rest. You need to go right back to your room. I'll bring you that special chicken noodle soup you always like," Kimberly said.

"Mom, I'm fine. I don't need your friend's chicken noodle soup. I have to go." Halen groaned.

"I'm an adult. It's time I started becoming more independent."

"You tried that before and look what happened. You were kidnapped, held captive and forced to do unspeakable . . . ugh." Kimberly shook her head at her own graphic imagination.

"Mom, you can't keep me bottled up. I am a grown woman. I need to build my own life."

"A lot of good your decisions have done for you," Kimberly scolded. "I worked all these years to protect you, and this is how you treat me."

"Mom, I know I've treated you bad. I want to fix that, but I can't do that while you're smothering me." Halen moved closer to the door. "I want you to be proud of me."

"I am proud of you." Kimberly's lip started to quiver.

"Of what, Mom?" Halen inched back into the foyer. "What have I done that makes you proud? Did the drinking and drugs make you proud?"

Kimberly stared back at her daughter, searching for something convincing to say.

"Well, I'm not proud of me," Halen continued. "I need to find myself and become a responsible adult. I can't do that here."

"You are still sick. You need to get back into bed until you're better." Kimberly trembled as she faced her down. But a moment later, Halen's question registered. "I am proud of you, baby. We made movies together, and we . . . I would be prouder if you would get back in bed and I'll bring you some soup."

Kimberly had half turned away when Halen spoke. "I'm not eight anymore. You need a dog. A dog who will love you and demand that you take care of it all day, every day. When I get home, we'll talk and see if we can find you a puppy."

"I don't need a puppy." Kimberly stomped her foot. "I need you to get back in bed. You are still sick."

Kelson Rossi walked out of his home office, heading for the kitchen. He'd just reached for the refrigerator handle when he was interrupted.

"Kels, tell our daughter that she is still sick and needs to stay home," Kimberly demanded.

Kelson looked at his wife, then at Halen. "You're still sick and need to stay home," he said in a flat, unemotional tone. He looked at Halen, then opened the refrigerator. "Halen, if you feel well enough, then go."

Kelson had been little more than the bill payer of the household. He didn't go to the acting classes, award ceremonies or auditions. He didn't give much for fatherly advice, though he was an encyclopedia when it came to the law. Halen felt he would rather have had just the trophy wife, minus the child.

"Go," Kelson said. "You have a life to live. Go live it."

Halen was a little surprised by the simplified pep talk. It was just one of the very few encouraging things he had ever said to her.

"Thank you," she said with sincerity, and stepped out the door.

Before this confrontation, she had spent two days sleeping and letting her body heal itself from the double overdose. Her mother had checked on her consistently, bringing her food and medicine and tending to her every need. Halen appreciated the attention until it became smothering and she wouldn't let her get out of bed to exercise.

Halen knew it was time for her to get up and do something. With medicine from the doctor, the body aches, nausea and sniffles subsided, and for the first time in three days, she felt somewhat normal.

The months she'd spent in the mountains had forced her to get off drugs. The intense training taught her to strengthen her mind and that there was more to life than seeking the next high.

If you don't know what bad really is, you will never know good. It was a phrase that Tracer had used almost daily as he nearly beat the hell out of her until she learned to defend herself from his abuse.

At times she had refused to fight back and surrendered herself to die. She just didn't care. When she refused to play his game, he dragged her back and forth between the frigid cold and the steaming hot water until she fought back one more time. The continued abuse had sharpened her mind to focus on overcoming the obstacle in front of her. The chills from the heroin withdrawal reminded her to steel her mind and focus on the demon in front of her.

She had to get her life together. She had to find out what happened to her. She had to find out more about the man captured on CCTV. She had to go see Deenya.

37

The knock on Deenya's door had gone unanswered. Halen stood there for several minutes searching for something to tell her what to do. The hallway to either side was as empty as her thoughts on where to go next. With a sigh, she returned to the elevator and descended to the lobby. Deenya must be out somewhere enjoying the challenges of her new job.

At the front desk of the apartment building, she was met by a flock of reporters who had been tipped off that she was in the area. Cornering her against the counter, the group cast a blur of questions at her. Cameras and phones were pushed out to the extent of the reporters' reach, each seeking to capture an image or video to complement any story they could develop. Any bit of information could be enough to make the headlines and become the catalyst to launch careers and help companies surge in sales with a juicy clickbait story.

The throng of bodies pressed in on her, crushing her personal space. One woman shoved a phone in front of her with an image of the young man she had danced with at the club. He was lying on top of a beach towel in a cluster of bushes, obviously deceased. Halen reached out, grabbed the phone and broke it across the edge of the counter.

The reporters gasped at the sudden act; some took a step backward. The instant change in atmosphere jolted Halen back to the real world and the mistake she had just made. She had reacted to the image, afraid she might have been responsible for the young man's untimely death. Now she wanted to run, needed to run, but there was nowhere to go that would be safe from the reporters.

She couldn't think with the onslaught of questions blazing at her like bullets from a machine gun.

"Miss, back here," came a voice from behind the counter.

Halen turned to find a young man holding a door open to the back office area.

Seeing the opportunity to escape the press and their questions, Halen sprang effortlessly over the counter and ducked into the back office. The young man closed the door, muting the questions and the quests for answers.

"Thank you," Halen said. She turned to the young man. His face was flushed like a child's after a first kiss.

Halen looked at his name tag. "Nick. Oh, thank you, Nick. That was crazy. I really wasn't prepared to face cameras and answer questions." She glanced around the back office for another escape route. Nick, still flushed with his jaw hinging, tried to form a coherent sentence. Halen hesitated after seeing that her hero had become a useless starstruck statue.

She looked around the maze of halls and back offices meant for the building's employees. A flicker of light came from a room next to Halen. She backed up a few steps and peered inside. As she had thought, it was the surveillance and security area. Banks of screens lined one entire wall, constantly switching between camera feeds. The heat from the computers, monitors and other equipment gave a hint of a burning plastic smell.

"Y . . . you're welcome." Nick finally found his voice. He still had an exuberant smile, but the red on his face had dulled a bit.

"God. What do I do?" Halen looked at the monitors and the cluster of people still milling around the office lobby. A young woman slunk around the end of the counter and put an ear to the door they had just gone through. She held a recording device in her hand and gently placed it against the door. Halen looked closer at the screen, then back at Nick, who was also leaning forward to see what the woman was doing.

"Does she have a listening device?" Halen asked. "Is she listening through the door?"

Everything on the monitor indicated that she was doing just that.

"That is flipping rude and illegal," Halen whispered to Nick.

"I got this," Nick said and turned to a room across the hall. He reemerged with a large cup, wrapped his lips around the straw and pulled hard on the drink. Stepping close to the door, he paused, waiting for a few seconds. Halen could see the strain on his face as he focused his superpower. He twisted his body, putting the slightest pressure on his stomach.

A roar erupted from his gut, vibrating the door. Halen watched the monitor along with the security guard who had just arrived. The woman on the other side of the door backed away, peering at her recorder as if it had suddenly become contaminated with something that might also infect her.

Halen's mouth dropped open in surprise and excitement—the reporter had gotten a small bit of karma. Nick straightened and gave a slight bow. Halen congratulated him with applause while the big security guard rolled his eyes. Apparently, he had been witness to Nick's superpower before.

"I'll go kick that mob out of here," the large man said and started for the door.

"Um," Halen started. The two men turned to look at her. "I haven't done any sort of official interview since I've gotten back."

"What are you saying, Miss Kettleman?" the large security guard asked.

Halen read his name tag. His eyes were bright and friendly, though she would hate to see what he was like if she got on his bad side. "Juan, Nick, if you could spare a conference room for a few minutes, I would like to answer a few of their questions."

"Okay," Juan said.

"Except for that one who was trying to listen through the door. You can kick her out of here."

Halen looked between Juan and Nick, seeking their approval.

"We got you, Miss Kettleman." Juan stepped through the door and shut it behind him.

"Nick. Wow. What a talent."

Nick grinned like a child who had won a first-place ribbon for finger painting.

"So the reason I came here was to look at the videos from a few days ago. A man brought me to my friend's apartment and left me at her door. Is it possible for me to view that footage? My brain was a little foggy for the last few days, and I'm trying to piece things together."

"Oh. You're that girl." Nick connected the dots. "The police impounded the memory cards."

"Shit." Halen ran her hands through her hair. She turned to look down the hall toward the back offices.

"Okay." She spun in a circle, looking for an option. Something that would inspire her to think of a solution. She spun again in the opposite direction, looking at the elegant trim molding that offered little to suggest an answer. She stopped and sighed. Her arms flopped back to her sides. "I can do this. Do you have a powder room?"

Nick looked at her blankly for a moment before he realized what she was asking. "Oh, sorry. The ladies' room is down the hall and to the left."

Halen followed his directions. Her nervous bladder had suddenly become a concern, as she would be facing the paparazzi without anyone to back her up. No friends, no manager, not even her mom would be there to handle damage control if she should slip up. She started to sweat. This new version of herself was going to take a bit to get used to. To not run from a confrontation took effort, and she had seldom put forth effort for anything besides acting. She knew how to act from a script or under direction, but this was unfamiliar and far from comfortable.

She fussed with her hair a bit and wished she at least had a tube of lipstick, but her pockets were empty. A woman came into the restroom, walked purposefully to a stall and closed the door. Halen assumed she was part of the apartment building staff or possibly a resident. But through the mirror, she saw a phone peeking out from under the stall.

Rage boiled through her veins at the disrespect and violation of privacy. She messed with her hair again, then stepped back to straighten her clothes, all the while keeping the phone in sight in the mirror. She had backed up nearly to the stall where the woman was filming from. In a flash, she whipped around, snatched the phone out of the woman's hand and marched out of the lavatory.

Back in the security room, Juan greeted her. Nick stood nearby with his childlike grin, ready to jump to Halen's bidding like a trained puppy.

"All the reporters are in the conference room, Miss Kettleman." Juan waited, ready to escort her. She mentally prepared herself for the firing line of reporters.

"Thank you, Juan." Halen sighed deeply and looked up to the large man. "Okay. I'm ready."

"I told them we needed to have this room back in thirty minutes for an upcoming event," Juan told her.

"Oh."

"I told them they would all have an opportunity to ask you one question each." He led the way down the hall. "I also told them they would not be allowed to take any photos."

"You know they're going to want photos."

"I know," Juan said over his shoulder. "You can amend that if you like, and if they behave."

"Thank you, Juan."

"No problem, Miss Kettleman."

"Juan."

"Yes, Miss Kettleman."

"Call me Halen. Please."

Halen entered the conference room, expecting to be assaulted by a volley of questions. The assembly of paparazzi sat obediently waiting for a chance to be the first to ask a question. Each sat with a pen and a notepad; some whispered to their neighbors.

The whispers halted when Halen entered. She scanned the room and found a line of phones on a separate table. She cast Juan a questioning glance.

"I told them they had to leave their phones on the table and take notes old school." He gave her a wink.

Halen smiled. The ground rules had been made perfectly clear, and any violation would be met with the large security guard escorting them out of the room.

"Thank you, Juan." Halen turned to the small assembly. "Well. Surprise. I'm not dead."

A chuckle spread through the group. Halen pulled out a chair and prepared to sit. "I suppose everyone is eager to know where I've been and what I've been doing."

Smiles and nods spread across the group. A few scribbled down every word she said. Halen made a final scan of the collected faces and took a deep breath.

"Honestly, I was kidnapped." Halen breathed a sigh of relief, having said out loud what she had been keeping bottled up.

"Were you assaulted?" a young man with a boyish face asked.

"The short answer, yes. What was done to me was at times horrific," Halen said, standing poised and calm.

"Were you assaulted sexually?" the man asked again.

"One question per person, please. I don't have a lot of time. This room will be needed again shortly." She turned from the man and sought out another eager hand waving in the air. She pointed to the young woman next to him, thinking to just go down the line so everyone would have an opportunity to ask their question.

The woman straightened and cleared her throat. "Were you sexually assaulted?" The woman sat ready to scribble Halen's answer.

"Oh, I see. Sex sells. Gets a passel more clicks than regular old assault," Halen mocked with an British accent. "No. Sorry, no extra clicks for you."

She started to relax and banter with the people before her.

A thick woman in the back of the group raised her hand, then spoke up when called upon. "Where—"

Juan was suddenly right there between the group and Halen. "Young man, I told you no pictures." A large hand reached out and seized the reporter's hand. "Come with me. You agreed to the rules, and you broke them."

Juan kept a large meaty grip on the camera and the hand that held it. He led the man to the table, where he gathered his phone and escorted him toward the door.

Halen turned back to the group, who stared wide-eyed at the security guard escorting the man out.

"Well, I hope you guys have more respect than that guy did." Halen fixed a glare on them, wondering if anyone else was going to step out of line. "I don't have time for that and neither do you. Two questions are gone, and more importantly two answers. Am I correct?"

Most of the group nodded while a couple answered with yeses.

"You bitch."

All eyes turned to the open door Juan had just left through. A woman marched up to Halen, her face tense and angry. Halen was sure someone had replaced her thong with a thorn.

"Give me back my phone," the woman blurted out.

Halen pretended to be surprised by the accusation. "What phone are you talking about?"

"You know damn well what I'm talking about," the woman hissed.

"I did find a phone in the bathroom. I was going to turn it in to the front desk. Can you describe the last photo taken with it?"

The group of reporters sat with saucered eyes, dumbfounded at the bravado of the woman verbally attacking the starlet. The woman glanced to the group, realizing the trap she had been led into. Her face flushed while her eyes desperately sought a solution to alter her original intentions.

Halen pulled the phone out of her back pocket. She swiped the screen, showing the woman that she had unlocked it.

"How'd you know the code?" the woman asked.

"Your pattern is etched into your screen protector. It only took me two tries to get in. You should maybe find a different line of work, because you are terrible at this." Halen glanced to the other reporters, who were devouring every word and scribbling on their pads of paper.

The woman redoubled her anger and focused it on Halen. Her jaw clenched as the rest of her face turned scarlet and scrunched into a scowl. She launched forward, swinging a roundhouse fist for Halen's face.

The wild swing whipped through the air like a comet on a collision course. Halen met the woman's punch with her own right hand, but not with a fist. Instead, it held the woman's phone. Glass cracked and the snap echoed through the room. The fancy phone broke as the reporter's fist struck it. Shards of glass fell when it buckled. Horror quickly turned to rage as the woman watched her phone fall to the floor, broken, bent and completely worthless.

She stepped forward, swinging again with the other hand. Halen stepped into the swing, catching the woman's arm and using the momentum to upend her and slam her onto her back. As she hit the floor, air rushed out of her lungs. Halen kept hold of the woman's arm just as Tracer had instructed her, twisting it so she could apply pressure at the elbow and force her to move where she directed.

"Let this be a lesson that honey works better than vinegar. Do you understand?" Halen growled down to the woman.

The woman stared up at Halen, struggling to pull air into her lungs when she finally nodded.

Juan appeared a moment later and gripped the woman's hand. He waited for her to catch her breath and helped her onto her shaky legs before escorting her out the door.

38

"Miss Kettleman—Wow, that was awesome," Nick gushed.

Halen took a sip of the lemon water Juan had given her. "What was?" She ran the recent events through her mind, trying to figure out what Nick was talking about. She had spent just short of thirty minutes answering questions from the group of reporters and posing for a few pictures. One man asked if she would flip him like she had flipped the rabid woman. She politely declined and thanked the reporters for their commitment to their readers and fans.

Nick continued to spew his admiration. "Flipping that woman over you and neutralizing her. I didn't know you could do that."

Halen hesitated, backing away from him half a step, evaluating his intentions. He looked at her with eager eyes, like a child waiting for the rest of a story.

"It was something I learned recently," Halen said.

"From that man in the video?" Nick asked.

His demeanor gave Halen pause. It felt a lot like he was leading her into a trap. A trap she didn't want to fall into.

"Yeah." She fibbed, knowing any answer she gave wouldn't satisfy him. "Look, I've got to go."

"But—"

"Sorry, Nick. I really have to go. I need to find my friend and take care of a few things." She did have to find Deenya, but she didn't have anything urgent on her to-do list.

"B-but . . ." Nick stammered.

Halen turned to walk out the front door.

"The man in the video is not the same man as on the news," Nick blurted out.

Halen stopped and turned.

"I don't think he's the same guy they found on the beach." Nick waved a data stick in the air.

"When will you hear back from them?" Deenya asked.

"Sometime in the next few days. They say they have a few people moving out soon and will let me know which apartment opens up first."

"I hope it's one on this floor," Deenya said, scanning the computer screen.

"Me too," Halen said.

"Why can't she just stay here?" Cheshlan called from across the room.

"Because, sweetie, she's a big girl now and needs to stand on her own two feet. Just like you will have to someday."

Disappointed, Cheshlan looked at her feet for a moment, then popped her head back up. "She can move across the hall."

"Sweetie, someone already lives across the hall," Deenya explained.

"Maybe they have an empty room." Cheshlan worked every angle she could to have Halen move as close as possible.

"Chesh, I don't think they would like the way my feet smell," Halen said, dodging the commitment.

Cheshlan walked around the couch and picked up one of Halen's feet. After giving it a big whiff, she set it back down, crinkling her nose.

"Well?" Deenya asked.

"It smells like weird strawberries," Cheshlan said and turned back to her TV show.

Deenya laughed and Halen rolled her eyes.

"Can't argue with an expert," Deenya said, grinning at her friend.

Halen threw a pillow at her. "You hush."

Deenya leaned back to the computer screen. "Look here. See how he tips his hat down."

"Yeah." Halen studied the video footage of the man carrying her into the building until he left. Even freezing every frame, they were never able to get a clear image of his face.

"I think he knows where the cameras are and is purposefully hiding his face from them," Deenya said.

"He looks like the guy I danced with. I remember the red striped shirt, and he was fairly tall. Yet it doesn't look like him either. Could he have a twin or a brother?"

"He could, I guess," Deenya admitted. "So this guy who kidnapped you—he told you he was paid to kill you and make it look like an accident?"

"Not in as simple of words." Halen shifted her feet up onto the couch and pulled a pillow on her lap, hugging it tight. At Deenya's expectant gaze, she continued. "He mentioned that he specialized in making peoples' deaths look like accidents."

Deenya covered the small gasp coming out of her mouth. "Oh shi—" She clamped a hand over her mouth tighter to prevent spilling the explicit word. "He's a serial killer?"

"No," Halen said. "He's a contract killer—a hit man."

"Holy fu—" Deenya once again clamped her hand over her mouth and looked over at Cheshlan, who was engrossed in a favorite show. "A hit man?" Deenya said a little quieter.

Halen nodded.

"Why didn't he kill you?" Deenya scooted closer and closed the laptop.

"Do you know that birthmark I have on my side?" Halen asked.

"Yeah, I remember. I always thought it looked like a funny-looking ice cream cone."

Halen shifted and pulled up her shirt, leaning a bit to the side to give Deenya a good view of the port-wine stain.

"That doesn't look like the ice cream cone I remember."

"Tilt your head the other direction." Halen leaned forward more.

Deenya tilted her head, then looked again. "Oh my god." She covered her mouth and laughed out loud. "Oh. I'm sorry. I don't mean to laugh. It caught me off guard when I finally saw it."

"Yeah, the middle finger, right?" Halen put her shirt back down.

Deenya nodded. "What does that have to do with the guy that kidnapped you?"

"Well, when I stitched him back up from the grizzly attack—"

"You were attacked by a grizzly?" Deenya leaned forward again in anticipation, as though a few inches would help her get the news faster.

"He was attacked. Not me," Halen said. "When I was first stitching up the claw marks on his side, I didn't see it right away because I had to get the wound to heal from the inside out. When I was able to stitch the skin back together I saw it."

"Saw what?" Deenya asked.

"He had a port-wine stain on his side that looked almost identical to mine." Halen sat back, waiting for the connection to be made. She could almost see the gears working inside her friend's head.

"Oh fuck," Deenya blurted out.

Cheshlan turned, her eyes wide in disbelief. "Mom!"

Spinning toward her daughter, she begged, "Oh, sorry, sweetie. I didn't mean to say that word."

THE HIT

With one hand on a hip and the other wagging a finger at her mother, Cheshlan said, "You really need to work on an alternative vocabulary."

"Mom, I'm home!" Halen called out after setting her bag down.

"In here, baby!" The voice rang through the house.

Halen made her way through the expansive house, following the sound of her mother's grand piano. Kimberly had justified the purchase of the piano because the former resident had a corner of the house that was perfect for optimizing acoustics. The piano stood just off center of a small stage, allowing room for a second or third artist to perform. Halen hadn't bothered to learn the piano. Her mother hadn't either. She just liked the way it looked in that location. A cello stood on a stand next to it. A guitar, violin and other instruments hung on the wall behind the piano, polished, in tune and ready to ignite the air with sound.

The housekeeping staff were the only ones who touched the instruments and only to clean them. Kimberly had a professional musician stop in every other month and before special occasions to make sure they were in tune should a guest feel the urge to play something. The instruments had sat on the stage doing more listening than speaking.

A twinkle of keys grew louder and cascaded a harmonious melody through the house. Halen rounded the corner. Her mother sat on a white leather couch, listening to the blend of sound and nodding along with the lulling melody. Halen looked at the artist sitting on the piano bench and found dark, tight curls that hung almost to the woman's shoulders. Her slim, athletic frame leaned and swayed gracefully with the tempo of the music, and her head wove as if emphasizing the next set of notes.

The soothing harmony conflicted with Halen's internal hackles as she realized that Greta was playing. She didn't know why she felt tension toward the woman; there was no obvious reason. If anything, Greta had been more than accommodating, especially since Halen had been so rude to her.

The music spoke to Halen and lulled her into a better mood. If she was going to turn her life around, she had to be open-minded and apologetic to everyone from her past. She pressed away the tension she had toward Greta and gave in to the melody.

For a few years, Greta had been a regular visitor to their house and a part-time resident. It seemed that in Halen's absence, she had continued to come over, just as she always had, and Halen reasoned that Greta must have been a significant comfort to her mother. Halen quelled her internal conflict in light of the new revelation. She couldn't fault her mother for seeking comfort from her friend—a comfort they both needed.

If Greta had kept her mother mostly sane through what must have been a devastating time, then she owed her a debt of gratitude. She could only imagine the pain of losing a child. She thought of Cheshlan and how attached the two of them were becoming. For a moment, she thought about the pain she might feel if something were to happen to the little girl. Whatever she felt, she was sure Deenya would go through a hundred times the anguish if something were to happen.

Halen quietly walked around the couch and sat an arm's length away from her mother. Kimberly reached out and Halen met her halfway. She gripped her hand and gave it a loving squeeze, then scooted closer. Greta continued playing, and Halen allowed herself to enjoy the music. Greta finished the piece, then launched into another.

Halen scooted closer, enjoying the intimate moment and letting her guard down. She knew it wouldn't last, but for a moment, she dissolved into the world that was. A world she'd ruined little by little, starting so long ago. By the end of the song, Halen was leaning against Kimberly, cuddling against her shoulder as if she were a small child.

Later, Halen sat across the table from Greta, with her parents on either end. Gourmet takeout had been dished onto dinnerware and set around the small kitchen table instead of the formal dining hall.

Kelson was his normal quiet self. He said little and asked for little, but when he asked for something, Kimberly promptly obliged, mostly because she was afraid he would leave and take his money with him, leaving her alone and insecure.

The silverware clinked against the white dinnerware. Wine gurgled into the stemware as Kimberly walked around the table, topping off everyone's glass before sitting down. Halen had only taken a sip from hers, while her mother filled her glass for a third time. Greta focused on her plate, dashing a bit of salt on her meal before automatically handing the shaker to Kelson.

Kelson had always been distant with Halen. He was a workaholic, preferring to be at the office rather than at home.

When Greta passed the salt, Halen recognized the familiarity. Her ex-friend had anticipated that her stepfather would need it. In the exchange, Halen thought she saw Greta's pinky finger reach out and give the slightest brush against Kelson's hand.

Halen shook it off. It was probably no more than Greta being here so often that like anyone, she had learned when someone would want something at a particular time. People were creatures of habit, and learning those habits was the same as working together with someone, like Halen had with Tracer. She'd learned his behavior, his preference for coffee and the way he rolled the dice in their backgammon games. She turned her attention back to her salmon and tried to put those thoughts from her mind.

The salmon had been expertly prepared, as Kelson wouldn't settle for less. He never did. Everything he did was done to perfection. He left nothing to chance, and it showed in everything he did, especially when it came to his work.

"Oh, this is wonderful isn't it?" Kimberly said, breaking the silence. "We're all back together. Kels is being considered as a full partner. Greta just landed a role on *Guilty Rich*. And Halen, my sweet Halen, is home. She has an audition with Drake Benguardie for his new film. They're filming in Tuscany. Oh, I know we'll have a wonderful time. I've always wanted to go." Kimberly babbled on, barely touching her food, though the bottle of wine was now all but empty.

"Oh. Greta. Thank you for the wonderful music this evening."

"You're welcome, Mom," Greta said, then took a healthy bite of salmon. Halen had heard Greta call her mother that before and it had never bothered her. Now it felt odd. It wasn't the fun joking way she had always said it before. This time it was serious and intimate. She wondered if her absence had drawn them deeper into a mother-daughter relationship.

Small talk accompanied the rest of the meal, with nothing else out of the ordinary taking place, yet Halen felt uneasy. By the time the four had dispersed from the table, Halen was exhausted. The impromptu interview, an hour of being Cheshlan's best celebrity friend and the surprise of Greta visiting for the evening were all too much. And she still had to tell her mother that she was moving out.

39

Halen woke and looked at the clock on the nightstand: it was just after 3 a.m. Something felt off. She felt like she was being watched. A sliver of light coming through the cracked door drew her attention. She thought she had closed it. Maybe it hadn't latched and it popped open on its own.

A small slit between the curtains revealed a black sky with distant city lights from across the Biscayne Bay. They weren't the stars from the Canadian wilderness, and they didn't give her the unbelievable smallness she felt when looking up at them. These made her feel distant and disconnected and suppressed.

She slipped from between the covers, careful not to disturb them. The ambient glow coming through the curtains made it appear that she might still be under the thick comforter. Leaving the warmth of the covers behind, she roamed the cool, air-conditioned room. Something still felt off. Like she wasn't alone.

THE HIT

She looked around her room. Nothing seemed to be out of the ordinary, yet she felt uneasy. She sifted through her closet and found a black Darth Vader bathrobe she had been given as a gag gift.

Putting it on and pulling the hood up over her head, she slipped out of her room.

The hallway was quiet. Nothing stirred. Halen was happy that her mother didn't want a dog, as cleanliness and order were her top priorities, and Kelson never had the time for any pet. Halen was glad for it in this case, as a dog might alert the house that someone was sneaking around.

She walked to her mother's bedroom door and leaned an ear close to it. Soft, gentle snoring came from within. She was fast asleep. She slipped to Kelson's door next. She listened but couldn't hear anything. Turning back, she went to listen at the guest room where Greta was sleeping. She heard the rustling of blankets, then all was quiet.

Leaving the confines of the house, she made her way to the lush grass of the yard. Her bare feet sank down into thousands of blades tickling her toes and the soles of her feet. She remembered the brutal treatment and lessons from Tracer. It had heightened her awareness of all things around her, and it had stuck. She was feeling the thousands of blades like she was feeling the grains in the rock floor of the cave.

Something had caused her to wake up in the still of the night. Something she had to find. The solar lights next to the concrete and the lights from the city illuminated her path enough to keep her from stepping on her mother's flowers.

She glanced around the yard. A deep shadow in the corner drew her attention. The neighbor's cabbage palmetto draped its large leafy hands over the eight-foot wall, creating a concealed perch. The spot called to her. Gripping her toes on part of a Mediterranean-style statue, she clambered up the wall and turned to face her parents' yard. The slightest of breezes ruffled the foliage around her. She sat unmoving, listening to the night. Water lapped gently at their boatless dock.

Kelson had never bought a boat; his intense work ethic prevented such luxuries. And he wasn't one to entertain clients. That was his employer's job. Kimberly had insisted on the property, as many of her friends had boats and would stop by semi-frequently along with the growing elite circle that gravitated to Halen and her celebrity status.

The high wall reminded her of sitting outside the cave overlooking the valley and the encounter with the lynx. She liked the lynx and was fascinated by his enormous feet. Though she couldn't measure them, she thought they were as big as her own hands. She imagined playing a friendly clapping game like she did when she was younger, and how her hand might have seemed dwarfed by the cat's paws. She wished she could have another encounter like that one. The chances of that were next to zero. But she was warmed by the memory, and it was something no one could take away from her.

The night was quiet. Halen intermittently closed her eyes to listen. Water lapped at the dock. A car raced away in the night. Crickets chirped from the bushes, and the occasional breeze rustled the leaves. A door opened and closed on the property behind her. The owner escorted his elderly dog out to conduct its business, then back inside after a few minutes. The light extinguished and Halen turned her attention back to her parents' yard.

In a dark corner opposite her, she thought she saw movement. She blinked and looked again. Something was out of place in that area of the shrubbery. She studied it, trying to work out the shape. It couldn't be a person; the shadow looked far too lean to be a person hiding in the bushes, yet she felt something was there.

A latch clicked shut. Halen's eyes darted to the noise, then back to the suspected shadow. Nothing looked any different, yet something felt different. The shadows looked the same, swaying with the breeze that disturbed the needle palms. She didn't see anything out of the ordinary. But when she looked back at the latched door, a slim shape tiptoed across the tiled sidewalk. Halen stretched her frame to peer through an opening in the palm leaves. The figure was heading to the pool house.

It was Greta. Halen followed the woman with her eyes until she disappeared inside the small building. A light turned on inside. Her shadow on the curtains showed her crossing the room, and a short while later, the light went out.

Halen glanced around the yard, looking for anything else that might be out of place. Her mind jumped back to the cave and something Tracer had taught her. They had spent hours watching the wildlife go about their daily business of just surviving. In a way, this was no different. This was an assurance of survival. The muffled sounds coming from the guesthouse were the result of survival.

She started putting the pieces of the puzzle together. Greta was boosting Kelson's ego and sense of virility in exchange for supplementing her extravagant lifestyle.

"This is your way of survival." Halen spoke quietly to Greta, who wouldn't in a million years guess that she had been discovered by Darth Vader sitting atop an eight-foot wall. Halen's bedroom door being ajar must have been the result of Kelson looking in to see that she was sleeping soundly. She wondered what was in it for him. He could have any woman—why someone as young as Greta?

Was it a midlife crisis? Was it spurred by Kimberly's withdrawal and lack of affection when Halen had disappeared? She knew Kimberly never initiated intimacy and only rarely obliged Kelson's advances. She didn't know why, and it wasn't for her to ask. From friends, Halen had learned that her mother had gone into a deep depression and eventually went into therapy. Medication and intense counseling helped her cope with Halen's presumed death.

Halen was back now, and her mother had become more controlling, or at least she tried to be. She would shoo Halen's friends away. Most of them were bad influences anyway. Her lifestyle was different now. She didn't want to be encircled by admirers, except for Cheshlan. She didn't want to go out, especially after almost dying at the hands of someone she would have thought was a friend. She couldn't pinpoint or guess who it might have been, so she decided to make herself scarce to all her friends.

Greta was somehow an exception. The two of them had been close, finishing their educations together at a private high school. But in the past year, a snide remark about Halen's acting rubbed her the wrong way—though after listening to Tracer explain why he thought her acting was poor, she realized it was likely true. She booted Greta to the side and found a new bestie who would shower her with praise.

Shortly after their falling-out, she had been abducted. Her mom went into a depression, and Kelson dove more into work, as he was not a person who remotely understood the emotional needs of a woman. Halen had never really bonded with Kelson when she was growing up, as he was always working, and he was boring. Law was the ultimate boring subject to her.

Although Kimberly complained about the hardships of parenting, Halen could see now that it was a ploy for attention. She did little more than shuttle her from one class or event to another, seldom staying for the duration. Minders on the sets made sure Halen ate, finished her homework, played games and in general raised her. Advice came from many people she'd charmed at a young age, but no one was ever a permanent figure. Everyone moved on. Maybe it was that consistency she lacked growing up that caused her to make poor decisions.

Somehow Halen had survived her dangerous lifestyle. Now she was sitting on a wall, looking out across her family's yard like a Peeping Tom. She would have liked to compare herself to a wise, discerning owl, but she wouldn't want to offend those majestic creatures. The more she observed what was going on around her, the more foolish she felt. She now felt silly sitting on the wall, but she had learned some things about her family. It was time to quit her alley-cat patrol and go back to bed.

Reality hit her as hard as her feet hit the ground. She didn't feel upset, just disappointed. Disappointed that she was blinded by the route she was on because she hadn't known any other kind of lifestyle. She hadn't known anything less than luxury. Private cars would carry her and her mother anywhere they needed to be. They seldom waited for a table at a restaurant. When the crowds became too much at a store, her mother paid to have them close the doors for a private shopping session.

Halen had never been in want of anything until Tracer had taken her deep into Canada. She'd been without traditional shelter and was stripped bare of all material possessions, yet it had somehow become a magical and spiritual time in her life. She couldn't see it then, but she could now.

Walking across the lawn, she paused to look at the sky. Only a few stars were bright enough to reach through the city's glare. She felt like one of those stars she couldn't see, suppressed by the corporate world sitting just across the bay.

Halen made her way back to the house and slipped under the covers. It would upset her mother, but she would have to leave. She couldn't stay with all the hidden theatrics, all the fakeness that clouded her parents' house. It wasn't even a home.

Thoughts of why, how, who and when raced through her mind as she lay awake contemplating the new information. Sleep finally claimed her, hours after both Kelson and Greta had slipped back into the house and to their respective rooms. She concluded that she would move out permanently when morning came, whether there was an apartment on Deenya's floor or not.

40

"Set the couch over there," Halen said, stepping out of the way of the movers.

The husky men set the leather sofa down and attached the feet back to its base. She turned back to a box and began pulling framed pictures out, considering where she might hang them. Most of her clothes were left at her parents' house. They just didn't fit her sense of style anymore. She was no longer a partying teen. She wasn't a sophisticated lady either. She didn't know who she was. She was transitioning into an adult without a road map.

"We'll be right back with the bedroom furniture," one of the movers said. The four men left, taking the dollies and straps with them to handle the next load of furniture.

"Oh. Thank you. I'll leave the door unlocked. Just knock first, then come in," Halen said as she looked for the package of picture hangers she had bought. The door closed and she began to hum.

Cheshlan would be there as soon as school let out for summer vacation. Then Halen would have a permanent shadow for three solid months. She realized she only had this last week to make good on her promise to attend school lunch with her. Maybe she would go tomorrow if the movers didn't take too long.

She continued unpacking, waiting for the next load of boxes and furniture.

The knock sounded. Halen jumped. "That was fast." The door didn't open. "Come in," she called out.

She pulled out more pictures and arranged them on a counter, then rearranged them, trying to decide where each one would look the best.

The usual grunts and squeaky wheels didn't accompany the door opening. Halen turned.

Her mother stood just inside the door, hands folded in front of her. She had to have stopped by the salon, as her highlighted shag framed a pleasant face. Halen had told her mother she would look good in the style during one of their moments of peace, and she was right. She looked fresh and stunning, like she was ready to take on the world.

She smiled at Halen. "Hello." Her voice was quiet and sweet. It felt inviting and somewhat unsure, like she was asking if it was okay to be there.

"Hello," Halen said. The two of them had argued that morning, and her reply was a little clipped.

"You hurt me this morning," Kimberly said.

"I know, Mom. I'm sorry. I shouldn't have acted the way that I did."

"It hurt, Hay."

"I'm sorry for telling you all those hurtful things, but . . ." Halen paused, thinking of a polite way to say it.

Kimberly stiffened. "Go ahead and rip my heart out. That's all you seem to want to do."

"Mom. I don't want to do that. I want you to be proud of who I am. Who I am becoming. I realize I was a snot, evil and vindictive. I am not that person anymore."

"You are. You just don't see it."

"How am I being mean, Mom? How am I being such a horrible person?" Halen leaned on the kitchen counter while nervously tapping her finger against the granite top.

"You're moving out—that's what you're doing!" Kimberly cried.

"Yes, Mom. I have to. That's what kids do. They grow up and they leave. It has been a recurring phenomenon for millennia."

"You can live in the pool house. I won't even charge you rent." Kimberly looked at her with expectant eyes.

"It's not about the rent, Mom."

"I can charge you rent if you want."

"Mom. You're smothering me."

"Oh, nonsense."

"Mom, I need to learn to stand on my own two feet. I can't—"

"You're standing on your own two feet right now," Kimberly interrupted.

"It's a figure of speech, Mom."

"You can live your life from home. Just move into the pool house. There's no need to go anywhere. You have everything that you need here," Kimberly suggested again.

Halen swallowed back the bile in her throat. The pool house was now forever tainted, giving her reasons to avoid it like the plague. "Mom. Just no."

"You can. I'll even help you pack." Kimberly moved around the kitchen counter and began gathering the framed pictures Halen had just unpacked. She hurriedly wrapped them with the discarded packing material and stuffed them in a box.

"Mom!" Halen grabbed a picture and set it back on the counter. "I'm staying here. This is my home. If you're not going to respect that, then you need to leave."

"Halen, you're just tired. Come home and get some sleep. You'll feel better." Kimberly reached for another frame. Halen slapped it down, breaking the glass.

"Dammit, Mom." Halen grabbed the frame, her hand catching on a piece of glass. Blood oozed out of the deep line. She hissed, then growled through her teeth. "Fu . . . fart."

"Oh. Sweetie, let me see." Kimberly tried pulling Halen's hand around to see the cut.

"DAMMIT, MOM." Halen elbowed her away.

"I'm just trying to help," Kimberly spat back.

"I don't need your help. Didn't you ever want to do anything on your own?" Halen demanded.

"Just let me—"

"No, Mom. Can't you take a flipping hint? Leave me alone." Halen wrapped an old T-shirt around her hand. "I'll come by in a couple of days to get some more of my things."

"Let me take you to the clinic," Kimberly offered.

"Mom." Halen managed the sternest voice she could without growling at her mother. "Go home. Thank you, but please go home."

Kimberly pulled an oil lamp out of her bag and placed it on the counter, then turned and left, shoulders drooping, eyes fixed on the floor just in front of her feet. She disappeared out the door and down the hall to the elevator.

Halen squeezed her wound shut and held it tight. A minute passed as she contemplated what to do next. The oil lamp put off a strong potpourri fragrance that made her nose crinkle. The throbbing in her hand hammered at her sanity. A whirlwind of thoughts added to the nauseating effect from the cut. Sounds blurred, along with her vision. She moved to take a step and her knees gave.

Crickets chirped noisily, beckoning Halen to the edge of consciousness. The urge to pee brought her further out of the black abyss of a dreamless sleep. Realizing she was soaked from the waist down brought her fully awake. She thought she had wet her pants sometime during the night; now she was cold.

Her hand still stung and throbbed. The throbbing pulled her further from her dreamless sleep. She was cold and she couldn't see. Moving to cup her injured hand, she felt it drag through water. The crickets continued to chirp.

THE HIT

She knew her hand was there somewhere. She just couldn't find it, yet it stung. She felt around in the dark water. *Did I fall asleep in the tub?* She felt as though she was sitting up, but even the logic that water was down and air was up didn't feel like it fit in her situation. Somehow she felt as though it were sideways, and all she had to do was take a step forward and she would be out of the water, just as if she were stepping through a door.

She blinked against the inky blackness of the night, but it didn't improve her sight. She closed her eyes and used her other senses to tell her where she was. The shivering became more pronounced—on the edge of becoming violent. *Did the power go out?* Halen reached to her sides for the edge of the tub. Her left hand hit a solid wall, while her right hand reached on forever. She pushed it down to feel the bottom of the tub. It met hard plastic, then slipped off into a hole.

She jerked back in a panic. Familiarity made her muscles respond automatically, and she lunged her hands to the steering wheel.

Water sloshed as they came up and clenched the wheel. Cold water splashed her upper body, and she gasped. She was more than fully awake now. Fragments of questions poured forth. *How did . . . Car? Water? Lights are . . . Metallic taste . . .*

Halen reached for any switch. A motor whined. Its steady back-and-forth whirling told her it must be the windshield wipers. There was power there somewhere, and somewhere there had to be a light. She felt on the dash for any type of switch. Turning one knob had no results. She turned another. Nothing. She found the blower vent and wiggled the louvers up and down. Not even that would turn on a light to allow her to see where she was and why she wasn't in her new apartment. Eventually she hit a button that briefly illuminated the interior of the cab. Fumbling in the cool water, she hit it again and pushed it until it clicked. Green arrows lit up the dash, and yellow lights strobed at the corners of the vehicle. Realizing with blatant certainty that she was in a car, she reached for the turn indicator and twisted the handle. With two small pops, light shattered the mysterious night.

Her vision was still somewhat obscured. Two rows of teeth snapped together as a creature peered through the window.

"OH SHIT!" Halen screeched in surprise. Her heart hammered in her chest. Adrenaline surged from within every hidden crevice of her body. Looking around at the rest of the car, she realized the windows were down on either side. She reached for the window buttons. Only the driver's side window rolled up, while the other faulted and remained static.

The smell of swamp and alcohol permeated the inside of the car. Beer bottles and an empty whiskey bottle floated on the water, and a convenience store cup along with a couple empty soda cans completed the odd assortment. She tried to get her mind to work through the shivering cold that rapidly negated the surge of adrenaline. She forced herself to think, to come up with any type of solution. The trouble was that there seemed to be a million problems that required an immediate solution. She was wet. She was cold. There were two ancient predators just inches away on the other side of the glass. And more would probably soon arrive once the feeding frenzy began. She was in a car that wasn't hers and she had the taste of alcohol in her mouth, along with the metallic taste of blood. A quick exploration with her tongue found that two of her upper teeth were loose, and her lip was swollen and tender.

Half-submerged in the water, the alligator leaned against the windshield, stopping the wipers and causing the fuse to blow. He had found the hood of the car and was warming himself from the cool night air. His smaller companion, who was more adventurous, slid off the hood into the swampy water. Though smaller, it could still tear her limb from limb.

The lights went out, leaving Halen in complete darkness. She panted as her anxiety shot to the moon. The alligator that had slipped off the hood had become an immediate concern. Fear of the night and the creatures surrounding her sent her adrenaline into overdrive. Her heart raced and she sensed something large crawl through the window of the car and bump into her. Her hand pushed against jagged teeth.

Wild thrashing churned the water inside the car as the predator came to taste what had been delivered to them. Teeth sank deep into her shoulder. Halen reached for anything to fight off the monster. Her hand grasped the bottle of whiskey, and she shattered it against the dash of the car.

41

"Have you seen Halen?" Deenya peered at Halen's mom through the ornate archway of the front door.

"No. Is something wrong?" Kimberly asked.

"We were supposed to go to her place and help set up her apartment yesterday, but there was no answer when I knocked. We called security to do a wellness check. They said they could only do one if an officer was present. The police said that it had to be twenty-four hours before they could—" Deenya's concern deepened the creases on her face.

"I don't know why she agreed to that." Kimberly interrupted. "She told me she was going to move back here; I know she said she would move there. She says a lot of things she doesn't mean. She said she was sending all the furnishings back and she was bringing her things back home."

"She seemed so happy to start her own life." Deenya lost focus and looked inward. "Juan even said he saw her dancing around her new apartment and that she was going to invite us to a small housewarming party this weekend."

"I'm so sorry that she deceived you." Kimberly pulled the door close to her side. She hadn't invited Deenya in, and inferred that she wasn't welcome by holding the door close to her side.

Deenya knew they had been cut from different cloth. Kimberly was obviously silk while Deenya preferred the comfort of denim.

She hoped she could get a straight answer, but Halen's mother was not offering any logical information. "Is she here?" Deenya asked.

"No," Kimberly answered, short and quick.

"Do you know when she'll be back?" Deenya sought a ray of hope for her friend and a cure for the empty, sick feeling in her stomach.

"She said she would be here sometime late tonight." Kimberly shifted her feet in agitation.

"When she gets home, can you have her call me? Please," Deenya pleaded.

Kimberly studied her for a moment before answering with a flat and emotionless tone. "I'll tell her you stopped by." And she unceremoniously closed the door.

"I don't get it, Juan," Deenya said, inviting the big security guard into her apartment. He had completed his shift and came to help sort out the mystery.

"Halen's mom seemed almost cold. She basically said that Halen has gone back to her old shallow and superficial personality."

Juan nodded. "When she did the interview downstairs in the conference room, she was genuine."

"Right. I got that too. Her returning to her parents' house just doesn't seem right. If that's the case, she isn't doing it of her own free will," Deenya said.

The doorknob twisted, drawing her attention. It opened and Cheshlan scrambled through, peering at her mother with expectant and hopeful eyes. "Did you find her?"

Deenya exhaled in defeat. "I'm sorry, my little punkin. She's not at her parents' house."

Cheshlan slumped just inside the door. She had become a puddle on two skinny legs. Legs that grudgingly carried her to Deenya to lean hopelessly against her and whine into her shirt. "Is she gonna be alright?"

"I sure hope so." Deenya rubbed Cheshlan's back, but she began sobbing. "Hey, hey. None of that. Crying won't do you any good. Let's try to figure this out. There's always a solution somewhere." Cheshlan continued to sob into Deenya's shirt. "Hey. Remember what I tell you. You can always figure things out. And"—Deenya waved a hand around the room—"the three of us will be able to figure this out."

There was a knock at the door. Deenya opened it to find a slim man with body armor tucked under a pressed shirt. He didn't look muscular, but tough and wiry. A white scar circled partway around his eye. Deenya looked at the man's badge and ID as he introduced himself.

"Hello. I'm Detective Roberts from the Miami Police Department." He handed over a card.

Deenya accepted it, studying it for a quick moment before turning her attention back to the officer.

"I'm looking for Halen Kettleman. Do you know where I can find her? I have some follow-up questions for her."

Deenya looked at Juan, then back to the detective. "No. We don't. I was supposed to help her move in and put things away, but she hasn't answered her door and we can't get in."

"Do you think she went out with friends, maybe on a trip somewhere?" Detective Roberts asked.

"I don't know. She's been pretty adamant about not being around any of her old friends. She said she wanted to be a better person and her old friends aren't a good crowd to be around. I don't feel that she would disappear like this," Deenya explained.

"What did you talk about the last time you spoke with her?" Detective Roberts asked, absently rubbing his left forearm.

"We talked about the furniture she had just ordered and that it would be here yesterday afternoon. She double-checked with me to make sure I was coming up to help arrange things and help her unpack."

"You say she was moving in?" The detective shifted his feet, looking over his shoulder down the hallway.

"Oh, sorry, would you like to come in?" Deenya asked. After he stepped in, she looked to either side of the hallway, then closed the door. "Don't you usually have a partner working with you?"

"Not all the time." The detective stood just inside the door and waited for Deenya to answer his question.

"Yes. She was excited about moving in. We all were excited about her moving in. Juan is like my big brother. He works security here."

Detective Roberts turned to Juan. "Have you been in her apartment?"

Juan shook his head. "I was never invited."

"What about the wellness check?" Detective Roberts asked.

"It hasn't been twenty-four hours," Juan said. "And there has to be a security officer present."

"Can you call a security officer?" Detective Roberts said. "Since I'm here, we can check."

"Juan works here." Deenya turned to Juan. "Can you open the door so we can do a check?"

"No. I can't."

"Why not?" Deenya asked. Her anxiety was already at its limits.

"Only someone who is on duty can do that. My shift ended an hour ago. Let me call Mike, my supervisor. He should be in by now." Juan pulled a phone from his pocket and dialed his boss's number.

"There's blood over there," Juan pointed out.

THE HIT

Detective Roberts turned and looked where the big man was pointing from his position in the doorway.

"Oh my god. Do you see her?" Deenya called from behind the wall of men.

"No. It looks like she might have cut herself on some broken glass. I wouldn't think it's enough to be serious," Detective Roberts said.

"What does that mean? Of course it's serious," Deenya complained as she tried to peer around Juan. "She's been missing since yesterday."

"There's more on the floor," the detective said. "It's dried and crusty. Probably been there since yesterday." He looked around the room, then checked the other rooms before returning to look at the blood again. "She's not here."

"What about the blood?" Deenya managed to push Juan out of the way and step into the room.

"It's not alarming, but it is concerning."

"It's alarming. It's all alarming." Emotion flowed out with her words. "Something happened to her. Someone has been trying to kill her. She told me a hit man tried to kill her. Then there was the accidental overdose that I don't think was very accidental. Now she's gone without a word. Someone's still trying to kill her. I just know it."

The detective paused from his investigation and eyed Deenya but didn't ask anything further than what she had volunteered.

Tears forced their way to the corners of Deenya's eyes. "I just got my friend back. She's a good person now, full of depth, witty and smart. Where is she? Oh please, God, she can't be dead."

"She's tough," Cheshlan's small voice called from behind them. The group turned to look down at her, and she stared up at everyone. "She told me how she faced down a giant cat with teeth bigger than my head."

The detective absently rubbed his arm as the four adults stared down at Cheshlan.

"What are you doing here?" Deenya said. "I told you to stay in the apartment."

"Mom, I gotta know," Cheshlan pleaded.

"We all do, sweetie," Deenya said.

"It looks like it might have been significant enough to require stitches. Have you called any hospitals or clinics?" Detective Roberts asked.

"Yes, and we also called the jail and as many of her old friends as we could get ahold of. I asked about her on her old social media accounts. No one has seen her."

"Did she go on a trip? Maybe back to Montana?" he asked.

"Not that I know of. I couldn't get in touch with any of her friends that were up there."

"Is that blood?" Cheshlan asked, squatting down and looking at the carpet.

The adults turned to look at the young detective as she gripped her toy pony in one hand and twisted her fingers around the mane with the other.

The detective squatted down alongside Cheshlan. "Good eyes," he said. He rose and walked a few steps further down the hallway. Another lone spot of blood started the beginnings of a trail. "Juan, right?" he called. "Do you have surveillance of this hallway?"

"No, sir." Juan pointed to the empty box recessed into the ceiling. "The cameras are down. The new ones haven't arrived yet."

"What about cameras in other parts of the building?" Detective Roberts called over his shoulder as he walked down the hall, stopping momentarily to examine the floor. The small crowd started to follow, keeping to one side of the hall or the other so as not to step on potential evidence.

"Yeah. There are others," Juan said. "I can go down and look."

The detective stopped at a double set of doors. "What's behind these doors?"

"That's the utility room and the freight elevator," Mike, the security supervisor, offered. "Moving companies sometimes use the elevator to bring up larger items." He stepped forward to punch in his security code.

"I'll meet you at the front desk if I don't find anything." The detective disappeared through the double doors, escorted by the security supervisor.

"Why would she go through those doors?" Cheshlan asked, putting words to everyone else's thoughts.

"No lo sabemos, pequeño," Juan said more to himself than anyone else, then translated. "We don't know, little one."

"Maybe she was helping with the furniture and was injured," Deenya suggested, while she dreaded a much more sinister reason.

Juan turned to the regular elevators and pushed the call button. "Something don't feel right," he told Deenya. "I think whoever's out to"—He checked his words, glancing at Cheshlan clinging to her mother's side and devouring every word they were saying—"make her look silly, is still out there."

"I think so too." Deenya picked up on Juan's coded words. "From what Halen told me about the player from Montana, I think he switched jerseys."

"I don't know anything about that. Halen hasn't mentioned much about her past. The fact that she's here and her personality has flipped a one-eighty as you say, that should mean something."

"It has. I'm just worried that something has . . . you know," Deenya said.

"I don't think I've seen any of her movies. I really don't know much of what she used to be like."

"Do you watch *ET*?" Deenya asked.

"I think my dad said something about that movie, from back when he was a kid. She's too young to have been in that, isn't she?"

"No."

"She's not too young?" he asked.

"Oh my god, that movie is so old," Deenya said. "No, I mean *Entertainment Tonight*."

"What's *Entertainment Tonight*?"

Deenya sighed. "It's like a news station that only talks about movies, TV shows and what the stars do when they're not filming. Where have you been?"

"Working," Juan said.

"Working?"

"Yeah. My mom was a single mother for my whole life. She worked hard. So I did too. I remember being Cheshlan's age and folding towels and sheets at a hotel. I swept the parking lot. I learned to fix things. I sold drugs just one time and gave her the money to pay rent. She beat my backside till the sun came up, then used the money to pay rent. I never did that again. A few months later, we were evicted anyway."

"I'm sorry you had to go through that." Deenya rested a hand on the big man's shoulder.

"Mi mamá called it character building," Juan said.

"Kudos to your mamá. It doesn't look like she skimped on any building blocks."

"You calling me fat?" Juan teased.

"No. Your mamá had to build a big strapping lad to carry that big heart of yours." Deenya surmised from the little she knew of the gentle giant.

She watched his face curiously. His darker skin turned a muddled mix of red and brown. Deenya cracked a smile at his humility and was about to comment on it when the elevator door opened.

Two suits stepped out of the steel box. A badge hung from each of their belts. Deenya recognized the faces of the two detectives who had knocked on her door before.

"Oh. Detective Milton," Deenya said in surprise. "Detective Perez."

"Deenya. We were just coming by to follow up on that missing person report about Halen Kettleman."

"Oh. You just missed Detective Roberts."

"Detective Roberts?" Detective Milton looked at his partner, then back at Deenya. "We don't have a Detective Roberts in the precinct."

42

Blood leaked drop by drop through a hole in the plastic bag, then soaked through the canvas. The bag swayed in rhythm to her offset stride, casting the dripping blood at random angles to the concrete below. An aged and tattered army uniform hung loosely around her as she clutched the straps of the backpack. Her mud-caked jeans had lost their flexibility after the sun had dried the Florida muck to them. Ill-fitting boots clomped against the sidewalk. Occasional bits of mud fell from the soles, though most of it had been walked off long before. The grayish-white bits of marl rolled to the sides of her path.

Pedestrians gave her a wide berth so not to disturb her determined face and undeviating steps. Curious and questioning looks came from all around as more and more people noticed the unkempt oddity striding through a refined and polished part of the city. Even the stately, pristine windows seemed to grimace at the violation and indecency.

The city streets boasted high fashion both day and night. Any violation of this was viewed as a mockery of the societal norm. With the high taxes of the district came the benefits of an attentive police force. Wait times were minimal if one were to call for help.

Bystanders held their phones to their ears, but she didn't care—they were welcome to call the police. Most, however, pointed their cameras at her, probably taking a video to post on social media.

The populace chose the afternoons as their prime social bonding time, treating themselves to a few of the many indulgences the area had to offer. Police were sure to show up soon to check out what a few had certainly called in to complain about.

She marched past the fancy galleries, clothing boutiques and real estate offices. She was not the least bit interested in the neatly dressed mannequins in the windows, the flashing lights or the music that tried to lure people in to separate them from their money.

The one thing she was interested in was an attorney's office—one with a specific person who worked there. She reached a hand out and hauled back on the handle, swinging the mahogany door open. One last drop of blood tainted the concrete just outside the lawyer offices of Sterling and Beckman.

"Hello. Can I help you, Miss?" The receptionist's voice started off bright and cheery, then faded to uncertainty.

The visitor quickly evaluated the attorney's office. Turning her head to the right, she spied the room her target was supposed to be cowering in.

"Ma'am. You can't go in there." The receptionist moved to get up but was too late.

She heaved the door open and strode through on shaking legs. Once through the doorway, she slid the strap off her shoulder and ripped open the backpack, sliding a bloody and mangled head across the conference table. Men and women jumped backward, some toppling over their own chairs and spilling to the floor before scrambling to the edge of the room, away from the grotesque mess that leaked across the table and soaked into the scattering of papers and two laptops.

A paltry man screamed as the crimson-colored teeth glistened in a menacing grin. He scrambled away from the severed head. The sharp teeth promised savagery, but the alligator had already taken its last bite.

Kelson staggered back a step from his position near the far end of the table. "Halen!" Shock and confusion ripped across his face.

Halen stared piercing daggers at the man.

Kelson's boss, Dale Sterling, stepped forward. "Halen, wow, you look like—"

"Dale! Zip it." Halen held a hand up to the prominent lawyer. "Unless you want charged for attempted murder like the piece of shit stepfather that I'm unfortunate enough to know."

Halen's eyes didn't waver from Kelson. Her words didn't surprise him, but the sight of her worried him immeasurably. Halen saw it in his eyes. "What's the matter, Kelson? Afraid your little secret sprang a leak?"

Kelson remained silent. His eyes cast about for an exit, but he was cornered at the far end of the room. Several people stood on either side of the table, making it less than convenient for him to slide into oblivion.

"Your boy Blondie squealed like an overloaded washing machine." Halen held her stepfather's focus. "As soon as he got over the shock of seeing a ghost and watching me dump a couple bricks of cocaine into his toilet, he figured he was more afraid of what his supplier was going to do to him versus the law.

"Seems he owed you a favor. Or is it that you've become the hub for the Miami elite? I should know, I used to steal from your stashes. I figured, hell, you won't say anything. You're far more crooked than I ever imagined you to be. So what is it, Kelson? Why'd you take out a two-million-dollar life insurance policy on me? You're in debt, aren't you? You owe a scary amount of money to someone, don't you, and you needed a quick fix."

Kelson fidgeted, glancing from face to face, trying to judge the reactions to the accusation. He looked back at Halen.

"Is there someone out there who scares you worse than me?" Halen tossed the backpack on the table.

"I don't know what you're talking about," Kelson said.

"Oh. You don't?" Halen raised an eyebrow at her supposed father figure. "I don't either, but I know you have them and I know you'll have to answer to them when it comes time to pay up. I know you're running on credit and the masons are complaining about a shortage."

Kelson's eyebrows lifted.

"That's right. And the killer that you sent to Montana"—Halen waited for Kelson's brain to comprehend the sudden turn of events—"sends his calling card."

She pulled a round drink coaster from a pocket and tossed it to her stepfather. He picked up the stained coaster and read the advertisement: *Wade's Pub and Grub—best wood-fired pizza in Miami*. He righted the coaster, looking for a message, then turned it over. His breath caught, then he stumbled a step back. His hands shook the moment he saw the letter. On the back, written in blood, was his first initial with a line drawn through it. It was the calling card of fear and a promise that what was coming would be agonizing, and law enforcement wouldn't be able to hide him.

Halen hoped he knew of the rumors, that the initial would have been written in Kelson's own blood. She saw him wince. He had to know something of the man he had hired to follow her to Montana. With that kind of recognition, she knew he would be worried for a good long while. Tracer was dead. There was no coming back from the raging river that had swallowed him. The police would follow a trail to Kelson soon enough. If not, then the allegation she had made against him in front of his boss and their clients would ruin his career.

THE HIT

To have him committed to a mental hospital like some of Tracer's other victims was too much for her to expect, but the worry in his eyes was enough to send a clear message. He knew she wasn't to be taken lightly; doing so could cost him even more. To watch his life crumble before him was worse than simply being killed. If he was killed, he wouldn't have to face his peers.

She had done all she could do. She had exposed his crime to the world. The world would have to contend with him now and she would sit back and watch. His death was inevitable, and whether it was just his career or his life remained to be seen.

"Tracer said he'd be in touch," Halen lied, staring at the now pale-faced man. His dark blue suit suddenly became even darker as his need for the restroom had switched to a need for a change of clothes.

Halen felt a twinge in her shoulder that her adrenaline and anger had hidden. She reached up and felt a tooth that had lodged there when the alligator had attacked. She gripped the tooth and pulled the inch-long saber out. Blood oozed out of the puncture and soaked into her mud-smeared shirt. She turned, leaving the shock of people standing around the perimeter of the room. The severed head continued to grin at the lawyers and businessmen. Even in death, the alligator had lived up to its frightening reputation.

Halen walked out of the building, turning the alligator's tooth over and over in her hand.

43

"Stop. Give back my lunch!" Cheshlan screeched, pulling the small bag of carrots away from a classmate.

The noise from the cafeteria rivaled that of jet engines. Attempts to quell the chaos had been fruitless, as it was the last day before summer vacation. All work was finished. Books were nearly all turned in. Graded papers and art projects filled backpacks until they were bursting at the seams. Teachers stood talking among themselves in pairs on either side of the room, waiting for the day to be done. Though their work wasn't done, the last few days would be quiet and uninterrupted as they finished calculating grades and typing out final comments.

Cheshlan talked excitedly with her friends about upcoming summer activities. Some friends were going away to the mountains, some were visiting other relatives.

THE HIT

One girl talked about being the flower girl in her older sister's wedding. "What are you going to do, Cheshlan?"

"My mom's new boyfriend is going to take us on the set of a new horror movie he's making. It's going to be on Nic," Cheshlan explained.

"Nuh uh," a chunky boy with curly brown hair said. Crumbs spewed from his mouth and onto the floor as he chewed and tried to talk at the same time. "You don't know any movie stars."

"Yes I do. She's coming to lunch," Cheshlan argued back.

"I don't see her," the second-grade boy said.

"You probably don't even know what a camera is," his buddy chimed in. The two laughed, ribbing each other.

"She couldn't remember a single line from a movie," the second-grade boy said.

"I do know movies," Cheshlan protested.

"No you don't," the boy said.

"I do too."

Cheshlan's friend came to her defense. "Yes. She does. She knows every line to *Stories of the Witch's Stew*."

"You don't know every line of *Stories of the Witch's Stew*," the boy challenged.

"Yes, she does," her friend said with complete confidence.

"Say it, then."

"What part?" Cheshlan's friend asked.

"The part where she enters the witch's basement," the boy said.

Cheshlan began recounting the movie. "Shawna says 'Hold my flashlight.' Then she reaches for the light switch and tries to turn on the basement lights. Julia says 'Let's just go tell the police.' "

Students stopped eating and listened to Cheshlan recite the story, looking for any inaccuracies, as most knew the movie she was recounting.

" 'The police won't believe us. We have to get some kind of proof.' The light switch doesn't work and the house groans. Julia says 'I'm scared, Shawna. We have to leave right now.' " Cheshlan contorted her voice to differentiate between the two characters and continued in Shawna's voice. " 'Quit being a mini-Kay.' "

"What's a mini-Kay?" a boy asked.

Cheshlan's friend sat forward. "It's a miniature Karen."

"I am not a mini-Kay," the second-grade boy announced to the group.

"No. You're a mini-Kev—miniature Kevin," Cheshlan's friend chided.

The group laughed.

The second grader huffed. "You still don't know the whole movie."

"Yes she does," her friend fired back.

"I don't hear anything." He cupped a hand to his ear, leaning across the aisle from the adjacent table.

"Shut up, mini-Kev," a third-grade boy commanded, who apparently wanted to see if Cheshlan knew all the lines verbatim.

After a brief chuckle, Cheshlan continued. "So, Julia says 'Why do you call me that?' And Shawna says 'Because you think that everything needs to be given to you. You never take responsibility for what you do wrong. You were supposed to watch your brother along with mine. You didn't, and now we have to find them before two a.m.'

"Then Julia shines the flashlight through the basement, looking for the black wardrobe. When they find it, Shawna reaches up to open the cabinet door," Cheshlan said, changing her tone dramatically. "Julia snatches her arm. Shawna jumps, jerking the door open just a crack. They stare at the tiny opening. A black mist swirls out and around their feet and the door opens wider. The hinges creak and they hear a raspy voice behind them."

The students all leaned in a little closer, waiting for the famous line from the movie.

Cheshlan's eyes grew as big as the boy's when she heard the grated voice. " 'Children's ears and children's tears feed my blackened soul.' "

Halen grinned at Cheshlan after growling in the boy's ear. The boy screamed and spun to the creepy voice, tipping his tray over into his lap. Halen stepped back also and looked at the children surrounding her. Dozens of wide eyes now stared back. Some kids covered their mouths, while others dropped theirs open. The awkward silence was quickly broken by a girl who screeched uncontrollably and triggered the rest of the lunchroom into a near riot.

Some stood and hopped in place, not knowing what to do with all their excitement. Teachers turned to the commotion, looking to hush the noise. Two teachers raced to grab a boy who was jumping up and down on a cafeteria bench, while others closed in on the students, looking to understand why they were screaming abnormally loud. The assistant principal stood from her lunch and approached Halen, who had clearly sparked the pandemonium.

"Excuse me. Can I help you?" the assistant principal asked.

"Sorry. I just came here to have lunch with Cheshlan. I didn't mean to cause a stir."

"Well, one has been caused. I know it's the last day of the school year, but as you can see, this was not what we were prepared for." The assistant principal flipped a strand of hair over her shoulder in blatant irritation.

"I apologize. I just came because I promised Cheshlan that I would have lunch with her."

"And I'm in charge of keeping everything under control." Her condescending tone was all too apparent. "Now, I'm going to ask you to leave. I have to get this madhouse back under control." The assistant principal turned to the crowd, putting her hand in the air, signaling for silence. "Quiet down."

The students continued to scream and yell among themselves about the visitor to their school.

"Oh, sorry. Maybe I can help?" Halen offered.

"How can you help?" the assistant principal scoffed. "Do you have a teaching degree?"

The indignation of her tone sparked a challenge in Halen. This woman mocked her with her title, education and years of teaching experience, but Halen had one thing the principal didn't. She had leverage. She had what the students wanted. "What are the students doing after lunch?" Halen asked as she formulated a plan.

"They will go back to their classes and probably watch movies until the end of the day," the assistant principal said.

Halen nodded. The noise in the cafeteria had become explosive. The teachers' shushing was doing little to calm the half-pint mob. Lunch was almost done and they had to get the students back to their classes soon. The assistant principal yelled louder and louder for the students to sit down. Some did, but the rest continued their freak-out.

Halen walked to the edge of the cafeteria and stood on a vacant chair. She let out as shrill a whistle as anyone had ever heard. In an instant, the roar ceased. She peered across the sea of tiny, expectant faces.

She had a plan, but it called on her to pull multiple rabbits out of a hat and maybe even an alligator. A thought sparked as she pulled the alligator tooth out of her pocket. She considered its significance, then returned her gaze to the sea of faces that were enthralled, waiting for her to speak.

Halen had leveraged her fame and connections to spark an impromptu assembly. She spoke a few words to the students and promised them a special event if they would clean their tables and file back to their classes in an orderly manner. She made a few phone calls and prayed that her contacts would help fulfill the promise she had just made.

The principal waved a hand for the students to settle down, while the assistant principal stood to the side of the gym, privately seething at Halen's takeover of the unruly children. Halen had given her the recognition for the idea, and the students were enthralled to see real-life stuntmen and actors in an assembly instead of watching a movie in their classrooms.

Out of the four phone calls, three of Halen's contacts showed up. Joe, a stunt choreographer, redirected his van and crew from going to a set. Jamal Gregory, a karate instructor, brought a few of his students, while Detective Milton dispatched a couple of police officers to the school to help with the activities. Halen stood to the side with Joe and Shifu Gregory as they made final adjustments for their presentation.

The principal finished her introduction and handed the microphone over to the police officers.

"Good afternoon," Officer Jones said. "Is everyone excited about summer vacation?"

"Yeah!" the children screamed in unison.

"Is everyone excited about who is here today?" Officer Jones started amping up the crowd.

Again, the crowd erupted in cheers and applause.

The officer grinned as he set up his next ruse. "Thank you. I'm so happy to be here for you."

"Nooo!" the students said in unison.

"You don't want me here?" Officer Jones fed into the crowd.

"Yeeesss!" the students yelled back. "We do!"

"Who are you talking about? Are you talking about Officer Jenna?"

"Nooo!"

"You don't want Officer Jenna here?"

"Yeeesss, we do!"

"Well, I don't understand. Who do you want here?"

"Halen Kettleman!" the students said, entirely out of unison.

Officer Jones cupped a hand behind his ear. "Who?"

"Halen!" they said louder, and somewhat in time with the rest of their classmates. A number of them pointed to Halen, who stood off to the side talking with her former stunt coordinator and the karate instructor who had also helped choreograph some of the fight scenes she'd been in. Her stunt double did most of the fight scenes, but she had to be there for the close-up shots.

The stunt coordinator elbowed Halen and pointed to the crowd. She turned to see the excited and cheerful faces. She would have to play co-host at the impromptu event, but there was little doubt that she was the main attraction.

She pointed at herself. The children cheered. She pointed at the stunt coordinator.

"Nooo!"

Halen pointed back at herself. The audience cheered wildly. Halen grinned and stepped forward to help Officer Jones explain what they were going to see.

She waved a hand at the assembly. A mild cheer encouraged her to take center stage. Officer Jones put an arm around her shoulder.

"This has to be extra exciting for you guys," Halen said. "You must have been really good students this year for your assistant principal to have us here."

Halen looked out at the students. All had eager eyes and were ready to hear whatever she had to say.

She looked at Officer Jones, then back to the crowd. Her heart quickened and her palms began to sweat. Panic flooded through her, as she was now faced with something scarier than a mountain lion or an assassin. Another bite from an alligator would be preferable to public speaking. Stumbling over her words in front of so many hopeful minds was not what she had in mind when she stopped by to have lunch with Cheshlan.

Officer Jones handed her the microphone, gave her a smile and a pat on the shoulder, almost as if to say good luck. It seemed that he recognized her anxiety and of course knew of her turbulent past.

Halen took a hesitant step forward and tapped the microphone out of nervousness. She looked out across the audience at some of the hopeful eyes that peered back at her. She had called this assembly and was greeted with mild to wild enthusiasm. Now she had to deliver on what she had promised. To do that, she had to unclench her jaw and say something.

Her mind scrambled. Her jaw fell open, but nothing came out. With every passing second, it seemed her throat was being choked off tighter and tighter. She gripped the microphone with both hands and twisted it, then spoke with a quavering voice. "G-good afternoon."

"The microphone is off," a teacher called from the audience.

THE HIT

Officer Jones stepped up, flipped the switch back on and handed it back to her. He leaned in close to her ear. "Relax. You'll do fine. Just tell a story."

Halen nodded. She looked at the microphone and moved her hand away from the power switch.

"Sorry, guys. This is my first time speaking in public. I'm a bit outside my comfort zone."

"But you're an actress," an older boy said. "You're in front of millions of people all the time."

Halen nodded. "Yes, I am. But, there are a few differences. What you see on TV or in the movies isn't live. We don't create the lines on the spot. The words that you hear were written down on a piece of paper called a script. We practice saying those words over and over until we get them right. Sometimes there will be adjustments, but mostly we say what someone else wrote.

"Here, I don't have a script to read from. I don't know what to say that will inspire you."

Halen heard snickers to either side and caught the smirk of a couple teachers guarding the perimeter. A plump woman smiled and gave her a reassuring nod while the vice principal continued her skeptical scowl. Halen could almost feel the negative energy flowing from her and avoided further eye contact. The principal had assured her that they had a golden opportunity to ingrain an important safety lesson into their students to help keep them safe over the summer.

Halen had faced an uphill battle organizing the event in the short hour she was given. It helped that her stunt coordinator and her martial arts instructor each had children attending the school and willingly agreed to help her. She looked over her shoulder for support from her former coworkers. They gave her a nod and a thumbs up, encouraging her to continue. Officer Jones stood just behind her, ready to step up to support her.

She turned toward the crowd and took a deep breath, then reached in her pocket and retrieved the alligator tooth that she had fastened to a leather thong. She was going to give it to Cheshlan, but another thought came to mind.

44

"I think I'd rather face down a mountain lion or an alligator instead of standing up here giving a talk in front of so many people. I hope you forgive us if we stumble a little because we haven't had time to *rehearse*." Halen checked to see if everyone was following and not getting lost in other things. "I was abducted several months ago. It was really frightening and I was very scared. I was held captive for a long time, but eventually I was able to escape."

"Were you hurt?" a girl asked from the back row.

"Yes. At times I was hurt. Other times I just felt lonely, but I was able to think my way through it and survive." She stepped forward with a bit more confidence.

"How did you survive?" a boy asked.

Halen glanced at the clock, over to her friends, then back at the students. "That is a long story for another time. Today we want to show you a few things that will help keep you safe so you don't have to worry about surviving something bad." Halen backed up a couple steps. "To keep from being kidnapped, what should you do?" Halen slapped a hand on Officer Jones's shoulder.

"Call Officer Jones!" the students said in unison.

"Or any officer," Halen said. "Every officer on the police force wants you to be safe and grow up to do amazing things. So we want you to do things in a way that will keep you safe. So what is the number you call to get ahold of Officer Jones or any other officer?"

"911."

"That's right. Our job today is to give you some tips and tricks so that you won't end up like I did, or worse. We want you to do just a few simple things that will help you have a safe and happy summer vacation." Halen turned and waved a hand at her stunt coordinator.

"This is Joe. Joe is a stunt coordinator. He has worked on many different projects in the film industry and has worked with me personally to see that I can do stunts safely when I actually need to do them for a film. He looks really big and mean, but he has a bigger heart than anyone I know." Halen swung an arm around the big man's shoulders. "Joe, you have a child who goes to school here, right?" Halen asked.

Joe stood quietly.

"What's your child's name?" Halen asked.

"I'm not going to tell you that," Joe said.

"Come on, you know me. You've worked with me," Halen pleaded.

Joe shook his head. "No. I'm not telling you."

Halen turned back to the audience. "See? Right there, Joe's child is safer because I have no idea who they are. I don't know if they are a boy or a girl, so I won't be able to find Joe's child among all these faces. Since he hasn't said that he has a child, I don't even know if he does have one."

She turned back to Joe. "Joe your child is safe because you wouldn't give up their name. That is admirable. Now, for real, what's their name?"

Joe stood grinning, shaking his head. "No. I'm not going to tell you."

"Oh, come on, Joe. Just tell me what their first name starts with," Halen pleaded.

"No." Joe just shook his head.

Halen turned her attention to the captivated audience. "Joe's child, if you are in here, your father loves you so much. He won't even give your name to a movie star."

The audience laughed.

"See guys, his child is safe because he didn't even let a movie star know their name. Do you think he'll tell a complete stranger?"

"Nooo."

"That's right. Even parents don't talk to strangers about their families. And you shouldn't volunteer your friends' names to complete strangers or to people you only know a little bit. You should always check with your friend's parents to see if it's okay for that person to know who they are."

Halen turned to Joe. "Joe, we need a volunteer from the audience. Can you pick a volunteer for us?"

"I can do that," Joe said.

"Joe needs a volunteer," Halen announced.

A few hands shot up, while others rose hesitantly. Joe made a big deal of looking over the volunteers before selecting a tiny little girl who hadn't even had her hand raised. He lifted her off the floor and brought her out in front of the rest of the school.

"Hi, Joe's volunteer." Halen shook hands with the beaming little girl. "Thank you for helping us today."

The little girl nodded, grinning at Halen, apparently lost for words. Halen released her hand and Joe escorted her to stand just a few steps away.

"Joe and his volunteer are going to show you how easy and fast it is for you or someone you know to disappear. Let's say that this little girl here, who we will call Avera, since Joe won't point out who his real child is . . ."

A few snickers from the other students in her class confirmed what Halen suspected. The girl stood obediently as her father took a few steps back.

"Avera is just walking down the street. She's all by herself and just minding her own business. She's looking at the flowers and the trees and doesn't see the person sneaking up behind her. In just a few seconds . . ."

Joe launched at his daughter, swooped her up in his arms and ducked through a hastily set up frame and drew the curtain.

"He's in his car and gone. Five seconds can change your life. Today we're going to show you a few things that will help you stay safe and have a great summer."

"But she's tiny. Anyone can pick her up."

Halen looked at the older student. "Yes, the smaller a person is, the easier they are to pick up. I'm an adult, and I was still taken against my will."

"But you're a girl," the boy said.

"That is true."

"Guys don't get kidnapped," the boy said.

"Yes, they do," Officer Jones said.

"They couldn't get me." The boy was becoming more defiant, looking to prove himself among his peers.

"It can happen to anyone," Halen said.

"Not me," the boy affirmed.

Halen sighed at the losing argument. There was no way she would be able to convince someone who was this obstinate—at least not with words.

"Prove it."

Everyone turned toward the husky voice. A man in a tattered denim coat stood just inside the gym doors. Scars intermingled with the callouses on his hands. A week-old beard hid his face. He took a few steps further into the room and turned to the boy. "Dill. Come on up and prove it."

"Why should I?"

"If you can fight someone off, then I'll let you stay with your mom this summer. If you can't, you have to stay with me the whole summer," the boy's father said.

Dill hesitated.

"Deal?" Dill's father asked, one thumb hooked in a pocket.

"I don't want to go to Georgia," Dill huffed.

"Then you better show that you're big enough to avoid being taken."

The fourth grader stood and made his way around to the center of the floor.

"How do I know you won't cheat?" Dill asked.

"Dill, there's no such thing as cheating." Officer Jones said, stepping up next to Halen. "This isn't a game with rules. This is the real world. A criminal won't stop just because a rule is written down on a piece of paper."

Dill stood, trying to be defiant with every fiber in his body. Halen could see the anger in the young man—she had had that kind of anger toward Tracer. She knew the lesson would be a hard one, but it would be one that would stay with him for the rest of his life. One day, he might look back and be grateful for that harsh lesson, like she was for the lessons Tracer had taught her.

"To top it off," Halen said, "I'll throw in this alligator tooth." She held it up, showing the crowd. "The alligator who bit me left his tooth behind. I was going to keep it for myself, but if you show us that you can keep from being captured, then I will give this to you."

Dill's eyes lit up. He wanted that tooth. He wanted to prove himself in front of everyone.

"I'll show you. That tooth will be mine," Dill glared at Halen.

"Confidence is a good thing. Overconfidence is not." Halen watched the boy as he stood in defiance. "Shifu Gregory, can you help me with this?"

"Sure, no problem." The martial artist strode up next to Halen.

"Shifu, do you think overconfidence is good?" Halen spoke into the microphone.

"He won't get me and nobody else will either," Dill said.

"I hope we'll never have to find out," Halen said.

Shifu Gregory stepped up. "Are you ready, Mr. Dillon?"

"Yes," Dill said.

Shifu Gregory stood relaxed next to Halen. Everyone was quiet, waiting for the action to begin. Dill stood just four steps away from the two, with his back to them.

"It's been like ten seconds. I win. You need to hand over the tooth now," Dill said, turning around.

Shifu Gregory propped an elbow on Halen's shoulder with no intention of making a move. "Time hasn't started yet," he said. "Time starts when someone grabs you. Then you have five seconds to get away from them. See, an attacker won't make any move until he knows you aren't expecting anything."

Dill maintained a determined face, challenging the martial arts instructor.

Shifu Gregory continued. "Sometimes the attacker will purposefully create a distraction like setting something on fire. Most people are mesmerized by fire." He turned toward the students. "If something happens to you, try yelling 'Fire, fire!' instead of 'Help, help!' People will want to help put out a fire and will want to see what's going on and they will help. But the best thing to do is never go anywhere alone. You have plenty of friends sitting around you who would love to hang out with you. That way, when someone like me is distracting you . . ." Shifu Gregory turned to Dill. "You have a friend who is watching your back."

Dill tilted his head in confusion. The words were lost on him. Then he became even more confused when Shifu Gregory smiled. A hand grabbed Dill around the middle and another cupped over his mouth. The powerful arms spun him upside down, disorienting him in a matter of a few seconds, and carried him behind the curtain.

"Three seconds," Shifu Gregory said to the students. "It can happen that fast. We want you to be safe and see you back here next year, except for those going on to middle school. We will come visit you there."

"You made me pee." Dill's voice came from behind the curtain.

Laughter erupted throughout the room. Shifu Gregory held up a hand to quiet the students. "Biological warfare. Thank you for reminding me, Dillon. If you are being attacked, by all means, spit on them, throw up on them or go to the bathroom on them. What attacker will want to take you then? It might be a little embarrassing for you, but not as bad as for your attacker. They want easy targets, not hard, unmanageable ones. Only moms run to clean up vomit. Everyone else will run away."

The audience laughed.

"You'll have to go home and thank your mom for being that one, right Shifu?" Halen said.

"Right." Shifu Gregory continued, "Travel to and from places in groups, with an older sibling or with a parent. Don't go into dark alleys. Stay on lighted streets. Know which neighbors have cameras, and be ready to run to one of them.

Sometimes pointing it out will make the attacker run away."

"That is some great advice, Shifu." Halen turned to the students. "Is there anyone else here who thinks that they are safe from being attacked?" Halen held up the alligator tooth. "Anyone think it would take Shifu Gregory longer than five seconds to kidnap them?"

Dill's father had escorted him out the side door where he wouldn't have to face his peers with his accident. The rest of the student body looked around for anyone brave enough to make the attempt and possibly embarrass themselves by wetting their pants. Movement came from Halen's left. Shifu Gregory nudged her to look. A tiny hand pushed a remote joystick forward. An electric motor hummed, moving the heavy wheelchair forward.

An aide accompanied the little girl. She spun the chair around the edge of the assembly and up to Halen and Shifu Gregory.

Halen slapped the instructor on the back. "Five seconds, Shifu. Five seconds."

Shifu Gregory puzzled over the challenge. He looked at Halen, who had taken a step back, giving him room to work.

"That's cheating. She has a bodyguard," Shifu Gregory said.

The little girl waved a hand for her aide to step away. She grinned up from her wheelchair, daring Shifu Gregory to try anything.

He looked at Halen, then back at the tiny figure in the chair, then back at Halen. He held his hand out and Halen put the tooth in his hand.

"For making a martial arts master look like a fool, we bestow upon you a symbol of courage and intelligence."

45

Mike Denahy had worked for the Miami SWAT team for nearly a decade, and he had served his community faithfully for those years. Life was good and he made a comfortable living. His son and daughter were growing and would soon be starting school, but a ghost from the past had circled back around to find him.

"Why me?" he grumbled to himself. The rented van wasn't conspicuous in the bustling city, though he felt that it stood out like a sore thumb. He had scouted the location a week before and found a suitable place where he could observe from a distance. That was what he wanted in every conceivable way—distance from the drugs he had peddled in the past, distance from that lifestyle, distance from the man who blackmailed him, distance from this city and distance from the person in the sights of his scope.

His bags were already packed. He had accepted a job on the other side of the country. He and his small family would be starting over as soon as he pulled the trigger. He had pulled that trigger many times before. This time was different, but he forced himself to think of it as the same. The person in his scope wasn't any different from the people, or rather targets, in Afghanistan. It was a squeeze, a recoil and a clean slate. His debt would be paid and he would be free to start his life somewhere else.

His PTSD led to drugs which led to parties and a bouncer gig where he met Kelson. Kelson helped him straighten his life out but reserved a few favors in return. This was the last favor Kelson would call him on. One simple task and he would be free.

His wife and kids were the gems that he lived for now. From morning to night, he lived for them. He did everything he could to make their lives as beautiful as possible.

Colorado would be their new home starting tomorrow. Their life here would be done. All he had to do was pull the trigger.

The balcony door was wide open. As soon as the target came into view, he would fire. It was an easy shot. He had made longer shots many times before. The roof of the parking garage was less than two blocks from the condominium. He had full view of everything on the side of the building. Only one person had to walk out onto the balcony and sip their morning cup of coffee. Just one, and he would be done.

Summer break had started. Halen was fully aware of it, as she had three small girls scattered across her living room. They had spent the evening watching a series of Halen's monster movies before the three had finally run out of battery around two in the morning. Pulling a corner of a blanket up to cover a tiny figure made her smile.

She folded a pizza box lid to cover the now-dried wedges, then set it next to the trash. Searching through the box of new dishes, she unwrapped a couple and put them in the cupboard. When she found the coffee cups, she unwrapped one of the six and set it on the counter. She then unboxed the coffee maker and read the care information and directions.

Domestic chores were new to her. The single-cup coffee maker took an hour to unpack, wash and assemble. Torn boxes, plastic bags and white Styrofoam littered the floor in a corner of the kitchen. Halen grunted at the mess she had made and pushed it into a tighter pile as the water trickled through the K-Cup into the porcelain mug.

The coffee finished, she sipped the bitter cup just to conjure a memory of the months in the mountains without the luxury of cream or sugar. The coffee sparked the scent of pine and the feeling of fluffy soft fur from the lynx. She vowed to make the first bitter sip her own little ritual.

Halen set the cup down and pulled a box of sugar out of the bag of groceries she'd had delivered the day before. Prying at the cardboard became a more formidable task than she had thought. The glue was unrelenting and forced the paperboard to yield. Halen fished out a steak knife and turned back to the box. Even though the knife was sharp, the package yielded to the pressure, folding around the blade.

Holding the box firmly, she pushed harder on the blade. The paperboard had become pliable and resisted being opened. Halen pushed harder still. The paperboard finally gave. The knife slid through both sides of the box. The sharp edge slid easily once it had momentum, slicing the box top open.

She lost her grip on the box, and sugar spilled across the table and onto the floor. Halen gasped and stepped back to view the fallout. Frustration tripped her give-a-damn button. Air escaped her lungs, and her shoulders slumped in defeat. She looked around the kitchen and realized she had neglected to order a broom and dustpan and, for that matter, a vacuum and a trash can. She would place that order post-coffee.

Grabbing a fistful of sugar off the counter, she plopped it in her cup, then dug through a box of silverware until she found a spoon and pried it from its packaging. She grabbed the bottle of caramel macchiato from the refrigerator and peeled the security foil off the container. After adding the creamy liquid, she blended the morning tradition and walked out of the kitchen. White granules clung briefly to her feet before being wiped on the carpet.

After tiptoeing through the scattered couch cushions and leaving the rumpled blankets and empty pizza boxes behind, she leaned on the balcony railing, enjoying the late morning sun. The mess in the kitchen could wait.

The view of the Miami River seemed tranquil compared to the buzz of the roads. It was the hour after the first punch of the clock. People still rushed to get through traffic, hurrying to one place or another just to earn a paycheck.

She would have to face that someday. Her early success as an actress had provided her many things that most people would never get and some would never want. She didn't want some of those things anymore. She could definitely do without the drugs and the leeching friends. She knew she had to decide on a career. She had enough money in the bank to live frugally, by Hollywood standards, for about a year. She had to do something, and she had to figure that out sometime in the next few months.

At least she hoped she had a few months. The knowledge that her stepfather was still out there and was a potential threat weighed heavy on her mind. She had called his bluff and let his bosses know that they might want to rethink their association with the man. The fact that she had let him know she was onto him should have cooled his desire to kill her. If he was still after the life insurance money, he wouldn't have a chance to claim it now. The insurance company would look long and hard at the case for any foul play. In that aspect, she felt relatively secure that no one would be able to collect on any of her life insurance, but that didn't mean she wasn't still in danger.

She bent her head to taste the caffeinated nectar and flinched at the overwhelming taste of sugar. The cup shattered in her hand, sending the hot sticky liquid in all directions. Shards from the cup spattered her face, and Halen collapsed on the balcony.

Cussing, Mike slammed another shell into the chamber of his rifle. Her last-second flinch allowed his bullet to smash into the building after it had shattered her cup. He sighted through the scope and pointed the long barrel at the missed target. The silencer left barely a whisper outside the cab of the van, but the surprise he was counting on had failed and the easy score was gone. He sighted in again.

Halen was gone. He looked through the open door. She wasn't there. He looked through the windows. Nothing stirred. He looked at the balcony again and saw a foot. She was down on the balcony. She had to be making herself a smaller target, but if that was the case, why wouldn't she dive back inside where he had no chance of seeing her? If she was alive, that's what she would have done. People panic and run when they hear gunshots. They don't know which way to go, so they run in a direction they feel will be safe. Sometimes that was toward the danger and they didn't even realize it.

He searched the scene to see if he had been successful. He knew he had hit the coffee cup. Could the cup have shattered and killed her with multiple shards, like a shotgun? He peered through the scope, searching for any movement. He followed the foot up, looking for any twitch of muscle. The metal balcony frame around the glass left a sliver of an opening between the floor and the steel pipe.

From that angle he could see the back of her head and part of her ear. A fly landed on her ear. He watched as it crawled around on her. She didn't move. He knew his task was to kill her, and firing a second shot was as dangerous as telling the police that he had done it. A single shot would leave people guessing as to his position. A second would all but point directly at him, but he had to make sure his job was complete.

Training the crosshairs on the tip of her ear, Mike squeezed the trigger gently and steadily.

"Mike!"

The voice startled the former sharpshooter. He spun and looked toward the voice.

"Kelson?" Mike said. "What the hell are you doing here?"

He stared up at the figure who had interrupted his shot at freedom. "I got her, Kelson. She's dead on the balcony. The job's done. I don't owe you anything anymore."

The man stood for a moment, staring. In a flash, he pulled out a pistol, shoved it into Mike's ribs and pulled the trigger.

Mike felt the jolt, but he didn't feel any pain at first. He felt panic. He instinctively knew it was bad. He wasn't dead but he would be soon. He had to get out of there. Even though he was shot, he still had a few minutes. He had to get somewhere and call for help. If he was caught there, there would be questions to answer.

He tried to move his legs, but they failed to comply. He was paralyzed. And Kelson had vanished as quickly as he had appeared in the doorway of the van.

Mike was alone and he was going to die.

All his planning and doing the right things had gotten him nowhere. The shock was wearing off, and he started to feel the turmoil writhing within him. He knew it was more than he could recover from.

He had to call his wife. Even if he lived, he would never be able to make a phone call as a free man again. With trembling fingers, he fished his phone out of his pocket while his other hand covered the hole that was letting the life drain from him.

"Hey, honey," he said, trying to keep the alarm out of his voice. "I love you, and I have to tell you something."

Kelson had spent much of his time quelling the fires at the law firm the previous week. A lot had gone down really fast. Some things he was able to explain away, while others he dodged or minimalized.

This morning, he headed to work preparing for more damage control: Explaining that Halen was under a lot of stress and that the episode the week before was likely a nervous breakdown. Promising therapy and suggesting that the outburst was likely a reaction to her mother and him temporarily restricting her bank accounts.

He had said that the severed alligator head was part of a movie prop. Now he had more explaining to do, and he needed to plant some evidence to corroborate his story.

Kelson almost made it to his office when he realized he had forgotten some paperwork in the back seat of his car. It was nearly two blocks back to retrieve it.

THE HIT

As he turned a corner, a man stumbled and bumped into him. Kelson caught him and helped him regain his footing. He locked eyes with the man. The narrow face staring back at him spoke of an ailing man who might have been sick recently. His skin drooped on his cheeks, and bags hung under his eyes. A patch of skin lifted off his neck like a flake of tree bark, and a white scar circled partway around his right eye.

The brief encounter ended as quickly as it had started. The man thanked Kelson and apologized, then stepped around the corner and disappeared into the crowd.

Kelson continued on, rounding the corner in the parking garage. He fished through his coat pocket for his keys. Along with the keys, he felt something heavy and solid. He knew what it was, and he knew he hadn't put it in his pocket that morning. His blood went cold. He looked down into his coat pocket to verify what he had felt. The small gun almost glowed with its ivory handle. The muzzle of the short barrel didn't look as pristine as the rest of it. Something dark coated the tip.

He rounded the corner and froze. Flashing lights and police vests swarmed most of the second floor in the parking garage. The blue uniforms seemed to congregate around his vehicle, alarming him even more. Two officers approached him, one directly and another from the side. A detective quickly approached from the group of officers by his car.

"Kelson Rossi?" the detective asked.

Kelson began to sweat. "Yes."

"You're under arrest."

46

Halen clenched her teeth as the doctor extracted a glass shard from her cheek. The shots to numb her didn't quite reach the area where the doctor was working. When he pulled out the sharp piece of the ceramic coffee mug, he clinked it down into a pan alongside others. He turned toward the x-ray and back to Halen a couple times, then patted her on the knee.

"That's all of the larger pieces. Anything else will likely fester and work its way to the surface. You may have to come back in for those. Don't be surprised if you see tiny spots turn up. If you have persistent redness, you'll need to come back and see us."

"Thank you, sir."

"You're welcome. I'll have the nurse draw up the discharge papers and we'll get you on your way." The doctor stood and disposed of his gloves, then turned back to Halen. "Send the detective in?"

Halen sighed and nodded her head.

"Yeah, send him in," Deenya verbally affirmed for Halen. She turned to Halen. "You okay?"

"Yeah," Halen said flatly. The word felt unnatural and unemotional.

"You don't sound fine."

"Am I supposed to be upset and distraught?" Halen asked.

"I would be," Deenya said.

"Guess I'm getting used to people trying to kill me."

"I don't know how you do it."

"When the shock of almost dying over and over wears off, it ceases to be an extraordinary event and becomes a plain old Thursday."

Deenya smiled at Halen's offhanded joke.

"You gonna tell the detective?" Deenya asked.

"Let's see what he has to say first."

Deenya pulled up a chair. "Do you think they'll catch him?"

Halen shook her head and flicked her eyes toward the door. Through the break in the curtain, she saw Detective Milton's dark skin as he reached for the veil before pausing. Detective Perez was just a step behind him.

"Miss Kettleman, may we come in?" he said.

"Hey DM, hey DP." Halen lisped through the greeting. The numbing shots were now in full effect.

"Miss Kettleman." Detective Milton nodded. "Do you know who shot at you?"

"I'm guessing one of Kelson's henchmen," Halen said.

"Do you know a Mike Denahy?" Detective Perez asked.

Halen scrunched her nose while searching her memory. The few seconds it took to scan her memories yielded a second nose scrunch and a shake of her head. "I don't recall the name."

"Do you know why Kelson tried to have you killed?" Detective Milton asked, looking over his notepad at Halen.

"Insurance."

Detective Milton made a note in his book. "Do you know why he wanted the insurance?"

Deenya cleared her throat, and Halen looked over. "Hay-Hay. Lawyer. Even if you want to help, it's best to consult with a lawyer to make sure nothing you say will come back to bite you in the butt."

Detective Perez exhaled in disappointment.

"Yes. I will need a lawyer," Halen said. "I want to cooperate, but I need to make sure I do it in a responsible way and I'm protected."

Detective Milton sighed also and began to fish out a card. "I hope you will reconsider. We may not be able to hold him."

"Well, I'd hate to say something and you take it out of context, twist my words or otherwise. Even you are instructed not to say anything without consulting a lawyer, correct?"

Detective Milton looked as if he were a statue. She wondered if he was even breathing.

"See," Halen said, "even you can't or won't answer that question without a lawyer's approval."

Detective Milton sighed in defeat. "Miss Kettleman. It's imperative that we get some information from you concerning this matter."

"And it is imperative that I be represented properly," Halen fired back at him. "So unless you want to take some acting lessons or critique a movie, I believe we are done."

Detective Milton gave another defeated sigh. "Alright. Please call us as soon as you secure legal representation."

Over the following weeks, Detective Milton and Halen's lawyer kept her posted on the findings of their investigation. The drama in the weeks following the attempted assassination simmered, then cooled. The man who had shot at Halen had lived long enough to confirm that Kelson was the one who had shot him. It had seemed as though Kelson might have been trying to save Halen from being killed until documents surfaced naming him and her mother as the beneficiaries of a multimillion-dollar insurance policy. It also didn't help that the pistol recovered from his pocket matched the bullet retrieved from Mike.

Halen had mixed feelings learning that her former home had been searched. She had closed the door on that part of her life. Though they had found substances in her room, her lawyer argued that Kelson could have easily placed them there.

Her lawyer told her that they found significant information that would put Kelson away for years. It took several days, but the detectives managed to decipher the cryptic scribblings of the desperate man.

The development of evidence brought charges on several people associated with Kelson's illegal side hustle. Arrests were made at the insistence of an energetic prosecutor. The wealth behind those who were indicted brought a barrage of lawyers who swiftly whittled most charges down to a slap on the wrist or had them dropped entirely. The few who couldn't afford an attorney or had their finger in a little too deep had to satisfy the public's desire for justice.

Detective Milton called Halen early one morning and told her that a fight had broken out in the dayroom and that Kelson had been severely injured. The detective said the fight wasn't targeted at her stepfather, he just happened to be in the way. While being transported to the hospital, he had died from his injuries.

Halen hung up the phone knowing he wasn't collateral damage from the fight. He was targeted—most likely by friends of those who were on his coded list.

Would she be targeted? She knew a few people on that list but didn't remotely know the extent of their involvement in Kelson's illegal distribution of drugs.

She was satisfied though. Tracer had told her that it wasn't always about killing. It was about persuasion. If that meant killing someone, innocent or not, he hadn't blinked an eye. In Kelson's case, it was a statement that told the rest of that elite circle to be mindful of the underground network. But

Tracer was dead now. She had used the alligator's blood to smear on the coaster and claim it was Kelson's. She wanted to see the man falter when she told him that Tracer would be looking for him.

Halen had told her attorney the entire story—from her abduction to her meeting with Detective Milton at the hospital—but excluded the part where she thought Tracer was her father. With her lawyer's guidance, she worked her way through all the questions, providing true and satisfactory answers to the detectives.

Halen's mother had withdrawn and moved out of the house to stay with a friend, as her house had been seized in the investigation. Halen had already collected her important personal belongings and left that part of her old life behind.

In three weeks of being entirely on her own, she had successfully cleaned and organized her apartment. Cheshlan had been an almost constant companion, whose enthusiasm for helping her was bordering on annoying. Halen was impressed at how the child combined different artwork and furnishings to create tasteful decor.

With the drama of Kelson behind her, she focused on the future, and the future lay scattered across her carpet. Emptying the vacuum canister did not go as she had intended. When she pressed a button, the bottom fell open and debris flew around the apartment. In frustration, she changed clothes and went downtown for coffee with Deenya, leaving the mess to be cleaned up later.

"I wish I could have seen that," Deenya said between snorts of laughter.

"I'm sure you would have loved it." Halen took a sip of her iced coffee. "I would have made you help clean it up too."

Deenya shook her head, still snorting and trying to sip her drink.

Halen searched for anything to change the subject. "How are you and Clayton getting along?"

Deenya heaved a sigh to compose herself, then looked at her best friend. "I wanted to ask you about that."

"About what?"

"About maybe watching Cheshlan this weekend." Deenya played with her straw, trying to gauge what Halen's reaction might be.

"She's over at my house more than she is with you. Before you know it, she's gonna start calling me mom," Halen teased.

"I know. I need to keep her home more," Deenya said.

"I'm assuming there's a reason you want me to watch Chesh."

"Yeah. Chesh has been on every date with Clayton and I." Deenya took a sip of her drink, the straw lingering between her lips a little too long.

"And."

"Well, he asked me to go with him to his parents' houseboat in the Keys."

"Oh. You want to go make some waves," Halen teased.

Heat flushed Deenya's cheeks.

"A man like that, I would be disappointed in you if he returned here with less than a Cheshire grin."

Deenya looked at Halen hopefully. "So, you'll watch Cheshlan?"

"Yeah. You knew I would," Halen said.

"That's why I didn't bother to ask anyone else." Deenya grinned, heat still flushing her cheeks.

Returning to her apartment, Halen ran into Juan. She vented her frustration about the vacuum, and he showed her how it worked. She revacuumed her living room, asking Juan to stay just in case the machine fell apart again. When she finished, she thanked him and walked him to the door.

She rolled the vacuum back into the closet and pulled out the mop to finish the kitchen floor. Turning around, she came face-to-face with the muzzle of a gun.

47

The steel muzzle looked cold, but Halen knew it would get extremely hot with just a flick of a finger. Her life would end in a fraction of a second. Nothing would be able to bring her back.

It was as if her life was reeling backward. She saw in her mind's eye Juan's face light up when she asked him out. She saw him patiently explaining the vacuum mechanics, her coffee with Deenya, the explosion of dirt as it scattered around her apartment. She saw the fight with the alligator, the mountain lion on the cliff and the dead grizzly. She saw the eyes of the lynx and felt its purr vibrate through her soul. Then she saw Tracer's eyes staring at her.

In the cave, Tracer had stared at her for countless hours. At first she thought he was a pervert with deviant fantasies. Now she understood he was faced with probably the biggest decision of his life. He was evaluating if he should kill his only child or not. She recognized now what he had wondered for months. He either couldn't, wouldn't or he saw that she was worth more than the spoiled brat she had been.

She saw it now. She was worth saving. She was worth his sacrifice when he tackled the mountain lion over the edge of the cliff. She was worth the blood, sweat and tears from all his lessons.

The cold steel of the gun in front of her wasn't a lesson—it was her test. It was her decision to live or die.

Kimberly squeezed the trigger.

Halen's heart stopped. She couldn't believe that her own mother had pulled the trigger. She had squeezed it hard. Halen clamped her eyes shut, waiting for the lead to smash into her, ending her life.

Behind her closed eyes, she saw Tracer and the glint in his eye when she had disarmed him as he held a pistol to her face, just like her mother was doing now. That glint grew into a smile—a smile she had never seen before or after. He never smiled like that.

When Halen opened her eyes, her body was already in motion. The pistol flew across the kitchen, clattering onto the counter, bouncing off the backsplash. Halen spun her mother's arm behind her and gave her a shove into the door of the wall closet. The flimsy door broke under her weight, and Kimberly scrambled up and lunged for the gun.

Halen threw herself at her mother, trying to knock her feet out from under her, but missed.

She had never seen her mom move that fast before. The neatly pressed peach-colored pantsuit didn't suggest speed, but she had slipped past, and Halen only raked the fringes of her clothing.

Kimberly darted for the pistol, swooping it up and turning on Halen. She clicked the safety off and squeezed the trigger.

The small pistol bucked in her hand. The slug tore through Halen's shoulder, but Halen was already lunging. She had her mother in her crosshairs, and nothing was going to deny her the right to her own life and being happy. She reached for the gun, slamming a finger down in between the hammer and the firing pin. The hammer came down on her finger, pinching the tender flesh. Halen didn't feel it. She only felt anger. She wanted that gun out of her mother's hands. She wanted the threat to end. She wanted a boring life.

With both hands on the weapon, she forced it up and away from herself. Halen's finger slipped out from between the hammer and the firing pin. The pistol bucked again, this time sending a bullet into the ceiling. A loud banging came from the door.

"Halen, are you alright?"

Halen heard Juan's voice but was afraid to answer for fear of losing the struggle between her and her mother. She had to gain control of the gun or bad things were going to happen. Halen stretched her arms out, pointing the gun further up. She and her mother spun in circles, trying to gain leverage over each other. Kimberly kneed her in the groin, then in the gut, knocking the air from her lungs. Kimberly screamed, firing two more shots into the ceiling. Halen forced the muzzle of the gun toward the closet, where her mother emptied the rest of the bullets into the door.

A crash and a thud rattled the room. Two large arms enveloped Kimberly, trapping her arms to her sides. The pistol rattled to the floor. Seeing Juan's hands locked tightly around her mother, Halen quickly kicked the pistol down the hall and into the bedroom, then shut the door. When she looked back, Kimberly's feet were six inches off the floor as she struggled against the mighty strength that held her.

Halen grabbed her phone and called 911. "I need police."

"My mother tried to kill me," she said between gasping breaths.

"You killed my husband!" Kimberly screamed.

Halen looked at her mother with a mixture of hurt and contempt. "I'm at the Riverside Apartments. Apartment 561."

"It happened just a minute ago. She tried to shoot me." Halen paced the floor, adrenaline still surging through her. "Yes, she's still here . . . No. Security has her detained for now."

"LET ME GO!" Kimberly screamed as she continued to thrash. Juan tightened his grip on the woman. "You're supposed to be dead."

Halen set the phone down but didn't disconnect from the call.

"Why, mom? Why should I be dead?" Halen yelled back at her.

"I should have aborted you. You've cost me everything."

Halen flinched at her mother's comment, but she wasn't shocked into sadness. She was still too angry for any sadness to gain a foothold in her emotions. "I helped you build everything that you have," Halen said, fists clenched at her sides.

"You killed Kelson," Kimberly said and began thrashing against Juan again.

"Kelson tried to kill me!" Halen barked. "He tried to have me killed several times."

"Why couldn't you just die in Montana like you were supposed to?" Kimberly screamed.

"You sent an assassin to kill me?"

"No. He was just going to help you have an accident," Kimberly growled. "But you had to fuck that up too. You were always a fuckup."

"You pushed me into acting. You pushed me into being the best actress I could be, and you helped me create the career that gave you everything you ever wanted," Halen argued.

"You . . . I should have raked you out with a coat hanger as soon as I found out. My parents wouldn't let me. They said I'd burn in hell. I told them that I didn't want any children. They forced me to keep you. Then they forced me not to put you up for adoption. My life has been hell because of you." Kimberly spit at Halen.

Halen dodged her mother's feeble attack. "Why didn't you just run away?" Halen asked. "Why didn't you leave me with your parents and start a new life?"

"Because they wouldn't have given me anything. So I played the good child and doting mother to play into their stupid family morals," Kimberly said with an edge still in her voice. "All to get an inheritance. They cut me out of their will and gave it all to charity. Everyone loved them, but they didn't love me."

"Why?"

"They said it was God's will. Self-righteous pricks."

"How did you get pregnant in the first place? Didn't you use protection?" Halen asked.

"It wasn't my fault. I was raped." Kimberly's growl withered to a sob, and she went slack. Juan grunted against her weight to keep her upright. Kimberly didn't shed any tears. Halen couldn't remember a time when she had ever actually cried. She was always strong, proper and had an answer for everything.

"They took turns screwing me. I woke up halfway through and begged them to stop, but they laughed and chanted for the next guy to stuff me."

"Why didn't you fight them off?" Halen asked, with more compassion in her tone.

"Because I was too goddamn drunk," Kimberly spat. "I never wanted kids but they fucking gave me one, and my parents made me keep it. Fucking God's-child bullshit. You're not God's child. You're a fucking demon straight from hell." Kimberly spat again, this time staining the bottom of Halen's shirt.

Halen didn't flinch. She didn't want to show this woman that what she had said affected her in any way. She stood with a straight face, forcing back the tremendous emotion that compelled her to scream at the top of her lungs. She wanted to cry, to laugh, to scream, to rage, but she couldn't. She could only attempt to listen. To try and digest all that her mother was saying. If not digest it, at least file it away where she might be able to recall it all later. But it didn't wait. It was all there, all together at one time like an avalanche racing toward her, burying her with things no one should have to hear.

She turned away, retreating into her mind. Her mother had dropped multiple bombshells, each one compounding the other. Her mother was a fraud. She wasn't a mother at all. She was a dictator. For years, Kimberly hid behind a smile and made Halen work to fund their lavish lifestyle. When Halen began falling out of the limelight and into a vomited puddle, Kimberly sought to rid herself of the embarrassment. Many stars had met untimely deaths; her mother expected her to do the same.

Halen was tired of the deception, the fakeness of her parents. And she was tired of being used. She was appalled at her friends who tried to use her celebrity status, but her mother had secretly been the worst offender of them all. For the first time in her life, Halen wanted truth and honesty that was built on a solid foundation. She didn't know how to achieve it, but she knew it wasn't anywhere near this woman who claimed to be her mother.

The rest of her family—her grandparents or any other relative—was a total mystery. Her mother never talked about them. When she'd asked, Kimberly just said that they died when she was young. She wondered if that was a lie as well. Kelson's parents accepted Halen, but she hadn't been afforded many opportunities to get to know them.

Then there was Tracer. No last name, no past and no future, because he was dead. Yet she felt more connected to him than anyone else. The birthmark on his side wasn't definitive proof that he was her father, but somehow she felt that he was. He definitely wouldn't make father of the year. But hadn't he done what fathers did? Try to protect their daughters from the evil in the world?

Halen felt alone. She felt close to only one person, and he wasn't there. He was gone, leaving her utterly alone.

A groan came from Juan, followed by a rage-fueled scream. Halen looked up in time to see Kimberly lunge at her. Her manicured nails hooked like claws ready to rip flesh from bone. This woman wasn't her mother. This woman belonged in an asylum.

Kimberly charged. Her wild eyes were desperate for her own twisted vengeance. Tracer had rushed Halen many times, but his movements were more calculated and deliberate. Kimberly was like a stumbling child.

"Police! Stop!" an officer yelled from the door as he lunged for Kimberly.

It was too late. Halen had trained all winter to defend herself, and her reaction was instant. She pushed the woman's arms to the side and hooked a solid fist to her head. Kimberly fell like a slab of meat onto a butcher's table.

48

Regina Benton shook the rain off her umbrella and dried it with a towel. She hummed hymn after hymn as she tidied up from her son and daughter-in-law's visit. She had just received the best news she could think of, and the hymns rejoiced that news. She had so much to do in preparation for her first grandchild. Her mind spun in circles as she wondered what to do first, but she settled on just cleaning her house.

She set out a pad and pencil, wrote down a few initial thoughts, then started for the kitchen, where their dinner dishes waited. Glancing at the table, she saw the mom-to-be's scarf. She picked it up and gently laid it over the back of a chair, knowing they would be back the following weekend for Sunday dinner.

Regina turned to the dishes and filled the sink with sudsy water. She was elbow deep into cleaning a pan when the doorbell rang. She smiled, knowing that the scarf was her daughter-in-law's favorite.

Drying her hands and grabbing the scarf, she headed for the door.

The storm had not abated. If anything, it had increased to a dull roar, pounding heavy drops on the roof. She opened the door to find a slender figure soaked to the bone. Strings of hair clung tight to her face. A light jacket hugged her skin as if it were a part of her, and her shoulders hunched against the cold rain.

It took a minute for Regina to register who it was. She had never seen Halen without her looking like she had just stepped out of a magazine. Now she looked like a pathetic drowned kitten and not the snobbish socialite she had known.

"What do you want?" Regina's stern voice reflected her mood from her previous encounter with the starlet.

"A mom." Halen's tears flowed like rivers down her face, mixing with the rain and falling to the steps.

Halen woke with a start and looked around. Her surroundings were foreign to her—a collection of antique furniture and tiny ceramic cat figurines. She was in a large T-shirt that didn't belong to her. Her clothes were neatly stacked on a chair next to the bed. Slowly, the night before came back to her. She had divulged every detail to Regina, keeping her up for hours as she unloaded her emotional baggage. She told of her abduction, her training, her encounter with the lynx, the mountain lions, alligators and the several assassination attempts.

She told of her suspicion that Tracer was her father and that she would never see him again because he had been carried away in a flooded river.

Regina listened intently, only asking a question or two as Halen cried her story out, at times sobbing uncontrollably into the woman's lap. Sometime late into the night, Halen finally drifted off.

Halen smelled food cooking and the strong aroma of coffee. Sliding out from under the covers, she dressed quickly and made her way to the kitchen. On the table were two place settings and an open laptop. Regina hummed a tune as she tended to the stove, cooking grits and scrambling eggs. It was like a dance she did, with everything timed in perfect harmony. Stir eggs, flip ham, add salt to the grits, open the oven and pull out a pan of towering, perfectly browned biscuits.

"Good morning," Halen said meekly.

"Good morning, sweetie," Regina said, interrupting the hymn she was humming.

"I can see you have company coming over, so I'll just go. Thank you for listening last night. It really meant a lot." Halen started backing toward the door.

"Fool child, sit your bum down and have some breakfast. No one leaves here until they're rested and fed," Regina commanded. "Now sit so we can eat. Coffee?"

"Yes, please."

"I don't have any of that fancy coffee. I only get the south's finest." Regina grabbed the antique coffee kettle and poured the black silk into Halen's cup. The stainless steel percolator pot showed obvious decades of use, yet it looked clean enough to be repackaged if it weren't for the scratches and the occasional dent.

Halen took a sip of the black liquid and reveled in the aroma and bitterness. "Mmm. Good." It was better than what Tracer made. He didn't have the same brand that Regina had, and he wasn't consistent with his measuring.

"Tracer never made coffee as good as this," Halen said.

"You were fond of this man?" Regina asked.

"In a weird way, yeah. I don't think it would ever be a lasting thing, but it was nice for a time. Sometimes the coffee was strong, and sometimes weak, but I guess that in itself was the magical part of the moment."

"Mmm. Cherish those memories, because you won't be able to re-create them in any other way. You said a mountain lion came up and lay in your lap?" Regina took a sip of her coffee after mixing in the tiniest bit of cream and sugar.

"No. It was a lynx, like a bobcat. They have huge paws and long black tufts on the tips of their ears."

Regina got up to tend to the stove.

"Regina," Halen called after her. She waited until she turned back around. "Thank you."

"Girl, you were a tough one. Even I didn't see much future for you. This Tracer guy seems to have been the thing you needed in your life. I thank the Lord that he answered your prayers."

"I didn't pray for him though," Halen said.

"Mmm. Yes you did. You acting out like you did. You were begging for attention and discipline. It took someone who cared about what and who you will be in the future to be able to turn around that wreckage you were driving. Everyone looks for the right-now. They don't want to look into the future. The future scares them." Regina set the skillets on assorted hot pads in the center of the table. "Once you've seen the really scary stuff, you know everything else is surmountable and success is right around the corner."

"What are you typing on your computer?" Halen asked, changing the subject. "It looks like a screenplay of some sort."

"Well. The news that my son and daughter-in-law are expecting inspired a children's series. I want to make it for my grandchild."

"That's so awesome. How far along are you on it?" Halen asked.

"I got the idea just this morning."

"Oh. I would love to hear more about it. Only if you want to share with me."

"Thank you, sweetie. If I get to that stage, I can make some more coffee and we can talk then."

Halen smiled at the sincerity in her voice. The idea that she might have made another friend tickled her insides with joy. It was an odd occurrence. She didn't have to buy her anything, and it felt genuine.

"I'm looking for another project, if you know of any," Halen said. "I need to find something. My mother raided my bank account, and much of all their and my assets are tied up in the investigation. I need to find some work pretty soon. My bank account is tied up too, though my lawyer thinks he can get it released soon."

"I can give my agent a call. Ask him if he's willing to try to find you some work. Your reputation hasn't been the best."

"I know," Halen said. "I've been a stuck-up narcissistic b—" She quickly checked her language and looked at her host. Regina didn't look up but continued to fuss with her breakfast. "Well, you know what I mean." Halen took a bite of her eggs.

"Mmm-hmm. Yes, you were." Regina offered Halen a biscuit. "Everyone needs their butt whipped sometime in their life." Halen cast her a questioning look, then she continued. "I had my butt whooped by my momma's Bible. I heard my father say a four-letter word. I repeated it when I spilled my plate on the floor. My momma whipped my butt for an hour. Never said one of those words again."

"I kinda had the same thing happen to me. I said a word and was backhanded hard enough to hear bells ring. I still think twice before using that word."

The two women tended to their breakfast, and Halen even asked for a second helping of biscuits.

"What are you going to do now?" Regina asked after collecting the plates from the table.

"I don't know," Halen said as she helped clear the table. She set the dishes in the sink and looked around for the dishwasher. "Regina. Where's your dishwasher?"

"Never had one."

"Why not?" Halen asked.

"My hands do a better job," Regina said.

"But a dishwasher would save you so much time."

"Don't need one. I live by myself. Dishes take less time to wash than to load them into a machine," Regina said, turning on the faucet and dribbling in the green syrupy soap. Bubbles sprang to life, quickly covering the flatware. "A little manual labor never hurt anyone."

"Can I help?" Halen asked.

Regina smiled and handed her a towel.

49

The remnants of police tape clung to either side of Halen's apartment door. It was dented where Juan had crashed through to save her and to subdue her mother, and the doorjamb had been ripped from its frame. She was grateful and said as much to Juan before he had excused himself back to his job that night.

After the night at Regina's house, she stayed two nights with Deenya before the police released her apartment back to her. Upon entering, she found her entire apartment in disarray. Evidently the investigation required the search of her whole house. Furniture had been moved. All the new appliances had been shifted, and the sparse amount of food in the cupboard and refrigerator had been rearranged. It didn't look like they took anything, but the violation of her property made her skin crawl.

Halen shrugged at their overstep, knowing that they wouldn't find anything *because* she didn't have anything. Her entire past had been left behind in her parents' house. This apartment was a clean slate. If they were looking for evidence of past drug dealings, which she assumed they were, they would find nothing. It wasn't like she could do anything about the invasion. Filing suit against the city government just to prove the minor infraction would cost her more than she had.

She set to work cleaning up her apartment. The building manager said that they would have a new door installed the following morning. Though the frame had splintered and the door easily opened with just a push of a finger, the deadbolt still operated enough to keep the door shut against an occasional bump. It latched just enough to fool any random passerby.

With the majority of her apartment looking like the aftermath of a drunken house party, and knowing who had done it, she decided to wash everything and start over yet again. Deenya and Cheshlan would be over in the morning, but she didn't see any reason to wait. It was her mess, and she didn't want to burden her friends with it any more than necessary.

A brief thought about not using the dishwasher momentarily gave her pause as she reflected on Regina's words and work ethic. A split second later, she pulled the door open to load the machine. She would battle with the moral ethics of hand-washing dishes another time.

"Housewarming party?"

The voice made Halen jump. She spun around and stared at the man standing just inside the balcony door. His clothes draped loosely over his slight frame. They looked ill-fitting, like he might have gotten them at a thrift store.

"I thought you were dead," Halen said. The gnawing question that had stirred relentlessly in the back of her mind had just been answered.

"I am," Tracer said. "I died a long time ago. When I accepted that first job, I was no longer the child Bill and Florence raised."

"Can I get you a cup of coffee?" Halen asked.

"No, thank you. I won't be staying." Tracer looked nervously at the crumpled door and the splintered wood of the doorframe. Halen followed his gaze, then dragged a chair to the door and wedged it in under the handle.

Tracer didn't say anything, but his relaxed posture told her enough.

"How are you feeling?" Halen asked. He seemed a little worse for wear.

"I'm fine. Nothing to worry about."

"You recovered from that bear attack?" Halen asked.

"Yes. Thank you for what you did. You had every right to say those things to me. Though I wish you wouldn't have used that word," Tracer said. "I know you're better than that."

"I'm a better person than what I used to be, but I still don't think I'm good enough to be a friend to much of anyone."

"A little humility goes a long way," Tracer affirmed. "You are a good friend to that young woman and her daughter. They'll help keep you grounded."

"I don't think I could get rid of them if I tried." Halen huffed a laugh. "But I promise to do right by them the best I can."

"Good," Tracer said.

The quiet tension stretched on. Halen hesitated to ask the question she had been wanting to ask ever since she stitched up Tracer's side.

She had to ask. This was going to be her last chance. "Are you my father?"

Tracer seemed reluctant to answer. Seconds passed before he did. "I don't know."

"Do you know Kimberly Kettleman?" Halen asked.

"Kimberly Kettleman is a name I haven't spoken in twenty years. I had blocked out that part of my life for so long." Tracer stared off into the decades-old memories. "She was a sophomore at the same university I went to. She was pretty. I had a crush on her, but she was popular and I wasn't. I let it slip that I was still a virgin, and some frat boys took me under their wing and told me they were going to help me out.

"They took me to a party. Kimberly was there. They noticed that I was watching her intently. They said that they'd arranged for me and her to hook up in a back room, and they pushed me down the hall. I didn't know what *hook up* was. I thought it was alone time to talk first, then decide to become a couple, maybe even make it to second base."

Halen shuddered and shook away the image of her mom being felt up by Tracer.

"When I entered the room, it was dark. A girl was there who I thought was Kim. We kissed and she helped me out of my clothes. I thought that I was hooking up with Kim. She coaxed me to have sex with her. I thought that I was, until they flipped the lights on. Twenty people cheered and rooted for the show. The girl who had pretended to be Kimberly and helped me out of my clothes was standing off to the side cheering with her arm wrapped around the president of the fraternity.

"They held Kimberly down and forced me to continue. She was so drunk that she barely knew what was going on. When I tried to stop and leave, they held me there until I finished."

"That's why you don't like that word?" Halen asked.

Tracer nodded. "I've killed all but two of them."

"Oh."

"I never saw Kimberly again after that. When I was contracted for this job, I didn't deal with her. I only saw her from a distance. I didn't recognize who she was. I only guessed who you might be after seeing your birthmark."

"My name, Kettleman?"

"It's not an uncommon name. It didn't register until the bar in Montana. That is when I changed my plans, but I knew you'd still be in danger if I just left."

"That's why you taught me what you did."

"Yes." Tracer looked into Halen's eyes for a moment. "I guess I should hang it up. I've been looking for a good reason for years. I guess I have one now. There's no need to continue. It gets tiring, and I'm getting old."

Tracer handed a canvas bag over to Halen.

"What's this?" Halen looked at Tracer, then at the black bag.

"I took a job and a down payment. I didn't complete the job. I went to return the money as a breach of contract but couldn't find the client. When I did, I found that they couldn't receive the refunds. I can't keep it, I didn't fulfill the contract. Therefore, it must go to the next of kin."

Halen unzipped the bag and peeked inside. She pulled out two bundles, each a half-inch thick: one a bundle of fifty-dollar bills and the other a stack of twenties. She looked further in the bag and saw multiple bundles of all denominations. Her eyes went wide.

"How much is in here?" Halen asked in a whisper, afraid to say anything out loud, like it was a secret.

Tracer held up two fingers, then five, close to his chest. Halen mouthed the words *two-hundred-fifty thosand*.

"Yes," Tracer said. "The rest was to be paid after. Obviously I won't be seeing that."

"You could have easily retired to another country with this. No one would ever know." Halen half hinted at the possible option.

"I have enough," Tracer said.

"You can take this. I don't want it." Halen offered it back to him.

Tracer shook his head. "No. I didn't finish the job. I don't get paid. That's just good business."

"I know it's good business, but I'm not deserving of it," Halen said.

"You will be. Find something good to do with it. You know that you're going to play hell getting your money back from your parents. That stuff is going to cost you money. And you're going to need something to live on until then."

"I'd trade it all," she said.

"For what?"

Halen set the bag on the coffee table and wrapped her arms around the man, hugging him tightly. Tracer started to throw his arms up in defense but stopped. Halen sank her head down onto his shoulder and breathed deep the scent of his leather coat and the gentle fragrance of Polo. It was the best way she could show how much she appreciated him and the valuable lessons he'd taught her.

Tracer froze. Halen noticed that he didn't return the hug. "It won't hurt if you hug me back," she said, still clinging to him.

Tracer folded his arms around her, barely touching her.

"A little tighter please," she whispered into his shoulder.

He gripped her tighter, but Halen felt that his arms were like wood, stiff and unemotional.

Boom boom boom. The door shook with violent blows.

"FBI! Open up!"

The loud voice hadn't even died out when someone kicked at the door.

Halen turned to the noise, then back to Tracer. "Wait!" she cried out. "Where are you going?"

Tracer stopped, his hand gripping the rail to the balcony, and looked at her. The chair gave way to a third kick. Splinters shot in all directions as the wood fractured under the assault.

"FBI. Stop right there!" the officer said as Tracer jumped from the balcony with the bag full of cash.

Halen wanted to run after him but held her hands up as FBI agents swarmed her apartment.

Two agents bolted to the balcony and looked down. There was nothing. They looked to the sides and there was nothing. He had disappeared. Pistols drawn, they continued to watch for any movement. A whirl of fans buzzed to life two floors lower, and a large drone carrying Tracer flew out from the balcony.

The drone flew toward the Miami River. The streets were lit with red and blue flashing lights. There was nowhere to go. He couldn't outrun those on the ground with the drone. Halen heard a helicopter approach, and a loudspeaker announced the police presence in the air. Its giant spotlight lit up the night sky and focused on the drone.

An agent fired his pistol at Tracer. Halen was forced to her knees and handcuffed. She heard shouts and sirens. The buzz of the drone faded away and someone called through the radio to get boats into the river.

Halen resisted the urge to cry so it wouldn't be evident that she had an emotional tie to the man. She didn't resist and stayed frozen in place. Everything became a blur as she answered question after question into the early morning while her heart grieved.

It was winter again in Miami. Halen had just left Regina's office. She had partnered with Regina to help bring her children's show to the public. *Clay & Doey*, a claymation production, became a mild success during their testing phase. They used some old school technology and built an at-home DIY kit for kids to create their own claymation and submit them for a chance to be broadcast on a future episode.

Halen rounded the corner of sketch artists who were finishing up the design art for the at-home DIY kit. She entered her own office and sat down to the spreadsheet she had left open. Their budget had been stretched to the max. Any profits were going to be razor thin, and their producers expected the project to be further along. Halen had a few more strings to pull to get the project done, but they would for sure be in the red with another investor munching at any profits.

Halen leaned her elbows on the desk and ran her fingers through her hair, then pulled at her neck as she sat back. She needed an emergency sip. She tried to hide it, but she had heard whispers. It wasn't like she had to drive home. Her home was a ten-by-ten back room. Her parents' estate was still tied up in the courts, along with all her money, as it had been co-mingled with her parents' money and no one could say for sure who had what. She lost the apartment a month later and moved in with Deenya. She'd stayed for a few months, picking up odd acting jobs and helping where she could until Deenya and Cheshlan moved in with Clayton, with Deenya sporting an engagement ring.

Halen was left with the seed money from an investor for Regina's show. She used whatever influence she still had to scrape together enough money to rent a shabby studio where she became the producer and the night watchman, as it wasn't exactly in a desirable part of town.

She grasped the handle of a drawer where she hid several cheap bottles of wine. Her depression demanded company, and she didn't want to burden anyone else with her shortcomings.

Her hand was still on the handle as her eyes lingered on the computer screen and paused. The argument to refrain from drinking was quickly lost. Jerking the drawer open, she reached for the smooth, polished glass, but it wasn't there. In its place was a gift-wrapped box. The bright *Happy Birthday* lettering was plastered at all different angles in bright green, blue and red. A small card was taped to the top of the box.

She opened the card and read out loud. "Trade. No more booze. Deal?" Halen cocked her head and pulled the box out. In the drawer, it was plain to see that the three bottles of wine were gone.

Someone knew where she hid her wine. And someone was insistent on leaving a message. She looked around, but only saw people bent to their work, trying their best to get this project off the ground and get their names on the credit roll.

Halen slid a finger under the flap of paper and pried it up. She turned the box on all sides, gently undoing the paper and setting the bright colors aside. She pulled a letter opener from another drawer, cut the tape and opened the box.

THE HIT

Halen gasped. Inside was bundle after bundle of cash. Underneath was an old, weathered box. The corners were frayed and the print had faded, but she instantly knew what it was. She pulled the box out and set it on her desk. She was no longer concerned about the stacks of cash still in the box. She sat back in her chair and stared at the backgammon game that she had played countless times in an isolated cave in the middle of the Canadian wilderness.

The note on top of the box had only one word: *courage*. A tear tugged at her eye as she lifted the lid of the game. Inside, she didn't find the game—she found something more powerful than all the money that had sat on top of this box.

Her jaw dropped as she realized the significance of the gift. The hair stood up on her arms and neck as she felt the spirit of the bear wrap its energy around her. She slipped the loop over her head and let it settle against her chest, each of the ten claws radiating from her neck. Closing her eyes, she hugged the tufts of hair and the large four-inch claws from the grizzly that Tracer had killed.

Dear Reader,

Thank you for allowing me to share this story with you. It has been a great milestone for me, developing my writing and learning how to craft a captivating story. The challenge of keeping characters organized and interesting has kept me on my toes along with learning more tricks of the editing trade. Editing is the bane of my existence, but a necessary evil. I will do my best to shoulder this burden the best I can without sacrificing time to write the next book.

My job is never done as I choose to keep learning and developing new and interesting stories for your reading enjoyment, with the help of my editor, of course. The second book of the Secret to Life series will be out soon, continuing that saga of the Rington family. As for future stories, I am tickling the ideas for a YA steampunk series, a sci-fi horror series and a dystopian series that sends humankind backward in evolution. I'm writing a bit in each, waiting to see which one will consume my attention first and force its way into the spotlight.

You can find more of my literary works at storyteller-alex-r-price.com

Thank you for reading, and I look forward to seeing you in the next pages.

All the best,

Alex R Price

www.ingramcontent.com/pod-product-compliance
Lightning Source LLC
Chambersburg PA
CBHW051313190726
48290CB00001B/137